The fifth novel in an
original new paperback series
★ WAGONS WEST ★
about America's great
expansion westward.

TEXAS!

By the author of INDEPENDENCE!

★★★★★★★★★★★★★★★★★★★★★★★★

WAGONS WEST

TEXAS!

UNFORGETTABLE MEN AND WOMEN— THEIR DREAMS AS OLD AS THE HUMAN SPIRIT, AS NEW AS THE NEXT FRONTIER!

COLONEL LELAND BLAKE.
Summoned from the Oregon territory
in urgent secrecy, he is given charge of
America's newest wagon train—to Texas!

CATHY BLAKE.
She now joins her husband at
the head of the train.

WHIP HOLT.
invited by Sam Houston in person, he leaves
his devoted wife to go on a dangerous mission,
only to be stopped by a painful truth.

ELISABETA MANUEL.
Ravishingly beautiful, she gives her
body and heart to a traitor, hoping to
become his wife—but is forced
instead into bondage and betrayed.

ANTHONY ROBERTS.
Though American-born, he spies for the
British and Mexicans in Texas—driven by
savage desire to find and destroy the
American vigilantes who killed his father.

CAPTAIN RICK MILLER.
There is no better rider, no better marksman,
than this stalwart Texas Ranger who is
drawn overpoweringly to Anthony's woman.

★★★★★★★★★★★★★★★★★★★★★★★★

DANNY TAYLOR and CHET HARRIS.
Best friends who grew up together on the
first wagon train west, they now yearn for
wild adventure on the Mexican frontier.

MELISSA AUSTIN.
Young red-haired firebrand, the only
single woman on the trek to Texas, she has
made romantic rivals of Danny and Chet.

TENG CHU.
The great Chinese warrior and member of
a high Mandarin caste, he is ridiculed for
his strange attire, until his "strange"
weapons strike fear in the Americans ranks.

HEATHER MacGREGOR.
The oldest daughter of Scottish
pioneers, she throws herself body and soul
into the harsh life of a frontier woman.

ASA PHIPPS.
Nearly tarred and feathered for his
crude sexual advances, he is easy prey for
Anthony Roberts' schemes of treason.

HARRY CANNING.
Called away to build the Texas
navy, he is forced to leave his young
wife Nancy behind in Oregon

NANCY WADE CANNING.
Still very young, she has no
intention of staying behind—so she stows
away and follows Harry into peril.

ANDREW JACKSON.
From private sessions of his
"lions den" in Nashville, the former
Presidest pulls the strings behind
the politics of Washington, D.C.

Bantam Books by Dana Fuller Ross
Ask your bookseller for the books you have missed

WAGONS WEST ★ VOLUME 5

TEXAS!

DANA FULLER ROSS

BANTAM BOOKS

NEW YORK • TORONTO • LONDON • SYDNEY • AUCKLAND

TEXAS!
A Bantam Domain Book / published by arrangement with
Book Creations, Inc.
Bantam edition / September 1980

DOMAIN and the portrayal of a boxed "d" are trademarks of
Bantam Books, a division of Bantam Doubleday Dell Publishing
Group, Inc.

Produced by Book Creations, Inc.
Lyle Kenyon Engel, Founder

ISBN 0-553-26070-7

Published simultaneously in the United States and Canada

Bantam Books are published by Bantam Books, a division of Bantam
Doubleday Dell Publishing Group, Inc. Its trademark, consisting of the
words "Bantam Books" and the portrayal of a rooster, is Registered in
U.S. Patent and Trademark Office and in other countries. Marca Regis-
trada. Bantam Books, 666 Fifth Avenue, New York, New York 10103.

PRINTED IN THE UNITED STATES OF AMERICA

RAD   22   21   20   19   18   17   16

TEXAS!

NOTE

This is a work of fiction about Texas in the 1840s and the people who brought the Republic of Texas into the United States as the twenty-eighth state. While the general outlines of history have been faithfully followed and the spirit of the story is true, a few of the more complicated details of the record have been simplified, so as not to distract from the story.

Texas & Mexico 1846

Disputed territory between Texas and Mexico

● Towns and settlements

△ Battle sites

the route from Oregon

The Wagon train from Memphis

I

Captain Rick Miller, head of the criminal investigation division of the Texas Rangers, rode at a seemingly easy canter across the vast plains of the young Republic. Homesteaders whom he passed as they worked in their fields and with whom he exchanged friendly waves wouldn't have guessed that two of his Rangers following behind him were hard pressed to maintain his pace.

Tall and sinewy, with a physical strength and endurance that his slender frame did not indicate, Rick kept a constant watch in all directions, his pale eyes squinting beneath the blazing, shadeless sun. For six months the authorities had been unable to capture a gang of thieves who preyed on isolated farms and ranches. The day before, when a report had been received in Austin regarding the area in which the criminals were now operating, the task of killing or capturing them had been given to Captain Miller. Respecting the power of the pistol hanging from a holster at his belt and the rifle slung from his shoulder, Rick believed in shooting only when necessary, but at the same time he was sworn to rid Texas of lawbreakers. President Sam Houston himself had said, "I'd hate to have Rick Miller on my trail."

Although he didn't want to admit it to himself, Rick was pleased he had the opportunity to leave Austin—

1

with its grubby murders and robberies that were commonplace in a new civilization—and return for a time to the field. He loved the open spaces as much as he despised criminals.

One of these years, he reflected, he would leave the Rangers, find some property he liked, and settle down. He was in no great rush, to be sure. A man needed a wife for that kind of life. At the moment there was no woman who interested him, and, he had to admit, he was more than a little uncomfortable in the presence of ladies. The only women he had ever known had been harlots, and he had attended to his physical needs, then gone on his way.

Looking back, he took pride in the knowledge that he had come a long way since the death of his parents and his start in the Rocky Mountains, where he had lived for years as a trapper and hunter before migrating to Texas, where he had become a Ranger almost immediately. He had been wise to give up the life of a mountain man, which offered few opportunities these days. The great heroes of the Rockies were gone now. Jim Bridger had set up a trading post somewhere in the mountains, either in the Utah or Wyoming countries, and Kit Carson, the last he had heard, was in California. Sam Brentwood had become completely civilized and lived with his wife and family in Independence, Missouri, where he owned a supply depot that provided essentials for members of wagon trains heading westward. Even Rick's own hero, Whip Holt, had married and remained in Oregon after leading the first wagon train to that territory.

Smiling slightly, Rick shook his head. It was hard to think of Whip Holt as a married man. He guessed he himself could be tamed, too, if the right woman ever came into his life, but he shrank from the thought. He was too independent. And, he had to concede, assignments like his present job still gave him a feeling that he was performing a genuine service. He was not ready to settle down.

A cloud of dust on the horizon caught Rick's attention.

"Look yonder," he called to his two Rangers. Instantly he increased his pace to a full gallop.

His men did the same, silently cursing him. While it was true that Captain Miller had become famous because of his instinct for smelling trouble, they saw no need to exert themselves unduly on what well might be a wild-goose chase.

Rick's stallion responded to the slight touch of his spurs and ran steadily, his hoofs thundering on the hard, dry ground beneath his feet. It hadn't rained in weeks, much to the distress of the plains farmers, but a horse could make better time on such ground.

A farmhouse came into view in the distance, with two barns behind it, and when Rick made out five horses tied to hitching posts near the front door, he became even more alert. Signaling to the Rangers behind him to follow his example, he unslung his rifle, made sure it was ready for instant use, and cocked it.

An unseen woman's scream sounded from somewhere behind the house and was followed by a single shot. Then all was silent again.

Before Rick and his men could reach the house, five men, all armed, raced around to the front of the house, four of them carrying filled burlap sacks.

Rick and the Rangers had two choices: either they could dismount and shield themselves behind their horses, or they could continue to ride forward, taking a greater risk, relying on their momentum to achieve a victory in the face of odds that were almost two to one against them. Rick chose the latter course.

The man who was not carrying a burlap sack appeared to be the leader, and as he reached for his pistol, Rick instantly drew a bead on him with his rifle and squeezed the trigger. So certain of his aim that he reloaded without delay while still riding, a feat that few could emulate, Rick had the satisfaction of seeing the man crumple to the ground, a small, neat hole in the center of his forehead.

The Rangers fired a second or two later. One bullet

found its mark, and another man fell to the ground,
flinging his arms upward and dropping his burlap sack
with a crash as he died. The other Ranger missed his
target completely, but now the odds were even. Rick
fired a second shot as quickly as he could raise his rifle to
his shoulder, and again he was successful.

By now the two remaining thieves had placed their
burdens on the ground and were returning the Rangers'
fire with their own pistols. A bullet whistled past Rick's
head, close to his ear, but he did not flinch. Instead, he
felt angry. Timing his move carefully, he forced his
superbly trained stallion to a halt, at the same time
leaping to the ground and firing his pistol at one of the
remaining pair before they had the chance to reload. For
the third time he found his target.

The last of the robbers turned and started to run. Rick
had no opportunity to reload now, but he sprinted after
the criminal. Using his rifle as a club, he grasped the
weapon by its still-warm barrel and sent the stock
smashing into the side of the man's head. Blood spurted
from his head as he dropped like a felled log and lay
motionless, his sightless eyes fixed on the pale, cloudless
sky.

The two Rangers were not surprised at their superior's
accomplishments. Dispatching four of their five foes had
been a typical Rick Miller performance.

Leaving the Rangers to make certain that all five of
the criminals were indeed dead, Rick walked to the rear
of the house, then removed his hat when he saw the
tableau that awaited him. A man with the tanned face
and forearms of one who lived behind a plow was
stretched on the ground, a faint trickle of blood still
oozing from the spot on his chest where a thief's bullet
had killed him. Standing over him, dry-eyed, were a
woman with a lined, careworn face and two girls in their
early teens, who wept as they clung to their mother.

"Miller, Texas Rangers, ma'am," Rick called, announcing himself so he would not alarm the trio.

The woman looked at him and nodded, her face
blank.

"I'm afraid we got here too late, but those thieves won't do any more damage, not to anybody," he said.

"Thank God for that much," she replied in a dry, cracked voice.

He moved a few steps closer, then halted, feeling very much ill at ease. He had no idea that, when he spoke again, there was genuine compassion, even a touch of tenderness, in his voice. "We'll return your stolen property to the house for you, ma'am, and we'll remove the bodies of those bobcats so you won't have to look at them again. Is there anything else we can do for you?"

"Yes, please." Like so many who lived on the frontier, the newly widowed woman was eminently practical, even in a time of great tragedy. "I'll be obliged to you if you'll dig a grave for my husband's body. The girls and I have no heart for it."

"Yes, ma'am," he murmured.

"You'll find shovels in the near barn," she said, then led her children into the house.

Rick and his Rangers went to work digging a grave, fashioning a crude coffin, dragging the bodies of the thieves off the property, and throwing them into a gully, where the vultures soon would dispose of their remains, and then piling the stolen goods on the front porch. Rick noted absently that it was in need of paint.

There were several other chores that had to be done, and then Rick tapped at the door. The woman, still dry-eyed, opened it and stood on the threshold.

"It won't make up for the loss of your husband, ma'am, but I've put the thieves' horses in the big barn for you. I reckon you can get a fairly good price for them. They're all sound geldings. And here are the robbers' firearms, along with a purse that's filled with all the money they were carrying. Maybe all this will help tide you over."

An expression of gratitude appeared in her shocked, grief-stricken eyes. He became still more uneasy. If there was anything that upset him, it was being thanked for doing his duty. It didn't occur to him that he was going far beyond the call of duty, any more than he knew his voice and manner suggested a surprising inner, gentle quality that was at odds with his conduct when he tracked down criminals. He would have been astonished had anyone told him that he was a truly gentle man.

"What more can we do for you, ma'am?"

The woman hesitated for an instant, then said, "Would it be asking too much to bury my husband, please? My girls are taking it bad, but they'll accept his death as final once he's buried and they realize life must go on. That's why I hate to wait a day or so until the neighbors can gather."

As Rick well knew, the closest neighbors might live as far as five miles away. "It's the very least we can do," he said.

Again she hesitated. "Maybe you could read a prayer? I can fetch a Bible for you."

He had never read aloud, but duty sometimes made it necessary for a Ranger officer to do unusual things. "Is there something in particular you want me to read?"

She shook her head. "You choose it."

"Then," he replied, surprising himself as well as the widow, "I won't need the Bible."

A few minutes later the little group assembled behind the barn where the grave had been dug. The Rangers carried the farmer's coffin there and, at the widow's request, nailed it shut before her daughters came out of the house.

Rick knew without being told that she wanted the girls to remember their father as he had been in life. The woman called to her daughters, and when they joined her, she placed her arms around their shoulders.

Rick's instinct told him what to recite. He had been reared in a God-fearing home before the untimely death of his parents, and although he never spoke of his religion, his faith ran deep. His voice resonant but soft, he spoke the Twenty-third Psalm from memory:

The Lord is my shepherd; I shall not want.

He maketh me to lie down in green pastures: He leadeth me beside the still waters.

He restoreth my soul: He leadeth me in the paths of righteousness for His name's sake.

Yea, though I walk through the valley of the shadow of
death, I will fear no evil: for Thou art with me; Thy
rod and Thy staff, they comfort me.

Thou preparest a table before me in the presence of
mine enemies: Thou anointest my head with oil; my
cup runneth over.

Surely goodness and mercy shall follow me all the days
of my life: and I will dwell in the house of the Lord
forever.

At a nod from their commander the Rangers lowered
the coffin into the ground and began to fill the excava-
tion. One of the girls sobbed, and for the first time tears
trickled down the woman's cheeks. She brushed them
away. "That was beautiful." Her voice became firm as
she issued an order. "Mr. Miller, you and these boys will
stay to dinner."

Rick became fidgety. "We can't impose on you,
ma'am."

"Stuff and nonsense, Mr. Miller," she said. "Dinner has
been on the stove for hours, and if you don't eat it, I'll
have to throw it out. If there's anything that's a sin, it's
wasting good food when there are folks starving all over
the world!"

It would be an insult to refuse her hospitality, so he
agreed to stay.

An enormous bowl of beef stew was placed on the
kitchen table, and with it the widow served a large loaf
of crusty, hot bread and slabs of butter. The two young
Rangers ate lustily, and the teen-age girls recovered
sufficiently to engage them in conversation.

Rick had little appetite and pushed the stew around
on his plate. He could not rid himself of the thought that
he was eating a meal that had been intended for a man
who was now dead. It was absurd, he reflected, for
someone in his type of work to be so sensitive, and he
wished he could curb his feelings sufficiently to live up
to the hard-bitten image he presented to others.

"I'll drop in to see you whenever I'm out this way," he
said at last. "And if there's anything you want or need,

just send word to me at headquarters. I'll either come myself, or, if I'm too busy, I'll send one of the boys."

"That's right kind of you, sir," the widow replied. "As it happens, my son is due home in a month or two, so I reckon we can make out until then."

Rick was relieved. "How old is your son?"

"Twenty-three."

"Ah, then he's plenty old enough to do a man's work on your property. I was going to suggest that I could help find a hired hand for you."

"Oh, he's worked on the farm with his pa ever since he was a tyke, so he knows what needs to be done here. He just went off to St. Louis to pick up some newfangled wheat and onion bulbs that are supposed to stay alive during the dry spells here." She paused, then looked at him carefully. "Are you always this helpful to the survivors of folks who are killed by thieves, Mr. Miller?"

He felt color rising to his face and hoped it would not show beneath his heavy tan. "Well, ma'am," he said, "there's nothing in Ranger regulations that requires it. But the way I see things, Texas is putting up one whale of a fight for her existence. Between the weather and the threat of a new war with the Mexicans, who'll slaughter every last one of us if they win, we've got to stand together. It's the only way we'll survive." The discussion made him uncomfortable, so he turned to the two Rangers and issued a brusque order. "Help the youngsters clear away and wash the dishes, and we'll be on our way. We can reach Austin by late tonight if we push ourselves."

A few minutes later the widow escorted him to the front door, putting her hand on his arm for an instant. "Mr. Miller," she said quietly, "I want you to give your wife a message for me. Tell her she's a very lucky woman."

The embarrassed Rick didn't have the heart to tell her he was a bachelor.

He took the lead on the ride back across the open

fields, his stallion settling into his customary canter. With his broad-brimmed hat shielding his pale eyes, his rifle and pistol ready for immediate use in case of need, Rick Miller looked, once again, like a tough-minded law enforcement officer.

Cathy Blake tried to achieve a more matronly appearance by fixing her long, blonde hair in a bun at the nape of her neck, but the effort failed. Standing by the window of the commandant's house at the Oregon fort overlooking the Columbia River, she looked as young and pretty as she had before her marriage, when she had driven her lead wagon in the first train that had crossed the continent. She glanced at her two-year-old daughter, Beth, who was sitting on the floor, busily scribbling on scratch paper, then resumed her vigil. Her husband was due home at any moment.

She saw him when he left his office and started across the parade ground, trim and erect in the blue uniform of a full colonel in the United States Army, his physique lithe, his step light. It was absurd after being a married woman for years, Cathy thought, to feel a warm glow when she saw her husband. Perhaps she was an incurable romantic, something she had never suspected about herself.

As Lee drew closer, she noted that he was preoccupied, which was unusual. No, preoccupied wasn't the right description. His eyes were wary and guarded. But she told herself not to be concerned until and unless she had cause to worry. She opened the front door for him as he approached the steps, and they kissed.

Beth raced to the door, waving a sheet of paper. "Papa, look!" she shouted. "I make picture."

Lee swept her into his arms, hugged and kissed her. She was doubly precious to him and Cathy since they had lost their first baby through a miscarriage. But he merely glanced at Beth's scribbles. "Very nice," he said. "A beautiful picture, Beth."

Cathy noted that he didn't really look at the drawing.

Not that there was anything of substance for him to see,
but ordinarily he showed a great interest in Beth's activities.

Losing interest in the drawing now that she had been
praised, the little girl dropped it, grabbed her father's
gold-braided hat from his head, and squirming into a
sitting position on his shoulders, informed him, "Beth
want horsie ride."

Lee smiled but shook his head. "Not tonight, Bethie.
Papa is thinking about many things."

"Want ride!" she repeated, catching hold of his hair.

He pried open her small, chubby fists and held her at
arm's length. "That was naughty, and I disapprove.
Don't do it again." Without further ado he lowered her
to the floor.

Lee rarely was forced to discipline Beth, and the child
burst into tears. Tears always disconcerted Lee, and, as
he smoothed his rumpled hair, he looked helplessly at
his wife.

She picked up his hat, placed it on a peg in the front
hall, then silently motioned him into the sitting room
before she turned back to Beth. "You hurt Papa," she
said. "Poor Papa."

The little girl stopped crying, then ran to her father
and hugged him. "Poor Papa, poor Papa."

Although Lee returned Beth's hugs and kisses, he
looked relieved, Cathy observed, as she took Beth off to
the kitchen to be fed an early supper by Ginny Dobbs
Mullins, the wife of Lee's sergeant major, who worked
for the family part time.

"What's wrong?" Cathy asked as she returned to the
sitting room.

Lee wandered to a decanter, poured a small quantity
of whiskey into a goblet, and added a considerable
quantity of water to it. "Nothing, really. We need to
have a little talk, but I suggest we save it until after
supper."

"If I didn't have such a high regard for you, Colonel
Leland Blake, I'd tell you that you're the most infuriating
man alive. After that kind of a preamble, how can you

possibly expect me to wait until after supper? Goodness
only knows what I'd be imagining by then!"

He tasted his drink and made a wry face. "I don't
really want this," he muttered, walking to a window,
opening it, and throwing the contents into Cathy's flower
bed.

"Just what the peonies and marigolds need," she said.

He grinned at her. "Quality Kentucky whiskey is the
best fertilizer there is. I don't even know why I fixed
myself a drink."

Aware that he usually drank only when they had
guests, she felt certain something was bothering him.
Sitting in a straight-backed chair, she folded her hands
in her lap and announced, "I'm listening."

A light of warm amusement appeared in Lee's eyes.
"Sometimes you look exactly like Beth. Or vice versa."

"Stop stalling, Lee, or I shall forget I'm a lady. I can
scream louder than your regimental bugler can play that
dreadful brass instrument of torture."

He put his hand on her shoulders, kissed her, then
sank into the easy chair directly opposite her. "Stop
fussing. The end of the world isn't upon us."

"I'm so relieved to hear it," Cathy said dryly.

Lee settled back into his chair. "You've often heard me
speak of Colonel Bill Hawkins, my classmate at the
military academy. We were roommates in our plebe
year, we've always been promoted at the same time, and
we're still quite close."

"You correspond with him."

"Right. I had a letter from him today that was
squeezed into the official pouch the War Department
sent to me. Bill can get away with stunts like that
because he's head of the Military Secretariat." He
reached into an inner tunic pocket, removed a letter, and
unfolded it. "Maybe I'd better interpret it for you."

"In spite of any opinions to the contrary held by the
male member of this family—no name, mind you—I am
capable of reading simple English."

Lee chuckled and handed her the communication.
"Help yourself."

Cathy studied the letter at length, frowning, then handed it back to him. "This is pure gibberish. Not one sentence makes sense."

"When there are very private matters to be discussed," he said, "Bill and I always use a code we once worked out when we were on an intelligence assignment together. Any snooping War Department clerk who might have opened the letter wouldn't have understood a word. As I said, Madame Wise One, I'll interpret for you."

"I not only stand corrected, but I'm ready to jump out of my skin."

"Please don't. I've never touched smoother, softer skin."

She couldn't help giggling. "Vulgar."

"Accurate," he countered, then became serious. "Because of his official position, Bill is privy to all sorts of inside War Department information before anyone else knows about it. The gist of this letter is to tell me that there's a transfer in store for me."

"Oh." She caught her breath and tried not to appear too concerned.

"All Bill can tell me about it is that something big is in store for me. Winnie—General Winfield Scott, the Chief of Staff—has had several discussions with President Tyler about it. At the moment everything is being kept secret, but Bill says I should get an official communication before long."

"How long is that?"

He shrugged. "Your guess is as good as mine."

"Colonel Hawkins has no idea what might be in store for you?"

"Apparently not, unless the post is so sensitive that he didn't want to be the one to break the news to me informally. All I can say for certain is that it won't be a routine transfer to the command of a garrison in the Nebraska country or New England or the South."

Cathy listened carefully. She loved Oregon and her friends who she had met and grown close to on the wagon train. Yet she had known before she married Lee that no army assignment was permanent and that the day would come when they would be obliged to move.

"I've been thinking of every possibility. It could be that a new Indian war is going to break out somewhere."

"The Choctaw?"

"Not likely," he replied, grinning. "Andy Jackson taught them a lesson back when you were about Beth's age, and they haven't forgotten it. The puzzling angle of this thing is that Bill is sure I'll be able to take a few of my present people with me, like Sergeant Major Mullins. So I'd say that an Indian war is a strong possibility. Another is a post in Texas."

"The United States isn't sending troops into the Republic of Texas! That would mean war with Mexico, wouldn't it, Lee?"

"That would be my hunch, but I don't have the information that's available to President Tyler, the State Department, and the War Department." He reached for a pipe from the rack beside him, then filled it slowly and carefully, an indication that he was deep in thought.

"Why should Texas be so important to the United States?"

"The situation is simple, fortunately or unfortunately. Our country has a legitimate claim to the Oregon country, as you well know, but so does Great Britain. We've avoided an armed conflict here. So far. And it's my hope, as it is that of the British garrison at Fort Vancouver across the Columbia, that the dispute will be settled by diplomatic means. Texas is a different kettle of fish."

"In what way?"

"Hear me out," he said patiently, always impressed and pleased by her eagerness to learn. "Texas is a vast country and was virtually uninhabited for years. It was a province of Mexico, but very few Mexicans lived there. Americans are thrusting westward in great numbers, and have been for a number of years now. Naturally, there were thousands who were attracted—and are still attracted—by the fertile land in Texas going to waste. So

Americans migrated there in large numbers—and are still migrating."

"I know part of the rest of the story," Cathy said. "General Santa Anna, the President of Mexico, gave the Americans in Texas a hard time."

"Yes, it was very rough for them. Santa Anna is a tyrant, a dictator. So the Americans rebelled, and Sam Houston, who was Governor of Tennessee a number of years ago, won the great Battle of San Jacinto from Santa Anna. Texas became an independent country."

"Of course. But why are we becoming involved?"

"Because American citizens are still moving to Texas in huge numbers. The migration there is even greater than it is to Oregon. The day is bound to come soon when Texas will become an American state. They want it. We want it."

"But Santa Anna doesn't want us to become stronger at what he believes is his expense."

"Precisely," Lee said. "I'm talking about a factual situation that exists, not the ethical question of whether it's right or wrong for Texas to break way from Mexico and ultimately become part of the United States. The Texans will go to war to protect their liberty, and we'll do the same."

"That," Cathy said, "is the part that confuses me."

"Santa Anna," Lee said, puffing hard on his pipe and momentarily obscuring his face in a cloud of blue smoke, "is a no-good, vindictive devil. If he should regain control of Texas, he'd execute or imprison and torture every man who took up arms against him. He's said as much in so many words, which is why the opposition to him in Texas is so great."

"I can imagine what would happen to the American women and children."

"Texans who lived under Santa Anna's rule don't have to imagine anything," he said bluntly. "They know."

"And you think you may be given command of a regiment in a new war in Texas?"

"I honestly don't know what to think, which is why I'm whirling, Cathy." He picked up the letter again and tapped it with the stem of his pipe. "Now we come to the core of our personal situation. Bill Hawkins was very clear and very emphatic about one thing. He swears I'll be able to take my family with me on my new assignment."

She sighed deeply, and then a smile of relief and joy spread slowly across her face. "Hallelujah! As long as you and I are going to be together, I don't care where you're transferred."

"Not so fast," Lee told her. "I'll grant you we're playing a guessing game, but I'm worried. I can't believe the War Department would allow any officer to take his family into a war zone, regardless of whether we'll be fighting Indians or Mexicans. But there's no way on this earth that I'm going to subject you and Beth to any risks. I love you too much for that."

"I love you so much that I'll take any risks if we can stay together." Cathy impulsively jumped to her feet, went to him, and kissed him.

Lee returned her kiss with such ardor that she backed away, returning to her chair. "Beth hasn't gone to bed yet, and Ginny is still here, darling!" She tried without success to sound severe.

He grinned happily, but his face gradually became stern. "I will not permit you and Beth to be exposed to danger," he said. "And that's a definite, final decision."

"What would we do?"

"Suppose, for the sake of argument, that I take command of some unit in Texas and a war is fought there."

"There are a lot of women and children there right this minute!"

He ignored the interruption. "One sensible approach would be for you to move to New Orleans. It isn't all that far from Texas, and I could visit you whenever I'm granted leave."

Cathy shook her head so hard that the pins holding her bun in place loosened, and her blonde hair tumbled down her back. "I don't know a soul in New Orleans," she said.

"Another possibility worth considering is that you stay

right here in Oregon, where we have so many good
friends."

"We'd have to vacate this house."

"Sure. A new commandant will take over the garrison,
and the house will become his. But that's no problem.
We can establish a homestead and build a house of our
own there."

"What you mean," she said, "is that while you go
traipsing off to Texas—or wherever—I'd have to ask
friends to build a new house on the property for me."

"Something like that," Lee said lamely.

"A house where you won't have spent a single night. A
strange house with no memories."

"Cathy—"

She refused to be interrupted. "How far is it from here
to Texas?"

"Two thousand miles, more or less."

"With the Rocky Mountains to cross in order to get
there!" she exclaimed.

"Not necessarily. There are smaller ranges of mountains to the south—"

"Not all that small, I'm sure, and we'd be separated by
too great a distance. I wouldn't see you from the day you
left until months after the war ended!"

Noting that she was out of breath, he asked quickly,
"What do you suggest?"

She stood, planting her feet apart and clenching her
fists, creating the illusion that she was towering over
him. "You tell a regiment of hundreds of men to march.
And they march. You tell them to shoot, and they shoot.
You've made a family decision, which you've announced
to me. Now you'll hear my decision!"

Rarely had he seen her so ferociously earnest.

"Actually, I don't call it a decision. This is an ultima-
tum. Colonel Leland Blake, United States Army, I'm
issuing an order. As long as the War Department allows
us to stay together, we'll be together! And that, my
darling, is really final!"

Lee knew she had made up her mind, and that nothing
he could say or do would sway her. "You remind me of

that glue we made on the trail from the remains of a buffalo, remember? Smear it between two strips of leather, and nothing would tear them apart."

"I'm smearing an even stronger glue on both you and me right now," Cathy said.

He stood up, reached out, and took her hands in his. "At the risk of giving you a head so swollen it won't fit into that silly hat you wear to church, General Cathy Blake, you're the most wonderful woman in the world."

He drew her to him, and their kiss was long and passionate. "Be good," she murmured.

Lee glanced at the clock on the mantel over the hearth. "Ginny will be going home any minute, and it won't take long for us to put Beth to bed. I daresay, after the years I've spent in the army, that I can exercise enough self-discipline to be good for approximately a quarter of an hour."

"Ginny has put our supper on the stove. It will spoil if we don't eat right after Beth goes to bed."

"Let it spoil. We have a full larder. Besides, a meal is the last thing on my mind right now."

"You're incorrigible, darling," she murmured, her eyes shining.

"So I've been telling you for years. I'm glad I've finally convinced you."

They looked at each other, both conscious only of their deep love for each other.

"I'm a little shaky on my Bible," Cathy said softly. "I can never remember if it was Naomi who said it to Ruth, or if Ruth said to Naomi, 'Whither thou goest, there will I go.'"

"It was Ruth who said it to Naomi."

"In this family," she declared, "it is Cathy who says it to Lee, and don't you forget it, ever!"

The Madrid sunlight, almost uniquely clear and harsh, filtered into the parlor of a drab, middle-class house in the Spanish capital. Elisabeta Manuel, on whom a beam of light played, was dressed as dully as her surroundings as she sat upright in an old chair with a worn velvet seat, her hands folded primly in her lap. But the effect was misleading.

Her dark hair, rich and shining, cascaded down her back. Her forehead was high, her full lips were devoid of cosmetics, and her large, violet eyes, her most arresting feature, were luminous. Her slender, supple figure, although well concealed by her loose-fitting, high-necked dress, was little short of perfection. She was in her early twenties, but her air of innocence made her look much younger.

Anthony Roberts knew her sufficiently well, however, to realize that, properly displayed and enhanced, she would emerge as a radiant beauty. For several months, first in England and then in Spain, he had been searching for a young woman who was essential to the accomplishment of his devious scheme, and suddenly he had remembered Elisabeta. His hunt was ended, but he could not allow her to see how desperately he needed her, yet at the same time he had to overwhelm her, sweep her off her feet.

"Only a few days ago," he said in his fluent, unaccented Castilian Spanish, "I learned of the unfortunate passing of your dear parents last year. Your father was one of my closest friends, so I came to Madrid at once to offer you my condolences." That was a lie, of course; he had spent the past three weeks in Madrid.

Acknowledging his sympathy by bowing her head, Elisabeta was surprised. She had known, to be sure, that this man, who was in his late thirties, solidly built and charming, had cultivated her parents, but she would have called him an acquaintance rather than a friend. It was possible she was mistaken, to be sure. She had not been her father's confidante, and there was much about him she had not known. Certainly it had been a shock to discover, after living comfortably for all of her life, that he had left only a tiny estate. As a consequence she had been forced to depend on the charity of relatives who had taken her in out of a sense of duty rather than affection.

"It was not easy for me to find you," Anthony said.

"I am not surprised," she replied in her clear soprano. "My relatives are quiet, retiring people."

"So I found out," he said dryly, switching to English.

Ah! He had another unusual quality. He was fluent in both Spanish and English, usually speaking the latter with an upper-class British accent, yet occasionally sounding like an American. Her own English was almost faultless, thanks to the many years of devoted instruction she had received from Sister Maria at the convent school, but she had to admit that she spoke it with a slight Spanish accent. He had an Anglo-Saxon name, although she didn't know his nationality, and as a courtesy she addressed him in what she assumed to be his native tongue. "I hope I did not cause you trouble," she said politely.

"Trouble?" His laugh was rich and warm. "Dear Elisabeta, I would have gone to the ends of the earth to search for you." That much was true. Once he had thought of her as the necessary instrument to implement his plan and enable it to function, nothing would have persuaded him to end his hunt. "In any event, we are together now, that is what matters."

She was embarrassed because his comment sounded so personal. She had known few men, other than her father and several distant cousins, so she became flustered when she was complimented. Not that it happened all that often. In her present existence she met virtually no members of the opposite sex as she kept house for her relatives, who were so self-sufficient they had no social life and encouraged none for her.

Anthony knew he had to get her out of these familiar surroundings so he could apply his pressure forcefully. "This is such a glorious day that I wonder if we might take a stroll together."

The young woman hesitated. Never in her life had she gone anywhere with a man unless she had been attended by a chaperon, an old custom in which she had been reared. Several friends from the convent school had told her that times were changing, becoming more liberal, but she was inexperienced in such matters.

Instantly aware of her dilemma, he hastened to reassure her. "My dear Elisabeta, I give you my solemn word I am not a cannibal. I had a substantial breakfast, and I swear I won't carve you up and eat you for dinner."

She laughed a trifle nervously. Her uncle was away on business, and her aunt was out shopping, so she and Anthony were alone in the house. He was behaving like a perfect gentleman, so she saw no harm in going for a stroll with him. In the open, where they would see other people, he would need to be even more discreet. "All right," she said, making a daring decision. "I'll get my mantilla and shawl."

He nodded, hiding his exultation. He had won the first round, perhaps the most difficult. Now he had to advance at an even pace so he wouldn't alarm her.

Elisabeta left the room for a few moments, returning with a scarf of black lace that almost completely covered her lovely hair, and a thick shawl of black wool that further muffled her figure.

As they walked slowly, seemingly aimlessly, Anthony told her in detail about some of London's newest, most fashionable restaurants and about a number of exciting plays he had seen there recently. Elisabeta's sigh was inadvertent. "You lead such a glamorous life," she said.

"No more glamorous, I'm sure, than your life in Madrid, which is so alive." He well knew that she went nowhere, undoubtedly had visited no more than a few quiet dining places in her life, and had attended the theater only in the company of convent school classmates who had been chaperoned by nuns.

It wasn't accidental that they approached an outdoor café, where handsomely attired men and ladies in the latest fashions were sipping coffee or wine. Elisabeta couldn't help glancing surreptitiously at them. Step two was having its influence, he thought with satisfaction. "Shall we stop for some refreshments?"

She was tormented by indecision but suddenly made up her mind. No harm could come to her in this public place, and she could think of the occasion often during the endless, lonely months that stretched ahead for her.

Only a few very discerning men who were quick to recognize true beauty even glanced at Elisabeta, Anthony noted. How all that would change! He held her chair for her and then, as he seated himself, ordered a bottle of wine from the waiter.

Elisabeta's conscience bothered her, but she squelched it. She had been accustomed to wine all of her life, and by no stretch of the imagination could she be regarded as wicked if she drank a glass now rather than a cup of the bitter Moorish coffee that she disliked.

As they sipped their wine, Anthony Roberts described the wonders and challenges of the New World to her. He was a spellbinder, giving a superb performance, and he was able to refill her glass frequently without calling her attention to what he was doing. Summoning the waiter, he murmured a request for a bottle of potent Andalusian brandywine.

Elisabeta was enthralled by his stories. "You sound as though you've spent much time in America."

He was able to reply truthfully. "No, I haven't been there since I was a child. But the New World is much on my mind because I'm sailing there shortly from Málaga."

Their brandywine was served, the waiter placing the uncorked bottle and two glasses on the table.

Elisabeta was so enthralled, so engrossed in her own daydreams that she failed to notice the very generous portion that Anthony poured into her glass. "Where will you go?"

"I sail first to Havana, where I shall stay briefly. Long enough to see the sights, find the places that serve the best meals, and enjoy myself. Then I shall go on to New Orleans, in the United States. I am told there is no other city like it. And finally I shall go on to the capital of the Republic of Texas, where I shall attend to some business." He raised his glass in a toast.

Elisabeta raised her own glass in return, then sipped the brandywine. She was startled by the strong taste of it. By now, however, the wine she had consumed had lowered her guard somewhat, so she wasn't too concerned. "How I envy you the adventures you'll have."

"I shall sail in a few days," he told her. "As a matter of fact, I've been fortunate enough to have engaged a rather luxurious suite on board an old but splendid galleon." He waited deliberately while she absently sipped her brandywine, then quietly added, "How I hate to go alone."

Excitement, combined with the alcoholic beverages she had consumed, brought a blush to her cheeks, and her limpid eyes were shining.

Now was the precise moment to strike, Anthony decided. He had already planned this move carefully, searching every facet of his approach for possible weaknesses. He knew he had to be bold yet tender, self-confident yet supplicating. If she responded as he hoped, he would be able to fulfill the ambition that had consumed him since he had been a child. If she refused, he would be obliged to scheme anew, starting from the beginning.

Gently but swiftly, he took her hand in his. Elisabeta instinctively pulled back. Anthony looked crushed. She thought better of her gesture. He was so abject she felt sorry for him, and surely no harm would be done by allowing him to hold her hand. She returned it to the table and enjoyed a pleasant sensation when he tenderly placed his own hand over it.

"I don't quite know how to say this to you," he said, remembering every word of the speech he had devised for the occasion. "But I—well, I have loved you for a long time, ever since I watched you in your teen-age years, growing to womanhood. Shortly before your father died, I asked him for your hand. He consented—"

"He did?" That put a far different light on the matter.

"Indeed, but he asked me to wait a year, until you became more mature. I have waited for that year, and now I am here."

Elisabeta was totally confused. She had tried hard since the death of her parents to reconcile herself to the probability that she would live and die a spinster. She had no money to provide any eligible suitor with an appropriate dowry, and her relatives did nothing to promote her marriage to anyone.

So she had a clear-cut choice. She could continue, for the rest of her life, to live as she had for the past year, or she could visit strange and exotic places, enjoying luxuries she had never known, with the spice of adventure thrown in.

To be sure, she was not even remotely in love with Anthony Roberts, whom she scarcely knew. But her father might have arranged her marriage with Anthony, who had many factors in his favor. He had great charm and seemed unusually considerate. He was sophisticated and cultured, and he appeared well able to support a wife in a manner far more sumptuous than any she had ever known. Spurred by the drinks she had consumed, she nodded, unable to trust her voice.

Anthony felt a surge of triumph. The odds had been against him, but he had won her. Now he had to overcome the last, tricky obstacles, making his demands seem reasonable. "We'll take the late stagecoach today for Toledo and then go south."

She blinked in astonishment. "But we can't be married until the banns have been published and a whole week has elapsed."

His grip on her hand tightened. "I'm afraid there isn't time, dear Elisabeta. We'll miss our ship in Málaga if we stay in Madrid for an extra week. We'll be married after we reach the New World."

The girl caught her breath. "Surely you aren't suggesting we live in sin until then!"

"A mere technicality," he said, shrugging. "Believe me when I tell you that I love you and want to spend my life with you. What alternatives are there?"

"I—I don't know." Her mind was whirling.

"It would be absurd for us to travel separately, as well as exorbitantly expensive. I have no money worries, but I don't like to squander my fortune."

As one who had always been careful of her money, she could appreciate his feelings.

"Besides," he added with fierce, simulated passion, "I

want you so much I couldn't spend day after day in a platonic relationship with you."

Elisabeta turned scarlet. Encouraged by her reaction, he grew even bolder. "Until we go through the formality of a legal ceremony—which we will, at the first opportunity—we'll be husband and wife in the sight of God and in the eyes of each other."

No one had ever spoken to her that way, and she could feel her defenses melting away.

"We'll go first to my inn to consummate our marriage, and then we'll put Madrid behind us."

Elisabeta knew she was being swept off her feet without being given the opportunity to think clearly, and she protested feebly. "But that's too soon! I—I've got to go home for my belongings."

The last phase of Anthony's scheme was falling neatly into place. "Do you have any silk gowns that are your favorites?" he demanded.

She shook her head. "I've never owned any finery."

Having guessed correctly, he supplied the clinching argument. "I see no problem. We'll have ample time to buy you a complete new wardrobe before the stage leaves for Toledo."

The prospect made her dizzy.

Everything was falling into place, just as he had hoped. In order to make her totally dependent on him when he called on her to play the role he had chosen for her, he wanted her to have no ties with her past.

Also, she had to be transformed into a dazzling, ravishing beauty who would attract the instant attention and arouse the desire of every man who sought her. Therefore, the schedule for the rest of the day was obvious. First, he would take her to his quarters and bed her. The subsequent guilt that would overwhelm her would make it impossible for her to return to the house of her relatives, and she would cling to him. There would still be time to take her to some of the shops, in the oldest part of the city, near the Plaza Mayor, where the strumpets of Madrid worked and bought their gowns and shoes. For a reasonable sum he could buy her a wardrobe of eye-catching, figure-revealing clothes—she was so naive she wouldn't recognize the significance of what she was wearing. And if time became short before they completed their purchases, he knew a similar harlots' district in Málaga, which they could visit before they sailed. By the time he finished outfitting her, every man who saw her would crave her. She would become the perfect decoy.

Anthony paid his bill, stood and, drawing Elisabeta to her feet, looked at her with blazing, passionate eyes. "Come, my love," he said, and taking no chance that she might become panicky and bolt, firmly linked his arm through hers.

Harry Canning sat in his office on the Columbia River inlet where the shipbuilding company of Thoman and Canning maintained its headquarters. Once a ship's captain himself, he was no longer young, but he was still sound-bodied and vigorous, and his problem was mental rather than physical. He couldn't concentrate on the schedule for the new windjammer being built under his supervision because he was concerned about his wife.

He had known there was a considerable difference in their ages when he had married Nancy, but in spite of her flighty moments and her occasional impulsive acts, he had regarded her as a young woman endowed with common sense. He still thought so, although her behavior was far too often that of a pleasure-seeking adolescent.

He reminded himself that she was still very young, in her early twenties, but that wasn't her real problem. She was far too much under the influence of Melissa Austin, her best friend, who, although still in her teens, was imperious and strong-willed. Melissa invariably initiated some harebrained, thoughtless act, and Nancy always joined her, never thinking of the possible consequences. Perhaps, Harry told himself, he was being too severe. The young women sometimes created talk, as they had done when they had waded into the falls in the pool at the base of the Willamette River Falls, fully clothed, but

They hadn't actually harmed anyone, including themselves. Perhaps Nancy was right when, in moments of annoyance, she accused him of lacking a sense of humor.

A tap sounded at the door, and Harry Canning was relieved by the respite. He grinned when the tall, physically ungainly Danny Taylor came into the office. The one-time bound boy who had run away from his master and had made himself useful in so many ways to his fellow travelers was an adult now. He worked in tandem with his close friend, Chet Harris, who was somewhat shorter and stockier, on the farm owned by the latter's family. It was said that Danny was as clumsy as Chet was graceful, but Harry, long a judge of men, knew better. Danny was as reliable as he was quick-thinking in times of emergency, and behind his seeming physical ineptitude was a steady and dependable person.

"Got a few minutes to spare, Harry?" Danny asked as he sauntered across the office.

"Always, for you." The shipbuilder hoped Danny wanted to apply for a position. He would be a great asset, even though he would need to learn the business. Danny promptly dashed the older man's wishful thinking. "I need to have a private talk with you," he said.

"It won't go beyond these walls," Harry assured him.

"I'm not one to gossip, but I can't get my head set straight on my shoulders," Danny said. "Your Nancy and Melissa Austin are inseparable, and I guess you and Nancy are the closest thing to a family Melissa has had since her folks died of mountain fever before her wagon train even got to Oregon."

Harry nodded, although he would have preferred not to think of Melissa again for a long time. A hint of his wry humor appearing in his eyes, he said, "Well, you don't need me to tell you she's pretty."

"There's none prettier," Danny said fervently. "Man alive, when she stands in the sun, with that red hair looking like it's on fire, she's really something special!"

"What you're saying is that you're sweet on her."

"Sometimes I think I am, and sometimes I'm not so

sure." Danny spoke with his customary candor. "The trouble is that Chet is sweet on her. We're the best and closest friends, but we compete with each other, too, so I can't make up my mind whether I'm really falling in love with Melissa or whether I want to beat out Chet."

Harry chuckled. "That's being honest. What do you want from me, lad?"

"Tell me what she's really like. When she starts batting those green eyes at me, my heart starts jumping like a salmon leaping through the white waters of the Columbia."

"You may not like all you hear."

"If I'd wanted somebody to praise her to the skies, I'd listen to Chet!"

"First off, let's list her assets. She's exceptionally pretty, as any man who has eyes in his head knows. Equally important is that she's a decent, honorable person. Oh, I know she can't help flirting with every man she sees, but that's second nature to her, and she doesn't mean anything serious by it. She even flirts with me sometimes. My wife, who knows her better than I do, says she doesn't even realize she's doing it and that she'd give a rough time to any man who got the wrong ideas."

"I've figured that much myself."

"Her worst liability," Harry continued, "is that she's young, a problem she'll overcome automatically. I gather she was spoiled by her family because she was so attractive and an only child. After she lost her parents, everyone made a fuss over her."

"I was one of them," Danny interrupted.

"Everybody in the community flatters her. Even Whip Holt, who isn't fooled by her or anyone else, I'm sure. She's very appealing."

"Do I know it," Danny muttered.

"Too often, though, she behaves like a girl of eleven or twelve. She acts without thinking of the consequences, she does what she wants—sometimes just so she'll create shocks and raise eyebrows, I'm convinced—and she won't take advice. She has the stubborn character and the hot temper of a redhead." Harry refrained from adding that her natural strength as a leader had made a blind follower, at least for the present, of his own, almost as immature, wife.

"When I was a youngster," the introspective Danny said, sighing quietly, "I didn't know folks were so complicated."

"Well, you've grown up, but Melissa hasn't. Yet. I can't tell you what to do. Only you can decide whether you want to pay serious court to her. The only advice I can give you is that you might be wise to go off someplace and not see her for a time so you can gain perspective, even though you risk losing her to some competitor."

"Like Chet."

"That's the chance you'd be taking."

Danny rubbed his long jaw reflectively. "One place I'd sure like to go is Texas."

Harry brightened. "I wouldn't mind that myself."

"There's sure to be real fireworks there, and with the Willamette Valley becoming so civilized, life here is becoming kind of tame. But I have no notion of how I'd get to Texas or what I'd do there. So I reckon I'll have to sit tight and work things out in my head from right here."

II

The old man sat in a rocking chair on the veranda of his house, the Hermitage, and for a few moments he stared out across the rolling, green hills of Tennessee, his favorite view in all the world. Then, slowly, he poured himself a small amount of whiskey and filled his glass with water. Taking his time, he sipped the drink, savored it, and sighed happily.

His physician had restricted him to one drink each day, and this was his second, the first having been consumed several hours earlier, before dinner. But the physician was not present to reprimand him, and former President Andrew Jackson's three guests had no intention of reminding him that he was disobeying his doctor's orders. The "lion's cubs" did not rebuke the "lion."

By far the most physically prepossessing of the trio was Sam Houston, the conqueror of the Mexican dictator, Santa Anna, at the Battle of San Jacinto. Sam Houston had just been elected to serve another two-year term as President of the Republic of Texas, with his new term to expire at the end of 1845. Tall and heavyset, he slouched in his chair, his eyes shielded from the late afternoon sun by the high-crowned, broad-brimmed beaver hat that had become his political trademark. The days when he had been called "the Big Drunk" by the Cherokee Indians were long past, and he contented himself with a glass of fresh apple juice from the Hermitage's orchards.

Also drinking apple juice was a slender man who looked like meekness personified until the observer saw the steel in his gray eyes and the set of his firm jaw. James K. Polk, the former majority leader in the House of Representatives, never touched liquor because of a chronic stomach complaint. Completely at home in this house of his mentor, he stretched his legs out straight and relaxed in his chair.

The only member of the group slightly ill at ease in the presence of his seniors was young, dark-haired Andrew Johnson, a former tailor whose wife had taught him to read and write. Currently the majority leader of the Tennessee Senate, he was running for a seat in the U.S. House of Representatives, and his election was certain because of Andrew Jackson's support. Like his mentor, he had a glass of whiskey and water, but he left it untouched.

Old Hickory cleared his throat. "Boys," he said, "the way I see it, the settlement of the Oregon boundary dispute with Great Britain and the admission of Texas to the Union as a state are two parts of the same issue. This country is spreading out. Fast. What's that phrase you've been using in your recent speeches, Jamie?"

"Manifest destiny, Mr. President. We regard the expansion of our boundaries as the manifest destiny of the United States." Polk spoke with obvious sincerity.

Sam Houston grinned at him. "It's a great rallying cry. I wish I'd thought of it."

"Help yourself to it, Sam," Polk replied. "The sooner the American people become aware of our goals, the sooner we'll achieve them."

Old Hickory nodded. "Sound thinking, Jamie. If I'm right, it will take another two years for Texas to be admitted to the Union and make the damn British listen to reason and give us a fair border in Oregon."

Houston was disappointed. "Why that long, sir?"

"I have nothing against John Tyler," Jackson declared. "He means well, and he's a fairly effective President. But he has no political base, no political support of his own. Van Buren has killed himself by opposing the annexation of Texas, and I've written him as much. He won't win the nomination. That's why Jamie will be the next President."

Young Andrew Johnson spoke tentatively. "You think he can beat Senator Clay, sir? He's sure to win the Whig nomination."

"Henry Clay is a jackass," Old Hickory said. "He has a genius for taking the wrong stand on every popular issue. He's come out strongly against the annexation of Texas. And he's said flatly that Oregon isn't worth a war with the British. The people of this country demand the admission of Texas and a fair slice of the Oregon country."

Houston frowned, then sighed. "I hope you're right."

Jackson raised a thick, white eyebrow, and an amused gleam appeared in his blue eyes. "Have you ever known me to be wrong in my judgment of American popular opinion?"

"No, sir," Sam Houston admitted. "But two years is a long time to wait when Texas has so many problems. Immigrants are still coming to us from every state, but that's the only bright spot. We don't have the funds in our treasury or a national income to function indefinitely as an independent nation. Santa Anna keeps trying to nudge us into a new war by sending cavalry patrols across the border. We desperately need a navy to protect our coast along the Gulf of Mexico, and we don't have even one warship. I wish we could light a fire under President Tyler and Secretary of State Webster."

"Well, that won't happen," Jackson said flatly. "Daniel Webster is too conservative for his own good—or the country's. You'll have to be patient, Sam. And that brings me to the ultimate purpose of this meeting. We've got to coordinate our efforts so Texas and Oregon will fall into our laps by the time Jamie Polk reaches the White House. Sam, what are your most urgent needs?"

"A navy," Houston replied without hesitation. "Arms, munitions, and supplies for an expanded army. I'm getting a wonderful response to my appeal to the American people for contributions, but I need more. A great deal more."

Old Hickory turned to young Andrew Johnson. "When you win your seat in Congress, you'll inaugurate an immediate campaign for the expenditure of Federal funds to provide Texas with arms and gunpowder. How does that sound to you?"

"Great, sir!" Johnson spoke eagerly but somberly. "It's just what I've had in mind."

"In the meantime," Houston said, "maybe I'll accept that interest-free loan the British keep dangling in front of me."

"If you must, then do it," Old Hickory replied sourly. "It may not surprise you that I'm not overly fond of them."

The trio roared with laughter. Jackson had defeated the Duke of Wellington's veterans at New Orleans in the War of 1812, but even that victory had not satisfied him, and in his two terms as President, he had lost no opportunity to express his anti-British bias.

The old man laughed sheepishly, then sobered. "By all means, Sam, take their money. Just keep in mind that it is in London's best interests to see Texas maintain her standing as a separate and independent nation."

"I'm not forgetting it," Houston replied.

"Now, then." Old Hickory folded his sinewy hands in his lap. "Texas and Oregon must be kept intertwined in the public mind. Immigrants are going to Oregon by the thousands these days. New wagon trains are setting out from Independence, Missouri, every month or two. While the British procrastinate, we're occupying the region. Immigrants are pouring into Texas, too, but her situation is different. The friends of annexation, and that includes an overwhelming majority of Americans, will have to keep up the pressure for the next couple of years. Texas must be given first priority."

Houston was relieved.

"Once she becomes a state," the old man went on, "America will be so big and so strong that Great Britain will be very reluctant to fight another war with us. We continue to insist that we want the border established at fifty-four forty, but in time we'll settle for the forty-ninth parallel, which is reasonable and just. Jamie, we'll depend on you to keep Texas and Oregon linked."

"They're already linked," Polk said. "The question is how to dramatize the linkage."

"Ah, we'll soon come to that," Old Hickory declared. "The biggest problem, as I see it, is not the possibility of war with Britain, but war with Mexico."

"I wish I could predict what Santa Anna will do, but I can't," Houston said. "He's so vain he's become unrealistic. If *I* could beat him with my little army, as I did, he'd stand no chance in a war with the United States. But he's foolish enough to declare war, once Texas is annexed."

"There's also the possibility," Polk said, "that he'll be more pragmatic than that. According to the reports I've been receiving from Washington City, he may be willing to sell California to the United States. Certainly he's been weighing such a deal. But we can't make our policy contingent on what Santa Anna will or won't do. I believe we should simply forge ahead."

"Those are my sentiments, too," Sam Houston declared.

"You're right, both of you," Andrew Jackson said. "Now, how do we forge ahead? First, we encourage aid to Texas by private citizens' contributions. Sam needs everything from guns to farm tools. Then, boys, there's an angle none of you seems to have considered. We encourage the people of Oregon to help their brothers in Texas!"

They stared at him in admiration. He had become physically frail, but no man in America could match his political acumen.

"I suggest," he continued, "that all of us ask for the help of our influential friends. I'll start writing letters myself first thing tomorrow."

"Why don't you leave that burden to us, sir?" Polk asked, trying to be diplomatic. "The doctor has made it very plain that you're not to tire yourself."

Jackson stared at him, then at the others, with sup-
pressed fury. "Hell, I can dictate letters, and it's no great
chore to sign my name to them, you know. When the
future of this country is at stake, I refuse to pamper
myself because of what doctors say! By the Eternal, I'm
not dead yet, and while there's breath in my body, I'll
continue to serve my country!"

The snow-capped peaks that lay to the east of the
ranch located in the fertile valley near the junction of the
Columbia and Willamette rivers inspired awe, and Eulalia Holt never tired of the view from her kitchen windows. The population of the Oregon country was soar-
ing, with wagon trains arriving every few weeks, and
newcomers were claiming land eagerly, but the mountains were tranquil, and their serenity influenced the
ever-growing community.

Eulalia had good cause, as she well knew, to be
grateful for the blessings she enjoyed. The ranch, where
her husband bred horses, had prospered in the past four
years. Michael—or Whip, as everyone else called him—
no longer yearned for his old life as a hunter, guide, and
trapper and was content with his lot. Six hired hands
worked for him, and Eulalia had hired the wife of one to
help her with the housework. The Holts were prosper-
ing, and none of the new arrivals could have guessed
they had been penniless when they had come to Oregon
on the first wagon train.

In spite of their growing wealth and respected position in the territory, nobody worked harder than the
Holts. Toby, their two-and-a-half-year-old son, was one
of the reasons they did so, Eulalia realized, and they
would be equally ambitious for the other children who
would be born in the years ahead. She could vividly
recall the day when all of her earthly possessions had
been packed in the covered wagon that she, her late
father, and her brother had occupied when, after they
had lost their South Carolina plantation, they had joined
the first wagon train. And Whip, who had guided that

train, had been able to stow his belongings in a small saddlebag.

No wonder she appreciated her huge wood stove, sturdy table, and comfortable chairs. Wandering into the parlor, she let her hand rest on some of the fine furniture that had been purchased in Boston and carried here by ship. Her world was solid and secure, and she smiled as she went on to the small room that she and Whip used as an office. A chore she thoroughly enjoyed was that of keeping the ranch's books, and she loved seeing the profits mount month by month, year by year. Some of the newcomers couldn't understand why a beautiful woman still in her twenties willingly "buried herself" on the ranch, seeing only a few old friends socially. But these newcomers belonged to a different breed. The early settlers never allowed themselves to forget their lean years or the hardships they had suffered.

For the better part of the morning, Eulalia immersed herself in the columns of figures, and the time passed swiftly. Even before they sold the three colts that Whip was readying for market, the current month's profits would amount to four hundred dollars. Eulalia guessed she could treat herself to the expenditure of five dollars for a length of silk that she and her sister-in-law, Cindy Woodling, would make into a new dress.

The sound of approaching hoofbeats interrupted her work, and Eulalia looked out the window and smiled as she saw Whip approaching on his magnificent stallion. Whip's worn buckskins were comfortable, so she couldn't blame him for refusing to buy new clothes. But his broad-brimmed hat, which he had worn for at least ten years, was positively disreputable. She would get him a new one the very next time she went into town and then would burn the old one. There were times when a woman had to take matters into her own hands.

Eulalia's smile broadened as she watched Toby, mounted in front of his father. They sat erect in the same way, the boy's posture a copy of that of the father he so strongly resembled. Eulalia had insisted that Toby was

too young to ride with Whip, but Whip had overruled
her, and he had been right. Toby held himself with ease
and confidence.

Only when they dismounted did the young woman's
smile fade. Whip limped painfully as he and his son
walked slowly toward the house, and she knew the
arthritis in his hip was flaring up again. But she couldn't
let him see her concern, so she composed herself and
pretended to be working on the books again.

Toby raced into the room. "Mama!" he cried. "Papa's
new horse is going to have a baby. I want to go see it!"
Eulalia knew that Whip's new wild mare in the upper
canyon was about to foal.

"We'll talk about it at dinner, dear. Now come along,
let's get cleaned up." She poured water into a basin and
helped the boy wash. Then she joined Whip, who had
disappeared into their bedroom. She consciously adopted
a casual manner.

As she had anticipated, Whip had poured water into a
basin and was scrubbing his hands. He didn't want her
to see him walking.

"You couldn't persuade Toby to eat smoked venison
with you on the range, I gather." She sounded offhand.

Whip grinned at her. "He saw you baking chocolate
cookies before we left the house this morning. He made
it clear that he wanted to come home."

"He's already told me he wants to go see the new
mare." She saw that, after drying his hands, her husband
continued to stand near the table on which the basin was
resting, so she deliberately turned away from him.

"All three of us will go. We'll make an outing of it."
He started to cross the room.

Eulalia wheeled around before he could halt. "The
outing will have to wait. You and I are going into town
this afternoon. To see Bob Martin."

"Aren't you well?"

"*I'm* fine," she said pointedly.

Whip feigned ignorance. "Bob and Tonie are coming
for supper tomorrow night."

"That's a social occasion. We're paying a professional

call on our physician. You're having another arthritis attack."

"I manage just fine," he protested.

"You do not. That's why you were trying to hide it from me."

"There isn't a blame thing Bob can do for my condition. He's told me that medicine won't help. Rest won't help. I've just got to grit my teeth until my hip starts to feel better again."

She refused to back down. "He also said he wanted to see you the next time you felt crippled. So you're going this very day, Michael Holt, and I'm going, too, so I'll know you've actually seen him."

Whip limped as he fell in beside her, and they started toward the dining room. "You're a very bossy woman, Mrs. Holt."

"That's because you're too stubborn and too proud to take care of yourself when you're sick, Michael Holt. That's why you'll do as I tell you."

He placed a hand on her shoulder, halting her, then kissed her. "This is the only way I know to shut you up."

"Nothing shuts me up when your health is at stake." Eulalia refused to be mollified.

His sigh was exaggerated. "We'll do it your way, ma'am, because otherwise you'll nag me to death."

"We'll leave for town as soon as Toby goes to bed for his nap."

The boy was already in the dining room, wondering whether it would be safe to help himself to bread and butter before his parents arrived. He heard them approach and decided not to run the risk. Papa didn't care about such things, but Mama was a stickler for what she called "minding your manners."

The hired hand's wife appeared with a tureen of beef and vegetable soup, which Eulalia ladled into bowls. "Toby," she said, "I'm afraid we won't be able to go see the mare until tomorrow. I've got to take Papa into town this afternoon to visit the doctor."

In spite of the child's extreme youth, he knew that

something was wrong with his father, and he even
sensed that his father did not want to go to see the
doctor. But his mother obviously was insisting, and Toby
deemed it the better part of discretion to agree.

"Papa should go to the doctor," he said.

"Toby," Eulalia said, "you have more sense than your
father."

Whip glowered but remained silent. He still regarded
a call on a physician as a sign of weakness. He well
remembered the winter he had spent alone in the Rocky
Mountains, so debilitated by a raging fever that he had
felt certain he would die. Well, he had recovered, just as
his wounds had healed after a score of fights and battles.
To be sure, Bob Martin had told him there was no cure
for his arthritis and that he would have to accept the
approach of middle age. He appreciated his wife's concern, but he hoped she realized that a man who had
been active all of his life couldn't adjust overnight to a
new kind of existence. He would try, but the ache in his
hip made it difficult for him to think clearly.

Sergeant Major Hector Mullins was drilling a platoon
of U.S. Army recruits on the parade ground of Fort
Oregon, overlooking the junction of the Willamette and
Columbia, and his steady roar rolled across the open
area. When Hector was dealing with recruits, his voice
resembled that of an angry bull.

Colonel Lee Blake, the garrison commander, laughed
silently as he closed his office window. He needed to
concentrate on the mail that had just arrived from Washington City. On the top of the pile was a letter from the
Adjutant General, addressed to him, and he opened it
first.

The transfer that his friend Bill Hawkins had written
him about had come. But the post was not named in the
orders. Lee was directed to report first to army headquarters in Washington City. He was also authorized to
detach one member of his staff from present duties to
take with him on his new assignment.

He sighed and riffled through the mail until he found

another letter bearing his name. Written on War Department stationery, it was personal rather than official, and he immediately recognized the bold, distinctive hand of Major General Winfield Scott, the Army Chief of Staff who had long been his mentor.

You won't regret your transfer, Scott wrote. *I can't discuss your new assignment with you now, but I can tell you this much: I'm sure you'll detect the fine hand of Andrew Jackson. He wrote separately to President Tyler and me, suggesting you for the job.*

So! Old Hickory was responsible. To the best of Lee's knowledge, there was no insurrection of a major Indian nation under way. Knowing President Jackson's interests, he strongly suspected his new post would have some connection with the situation in the Republic of Texas. He could almost bet on it.

He read several other official communications, then went to the adjoining office of his executive officer, Lieutenant Colonel Eli Moser, a sheaf of papers in his hand.

"Congratulations, Eli," he said. "You're the new commandant of Fort Oregon."

Moser read his orders, then smiled broadly. "This is great. For me, at least."

"You can count on a promotion to full colonel within six months, you know."

"I'm sure of it. But what about you, Lee? Where are you being sent?"

"The War Department is being coy. They're not telling me until I reach Washington City."

"That means there's something big in store for you, Lee!"

"Maybe so." After spending all of his adult life in the army, Lee knew better than to waste time and energy in speculation. "I hope you won't mind too much if I take Sergeant Mullins with me."

"I'll miss him, of course. But I can't blame you for wanting him. There's isn't a better soldier in the army."

Lee returned to his own office and sent his orderly for the Sergeant Major.

Mullins saluted smartly. "I know I was makin' a ruckus out yonder, Colonel, but them recruits are hard of hearin'."

"Sit down," Lee said. "Mullins, I'm being transferred to an undisclosed new assignment, and I'm taking you with me."

Hector Mullins had spent many years in the army, too. "Yes, sir," was his only reply.

"We'll go to Washington City and pick up our new papers there. Not so incidentally, your wife may come with you."

The sergeant major grinned. "Me and Ginny will be ready to travel the minute you give me the word!"

Sergeant Major Hector Mullins, lying about his age, had been fifteen when he had enlisted in the army after the end of the War of 1812. He had fought in more Indian wars than he could remember, and now, although still in his thirties, he was a veteran with more than two decades of military service under his belt. It was no mean accomplishment that he had worked his way up to the highest rank a noncommissioned officer could achieve.

A bluff, hearty, and uncomplicated man, direct in his dealings with everyone, Hector had surprised his friends as well as Colonel Lee Blake, his commanding officer, by falling in love for the first time in his life. His marriage to Ginny Dobbs had seemed right for both of them. She had joined the wagon train to Oregon in the Rockies after traveling all the way across the Sierra Nevada when fleeing from San Francisco, no mean achievement in itself. She was a young woman with no false pretensions, no delusions of grandeur. Like her husband, she was practical and sensible.

So, when Hector came home for a quick meal at noon to the tiny house to which his rank as the garrison sergeant major entitled them, he anticipated no problems. Hugging her from behind as she stood at the stove, he allowed his hands to roam freely.

Ginny enjoyed the sensation but did not share his

playful mood. "Move back, Hector, or, I'll burn you with this spoon."

He released her, chuckled, and, removing his tunic, washed in a bucket of water he pumped from their well, then sat down at the kitchen table in his undershirt. He beamed when his wife brought their meal to the table. "Venison, eh? Don't tell me you bought this at the store."

"No," she said, "I stopped in at Dolores's inn this morning for a cup of tea while I was marketing, and she gave it to me. Her husband and his partner went hunting yesterday and between them brought down two deer. So they have more than they can eat at home and use at the inn. Dolores wouldn't let me pay her."

"I approve of friends like that." He cut the steak into two portions, placed the smaller but more tender portion on her plate and then began to shovel food into his mouth.

Ginny had made several attempts to improve his table manners after they first had been married, but he hadn't listened to her and she had abandoned her efforts. It didn't matter that he was rough and abrasive in many ways. She wasn't all that cultured herself, and what mattered was that they loved each other. In fact, she knew she would be lost without him.

"You look pleased with yourself," she said. "Did you have a good time his morning, scaring some new recruit half to death?"

"Guess again."

"You caught some troops breaking regulations, so you've locked them up."

"Wrong. The old man called me in for a confidential talk, so what I'm going to tell you can't be repeated."

"The old man?"

"I've told you a million times. Colonel Blake."

"He's your age," she said. "I don't know for sure, but he may be younger than you."

"It don't matter. In the army the troops always call the commander of their unit the old man, even if he's just started to shave."

Ginny sometimes enjoyed teasing him. "I'm not in the army. I always call him Colonel Blake."

"Don't get me all mixed up. What Colonel Blake told me is important. He's being transferred, and he's taking me with him. Seeing as how Mrs. Blake is going with him, he says it'll be just fine for you to come with me."

Her fork slipped from her hand, clattering to her plate, and she promptly lost her appetite. "Transferred to where?"

"Beats me," Hector said. "I've been stationed in so many places since I've been in uniform that I can't even remember most of 'em. And I don't much care. The old man is a great fellow to work for. You get along fine with his missus and pick up extra money helping them out, so I can't think of a better arrangement."

Ginny stared at him, caught her breath, and said, "What you're telling me is that we're leaving Oregon."

"Now you got it straight." Eating with great speed, he finished his meal, pushed his plate away, and, tipping back his chair of unpainted pine, belched happily.

Ginny moaned.

"If that venison ain't settling right, it'd be a shame to let it go to waste."

She handed him her plate. "Hector," she said plaintively, "I can't leave Oregon."

"What in thunderation do you mean, you can't? We don't argue when we get an order. First we salute, and then we do what we're damn well told."

"I just finished telling you, I'm not in the army." Her bantering tone had vanished.

He raised a bushy eyebrow, then peered hard at her, realizing she wasn't joking.

"I never had a real friend in my life until I joined the wagon train," Ginny said. "I behaved terribly for a while, but people were kinder to me than anybody had ever been. Some of those women are now my very best friends, and I'd be lost without them."

He became annoyed. "You happen to be married to me."

"I don't need to be reminded of that," she replied, flaring at him. "I'm going to be married to you until I die."

"Then you aren't staying behind in Oregon while the War Department sends me somewhere else."

"I have no intention of being separated from you, now or ever," she said.

He struggled for the patience it was so difficult for him to achieve. "Get things straight, Gin. It's a great feather in my cap that the old man wants me to go to his new assignment with him. I'm sure I'll even get a raise to the top pay an enlisted man can earn. When a full colonel of the old man's standing puts in a request for his sergeant major, it goes on his permanent record. I can stay on duty for another ten to fifteen years if I want, based on the strength of Lee Blake's request."

"You'll simply have to tell him your wife won't leave, that he'll have to find someone else. There must be a hundred sergeants major in the army."

The front legs of his chair landed on the kitchen floor with a jolting crash. Without rising, he reached for his tunic, then slowly fastened its brass buttons one by one. But his attempt to retain self-control proved fruitless. A garrison of close to one thousand professional soldiers jumped when he gave an order, but this slender young woman was defying him. "When I tell you to do something, Ginny Mullins," he roared, his deep voice filling the room and causing a small pitcher on the hearth mantel to rattle, "you'll goddamn well obey me!"

"I love you," Ginny said stubbornly, "I honor you, and I'll obey you in most things most of the time. But my happiness is at stake, and I'll be lonely and miserable if I leave Oregon."

He shoved back his chair so violently that it toppled onto the floor. Then, buckling on his belt because he always felt more comfortable in a crisis when he wore the full, prescribed uniform, he bellowed even more loudly. "Your problem is that you ought to have babies, like I've been telling you! Then you won't be so all-fired lonely."

Tears sprang to Ginny's eyes, and she began to sob. "I've told you again and again—I won't have children, Hector. I love you with all my heart, but that's one thing I can't do!" She pounded the pine table in frustration, causing the dishes to rattle.

Perhaps his domestic long-range military strategy was sound, Hector told himself, but his short-term tactics were a big mistake. Ginny had been orphaned at an early age, and every damn time he mentioned having children, Ginny became hysterical.

Well, maybe a good cry was what she needed. As sure as he wore the stripes of a sergeant major on his sleeve, he would accept the transfer that Colonel Blake had offered him. And his wife damn well would go with him.

The problem was that Ginny was no army private who could be directed to march on the parade ground for hours in full field equipment for disobeying orders. She was a fragile, loving female who had taught him what he had missed during all the years he had remained a bachelor. He cherished her, and her contentment was more important to him than anything else in the world— except doing, promptly, cheerfully, and without fuss, exactly what the army told him to do.

Lee stayed in his office until retreat, at sundown. From his window he thoughtfully watched the flag being lowered. Then, with the last bugle notes still echoing across the parade ground, he walked quickly to the commandant's house at the far side of the compound.

Little Beth, just two, her hair as blonde and her eyes as blue as her mother's, raced to the front door when she heard her father open it. "Papa, Papa!" she screamed in delight, even though she had last seen him at noon.

Hanging his hat, sword, and belt in the front vestibule, Lee swung his daughter to his shoulder, squeezed her tenderly, and went in search of Cathy. He found her in the kitchen.

Cathy took one look at her husband's face, then quickly went with him to the parlor.

With Beth still perched on his shoulder, Lee poured two small glasses of sack, placed them on a coffee table, and raised the wicks of the oil lamps she had already lighted. Then he handed her his orders and General Scott's letter. "Beth," he said, putting his daughter down, "it's time for you to put your dolls to bed."

"Dollies have to sleep," the little girl said solemnly, then went off to her room.

"How soon will *we* leave?" she asked him calmly as she finished reading the communications. She had not forgotten their previous conversation.

Lee knew that the War Department would not have said his family could travel with him if they had felt there was any danger to them. Sighing, he said, "I'm relieved of my present assignment immediately, as soon as I formally hand over command of the garrison to Eli. There's a convoy leaving early next week for Independence, so we can visit your sister and brother-in-law there before we go on to Washington City."

"It will be wonderful to see Claudia and Sam—and to let our children become acquainted. What does this transfer mean? Will we be going to Texas as you suspected?"

"I don't know for sure, but I think so. There's no point in guessing, in any case. We'll find out soon enough." Lee peered at her. "Honey, you seem so calm. Are you just putting up a front, or don't you mind leaving Oregon?"

"I mind it dreadfully," Cathy said. "But General Scott says that Beth and I are permitted to come with you, and our marriage is more important to me than life in Oregon—or any other place on the face of this earth!"

Lee cupped her face in his hands and kissed her.

Paul Thoman and Harry Canning, partners in Oregon's first and only shipbuilding yard, were also neighbors who shared the barbecue pit that was located on the boundaries of their properties. The Harvard-educated Paul, tall and almost painfully thin, threw more logs on the fire, while Harry turned the spit on which the meat was roasting. As always, they worked together in harmony, each of them knowing almost instinctively what the other would do next.

The contrast between their wives was much sharper. Lisolette Thoman was quiet and scholarly, like her husband, and she made few comments as she scrubbed the potatoes and shucked the corn for the barbecue. Nancy Canning was effervescent and lively, chatting animatedly with the guests while she washed the peaches, grapes, and cherries that would be served for dessert.

The center of attention was Melissa Austin. Endowed with an energy and zest for living that were the equal of Nancy's, she was launched on one of her long, breathless dissertations.

Neither Harry nor Paul paid the slightest attention to what she was saying. However, Chet Harris and Danny Taylor were hanging on to every word, their eyes riveted on her pretty face. They nodded in solemn agreement with her challenging assertions.

"I thought life in Oregon would be exciting," she said. "But it's just as dull here as it was back in Pittsburgh. Oh, an Indian or two comes into town from one of the Coast tribes, but they're harmless."

"Would you prefer that they scalp you?" Lisolette, who had been listening, asked. She was rewarded by her husband's deep chuckle. He had spent a year alone in the Rockies and could appreciate her point of view.

But Melissa just shrugged, and Nancy Canning was sympathetic. "I know what you mean, Melissa," she said. "I come from Pennsylvania, too, from a farm, and life here is very much like it was there. When you get up in the morning, you can pretty well predict what will happen all day. It wasn't that way when I first came here on the second wagon train. People were still dealing with the unknown, and all sorts of unexpected things happened."

"Most of them unpleasant," Lisolette interjected.

"But they were exciting," Chet said. "Danny and I joined every volunteer organization we could. Including the militia, once we were old enough."

"To me the question is one of challenges. Now we plow the land, sow crops, get rid of weeds, and haul in the harvest. Then we do the same thing all over again. With three growing seasons a year, we just keep doing the same things over and over again."

"Earning a good living," Lisolette replied. "Never going hungry. Having enough clothes to wear and a solid roof over your heads. Knowing that when you marry you'll be able to support your wives and children."

Paul and Harry exchanged glances, and the former nodded emphatically, proud of his sensible wife. He couldn't blame Harry for being somewhat dismayed. Obviously Nancy was still a romantic who wasn't yet ready to accept an existence as prosaic as it was profitable.

"If I had my way," Melissa said, "I'd take off for Texas tomorrow morning. Maybe that's because I have so much admiration for Moses Austin, one of the first settlers there, who happened to be a distant relative of mine. They've named the capital of the Republic for him, you know."

Harry Canning could remain silent no longer. "The farther people live from heroes, the more heroic they seem, and the greater their exploits become. I'm not decrying Moses Austin or any of the other founders of Texas. But I think some of our own early settlers can match them in skill and courage and daring. Look at what Whip Holt accomplished. Chet, you traveled on the first wagon train with him, and so did you, Danny. He performed miracles, almost. So did Lee Blake. And your own stepfather, Chet—Ernie von Thalman. And ladies like Tonie Martin. Just because she lives quietly as a doctor's wife these days doesn't make her any less of a heroine. She went through some hair-raising experiences when Russian spies were trying to kill her."

"I don't deny a word you say, Harry," Chet declared. "The point I'm trying to make is that those days are behind all of us. We now live in a humdrum world."

"We'll admit," Danny added, "that the situation can change overnight if Great Britain refuses to reach a

reasonable settlement with the United States over the
northern boundary of Oregon. Then we'll have a major
war to fight, with all of Oregon as the prize!"

"I pray that that war will never come," Lisolette said
devoutly.

"I don't believe it will," her husband assured her.

"Washington City and London are jockeying for position," Harry said. "It's like the card games we played in
sailors' taverns when I was a youngster. The players are
trying to bluff each other. In this particular game the
outcome depends on what happens to Texas. Once that
enormous area becomes part of the United States, the
British would be fighting a war they couldn't possibly
win. And they know it."

"Everything keeps coming back to Texas!" Melissa
said enthusiastically. "That's the place to be these days!"

Paul and Harry looked at each other again, then
suspended their efforts at the fire. "In yesterday's mail
pouch from the East, there was a letter from my father,"
Paul said, looking apologetically at Lisolette because he
hadn't yet discussed it with her.

Everyone present knew that the senior Thoman was
the principal owner of a major Boston shipyard.

"He wrote to me as soon as he received a letter from
old Andrew Jackson, who has been his friend for many
years. President Jackson explained that the Republic of
Texas desperately needs a navy. She has no ships at all.
The state of my father's business won't permit him to
send anyone off to Texas, so he wondered if Harry and I
might be interested."

"We've spent the whole day talking about the problem," Harry said. "There are all sorts of risks involved, so
the project would be a gamble if we decided to set up a
companion shipyard down in Texas. The profits—if
any—would be very small at first. But Texas is sure to be
admitted to the Union, and we'd have the first shipyard
there, just as we have the first in Oregon. So we're very
much tempted."

Melissa, sitting on a blanket, leaned forward intently,
her eyes shining. Nancy became tense and concentrated

her full attention on her husband. Danny and Chet were equally fascinated.

"We've pretty much decided," Harry said, "to go ahead—while maintaining our full partnership here, of course. Paul is needed here more than I am, so that means I'm elected to go off to Texas."

Nancy was ecstatic, and Melissa looked at her enviously. "When do we leave, Harry?"

"*We* don't," he said flatly. "None of the details are settled yet, and I have no idea how I'll be traveling there. But I'll be setting up a yard and living under very primitive conditions. I don't even know yet whether I'll be taking volunteer workers with me or whether Texas will provide me with manpower. There are all sorts of details still to be worked out. The one thing I do know— for sure—is that the uninhabited Gulf Coast of Texas is no place for a woman."

Nancy made no reply, but her jaw became set.

Harry went to her. "I would have preferred to go into all this with you in private," he said. "But what it boils down to is this. We'll have to sacrifice a year to a year and a half of our life together. Either I'll send for you after I get organized down in Texas, or I'll come back here, assuming I can find competent people to operate the yard for Paul and me. It just isn't possible to make plans of any kind right now. We'll have to steel ourselves to a separation."

His wife remained silent, her eyes burning, her full lips sharply compressed.

"You could take me with you, couldn't you?" Melissa demanded eagerly.

Harry shook his head firmly. "I said the Gulf Coast is no place for a woman these days," he replied. "If I can't take my wife, how in blazes can I escort a nineteen-year-old girl who isn't even married?" He shook his head in disgust.

Melissa was not squelched, however, and smiled brightly.

"If you take volunteers," Danny Taylor said, "count me in, Harry."

"That makes two of us," Chet declared.

"Not so fast," Paul protested. "You're in charge of the farm while your stepfather is in Washington as Oregon's official observer in Congress. What will happen to the farm?"

"My brother will stay here and run it," Chet said. "He loves farming, and if you listen to him talk, he had adventure enough to last him for a lifetime on the wagon train that brought us here. He's old enough to take charge now."

"I'll just have to see how things work out," Harry said, returning to the spit in order to put the finishing touches on the meat.

They ate a short time later, and Texas dominated the conversation.

"What kind of ships will you build?" Danny wanted to know.

Harry shrugged. "I have no idea. I reckon I'll have a few talks with President Houston or his Secretary of the Navy. Or somebody. All this is so new to me that we have no idea where we'll start. We haven't even settled the question of our compensation yet, although Paul's father warned us that—at first—we can't count on more than token profits."

"It seems to me," Melissa said, "that you're more patriotic than you let on."

Harry and Paul looked at her in astonishment. "If we weren't patriotic," the latter said quietly, "if we didn't believe in the United States and her future, we'd be back East instead of living in Oregon."

Nancy, who was eating very little of her meal, finally broke her long silence. "A woman," she declared, "can be just as patriotic as a man. Males don't have a monopoly on love for their country."

"Granted," Harry replied heatedly. "But we express our patriotism in different ways. I realize you're upset, Nancy, because I can't take you to Texas with me. But the truth of the matter is that there would be nothing you could contribute. What could you do there? Or you, Melissa?"

The red-haired girl shrugged.

Nancy Canning was even less impressed by her husband's rhetoric. "What can a woman do to help Texas?" she muttered. "I guess we'll just have to find out."

A fine rain was falling, but Oregon settlers paid no heed to inclement weather, and a crowd of three to four thousand people gathered at Fort Oregon to watch the brief ceremonies marking the transfer of command. A reviewing stand had been erected for the occasion, and the commander of the British garrison at Fort Vancouver across the Columbia River was seated there, along with his entire staff. One of the ironies of the continuing border dispute between the United States and Great Britain was that, after their initial difficulties, the officers and men of the two units lived harmoniously as neighbors.

Colonel Lee Blake read the War Department orders relieving him of the command and giving it to his deputy. He and Lieutenant Colonel Eli Moser exchanged salutes, and then the entire garrison, one thousand strong, paraded in honor of the outgoing commander. Standing to the left of Lee was Sergeant Major Hector Mullins, who was also being honored, and the enlisted men marched with a special fervor because they would never again hear this strict disciplinarian barking at those who were responsible for even minor infractions of the army's regulations.

Men, women, and children adjourned to the town hall, and the sun obligingly appeared, making it possible for the women preparing a gargantuan feast to serve the meal out of doors on the lawn. Sides of beef were roasting, as were lambs and turkeys, wild ducks and geese. Huge quantities of salmon, the region's greatest delicacy, were served both hot and cold, and there were mounds of crabs, oysters, and clams piled on tables, too. Someone jokingly remarked that the mountains of potato salad looked like the snow-covered peaks of the area. Corn was roasted in its husks, and women who had been cooking indoors appeared with huge loaves of hot bread.

There were apples, cherries, plums, pears, and peaches, as well as several varieties of melon, which had been placed on separate tables for dessert. Oregon was as bountiful as the early settlers had hoped it would be.

It was difficult for many of the old-timers to realize that Lee and Cathy Blake were actually leaving. Blacksmith Ted Woods and his wife, Olga, stood shyly, each holding the hand of one of their twin sons, and Ted, swallowing hard, expressed the sentiments of many when he said simply, "We'll miss you."

Eventually Lee moved off for a few last, private words with his old friend, Whip Holt, and both men, unaccustomed to expressing their sentiments, were embarrassed. "Keep your militia up to snuff, Whip," Lee said.

The rancher shook his head. "Now that you're leaving, I've decided to retire and turn the militia over to a younger commander." He lowered his voice. "I'm fine most of the time, but when my hip starts kicking up a fuss, I'm about as helpless as my son. Or your daughter." Wanting neither sympathy nor pity, he changed the subject abruptly. "Eulalia and I hope you and the family will be heading this way on visits. And when you come here, you'll stay with us. Or I'll skin you alive."

"We wouldn't dream of staying with anyone else. And thank you." Their old rivalries were buried in the past, as was Whip's one-time romance with Cathy, prior to her marriage. "Matter of fact, we're thinking seriously of moving back out here for keeps when I finally hang up my sword."

"That would be great!" Whip exclaimed. "You still don't know where you're being transferred?"

"It might be Texas, although I can't imagine what assignment I could be given there."

"I envy you," Whip said, then chuckled. "How I'd love to see old Sam Houston again. I still think of him as a hunter, of course, and I can't picture him as president of anything."

Stalking Horse, the Cherokee who had long been Whip's companion in the wilderness and now worked as his ranch foreman, had wandered close enough to hear the last portion of the conversation and joined in the talk. "If you see Big Drunk, give him greetings of Stalking Horse.'"

"I will," Lee promised, "But he isn't Big Drunk anymore. He proved at San Jacinto that he's a first-rate general, and as head of the Republic of Texas, he's been an exceptionally able administrator."

Whip continued to chuckle. "Maybe so, but I'll bet "I will," Lee promised, "but he isn't Big Drunk anyother man alive!"

The awkward moment of their parting had been bridged, and they went off to the tables for additional helpings of food.

Meanwhile, Cathy Blake had withdrawn to the rose garden on the far side of the town hall, accompanied by her two closest friends, Eulalia Holt and Cindy Woodling. "I'm glad this side of the building is deserted," Cathy said, "because it just wouldn't do for a guest of honor to break down and weep in front of all those people. Particularly when she's a colonel's wife. Women married to army officers are expected to keep their feelings under control."

"Well," Eulalia replied, sniffling, "I'm glad a rancher's wife may do as she pleases."

"Just listen to the two of you," Cindy said with forced heartiness. "You'd think the world was coming to an end."

"No," Cathy said gravely, "but this is the day it struck me that a very important part of my life is coming to an end. All of our belongings have been packed and will be sent after us, wherever we may be heading. And when we climb into that coach with Beth this afternoon, the curtain will come down on the happiest years I've known. I want to say this quickly, before I burst into tears, but you have no idea, either of you, how much your friendship has meant to me. How much it still means."

Eulalia nodded somberly. "We went through some terribly trying times together."

Cindy, ever the pragmatist, spoke briskly. "We'll keep

in touch by letter, Cathy, even if a single exchange takes months. And somehow, we'll arrange visits."

All three fell silent when they saw the solitary figure of a thirty-year-old woman, dressed for travel, walking down a rose garden path to a bench, where she sat and stared out miserably into space. It was apparent that she had not even noticed the trio.

The three old friends looked at each other, the pain of their own parting momentarily forgotten. Someone was in distress, and they moved toward her with one accord.

Ginny Mullins heard approaching footsteps, but she did not raise her head until the other women drew close. Then she said, "I'm sorry. I thought Hector was searching for me."

"Is the farewell party too much for you?" Cindy asked, smiling.

Ginny made no answer, but when she saw Cathy, she started to rise to her feet, ever mindful of the respect a sergeant's wife was expected to display to a colonel's lady.

Cathy immediately placed a hand on her shoulder. "Sit down, for goodness sake. There isn't a blue uniform anywhere in sight, and the way we behave when the men aren't around is strictly our own business."

Ginny thanked Cathy with a wan smile.

"If you want us to leave, just say the word," Eulalia told her. "If not, is there anything we can do to help?"

"Yes," Ginny said. "Hide me where Hector can't find me, where the whole regiment can't find me. That way I'll be left behind."

"It's that bad?" Cathy asked.

"Yes, it is, I'm afraid. Oh, I love Hector, and I know I'll go wherever he goes. He's my whole life, and that's the problem. Maybe if I had a child, as you do, Mrs. Blake, things would be different. But I know that will never be possible."

"Why ever in the world not?"

"Because I'm scared to death, that's why. Every time I remember my own horrible childhood—and it's always in my mind—I know I couldn't cope. I'm too frightened ever to have a baby. So Hector is all I have, except for the friends I've made here. I never had friends before I came to Oregon, and I don't expect to find others, ever again." Not waiting for a reply, she squared her shoulders and forced herself to walk back up the path.

For a few moments no one spoke as she disappeared from sight, her feet dragging, and rejoined the party-goers. At last Cindy said, "She's lonely and confused, but Hector will know how to improve her spirits. And she'll adjust fast when you reach your destination, Cathy, wherever you may be going."

"I hope you're right," Cathy replied, keeping her doubts to herself. She had seen the haunted expression in Ginny Mullins's eyes and knew that a great effort would be required before she regained her customary ebullience.

For the present, however, she had to put Ginny out of her mind. The convoy would be leaving at any time now, so she exchanged private farewell hugs and kisses with Eulalia and Cindy, then walked with them to rejoin the throngs of well-wishers. She was smiling steadily, and she knew that she wasn't merely play-acting for the benefit of those who expected her to be strong. The truth was that she was actually looking forward to the un-known future. A chapter in her life had ended, but a new chapter was about to begin. Unlike Ginny, the challenge excited her, and she was ready to meet it.

TEXAS

III

A portrait of Sam Houston's wife hung on one wall, and the Lone Star flag of the Republic of Texas stood on a stand in the corner. Otherwise, the office of the President in the ramshackle one-story frame building in the center of Austin was bare. A huge pine table, filled with documents and papers, served as a desk, and another, equally littered, was located behind his chair of unpainted pine. The floor was bare, the walls were whitewashed, and the only furnishings, other than several utilitarian tables with oil lamps on them, were a half-dozen ordinary kitchen chairs and several upturned barrels that could be used as seats when a large meeting was held in the room.

There was a brass spittoon that sat on the floor about ten feet from the President's desk, and as he read document after document, his new spectacles repeatedly sliding down the bridge of his nose, he let fly regularly at the spittoon with streams of tobacco juice. His aim was always accurate.

The government of Texas was conducted informally, and the President's clerk opened the door without bothering to knock. "Captain Miller of the Rangers is here to see you. He says he has an appointment."

Pleased by the break in his routine, Sam Houston nodded, then sighed as he shoved a stack of papers to

one side. The trouble with being the highest-ranking
executive in the Republic was that he rarely had a
chance to engage in physical exercise, and he envied
Rick Miller even before he came into the room.

Hard and lean, heavily suntanned, his sandy hair
flecked with gray although he was not yet thirty, Captain
Rick Miller moved into the chamber with the easy grace
of a natural athlete. He wore the customary "uniform" of
the Rangers, Texas's law-enforcement body, which con-
sisted of a broad-brimmed hat, an open-throated buckskin shirt, and buckskin trousers tucked into the tops of
his boots. On one arm was tied a frayed blue silk band
that was the symbol of his rank. Of far greater importance were the real marks of his authority, the brace of
pistols that he carried in his belt.

Like all 154 of his colleagues, he was proud of the
Rangers' boasts: "We ride like Mexicans, shoot like Ten-
nesseans, and fight like the very devil himself." Rick
Miller's experience in the hard world of the Texas frontier had made him a magnificent rider, a superb shot
with firearms of any kind, and a man at home in every
kind of fight from a formal battle to a saloon brawl.

President Houston well knew his reputation. "Rick,"
his friends said, "always fights to win. And he never
loses."

Recognizing the officer's talents, including his shrewd-
ly analytical mind, Houston had detached him from the
company he had commanded and had assigned him to
special duty. The President had never regretted that
decision during the past year. Miller investigated difficult murder cases, particularly those in which sabotage
against the Republic might be involved, and he was
available for a wide variety of other assignments. Perhaps his greatest virtue was his total reliability.

He saluted smartly. "Captain Miller at report, Mr.
President."

Houston offered him a plug of chewing tobacco.

"No, thanks, Sam," Rick drawled. He shoved his hat
onto the back of his head as he sat in one of the armless
chairs.

"You've been studying the maps and charts I gave you, Rick?"

"Yes, sir. The American maps of the Oregon country look pretty good, but the Mexican maps of the California and New Mexico provinces are worthless. As it happens, I know that country pretty well, so I'm not worried about it."

"You're ready to leave for Oregon soon?"

"Right this minute, Sam. My stallion is raring to go, and I've packed nearly everything I own into my saddlebags—including the two thousand dollars in U.S. paper money that you had the Treasury issue me."

Houston frowned. "Are you sure two thousand is enough, Rick? Texas may be hurting financially, but we're not all that close to being bankrupt. Remember, you're going off on a vitally important mission, and I'd feel safer if you were carrying an extra thousand or two for emergencies."

"I expect I'll be returning at least half of that two thousand to the Treasury, sir. As for emergencies," Rick added, grinning as he patted his pistols, "I'll call on my friends here. And on my rifle."

The President had to laugh, too. Then he sobered. "The man you're seeing in Oregon is Harry Canning, co-owner of the only shipyard up there. Keep in mind that he's as valuable to us as his weight in solid gold. Or a munitions train of gun powder."

"I won't forget it, Sam."

"Naturally, the credentials you'll take to him will authorize him to bring as many volunteers with him as he wishes. Preferably men who have had experience in building ships, although I don't want to be too obvious about that point. Canning and his partner are doing us a whopping favor, and I'd hate to empty their Oregon yard of workers who know their business."

What made Houston a great man, Rick thought, was his ability to see any given situation from the viewpoint of the people with whom he was dealing. It was a remarkable talent.

"Do you have any thoughts on how you intend to transport this Canning fellow here, Rick?"

"A few, sir, but I'd rather not spell them out because they might not be feasible. One way or another, I'll escort him safely to Texas. You can depend on it."

"I do, and so does the Republic," Houston replied. "As I see it, we'll have to wait another couple of years for annexation by the United States, and in the meantime our coast is so vulnerable that just thinking about it keeps me awake nights. Even after the protection of the American navy is extended to us, it will take many more months to assign a squadron, bring the ships together, and send them into our waters. So you can see how important Canning is to us."

"I understand all that, Sam. What confuses me is how we'll man the ships once they're built. It will take us at least a year to train a corps of sailors."

A gleam appeared in Houston's eyes. "That bothered me for a time, too. Until I thought of the obvious solution. Texas will start advertising in the newspapers of the Eastern Seaboard for veteran ships' officers and seamen. When you think of the response I've had to our other advertising—including the Rangers—you'll understand why I'm not worried."

"That's smart." Rick nodded in appreciation.

"Our biggest problem is bringing in top-level frontier leaders. No matter what some of the people in Washington City are saying, I know Santa Anna far better than they do, and I'm convinced he'll declare war when we join the Union. He's learned better than to send his armies into Texas, but he can bleed us white with raids. Obviously, I can't advertise for men who can command counter-patrols, so I've been writing to various people I know, inviting them down here. And Andrew Jackson, bless him, has been doing the same thing. But none of that is your problem. Concentrate on reaching Oregon as quickly as you can and bringing Harry Canning back here without delay!"

Rick hoisted himself to his feet, then pulled up his

gunbelt. "Mr. Canning doesn't know what's in store for him, Sam. He's going to set cross-country records traveling to Texas!"

The two letters, by coincidence, arrived on the same day. One, penned by Andrew Jackson's niece and signed in Old Hickory's distinctive, spidery hand, was succinct. In the event that war with Mexico broke out, which was likely when Texas joined the Union, the new state would need frontiersmen with wilderness experience who were capable of leading patrols of fifty to two hundred men on the Mexican border. Their duty would be that of repelling raiders.

He was writing, Andrew Jackson declared, because he knew Whip Holt would be a natural selection for such a position. That was all he said.

Sam Houston's letter was longer and more diplomatic. He knew Whip was married, had a child, and was operating a large, successful ranch. Therefore, he hated to ask an old friend to make a great personal sacrifice. But he felt compelled to write because the future of Texas—and with it the future of the United States—was at stake. Would Whip come to Texas for a year or two and train border patrols? The pay would be minimal, but he would be doing his country a great service.

Whip shoved the letters into a pocket of his buckskin shirt, saddled his stallion, and went out for a long ride, far beyond the confines of his own ranch. He did not return until sundown, after reaching the foothills of the mountains that lay to the east, and he knew what had to be done. The process of reaching a decision had been agonizing, but the outcome had never been in doubt. Never had Whip refused the call of duty, and he didn't intend to begin now.

Toby always ate his supper early, then was put to bed, and as Eulalia refused to allow anyone else to prepare the evening meal she and her husband shared alone, it was late when they sat down at the table and ate by candlelight.

The beefsteak was charred on the outside and rare on the inside, precisely as Whip liked it. The skin of the baked potatoes had been slightly blackened, making them crisp, and she had put the better part of a cucumber in his salad, as it was one of the few vegetables he enjoyed. All the same, he had almost no appetite, and he was more silent than usual, replying in monosyllables to his wife's talk.

Eulalia bided her time, waiting until they faced each other over mugs of hot, spiced tea before she asked quietly, "What's wrong, Michael?"

He fished in his pocket for the letters, then silently handed them to her.

She had guessed the letters were responsible for his strange mood. He hadn't mentioned them to her after reading them, and then he had vanished for the rest of the day. She scanned the two communications, her heart sinking to the pit of her stomach. One glance at Whip told her he had already made up his mind, that nothing she might say would influence him.

"You know as much about the ranch as I do, so I'm writing a letter placing you in complete charge while I'm away. Stalking Horse will be a big help to you, and so will that new hand, Bowman. You'll make out fine."

"What about Toby?" Her voice was an almost inaudible whisper.

"He'll be mighty glad to see me when I come home. I hope."

"I'll miss you horribly, Michael."

"I'll miss you, too. But I have no choice." Whip's jaw jutted forward.

He was giving her no alternative, either, and the stunned Eulalia sipped her tea in silence, not even tasting it. Even in her wildest flights of fancy, she had never imagined that her husband might return to the life he had known for so many years, and her whole world was crumbling around her.

"Aren't you being selfish?" she managed at last.

Whip shook his head vehemently. "Just the opposite,

dammit. I hate leaving you. And Toby. And the ranch I've worked so hard to build. But Andrew Jackson says I'm needed. So what else can I do?"

She had no reply. Former President Jackson was still his idol, and he was willing to sacrifice his own happiness and his family's because Old Hickory had called him to duty. It was not enough to remind him that he had done far more than his fair share of creating a larger, more prosperous America, that the very existence of the Oregon colony was due in large part to his efforts, determination, and courage.

All at once Eulalia loathed the scent of her tea and pushed away her cup and saucer. "When will you leave?"

"At dawn tomorrow morning. I'll wake up Toby so I can say goodbye to him before I go."

"So soon?" She had to fight the panic that welled up within her.

Whip nodded, making an unsuccessful attempt to smile. "It will be more difficult for both of us if I delay for a spell." He left his own tea untouched. "I think I'll head southeast through the Sierra Nevadas and then cut through the Rockies in the Colorado country. It's by far the shortest, fastest route, and I won't run into any Mexican cavalry patrols, not at this time of year."

His wife could only stare at him. "You must be mad. How can you even think of traveling alone across two of the world's most rugged mountain chains?"

"I spent a great many years alone in those mountains," he reminded her. "I know the way and won't need anybody to guide me. What's more, I respect the mountains, and I assure you I don't intend to take unnecessary risks. I aim to reach Texas alive and healthy."

There was nothing more she could say, so she rose swiftly, went to the kitchen, and began to wash the supper dishes.

Whip could hear her weeping and wanted to comfort her, but he was afraid his own resolve would weaken. So he went to the larder instead, taking bacon, flour, smoked meat, and corn. Then he sharpened his knife, cleaned the pistols and rifle he had always carried in the wilderness, and took from a shelf the bullwhip that had given him his nickname. All he needed now were some of the medicinal herbs he would take with him as a precaution and a warm blanket.

That night Eulalia slept poorly, and Whip was restless, too. Both were wide-awake long before dawn, and their final hour or two together passed so quickly that she could not recall the details later in the day.

The drowsy Toby responded to his father's farewell hug and kiss, then dropped off to sleep again.

Eulalia managed to remain dry-eyed until Whip had gone. She watched him from the kitchen window in the early morning half-light until he disappeared from sight, sitting erect in the saddle, and it was small comfort to realize he was wearing the new hat she had purchased for him. Only when he vanished did the full extent of her loss strike her, and then she wept hysterically.

But life went on. With Whip no longer there, she had far more responsibility, and she was so busy all day that she had no time to brood, which was a blessing. Late in the day her brother and sister-in-law came over from their adjoining farm for a visit, and Eulalia, glad to have their company, invited them to stay for supper.

They accepted, and just as she was wondering how to break the news to them, Toby came into the parlor and announced solemnly, "Papa went to Texas."

The startled Claiborne and Cindy thought the child had to be joking and turned to Eulalia. She could only nod confirmation.

"Why, in God's name?" her brother demanded.

"He had letters from Andrew Jackson and Sam Houston. They want him to train patrols for duty on the Mexican border, so there was just no way of stopping him. He kept saying it was his duty to go."

The pragmatic Cindy pondered, then shook her head. "He's lost his wits. Whip is no youngster, and I don't see how he can travel all that distance without—" She broke

off abruptly when her husband cast a warning glance at
her. "But he's tough," she added lamely. "One way or
another he'll make out all right."

Toby was allowed to eat with the adults, and after he
had been put to bed, Claiborne and Cindy inundated
Eulalia with practical advice. She was so heartsick she
paid little attention to what they were saying and could
only nod vaguely.

That night she had almost no sleep, and the following
morning she felt exhausted. But there was work to be
done, so she went about her chores doggedly, then rode
out to the range with Stalking Horse, returning for
dinner only after Toby had almost finished his meal.
This, she reflected miserably, would become her normal
routine for a long time to come.

With the help of Bowman, the best of the hired hands,
she sold a colt to one of the new settlers for a good price
and then inspected the barns and stables, making a
number of suggestions for their improvement. At sundown she prepared her own meal when she cooked
Toby's supper, and ate with him. She was clinging to the
boy too much, she warned herself, but for the present
she was so vulnerable that she knew she had to lean on
him.

After she tucked the child into bed, she returned to the
parlor and took a book from a shelf. Only recently a ship
had arrived with a cargo that included several thousand
books, and she had bought hundreds of them, pleased
because she now owned the largest private library in
Oregon.

But she could not become interested in the volume she
had selected, a novel by Sir Walter Scott, so she returned
it to the shelf and took another, a travel book by Washington Irving. She went to her chair, turned up the oil
lamp, and as she opened the book, she suddenly froze.
She could hear the slow pounding of a horse's hoofbeats,
and she well knew that no one would be paying a social
call at this hour of the night.

Eulalia peered out into the dark but could see nothing,
so she hurried to the kitchen, took her rifle from the wall,

and made certain it was loaded. Not since the early days had it been necessary for her to defend herself. Perhaps the word had been passed that a defenseless woman lived in the house.

A heavy knock sounded at the kitchen door.

"Who is there?" she called, her heart pounding.

A familiar voice replied, and she raced to the door, unbolted it, and threw it open.

A shamefaced Whip stood on the threshold. Eulalia threw herself into his arms, laughing and weeping simultaneously as they embraced and kissed. For the first time in all the years she had known him, she saw tears glistening in Whip's eyes, too.

He limped to a chair and slowly lowered himself into it, pain causing him to grimace involuntarily.

Wanting to give him a chance to recover before she asked any questions, she poured him a small glass of whiskey. A totally unexpected miracle had occurred, and she was grateful for it.

By the time she handed him the glass, he had composed himself. He downed the whiskey in a single gulp, then broke the silence. "I've never seen an old horse that can beat a two-year-old in a race," he said. "Matter of fact, there comes a time when old workhorses have to be put to pasture."

She sat at the table, too, and their hands touched, then held.

"Yesterday," Whip said gruffly, "I rode farther than I should have, and last night my arthritis flared up so bad that I knew I could never get to Texas. I've spent all of today trying to get back here."

Eulalia thanked the Almighty for preserving her husband and restoring his good sense.

"It looks like I'm home to stay," he told her. "I feel awful, letting Andy Jackson down, but I'd be of no help to the Texans with this confounded hip."

"You'll never know how happy and relieved I am to see you or how overjoyed Toby will be. He was lost without you. So was I."

"I'm glad I'm useful to some people." Whip sighed,

then his grip on her hand tightened. "Don't you ever repeat this to a living soul, but I'm relieved I'm here. Leaving you and Toby was the worst wrench I've ever known. I reckon I needed this experience to teach me that my wandering days are ended. From now on I'll be spending my evenings with you at the fire."

"It's where you belong," she replied, then kissed him again.

He was still concerned. "Honey," he said, "you put words together better than I do. Will you help me write letters to President Jackson and Sam Houston, telling them why I can't train border patrols for Texas?"

"Of course. And they'll understand. They're years older than you are, so I'm sure they have their aches and pains, too. And neither of them spends eighteen hours a day on horseback, you can just bet on that!"

He nodded, and for the first time his spirits began to improve. "Where do you keep your quill pen and ink jar?"

"We'll write the letters after breakfast tomorrow morning, dear," she said. "First things must come first." She hesitated. "Depending on how badly your hip aches."

Whip grinned at her. "It's never *that* bad," he said. Extinguishing the lamp, he carried a lighted candle in one hand, his other arm encircling his wife's supple waist, and together they walked slowly, purposefully toward their bedroom. A phase of their life together had ended, but another—richer, mellower, and more satisfying—was about to begin, while younger, more vigorous men pursued the dream of statehood for Texas.

Melissa Austin watched Nancy Canning trim the rose bushes in the garden outside her house and shook her head. "You aren't planning on staying here, so why are you doing all this work around the place?"

Nancy smiled. "For two reasons," she said, busy with her knife. "In the first place, the pruning needs to be done. And in the second place, Harry has no idea that I'm hoping to find some way you and I can go with him. He's convinced himself that I'm going to stay here when he goes away, and I don't want to upset him. He—" She broke off when she saw a stranger ride up to the front gate.

He was tall, slender but rugged, and when he dismounted with easy grace, tying his stallion's bridle to the gatepost, Nancy and Melissa saw that the dust on his boots was thick.

Melissa, who always used Chet Harris and Danny Taylor as measuring sticks, noted instantly that this man was far more mature. He exuded an air of self-confidence, his manner indicating that he knew what he wanted, then went about getting it. "He's handsome," she murmured, and couldn't resist the temptation to flirt with him as he walked toward them.

"May I help you?" Nancy called.

He removed his hat. "Captain Rick Miller, Texas Rangers. I'm looking for Harry Canning."

"I'm Mrs. Canning," Nancy said, intrigued. "Don't tell me you've ridden all the way to Oregon from Texas."

"In as straight a line as I could manage, ma'am." After his long journey Rick was in no mood for idle chat with two women. "Is Mr. Canning here?"

She shook her head. "You'll find him at the boatyard. About three-quarters of a mile toward the Pacific, right on the Columbia River."

He raised his hand to the wide brim of his hat, then departed without another word.

"You didn't even introduce me," Melissa said. "Men that good-looking don't come around every day."

"I was so surprised," Nancy said. "Just imagine, he's ridden here all the way from Texas. I'm not all that good at geography, but he's traveled a couple of thousand miles."

"You know what it means, don't you?" Melissa's huge eyes were shining.

"Well, I suppose you could say that Captain Miller hasn't come all that distance just for the exercise."

"Exactly. It won't be long before he takes Harry off to Texas, Nancy!"

"Hmmm. I'll insist that he stay here as our guest, so I'll be sure to learn the details of his travel plans."

"With any luck at all," Melissa said, "we won't be here much longer."

Nancy nodded, then put away her pruning knife. "I've changed my mind about the garden," she said. "It doesn't really need any more work."

A short time later Rick Miller was closeted with Harry Canning and Paul Thoman in the office they shared at the boatyard. "We aren't expecting you to build a place this fancy down our way," he said.

"We started from scratch here only four years ago," Paul replied proudly. "There's no reason the feat can't be duplicated."

"Well, we can supply you the manpower, Mr. Canning," Rick said to Harry. "Immigrants are pouring into Texas faster than we can get them settled. Trained manpower is something different. You said a few minutes ago that there are seven men who want to come with you. Are any of them shipwrights or carpenters?"

Harry shook his head. "These kids are all young fellows who want adventure. The demand for experienced carpenters is as great in Oregon as it must be in Texas. But that doesn't worry me. We trained our work crews on the job here, and I'll do the same in Texas. As soon as I find the right site."

"Sam Houston has already found it for you," Rick said. "You'll build your yard on Galveston Island, in the Gulf of Mexico. It's separated from the mainland by a bay that President Houston says is our best natural harbor. And if that's what he says, that's what it is."

"I've never heard of the island," Harry said.

"No reason you should. You'll be the one who puts it on the map. There's only a small village there now, with fishermen who obviously know something about boats— they may be of help to you. The island is heavily wooded, so you'll have all the timber you'll need, right at your doorstep. Just as you have it here."

"Sounds good," Harry said. "When do we leave?"

"As quick as you and your party can be ready. President Houston is in an almighty hurry to get you down there."

"Everything will depend on how much I've got to take along in the way of materials," Harry said. "Copper for hull sheeting, copper nails, wrought-iron plating, and studs. Not to mention tools—"

"You'll find most everything you need already waiting for you," Rick cut in. "Mr. Thoman's father has already sent us a whole shipload of building materials. They've been taken to Galveston Island, and they're being guarded by a company of our militiamen."

Paul smiled broadly. "Trust my father to do all that," he said.

"I have only one question for you," Rick said. "Have you or your young friends had experience crossing the mountains on horseback?"

"I've had none," Harry said, "and I feel sure the boys haven't, either."

"I spent a year in the Rockies as a trapper," Paul said, "but I'm afraid that won't help."

"Too bad you aren't coming," Rick replied. "Well, now. We'll do best if we can find a ship that will take us—along with horses for the whole party—to the southern part of California Province. Somewhere north of the Mexican naval base at San Diego, so they won't know we've landed. Then we'll ride straight across the Arizona badlands and the rest of New Mexico Province. There will be mountains and deserts to cross there, too, but the terrain isn't as rough as the Sierra Nevada and the Rockies, so we'll make better time. That means our first requirement is to find a ship."

"I'll sail you down the coast myself," Paul said and turned to his partner. "In the *Liz Lou.*"

Harry grinned, then explained to the Ranger. "We've specialized here in the building of commercial merchantmen for coastal trading. The *Liz Lou* is our newest schooner. We have several bidders, but she still belongs to us, and we can sail her with one of our own crews."

"Sounds fine, provided you understand the problem. If the Mexicans learn the purpose of this voyage, they'll send a squadron of gunboats out of San Diego to sink her."

"We'll take that risk," Paul replied without hestitation.

The hour was growing late, so they adjourned to the Canning house, where Harry told the secretly elated Nancy that he had already asked Captain Miller to stay with them. Lisolette Thoman joined them for supper, and it was not accidental that Melissa Austin was present, too.

Aside from displaying a flicker of interest when she revealed that she was distantly related to the late Moses Austin and Stephen Fuller Austin, Rick paid scant attention to her. There were more important matters on his mind, and he seemed unaware of her repeated attempts to flirt with him.

"First thing in the morning," he said, "I'll want to meet the lads who have volunteered to come with you, Harry. I reserve the right to weed out any I don't think are strong enough and resilient enough to travel with us. A ride of fifteen hundred miles across hostile Mexican territory patrolled by their cavalry will be no easy jaunt. And I can't wait for men unable to keep up a swift, consistent pace."

"Fair enough," Harry said. "I think all of the boys will qualify, but you're the expert, and I'll defer to your judgment."

"I'll want to inspect their firearms," Rick went on, "and their horses. No mares and no geldings ready for slaughter. We'll need stallions, for those able to ride them, and solid, healthy geldings for the rest. Can we buy arms and mounts here, if need be?"

"Ted Woods has put in a new line of rifles at his blacksmith foundry," Paul said. "And I'm sure Whip Holt will sell us any horses you may want."

"Perfect." Rick smiled apologetically at Nancy, then at Lisolette, but continued to act as though Melissa did not exist. "Sorry for all this business talk, ladies, but it can't be helped, and we'll soon be organized. Paul, how soon can you make your schooner ready for the voyage down the coast?"

"Seventy-two hours."

None of the men realized it, but Nancy and Melissa were listening avidly to every detail.

"What kind of troubles should we anticipate?" Harry asked.

"Indians, Mexican cavalry. Deserts. Not that I'm trying to scare you, Harry, but there are also snakes, scorpions, and a few hundred other natural enemies of man in the wastelands of New Mexico Province."

"I've known worse, I'm sure," Harry replied calmly.

Only Nancy saw Melissa shudder, and she glared surreptitiously at her young friend. She intended to show Harry she couldn't be bossed around and denied her fair share of adventure.

The little merchantman from Havana, the capital of New Spain, docked at the busy port of New Orleans, and loiterers near the wharves paid scant attention to the businessmen and traders who disembarked. New Orleans was the outlet for the agricultural products and the increasingly diverse manufactured goods of the states and territories of the American West, and buyers came from all over the world to purchase those wares. Truly cosmopolitan because of the roles that France and Spain had played in her past, New Orleans extended her hospitality to all foreigners and happily took their money.

The last man to appear on the deck wore conservatively tailored, English-cut clothes, Spanish boots and square-crowned hat, and carried a gold-handled walking stick. The idlers knew at a glance that it concealed a sword, which many newcomers to the United States carried, deluding themselves by thinking that the crude Americans who might assault them would have no idea they were armed.

Certainly no one who bothered to look at Anthony Roberts would have guessed that he was American by birth, that he still retained his American citizenship, and that he loathed his native land with a passionate, abiding hatred. This was the first time he had stepped on American soil in three decades, and he hesitated briefly at the top of the gangway.

Few people anywhere were aware of his background, which he kept secret. The son of a conscientious, conservative American father and a wealthy, half-English, half-Spanish mother, he had been born and spent his very early years in Hartford, Connecticut.

His father had been a strong-minded and stubborn man. Like thousands of other New Englanders, the elder Roberts had been strongly opposed to American participation in the War of 1812. But he had been indiscreet, and instead of confining his opposition to the ballot box, he had made inflammatory speeches in Hartford and nearby communities.

Then tragedy had struck. One night a drunken mob of self-styled patriots had broken into the house and dragged Roberts away. His body had been found the next day, hanging from an elm tree.

Mrs. Roberts had taken her son away at once, traveling first to Madrid and then to London, and for thirty years he had divided his time between those cities. Attending the schools of the well-to-do, he had been accepted as a peer and moved gracefully in high circles. For the past fifteen years he had augmented his considerable inheritance by selling British state secrets to Spain and Spanish state secrets to Great Britain. Increasingly adept in the practice of espionage, he had not only amused himself, but had found good use for the money. After all, his tastes were expensive.

His inheritance had included far more than financial wealth. His mother had nurtured within him the seeds of hatred for anything American, and they had grown through the years. At considerable cost he had kept track of as many of his father's murderers as he could and had developed an interest in Texas because several of them, along with thousands of other New Englanders, had migrated there during the Panic of 1837.

Now he had returned from Europe on a double mission. Great Britain had promised to pay him handsomely for any efforts that were successful in delaying, hindering, or disrupting the annexation of the Republic of Texas by the United States. The growth of any foreign nation—particularly her former North American colonies—made Britain's Prime Ministers and their Cabinets apprehensive.

Roberts's second mission was strictly personal. After a lifetime of waiting, he intended to obtain vengeance against the men who had hanged his father. To the best of his knowledge, at least six of them were in Texas, and he knew that three had business that brought them frequently to Austin, the capital.

As he stood at the head of the gangway, the taste of gall bitter in his mouth, a young woman approached and stood quietly beside him.

The loiterers gaped at her, and so did more genteel passers-by. By anyone's standards, dockworker or aristocrat, she was ravishing.

Tall and slender, she wore a traveling costume of black broadcloth that covered her from her throat to her ankles, but it fitted her so snugly that it emphasized every line of her feminine, willowy figure. Her high-heeled shoes and her erect, proud bearing further called attention to her body. Her black hair tumbled in waves past her shoulders, and on her head was perched a small square-crowned hat that looked like a miniature version of a man's headgear. In it she wore a scarlet feather that was a precise match for the rouge on her full, sensuous lips. Her features were chiseled, but her violet eyes were her most arresting feature, and she knew it, enhancing their appeal with a ring of black kohl around them and violet shading on her lids.

Elisabeta Manuel touched Anthony's arm with a white-gloved, slender hand, and he smiled at her.

"I must apologize again for bringing you to this barbaric land," he said.

"I am prepared to enjoy New Orleans," she replied. "We have been told it is a charming city."

Anthony had no intention of disputing the matter with her, but in his view nothing in the United States, by definition, could be charming.

They went ashore, where a steward had already summoned a carriage for them and stowed their luggage on the roof. Elisabeta looked around constantly, commenting on the French and Spanish influence on the architecture. Anthony made no reply.

When they reached their hotel, he registered them as man and wife. That, in her opinion, was quite fair because she regarded them as virtually married already, with only the technicality of a ceremony still to be performed. She realized, to be sure, that she still did not love him, but her gratitude to him was boundless, for he had rescued her from the deadly existence of living off the charity of relatives, and she felt she could never repay her debt to him. In addition he was generous, denying her nothing, and he had promised to marry her as soon as he settled some pressing problems that awaited him in the Republic of Texas. She hadn't presumed to inquire about the nature of that business, having been taught since childhood that ladies never pried into matters that did not concern them.

Naturally, Elisabeta had no way of knowing Anthony Roberts's real view of their relationship. He was flattered when they were seen together, her beauty creating attention wherever they went, and he had enjoyed buying clothes and jewelry for her. On the other hand, as a mistress she had given him far less satisfaction than had the women with whom he had lived in the past. She had had no previous sexual experience, and she automatically rejected his innovative pastimes, actually calling them perverted. The real reason he had brought her with him was his conviction that she could be useful to him. Her beauty was as potent a weapon as the knife he wielded so dexterously or the strong cord of thin silk strands with which he could strangle an enemy. In and of itself her appeal to men was harmless, but when it was utilized for his benefit, it could become even more dangerous than the sword he carried.

Soon after they arrived at the hotel, Anthony sent a message to someone he did not identify, then escorted Elisabeta to a lush garden set in the inner courtyard.

They sat at a table in the shade and were served a meal that surprised Anthony. The soup, which was called a gumbo, was delicious, and the chicken, fried and served with a rich cream gravy, was unlike anything he had ever eaten. Perhaps, he reflected, New Orleans was less barbaric and primitive than the rest of the United States. His long-held opinion of America was reinforced, however, when the wine he had ordered arrived: it proved to be so inferior that he refused to drink it.

As they were finishing their meal, a man appeared at the entrance to the garden and looked around slowly. He was middle-aged, ordinary looking, and only the red carnation he wore on the lapel of his coat set him apart.

The sight of that carnation instantly attracted Anthony's attention. "My dear," he said, "we've been traveling for many weeks. It would do you a world of good to go upstairs and rest."

Elisabeta smiled at him and shook her head. "You're always so considerate, but I'm not tired. I'd love to hire a carriage and have the driver show us the sights of the city."

His manner changed, and he became brusque. "We'll attend to that later. Right now, I must engage in a business meeting."

"I'm so sorry." She stood at once. "I believe I'm more tired than I knew, so I'll rest until you come for me."

Anthony stood at the table, making no move until she was gone. Then he slowly transferred his white linen napkin from his right hand to his left.

The man with the carnation came to him at once. "I was almost certain of your identity, Mr. Roberts," he said. "But I hadn't known that Mrs. Roberts was traveling with you. She's beautiful."

"Very beautiful, but she isn't Mrs. Roberts. Sit down, Mr.—ah—Franklin."

"Try our New Orleans coffee," the man said. "You'll find it has a flavor like that of the coffee served in the cafés of Paris."

Anthony obliged him by ordering a pot of coffee and two cups. He offered his guest a cigar, lighted one for himself, and then sat back in silence until they had been served.

"I trust your voyage was pleasant," the man who had been addressed as Franklin said.

Anthony nodded but had no desire to engage in small talk. "I was informed in Havana that your employer is interested in making a business deal with me."

"Indeed he is. He knows, of course, that you plan to work for the British—"

"Santa Anna must have good sources," Anthony interrupted.

"Our President sees to it that he is well informed."

"That's good to hear."

"It is understood," Franklin said, "that you'll be asked to engage in no activity that will conflict with the work you'll be doing for our friends in London."

"Splendid. I always live up to my obligations to my clients. What does Santa Anna have in mind?"

The Mexican go-between frowned at the repeated use of his superior's name. "Shall we just refer to him as the President?"

Anthony laughed. "No one can hear us, you know." He despised the conspiratorial attitude that so many engaged in the business of espionage adopted.

"Our problem is simple, and what we want from you is not complicated." Franklin spoke more briskly, apparently offended by the blunt rebuff. "As I'm certain you know, we maintain no diplomatic relations with the Texans. We continue to regard them as insurrectionists, and we hope to recover our lost territory at an appropriate time."

Anthony privately regarded that hope as overly optimistic. The Texans had already demonstrated that they were capable of defeating Mexico's army. So the best that could be accomplished now was his own goal of trying to prevent the United States from annexing the young Republic.

"Very few of our citizens are qualified to act as our eyes and ears in Texas. Relatively few could pass as

Americans and Englishmen, and none whom we've found are temperamentally qualified for the work. We've had a rather difficult problem—until we learned that you were traveling to Texas. So the President has authorized me to hold this meeting with you."

The man was long-winded, but Anthony told himself to be patient.

"All we would require of you is a regular monthly report. Anything of interest to us. Actions taken by Houston and bills passed by their Congress, as they call it. The rate of immigration, which we know is difficult to determine because so many Americans are going there at present. Anything and everything pertaining to their defense situation, which includes the size of their armed forces, their weapons, and so on. Any striking economic or political news. We glean very little from the Texas newspapers. Am I correct in assuming you intend to make your own headquarters in Austin?"

"That's my plan."

"Then you'd be a perfect set of eyes and ears for us, Mr. Roberts."

"Not so fast." Anthony pondered briefly. "Networks that pass along vital information often break down because communications are faulty. I've known two agents who have lost their lives because they were dealing with couriers who were untrustworthy."

"Ah." Franklin smiled broadly. "You need have no fears, sir. You will be dealing with no one. You won't know the identity of our couriers, and they won't know you."

"How is that possible?"

The Mexican chuckled. "A short distance from Austin, no more than a few minutes ride from the town, is a patch of woods. In it is a hollow tree. If we reach an agreement, I'll give you a map, which I'll ask you to memorize and then destroy. You will write your reports and place them in the tree on the first night of each month. There your responsibility ends. Our couriers will do the rest. And when you place your letter—or notes—

or whatever you care to write—in the hollow tree, you'll find your compensation for that communication awaiting you in the same place."

"Very ingenious," Anthony said, then added with emphasis, "I'm pleased to hear you mention compensation."

"What we ask of you is very easy and will not cause you any problems," Franklin said quickly. "The risks are minimal. And please keep in mind that we are a poor country. We cannot afford to pay fees on the scale paid by Britain, the most powerful nation on earth."

"How much?" Anthony's voice became harsh.

"In our pesos?"

"I am always paid in British pounds, or, failing that, American dollars."

"Dollars, then. Fifty dollars per month."

Leaning back lazily in his chair, Anthony smirked. "You've already told me my services are essential to you, that you can find no one else to do the work for you. So the question isn't one of the simplicity of the task or the lack of risk. We face a basic matter of supply and demand. Only *I* will be in a position to give you the information you need."

It was the Mexican's turn to become brusque. "How much do you want?"

"Double what you offered. One hundred American dollars per month, and I guarantee you'll get your money's worth."

The fee was still a bargain, but Franklin deemed it best to grumble. "You're holding us at gunpoint, but you give me no choice. We've struck a bargain, Mr. Roberts."

"With one month's fee payable in advance."

The Mexican sighed, took a wallet from an inner pocket, and counted out one hundred American dollars.

Anthony took the money quickly and pocketed it. "How will I get in touch with you if the need should arise?"

"It won't, sir. If we want special information, for which we'll make suitable payment, you'll find our request in the hollow tree. Like you, Mr. Roberts, we prefer not to complicate our lines of communication."

Himself abrasive, Anthony Roberts found few people in this line of work whose company he enjoyed, and he most emphatically did not include the Mexican. "I take it, sir, that our business is concluded."

"More or less. You're going on to Texas soon?"

"Without delay. I'll stay in New Orleans just long enough to arrange for sea passage to the Texas coast and to buy the horses we'll require for transportation from the Gulf to Austin."

"Then we shall expect your first report at the beginning of this coming month." Franklin coughed delicately behind a raised hand. "Did I understand you to say that the lovely lady with whom I saw you dining is not Mrs. Roberts?"

"I am a confirmed bachelor, sir, and I have no intention of changing my way of life."

There was a long pause before the Mexican representative said tentatively, "Perhaps, then, she is a resident of this city."

Anthony was amused. "She is not."

"Ah!" The exclamation, meaningless in itself, was an invitation to explain further.

There was no harm in telling him a few basics. "She is a native of Madrid, Mr. Franklin, and she speaks English with as much facility as her native Spanish."

"A lady of such great beauty, who would be at home in Mexico City because of her Spanish background, is a pearl of great value."

"I intend to make good use of her in Texas."

"I wonder," the man said tentatively, "whether you'd consider having her taken off your hands, Mr. Roberts. For a fair price, naturally."

Anthony studied him and saw he was serious. A fee that was high enough might prove tempting. If necessary, he might be able to persuade Elisabeta to accompany the fellow by telling her his own mission was too dangerous for her to go with him and that he would rejoin her in the immediate future. How Franklin would

handle her when she discovered she had been fooled was
not his problem. "What price would you consider equitable?"

"I am not lacking in personal means, although my
fund of American dollars is limited. Within a matter of
hours, however, I could obtain one thousand British
pounds."

The offer was large, and Anthony hesitated. His income from his inheritance amounted to only a little more
than one thousand pounds per year. On the other hand,
he would search long and hard before he found someone
as lovely, naive, and gullible as Elisabeta Manuel, someone he could bend to his will with ease. "I regret, sir,
that I'd require more than double that amount. But I'm
flattered. And," he added dryly, "I daresay the lady
might be, too, if I were in a position to tell her about it.
Which I'm not."

IV

Major General Winfield Scott, Chief of Staff of the United States Army, was as distinguished-looking as he was competent, and his political detractors, who suspected he wanted the presidency, did him a cruel injustice when they said he resembled an actor playing the role of a senior military commander. Gray-haired, with rugged features, he was tall and solidly built, wearing his well-tailored uniform with a flair. The creases in his tunic and breeches were sharp, his boots were highly polished, and his spurs of solid silver always gleamed. And although no one had ever accused him of undue modesty, he seemed unaware of the many medals that covered the left side of his tunic.

Colonel Lee Blake, who had served as a member of his staff, was at ease with him and felt at home in the spacious corner office of the new War Department building, built to replace the structure that British troops had burned to the ground during their occupation of Washington City in the War of 1812.

The General had not mentioned Lee's assignment but had been discussing the situation in Texas. "The Texas problem is intricate because of Mexico's continuing interest in her former province and Britain's determination to do all she can to prevent us from annexing Texas."

Lee nodded.

"Texas *will* be annexed, make no mistake about it. Then we'll be confronted with the problem of how Mexico will react, and no one knows what may be in Santa Anna's mind. I have a notion he doesn't know himself." The Chief of Staff laughed at his own little joke.

Lee smiled politely.

"We must be ready for whatever may develop. And Texas must be prepared, too, far beyond her present ability, to make her own adequate preparations." Scott glanced at the clock that stood on the mantel. "I'll say no more for the present. President Tyler is expecting us."

Lee was startled but knew better than to ask questions out of turn. His guess that his new assignment had something to do with Texas was now half-confirmed, but he had no idea why President Tyler wanted to see him.

They walked briskly, keeping in step automatically, as was the habit of military men. Soon they reached the executive mansion, now popularly known as the White House because it was repainted frequently to hide the scars made in the War of 1812 when the redcoats had tried to burn it down.

The President would see them shortly, a secretary said, and conducted them to an anteroom. To Lee's astonishment, Cathy was sitting there. She was bewildered and raised an eyebrow, and Lee shrugged, then presented the Chief of Staff.

General Scott bowed gallantly over Cathy's hand, then chuckled. "I took the liberty of writing a note to Mrs. Blake, asking her to join us," he said, enjoying their mystification when he offered no further explanation.

After a wait of only a few minutes, they were ushered into the President's office, and the lean, ascetic-looking John Tyler, the tenth President of the United States, rose to greet them. It was one of the ironies of history that, since he had announced his forthcoming retirement, the American people had just begun to appreciate him. Neither the nonentity nor the political hack he had been pictured, he was demonstrating clearheaded competence. His greatest handicap had been his sudden, unexpected elevation from the vice presidency when William Henry Harrison had died a scant month after taking office.

Lee stood at attention and saluted.

Cathy had never before met a President, and not knowing what else to do, she curtsied.

Tyler turned to Scott. "Have you told him, Winnie?"

The Chief of Staff looked aggrieved. "Certainly not, sir! I obey presidential directives."

"Your presence here is not accidental, Mrs. Blake," the President said. "I take great pleasure in administering the oath myself." He handed General Scott a Bible that rested on a table behind his chair, then turned to Lee. "Place your left hand on the Bible, raise your right hand, and repeat my words, phrase for phrase."

Before the astonished Lee quite realized what was happening, he found himself promoted to the rank of brigadier general. Cathy kissed him, the men shook his hand, and General Scott handed the young woman the single gold epaulet that was her husband's new insignia of rank.

Then the President rang a small silver bell to summon an aide. "Mrs. Tyler is expecting you to have tea with her, Mrs. Blake. You'll be taken to her while we have a discussion with General Blake."

General Blake. Lee enjoyed the sound of those words. But he returned to earth swiftly when the President motioned him and General Scott to a pair of chairs opposite his desk.

"The situation in Texas is critical and is growing more intense, General Blake," Tyler said. "It won't be too long before she has her own navy, we hope. Thanks to the efforts of someone from Oregon named Harry Canning. You must know him."

"I do, Mr. President. He's very competent and completely reliable."

"So I've been told. The Texas army, I'm sorry to say, is not in a position to defend the country at present. There's no lack of volunteers. But there are frightful

shortages of arms, including rifles and cannon. Their lack
of gunpowder is alarming. Their cavalry has horses, but
no sabers. Their sappers lack even such basic tools as
spades and shovels. Texas has been growing too fast for
her own good."

"If the British fail to prevent Texas from joining the
Union, and they will," General Scott added, "we don't
know what London will do next."

"We have reason to fear," the President declared, "that
Britain will encourage Santa Anna with money and arms.
In that event, Santa Anna would be in a position to
mount a serious invasion of Texas. We can't allow that to
happen. Do you have any questions so far, Blake?"

"Just one, Mr. President. According to what I've read,
private American citizens have been contributing funds
for the purchase of munitions for Texas. Is that information inaccurate?"

"No, indeed." A hint of a smile creased Tyler's long,
solemn face. "But those supplies are no more than the
proverbial drop in the bucket. Texas needs a tidal wave,
as you'll soon discover for yourself. On the recommenda-
tion of General Scott, which every general officer at the
War Department has agreed with, I'm sending you to
Austin as the military attaché at the United States Legation."

The puzzle was solved, and Lee was annoyed with
himself because the possibility of being given the post
had not occurred to him.

"Your principal responsibility," the Chief of Staff said,
"will be to ascertain the needs of the Texas army and
notify us accordingly. Then you'll be responsible, when
we send the supplies, for funneling them to the Texans."

"Yes, sir." Lee realized the task would be far more
complex than it sounded.

"You'll have your own compound at the legation,"
General Scott continued. "You'll have five junior officers
to assist you. All of them have already been in Texas
from six months to two years. You'll also have a cadre of
forty enlisted men, and I understand you're bringing
your own sergeant major to ride herd on them."

"I am, sir."

"Remember at all times," the President said, "that you and your subordinates are not permitted to join the Texans in any military endeavors. If you need a convoy for a freight wagon train of munitions, ask Sam Houston for the troops. Under no circumstances use your own. Your officers are there to advise and help you, your enlisted men will guard the legation. It won't be easy to remember you're on foreign soil," he added, his faint smile reappearing. "If you forget it, however, you inadvertently could start a war."

"I understand, Mr. President."

"And while you're at it, avoid politics there like the plague."

"That won't be difficult, Mr. President. I'm a soldier."

"Now," Tyler said, "there are two related matters that require discussion."

"Sir?"

"A wagon train is currently being organized for a journey to Texas," Tyler said. "There have been many trains in recent years, to be sure, but this one is special and takes on a symbolic significance. For one thing, it is far larger than any previously assembled. Almost one thousand people will be traveling to Texas. For another thing, they come from all over the United States, and I understand the party even includes some recent immigrants from Scotland. They're gathering at the town of Memphis and will go down the Mississippi River by barge and then make their way overland."

"It sounds impressive, Mr. President."

"This train," Tyler replied, "can do more to advertise American support than any other gesture we could make."

Lee nodded, unable to understand why he was being told about the venture.

"I've been wondering," the President continued, "whether you would be willing to meet the train at Memphis and lead it to Texas. As one of the leaders of the first wagon train to Oregon, you gained considerable national prominence, and Mrs. Blake is regarded as something of a heroine for her long journey across the country. We anticipate few problems, and your presence in the party would give a tremendous boost to the immigrants' spirits."

"You understand, Blake," General Scott added, "that the army can't formally order its new military attaché to Austin to lead a group of immigrants to Texas. But if you and Mrs. Blake choose to travel with them of your own accord, there's nothing the army can do about it. Your arrival in Austin will be delayed somewhat, I'll grant you, but we need time at this end to organize the munitions trains we're going to send, so nothing would really be lost."

Lee did not relish the idea of making another arduous trek in a cramped wagon, and he suspected that Cathy wouldn't like the prospect, either, particularly when she had to take care of Beth while he acted as the leader of the train. But there was no way that a man who had just been promoted to the rank of a brigadier general in the army could refuse a request from his Commander in Chief, even though it was an informal request. "Mrs. Blake and I," he said, "volunteer to accompany the wagon train to Texas."

A satisfied Winfield Scott sat back in his chair and relaxed.

President Tyler beamed. "I'm grateful to you, and I'm sure that President Houston of Texas will be equally appreciative." His smile vanished, and he hesitated. "My other request is strictly personal, and I make it only because of necessity. Are you familiar with the current situation in China?"

Lee was startled. "China? No, sir. We've seen few newspapers in Oregon, and I know nothing about what's happening in the Orient."

"China," Tyler explained, "has been closed to the West for thousands of years, but all that has changed. The Chinese have just been defeated by Great Britain in what the press has been calling the Opium War, and the Emperor has been forced to open his country to Western trade. Including our trade. The Tao Kuang Emperor has finally realized that he needs to modernize his army and navy, and some months ago one of his military experts arrived here from the Imperial City of Peking. Teng Chu is a rather remarkable man. Perhaps you'd like to explain further, Winnie."

"Yes, sir." General Scott chose his words with care. "Teng Chu has been visiting many of our military and naval installations, studying our weapons and learning about our methods of warfare. Obviously he holds a fairly high place in the Chinese army, although we've been unable to figure out his exact rank. He's rather— ah—unorthodox, you might say. We believe the reason the Emperor sent him rather than some other officer is because he speaks English. A very limited English."

"Teng Chu," the President added, "has just completed his tour of our army posts, navy bases, munitions plants, and so on. He has expressed a desire to visit Texas before he sails for Tientsin from New York. That has presented us with something of a problem. We got in touch with President Houston, who is agreeable to such a visit. But we're responsible for him, and we simply can't allow him to traipse around the North American continent unattended. Would you be willing to take him under your wing and escort him to Texas?"

Lee replied without hesitation, his own curiosity aroused about a military officer from the far side of the earth. "Certainly, Mr. President. But how will he get safely back to New York from Texas?"

Tyler deferred to General Scott.

The Chief of Staff shook his head. "The best we've been able to work out is to provide him with a troop of cavalry. They'll travel with your wagon train to Texas, so their presence should make your journey somewhat easier."

"Much easier, sir," Lee said but thought it odd that both the President and General Scott seemed very much relieved that he had consented to act as the Chinese officer's escort. Perhaps they weren't telling him all they knew about Teng Chu and his peculiarities. Well, he would find out soon enough.

The meeting adjourned, and they joined the ladies for tea. Mrs. Tyler, who was young and vivacious, chatted pleasantly, and the half-hour they spent with her passed quickly, but not quickly enough for Lee, who was anxious to bring his wife up to date on what was happening.

He had no opportunity until they walked back to their hotel, which was located a short distance from the White House. Cathy listened in silence, and when he was done, she still made no comment.

"What are you thinking?" Lee demanded.

"I'm glad you're going to be the military attaché at our legation in Austin," she said. "And I'm sure Hector Mullins will enjoy being in charge of security."

"That isn't what I mean."

"Well," she replied, sighing, "I suppose I feel the same way you do about traveling with another wagon train. I had thought those days were behind us."

"I'm more concerned about the Chinese officer," he said. "Not that I'm making light of the hardships we'll have to endure on another wagon train. But it will be a relatively short march through fairly civilized lands. It won't be anything like your trip across the whole continent in a wagon train."

"That's good," Cathy said. "Maybe I'm just getting old, but I don't think I could spend years on the trail again."

Ginny Mullins, who had volunteered to look after Beth whenever the Blakes were busy, became more morose than ever when she learned that another wagon train journey loomed ahead.

Her husband, who was delighted with his own assignment, tried to comfort her. "I wasn't with you the last time you traveled that way," he told her, winking at Lee and Cathy. "That will make all the difference. Besides, you heard General Blake say we'll have a whole troop of cavalry riding with us. Not that cavalrymen are in a class with foot soldiers, mind you, but I give you my guarantee that no harm will come to you."

Ginny looked bleakly into space.

That evening Cathy and Lee discussed the problem with their old friends, Ernie and Emily von Thalman, with whom they dined at the house that Oregon's official representative in Washington City had rented. "The poor woman feels like a fish out of water," Cathy said.

"I can understand it," Emily replied. "Ginny had no friends, no relatives, and the original Oregon settlers became her family."

"Don't worry about her," Ernie said. "Hector will straighten her out in time. I'm glad you were able to take him with you, Lee. But I don't mind saying that both of you will be badly missed in Oregon."

The reunion of old friends lasted well into the evening, and it was late by the time the Blakes returned to their hotel. But they were awake early because Lee wanted to obtain as much information as possible from the War Department about the wagon train to Texas. So they were the first guests to seat themselves in the dining room at breakfast. A smiling waitress told them what was being served.

Beth, unaccustomed to restaurants, nodded eagerly. "I want fish and steak and pancakes and eggs," she announced.

"She'll have a bowl of oatmeal, thank you, and a glass of milk," Cathy told the laughing waitress.

Service was rapid, and as they began to eat their meal, Beth pointed with her spoon. "Funny man," she said.

Walking toward them was a broad-shouldered Chinese, who stood at least six feet tall. His silver spurs, shaped like miniature dragons, jangled as he walked, and he was the epitome of dignity in what the Blakes were to learn was his "war coat," a loose-fitting garment of dark gray silk on which dragons, phoenixes, and other mythical creatures were embroidered in gold and silver. His face was broad, with a jutting chin and a firm mouth, and the humor in his dark eyes indicated that he had heard and appreciated the child's comment.

Lee immediately guessed his identity and stood. "Teng Chu?"

"You are General Blake." The Chinese bowed, then extended his hand Western style.

Lee presented him to Cathy, who invited him to join them.

Teng was pleased to sit with them. Beth continued to stare at him. "Little girl likes pigtail," he said.

Cathy was mortified. "Beth! Where are your manners?"

The Chinese officer waved a hand casually. "Is natural," he said. "In America, children see no pigtails." He gave the waitress an order almost as large as the meal Beth had wanted.

When he was served, he drew a pair of long, beautifully carved ivory chopsticks from one of his loose-fitting sleeves. Deftly cutting his broiled fish with them, he began to eat.

Lee and Cathy were almost as fascinated as their daughter, who asked to use chopsticks, too. His air almost that of a professional conjurer, Teng Chu produced another pair, then patiently began to teach the little girl how to use them.

To her parents' astonishment she was soon eating her oatmeal with them, holding her bowl close to her mouth. Teng Chu had won a small, devoted disciple, and not until she mastered the art of eating with chopsticks did he discuss his visit to Texas with Lee.

"I hear," Teng said, "that Texas is like China. Have many soldiers who fight on foot. Not enough guns. But win freedom from Mexico, anyway. That's why I want to learn what fighting men of Texas can teach me."

"You'll find they have no secret weapons," Lee said. "Their principal asset is their courage."

The Chinese officer smiled wryly. "In my country soldiers have courage, too. But English have better cannon and better rifles, so China loses war."

Lee had to concede that any nation possessing modern weapons had the edge in a war.

Sergeant Major Mullins, attired in dress uniform as was Lee, arrived to accompany his superior to the War Department, and it was plain that he took an instant dislike to Teng Chu, never before having encountered anyone quite like him.

When Teng announced that he would go to the War Department, too, Hector Mullins scowled. Noting this, Lee hoped there would be no personality clashes between them on the long journey they would be sharing.

They walked to the nearby War Department, and as they started down Pennsylvania Avenue, where cobblestones were replacing the old dirt road, they saw a half-dozen scarlet-coated troops coming toward them.

"British soldiers, I reckon," Hector said.

"Royal Marines," Lee replied. "They must be on their way to duty at the British Legation. They're probably part of the guard unit there."

As the two groups drew nearer to each other, the Marines caught sight of Teng, and not having noticed Lee's insignia of rank, they promptly began to taunt him. "Chinaman," one of them called in a rich Cockney accent, "go 'ome. We need the likes o' you to scrub the decks o' the warships that gave you such a bloody beatin'!"

Lee was afraid he would have to assert his authority to prevent an unpleasant incident, but Teng Chu elected to handle the matter in his own way. Reaching inside his loose-fitting coat, he produced a curved, double-edged sword that vaguely resembled a scimitar. It was narrow at its base, which was attached to a jeweled hilt, and then became broader, tapering again as it narrowed to a barbed point at its outer end.

The Chinese officer threw the sword into the air without halting or even slowing his pace, then caught it neatly by the hilt as it descended and, almost in the same motion, deftly lopped off a small branch from an elm tree. The Royal Marines gaped at him and fell silent.

Lee couldn't help chuckling. The marines saluted him smartly, and neither addressed the Chinese officer again nor even glanced in his direction. Even Hector Mullins was grudgingly impressed by the exhibition he had just witnessed.

Lee knew he needn't be too concerned about this

visiting foreign dignitary. Any man who could show
infinite patience with a small child and then, a few
minutes later, totally intimidate a half-dozen veteran
fighting men, was capable of taking good care of himself.

The final preparations for the departure of Harry
Canning's expedition to Texas were feverish. Paul Thoman was busy making his new schooner, the *Liz Lou*,
ready for the voyage, and Harry himself was everywhere, buying new rifles and pistols for members of his
party, supervising food purchases, and attending to
countless details.

Rick Miller, at his own request, arranged to spend a
day alone with Whip Holt. Shy at first in the presence of
the legendary mountain man, the Ranger gradually felt
more at ease as they rode on the range together, looking
for three geldings that the Texan wanted to purchase for
the coming journey.

"My friends down in Austin won't believe me when I
tell them I've actually met you and eaten a couple of
meals at your house, Mr. Holt," he said.

"I keep telling you to call me Whip. And what makes
you think your friends ever heard of me?"

Rick laughed. "There are hundreds of us who have
always wanted to be like you, Jim Bridger, and Kit
Carson."

"I can see where they'd admire Kit. He's quite a man.
So is Jim. But my confounded hip is so bad that I
couldn't even answer the call to duty in Texas!"

"There are plenty of us to do the fighting there these
days," Rick assured him. "I just hope we'll have real
peace one of these years. You don't know how I envy
you, Whip. You have everything a man could ever want.
A lovely wife and a strong son, a great ranch that's
making money. Everything."

"That's what I keep telling myself, Rick. But it isn't
quite true. When a fellow has smelled gunpowder for
enough years, he gets to hankering for another sniff now

and then." Whip suddenly became alert. "Now there's a
gelding for you. A three-year-old chestnut. He's almost
as powerful as this stallion of mine. I wouldn't hesitate
for a minute taking him off to the Rockies for a year—if
it weren't for my hip. And my family."

Rick refrained from mentioning that the era of the
mountain man was rapidly drawing to an end. Instead,
he watched the gelding cavorting in the field, then said,
"He's a fine-looking horse, and I'll take him. What do I
owe you for him?"

"Not a penny," Whip said firmly. "Not for this one and
not for the other two you've already picked."

"But that's not right, Whip. President Houston supplied me with special funds to bring Harry Canning and
his helpers to Texas. Good horses aren't cheap."

"You give all three of them to Sam with my compli-
ments. Tell him it's the best I can do for him these days,
seeing as how I can't come down to shake his hand in
person."

"I don't think I ought to accept," Rick said.

Whip met the younger man's level gaze. "I don't doubt
that you can outride me these days," he said. "But my
aim is still as good as it ever was, so don't go tempting
me to shut you up that way."

Rick realized it would be wrong to strip the veteran of
his pride, and for the first time he caught a glimpse of
how hard it had to be for a man of action to reconcile
himself to a life of quiet domesticity. "On behalf of
President Houston and the Republic of Texas," he said,
"I thank you for your gifts to us."

Whip's smile was pained, but he reflected that he had
made a substantial contribution to Texas's cause. At least
he could hold up his head again.

Melissa Austin, wearing a high-necked, ankle-length
dress of green calico, sat demurely on the horsehair
stuffed sofa in the parlor of the Woodling house, where
she was living, and poured steaming coffee for the two
suitors who had come to say goodbye to her. She had a

farewell scene to play, but she knew a great deal that they didn't, and although she was slightly amused, she had no desire to encourage either of them at present.

Danny Taylor, always the more studious of the pair, pointed to the black coffee in his cup. "You see that?" he demanded. "There's the proof that Oregon isn't a frontier country anymore. Now that the United States has established trade relations with the Ottoman Empire, we're importing coffee all the way from Turkey. There are folks who say it's a miracle that bags of it are brought to Oregon, but it's my contention this is part of the territory's natural process of growth and progress. Before long, folks here will be able to buy all the luxury goods you can get back in New York or Boston."

"I know what you mean." The chunky Chet grinned broadly. "It seems like a long time ago that we were drinking herb tea that winter we spent in the Wyoming mountains. Because that's all there was."

"Well," Melissa said, "I was drinking coffee back in Pennsylvania before I ever came to Oregon. I prefer it to tea."

Danny, who was painfully honest, couldn't help saying, "It's just as well, then, that you and Nancy Canning can't come to Texas with us."

Melissa stiffened. "Why is that?"

"I doubt if there's a single coffee bean in the whole Republic. Or very much tea, either."

"What do they drink there?" Melissa asked.

The two young men looked at each other. "Sage tea, maybe," Danny said.

"Or some other abomination," Chet added. "I'll let you know in the first letter I send to you."

"You've got to remember," Danny said, trying to be kind, "that Texas is still a frontier country. There are hundreds and hundreds of miles there where nobody at all lives. Or has ever lived."

"That's why I think it would be exciting to be going there," Melissa announced firmly.

"I like it," Danny said, "because I helped tame the Oregon wilderness. But I'm not like Whip Holt, who was happy to live by himself in the most remote areas of the Rockies for years."

"I've got to agree with you," Chet said. "The challenge lies in the taming. Building houses that are dry and warm."

"Shooting game until the herds of cattle and flocks of sheep start coming in," Danny said. "Knowing what wild roots and plants you can eat until you can start growing your own vegetables and fruit."

Melissa was wide-eyed. "I hope Texas isn't completely civilized by the time I get there."

"Oh, there will be plenty of discomfort left, I'm sure," Danny told her, smiling gently. "Speaking for myself, I'll be ready to settle down for keeps once we've helped with statehood for Texas. What about you, Chet?"

"Blamed if I know. I guess it depends on how rough a time we have down there."

"True," Danny mused. "We were just youngsters with no real responsibilities of our own when we came here. The burden fell on men like Whip and Ernie and Lee Blake. But we'll find out what it's like soon enough now."

"When are you leaving?" Melissa asked.

They looked at each other. "We're not supposed to say," Chet replied.

For the first time she showed a trace of annoyance. "I can't imagine what enemies of the United States I'd tell. Besides, if I wanted to know badly enough, I'm sure I could find out from Nancy. Her husband isn't keeping it a secret from her, you can be certain of that!"

Danny sucked in his breath. "We're boarding at nightfall tomorrow, and we're sailing soon after. Paul Thoman wants to leave at night so the British over at Fort Vancouver don't have too good an idea of what's happening."

"I won't tell a soul, I promise," Melissa said.

"Will we see you again?" Chet asked.

Danny waited anxiously for her reply, too.

Melissa shrugged and sounded indifferent. "If you want to come out any time before noon tomorrow, I'll be

here. But I'm going to be very busy in the afternoon."
She offered no explanation.

Each of them wanted to see her privately before they
departed, but she was continuing to maneuver them,
somehow making certain that both called on her simultaneously, which made it impossible for either to speak
his mind freely.

"I'll be here," Danny said, trying in vain to hide his
disappointment.

"So will I."

"Good. I'll see you then." Melissa, still seemingly
ingenuous, smiled at them impartially and conducted
them to the front door. Under the circumstances, neither
had the opportunity to kiss her.

Lee and Cathy Blake left Beth with Hector and Ginny
Mullins at the military compound in Nashville and, accompanied by Teng Chu, rode out to the Hermitage.
Andrew Jackson had invited them to dine with him, and
the Chinese warrior was eager to meet the former President and one-time Major General who was regarded by
most of his compatriots as the greatest of living Americans.

Old Hickory was frail, his almost translucent skin
tightly drawn, but for limited periods his vigor was
undiminished. The mantel above the fireplace in his
library and the bookshelves that lined the walls were
crammed with mementos of the full, honor-laden life he
had led. But the old man who sat in a rocker, a shawl
over his shoulders, was unpretentious in appearance as
he sipped the watered whiskey that his physicians no
longer bothered to prohibit.

Teng Chu fascinated the old man. "I don't suppose,"
Jackson said, "that you could give me an exhibition of
your way of fighting."

The Chinese bowed. "I am happy to show you our
special style of fighting," Teng Chu said.

A spirited stallion from the Jackson stables was saddled, and while Cathy went into another room to visit

with the retired President's niece, who acted as his housekeeper, the three men adjourned to the spacious grounds behind the mansion.

At Teng Chu's direction Lee set up some targets, each of them an apple from the Hermitage orchard; they were placed some distance apart on makeshift stands five to eight feet high.

Bowing again to the old man, the Chinese mounted the stallion. Reaching under his loose-fitting outer garment, he produced his scimitarlike blade, which he twirled over his head as he spurred the stallion to a canter. Measuring a target with care, he sent the animal hurtling toward it, and then he reached out in a single, decisive motion, his sword flashing in the early afternoon sunlight.

When he had thundered past the target, the viewers saw the apple, neatly cut into two pieces, lying on the ground.

Jackson applauded, and Lee was equally impressed. "Imagine having a whole regiment of cavalry that skilled," Old Hickory said.

"There are many such regiments in the Middle Kingdom," Teng Chu said, drawing to a halt beside them as his sword disappeared beneath his robe. "But our foot soldiers could not protect them with ancient muskets." Not waiting for further comment, he sent his mount forward again, this time riding parallel to the target that he selected.

They saw he was holding a very short spear in his hand, a weapon no more than eighteen inches long. At the appropriate moment, when the horse was moving at a full gallop, he let fly with the weapon, and the spear bored through the apple from stem to base.

A marveling Lee brought the spear, with the apple still on it, to the old man for examination. The weapon was even more curious than the two Americans had supposed. The shaft was made of bamboo, its hollow length filled with a heavy metal that may have been lead. The point was needle-sharp and made of steel.

"Remarkable," Old Hickory muttered. "Do you have many troops who can use this spear as you've just used it?"

"Many thousands," Teng Chu replied. Then he added, "Now I will show you one more weapon."

They watched him as he spurred the stallion. Reaching beneath his robe, the Chinese produced yet another weapon that the viewers could not see clearly. He was at least twenty feet from his target as he hurled it, and the apple resting on the stand disintegrated, with bits flying in every direction.

Lee ran forward to retrieve the weapon. It was unlike anything he had ever seen. About the size of a man's fist, it was star-shaped, with six points of steel, each as sharp as that of the short spear.

As Andrew Jackson examined the sphere, which still had a portion of the apple clinging to one of its points, Teng Chu dismounted and gave the reins to a groom. "In the Middle Kingdom," he explained, "this is called a falling star. It does not matter how the warrior throws it. If his aim is good, one of the points will strike the target."

"You've invented far more than gunpowder," Old Hickory said as they returned to the house. "This falling star is the most ingenious weapon I've ever seen."

"I will be honored if you will keep it," Teng Chu said graciously.

"I couldn't deprive you of it," President Jackson replied quickly.

The Chinese laughed. "In my baggage I have many others. In battle a warrior will use ten falling stars. Maybe twenty."

The weapon was placed on a shelf in the library near the bullet that Old Hickory had carried in his body for many years before it had popped out during his second term as President.

"If the Texas cavalry had weapons like these—in addition to their rifles," Jackson said, "they could win a battle even if they were outnumbered four to one."

"It is the rifles that make the difference," Teng Chu said, a hint of wistfulness in his voice.

"By the Eternal, you're right!" Old Hickory declared, striking the arm of his rocking chair for emphasis. "General Blake, I know of nothing more important for the future of Texas than the munitions train that's going to be assembled and sent on to you in the months ahead."

Teng Chu looked puzzled.

Lee felt compelled to explain to him. "Many wagons loaded with arms and munitions will be sent to Texas, each pulled by a team of twenty mules. Each will include cannon, rifles, powder—everything the Texans will need in case a new war breaks out."

"The people of Texas are fortunate," the Chinese said. "They have good friends in United States."

"That's because they're actually Americans themselves," Andrew Jackson told him.

Lee remained silent until dinner was announced. He was beginning to feel the weight of the burden that had been placed on his shoulders, and now, more than ever, he understood the significance of his new rank.

As Anthony Roberts had learned over the years, almost anything desirable was available to one who was willing to pay enough for it. Substantial dwellings in Austin were scarce, new arrivals in the Texas capital contenting themselves with log cabins that they built in haste. Most people lived in these cabins until their fortunes improved sufficiently for them to erect bigger homes. Anthony found it a simple matter, however, to rent a fully furnished two-story house of white clapboard, which was located only a short walk from the drab public buildings in which the offices of the young Republic were housed.

He and Elisabeta Manuel created a stir in the town when they moved into the place, the residents of Austin assuming they were husband and wife. Anthony made no attempt to disabuse anyone of the notion, and Elisabeta, still confident that he intended to marry her in the immediate future, followed his example. So the Cabinet members, as well as the senators and congressmen they soon invited to spend evenings with them, invariably addressed Elisabeta as Mrs. Roberts.

Not satisfied with just developing an active social life, Anthony also invested in a company that brought freight by wagon train to Texas from New Orleans. The venture had been floundering because it lacked capital, but his infusion of funds put it on its feet almost overnight, and its operators were certain it would begin to show a profit within a few months.

Thanks to these efforts, Anthony quickly attained his goal of establishing himself as a man of stature in the community. Elected officials of the Republic, spending months at a time far from their own homes in the vast country, were delighted to accept the generous hospitality of their genial host and his charming, lovely "wife," who made certain that guests never lacked food and drink.

It was only natural that the Texans should be curious about the couple, and Anthony unhesitatingly explained Elisabeta's background, telling those who asked that she was Spanish, that he had known her in Madrid for a long time, and that she was paying her first visit to the New World. But he was far more reserved about his own past, frequently replying vaguely to queries.

One evening, however, when a number of congressmen dropped in for cold meats and drinks, Elisabeta was astonished when he told a bald lie.

"What is your nationality, Mr. Roberts?" one of the guests inquired.

"As you can undoubtedly hear from my accent," Anthony replied, smiling, "I'm British. But I've long admired this part of the world, and I'm seriously thinking of renouncing my allegiance to the Crown and becoming a citizen of Texas."

The entire company approved.

But Elisabeta was puzzled, and later, after the company had departed, she continued to ponder as she cleaned up the kitchen. Returning to the parlor, where Anthony was sipping a final drink, she said, "You confused me this evening. I was so surprised when you said that you are a British subject."

He glared at her but made no comment.

The girl's violet eyes widened. "Why didn't you tell them you're really an American?"

"I prefer not to discuss it," he said harshly.

"All of the people here came from the United States, too, so I'd think you'd be proud to tell them you were born in Connecticut."

Anthony rose from his chair, went to her, and stood before her for a moment. Then, very slowly and deliberately, he struck her across the face with an open hand.

The totally unexpected blow was so vicious that Elisabeta staggered backward and would have fallen if she had not reached out and grasped a chair.

"Never mention to anyone—and I mean anyone at all—that I was born in America. You heard me say tonight that I'm a British subject. That's the story you'll tell in the future if you're asked."

The girl stood, one hand held to her smarting face. "But why lie about it? I don't understand."

"There is no need for you to understand," Anthony told her sternly. "You'll do as I tell you, no more and no less. That little slap was only a taste of what will happen if you meddle in matters that are none of your concern. This much you can understand, my dear—tell anyone in Texas that I was born in the United States, and I shall beat you within an inch of your life. Do I make myself clear?" He advanced toward her, his fists clenched, his eyes icy.

Elisabeta shrank from him. "Very clear," she murmured, certain he intended to make good his threat here and now.

He studied her for a few moments, and when he saw that he had succeeded in cowing her, he relaxed. "That's much better," he said. "From now on you'll do as you're told, and we'll have no problems." He gulped the last of his drink, then hastily left the room and climbed the stairs.

The bewildered Elisabeta remained in the parlor for a

long time, her face still aching. All she knew was that Anthony was no longer a considerate, kind gentleman, who appeared to be very much in love with her. His eyes had been those of a stranger, and his hard slap demonstrated his contempt for her.

She took his glass to the kitchen and washed it, then forced herself to go upstairs. The door of the bedroom she had shared with him since they had moved into the house was closed and locked, so she had to make up the cot in the tiny guest chamber at the end of the corridor. Perhaps it was just as well. Certainly she could not give herself to a man who had abused her.

She lay in bed, analyzing her situation. She no longer cared why Anthony had chosen to conceal his American citizenship from the Texans who had been their guests. Her own problems took precedence. Had Anthony struck her in a spurt of sudden anger, she might have been able to forgive him, but he had dealt her a nasty blow deliberately, and she was forced to conclude that he had been waiting for the right opportunity to show her his power over her.

There was no question in her mind that he had that power. She had literally no money of her own and had to depend on him for her very subsistence, even for the funds he gave her to buy food at the local market. She had no friends in Texas to whom she could turn for help.

She wanted to flee from Anthony, but there was no place she could go. She had relatives in California, now a Mexican province, but she could not go to them, any more than she could return to her native Spain. She had to stay here, continuing to pretend that she was Anthony's wife. It dawned on her that he had tricked her into accompanying him on this long journey to a strange, primitive land, and she couldn't even guess his purpose.

Fighting down the panic that welled up within her, she realized she would be compelled to tolerate this unsavory situation until she could find some way to solve her terrible dilemma.

V

Two hundred and fifty covered wagons were scattered over a large area of the waterfront facing the Mississippi River just below Memphis, and the horses, oxen, and mules that pulled these vehicles were grazing peacefully on the rich Tennessee grass. Each day for weeks, new wagons had been coming into camp, but the flood had subsided, and for the past forty-eight hours, no new wagons had arrived.

The future Texas settlers were eager to be on their way, and there were some who spent most of their waking hours watching the ever-growing flotilla of rafts that would carry them down the great river. Most, particularly those who had already traveled long distances to the assembly area, had already learned patience. No one knew when the party would depart, and in the meantime families lived on their own supplies of flour and beans, bacon and other smoked meats. Those who had funds spent money buying fresh vegetables from local farmers, and the poorest members of the company tried their luck each day fishing in the Mississippi, even though they were seldom rewarded with a catch.

Memphis no longer regarded itself as a frontier community. Founded in 1819 by Andrew Jackson, who had named it, the growing metropolis sat high on a bluff overlooking the river and was now spreading rapidly. The busy, prosperous inhabitants avoided the Texasbound immigrants and their campsite, but there were many residents who vividly remembered their own journeys through the wilderness in covered wagons, and every church in town took up food collections for this new generation of pioneers.

Individual campfires dotted the grassland, a scarcity of immediately available firewood making it necessary for a number of families to share each fire. Certainly one of the best tended was that of the MacGregors, who had just come to the New World from the highlands of Scotland, where Innes, the head of the family, had tended sheep. A broad-shouldered giant with flaming red hair and freckles, he towered above his tiny wife, Matilda, who was as dark as her husband was fair.

It was the MacGregor children, all five of them girls, who were responsible for the fire, and they tended it meticulously, thanks to the efforts of the eldest, Heather, who was fifteen. Even the youngest, Wallace, who had been given a male name before her birth by her father in the hope that Matilda would bear a son, performed her fair share of the chores, although she was only five. No MacGregor ever evaded responsibility.

As Innes strolled toward the site, an old musket under one arm, he paused to light his pipe and silently observed the members of his family. Heather kept the girls busy, as usual, sending them off to the forest southeast of the city for more wood, making certain they placed it in neat piles behind their wagon and herself placing logs on the fire to make certain it was used sparingly. As Innes watched, he saw seven-year-old Cara and five-year-old Wallace approaching, their small arms filled with wood. Like all of the MacGregor children, they had inherited his red hair and freckles. The family collie, Thistle, circled around the pair, frolicking yet making certain that no stranger tried to take their wood from them.

Innes told himself he was blessed with a fine brood, even though all of them, including Thistle, were females.

Starting forward again, he waved to his daughters, then called, "Where's Ma?"

Heather gestured toward the wagon.

"Mattie," Innes roared, "come out here, I've news for ye!"

Others nearby heard him and promptly appeared on the scene. The Howells, who came from the foothills of Virginia and were always cheerful in spite of their poverty, were a middle-aged couple, childless, who had become attached to the MacGregor youngsters in the weeks they had been neighbors. From the opposite direction came Asa Phipps, until recently a dirt farmer in Kentucky. Silent, with quick eyes that missed nothing happening around him, Phipps was also armed, his rifle far more modern than the weapon Innes carried.

Matilda MacGregor was the last to appear. She emerged from the wagon still carrying the quilt she was mending, and she lost no time reproving her husband. "Must ye bawl like a lost sheep? If people were asleep in any of the wagons hereabouts, you've waked them for certain."

"The whole camp will be awake soon as they hear the news." He beckoned to his children, his abrupt gesture indicating that they were to halt their work and gather around him. Aware of their curiosity, he enjoyed prolonging the suspense. "Great news it is I bring ye. We'll soon be on our way to Texas. In a few days now, at most."

"Oh, Pa!" Heather clasped her hands together, her expression blissful.

Asa Phipps looked at the Scotsman with disdain. "Every blame day we hear rumors that we're soon moving on, but we still haven't budged. I think we'll stay here until we run out of food and money—and starve to death."

"I beg to differ with ye, Mr. Phipps, but I know different," Innes said courteously and thereafter ignored the man, addressing himself to the others. "I was stretching my legs on a walk to the bluff yonder just now," he said, "when I saw a party of soldiers riding toward me. A troop of United States Cavalry. Fifty of them. And in their midst, grand as you please, was a general. Blake by name, with his wife and wee daughter and an elegant gentleman from the Orient riding with him."

Heather studied her father carefully. When he was in a mood, he enjoyed teasing the girls with highly embroidered stories.

Innes saw her expression and grinned at her. "I tell ye true, child," he said. "General Blake shook me by the hand. He's come to lead us to Texas, and he says we'll soon be on our way!"

"Why would a general in the U.S. Army lead a company of paupers to Texas?" Phipps demanded. "That makes no sense."

"Ah, but it does, sir," the gentle Howell declared. "Remember the story that made the rounds of the camp not four days ago? We were told that an army officer and his wife who were on the first wagon train to Oregon were joining us. And I read about it myself in a Nashville newspaper. So it must be true!"

Before Phipps could reply, a bugle sounded near the river, its sweet, high notes floating across the grasslands. Within moments people from a score of wagons began walking toward the source of that sound.

"We're being summoned, most likely," Innes said. "Girls, come with your ma and me."

Heather hesitated. "I'd best stay behind and tend the supper fire," she said.

"Lass," Matilda told her, "ye be too conscientious for ye own good. The world won't end if the fire dies out this once. Come along!"

The bugle continued to blare, and within a quarter of an hour the entire company, almost one thousand strong, was gathered near the bank of the Mississippi.

There a high-ranking officer climbed onto a boulder and gestured for silence. "Friends," he said, "I'm Lee Blake. My wife and I have had experience on a wagon train, having crossed the continent to the Oregon country on the first of them. I've been assigned to duty in Texas, and as a personal favor to President Tyler, we've come to help you on your own journey. I hear some of you have been waiting here for weeks, and I sympathize with you. We're going to push off down the Mississippi as fast as we can load the barges, a task we'll begin tomorrow morning."

"Why wait until then?" Innes MacGregor called in his deep voice. "I'll start this very night. What say ye, lads?"

Several volunteers raised their voices, and the chorus quickly grew.

Lee grinned at this man who possessed qualities of leadership that were unexpectedly coming to the foreground. "Thanks, Mr. MacGregor! Those of you whose wagons are loaded tonight will sleep on the rafts. No animals will be boarded until the very last. Now. I'll ask all work volunteers to report immediately to Sergeant Major Mullins, who will organize you into crews. For you women who have questions about wagon train travel that a man can't answer, my wife will station herself right here and do what she can for you. Let's get started!"

The men and older boys gathered around Hector Mullins, who showed them how to haul a wagon onto a river raft and lash it securely, and then they were assigned to groups, each consisting of ten or twelve men. The army cavalrymen—some of whom would sleep in tents on board the rafts made for them by the local garrison—pitched in, too.

Lee walked up and down the riverfront with Teng Chu beside him. Teng Chu shook his head in wonder. "No one pays money to these men to work like coolies?"

"They do everything themselves, and they will for the rest of their lives," Lee told them. "You'll understand better when you see them after we reach Texas, clearing their land and building their houses." He paused to watch Innes MacGregor, whose strength was so great that he needed only four men to help him as he pulled a large wagon onto a raft that was tied securely to stakes driven into the river bank.

Asa Phipps, who was taking no part in the volunteer labor, came up behind the pair and stopped short. "Damned if it ain't a real Chinaman. You, there!" he called, apparently regarding himself as a wit. "How would you like me to cut off your pigtail?"

The stupid question made no sense, but as Teng Chu turned, he saw the sneer on the farmer's face and realized he was being mocked. Before Lee could urge him to ignore the man, the scimitarlike blade appeared in the warrior's hand, and a moment later the sword was twirling menacingly in front of the astonished Phipps's face.

"I was just joking!" Phipps cried.

Lee started to intervene, then checked himself. Several of the future settlers' work crews had paused in their labors to watch, and although he had no idea what Teng Chu had in mind, he was content to allow the Chinese to handle the matter in his own way. Virtually none of the Texas-bound immigrants had ever seen an Oriental, and it was best they learn here and now that the warrior was a man of dignity who did not appreciate the scorn of strangers.

Phipps began to back toward the Mississippi, his lean face showing his alarm. Teng Chu continued to twirl the blade, which hovered no more than a hair's breadth from the tip of the victim's nose. The warrior's attitude was even more remarkable than his actions. His face was composed, showing no sign of anger, and there was a suggestion of amusement in his dark eyes.

Asa Phipps halted just short of the water. "Leave me be, you big bully."

The sword stopped twirling, and Teng Chu's gesture indicated that he was contemplating beheading the man.

The terrified Phipps took another backward step and fell into the water. With great difficulty he hauled himself to his feet, his clothes soaked and muddy. Seething but impotent, he climbed up the bank, slipped, and almost fell backward into the water again.

The onlookers roared with laughter.

When they grew a bit quieter, Teng Chu observed placidly, "This man has a mouth as big as the striped king of fish that lives in the River Yangtze. But he is not like the fish because he cannot swim." Showing his contempt for Phipps, he turned his back to the man and strolled off to rejoin a chuckling Lee Blake, the vicious sword vanishing again beneath his embroidered robe.

Lee was delighted. Not only had the unnecessarily unpleasant farmer been taught a lesson he would not forget, but Teng Chu already had won the respect and affection of this company of realists who judged a man by his actions. Word of the incident would spread, he knew, and henceforth the Chinese warrior would be welcome as a guest of honor in virtually every wagon in the train.

Innes MacGregor paused as, leading his crew to another wagon after loading one onto a raft, he deliberately made his way to Teng Chu. "Sir," he said, "I'm much obliged to ye. I've been wanting to give that sour-faced Phipps a drubbing for days in the hopes he'd learn some manners. You've not only saved me the trouble, but you've done the job far better than I ever could!"

Teng Chu smiled amiably as he took the Scotsman's measure. Then, to the surprise of everyone present, he volunteered to work with MacGregor and his crew.

Lee was impressed, knowing that in China it was beneath the dignity of a man of Teng Chu's class to engage in physical labor. This visit to the United States was changing the very nature of the Emperor's special representative, who was adapting to the American way of life.

Meanwhile, Cathy was surrounded by scores of women who were besieging her with questions about making homes for themselves and their families in the wilderness. There were so many who wanted information from her that she had to call on Ginny Mullins to help her.

For the first time since Ginny had learned that she had to leave Oregon, she became less morose. She, like Cathy, had acquired expertise in frontier dwelling, and she forgot her own feelings as she patiently explained how food supplies were accumulated, how clothing was made, and how primitive cabins could be transformed into comfortable homes.

When the night's work was done, most of the military went off to the local army post, where quarters were being provided for them. The rest took up their assigned spots on the rafts. Lee stayed on one of the rafts, while Cathy took Beth back to the post for the night.

Cathy had intended to remain at the post the following day, preparing the canvas-topped wagon that the army had purchased for her family's use. But she knew that the women of the caravan were waiting for her with more questions, so she hurried to finish her task, then took Beth with her and returned to the waterfront.

The men labored unceasingly, feverishly, and twenty-four hours later, after the horses, mules, and oxen were loaded onto rafts, the flotilla cut loose and began to move down the river, with the current of the Mississippi propelling the cumbersome, crude rafts.

The Blakes led the procession, and as Lee looked out at the fertile fields on both sides of the broad river, he grinned at Cathy, then turned to Teng Chu. "This kind of travel is positively luxurious," he said. "We'll tie up before sundown every night, and almost before you know it, we'll reach Louisiana. There's no cross-country marching, and we're moving through a settled, civilized area, where there's almost no danger of an attack by hostile forces."

Cathy glanced at the soldier who was steering the raft, then watched Beth playing with Wallace MacGregor, who was spending the day with them. She herself was inured to hardship, but she prayed, for the sake of all the children in the company, that the hazards and discomforts of the journey would not be too great after the company left the river and began the long overland march to Texas.

"There are fish in this river?" Teng Chu asked.

"Some, as I understand it, but not many," Lee replied. "The best fishing is in the streams that feed into the Mississippi. The current here is too swift, although some who have the knack are said to pull in an occasional fish. I can give you a hook and a line if you'd like to try your luck."

"Only the hook, please," the Chinese replied. Reaching beneath his robe, he produced a ball of marvelously strong line, made of intertwined strands of silk and cotton.

Beth and Wallace stopped their play and hurried to his side as he tied the hook to one end of the line. His face solemn but the twinkle in his dark eyes revealing his true emotions, he reached inside the robe again, then opened his hand.

The two little girls became excited when they saw a tiny dragon of porcelain, its color a fiery red. He attached the lure close to the hook, then threw the line overboard and allowed it to trail behind the raft, taking care that it didn't become snagged in the following raft.

"Small girls will catch fish," Teng Chu said.

Under his watchful guidance, Beth and Wallace took turns holding the line. Wallace was the first to bring in a fish, about ten inches long, which no one on board the raft could identify. But that didn't matter; the MacGregor child was ecstatic. No more than ten minutes later Beth had her first strike, and she jumped up and down, babbling almost deliriously, when Teng Chu removed the fish from the hook.

Lee had to concede that the warrior had a knack, as he had called it. Before the afternoon ended, the two little girls, "assisted" by Teng Chu, had caught a total of fifteen fish.

When a halt was called for the night, Sergeant Major Mullins, who had spent a two-year tour of duty on the Mississippi, pronounced the catch edible. That night the Blakes and the MacGregors dined on fried fish, and Beth and Wallace were so elated that they remained awake long after their normal bedtime.

Eventually they were persuaded by their mothers to retire, but they consented to sleep only after Teng Chu presented each of them with a red porcelain dragon similar to that which had been used as a lure. The warrior had become their idol, and thereafter both followed him everywhere, listening avidly to the stories he told them about Chinese dragons.

"When I grow up," Wallace announced solemnly, "I'm going to China and catch fish there every single day."

The voyage of about eight hundred miles down the Pacific Coast from Oregon to the southern portion of California in the *Liz Lou* was uneventful. Harry Canning had sailed in these waters for many years, and more recently Paul Thoman had come to know them, too.

Twice during the six days the party spent at sea, the cook came to Paul to complain that his food supplies were vanishing more rapidly than he had anticipated. On the second occasion Paul, who was not concerned, humored the man. "Maybe the lads who are going with Captain Miller and Mr. Canning have big appetites. Or some of our seamen may be heavy eaters."

"That's not what I mean, sir," the cook replied. "I take stock of my stores at the beginning and end of every day's meals. There ain't all that much missing, I'll grant you, sir. But every morning when I open the galley, something that we had the night before is gone. Day before yesterday, it was the leftover fish we had for supper. Yesterday, it was a mess of beans and sausages."

Paul was convinced that the man, who was semiliterate, was incapable of keeping an accurate count of what he had on hand. "As long as what's missing is only in small quantities," he said, "I wouldn't worry about it."

The cook shrugged and went back to the galley. He wasn't paying for the food, and if the ship's master was satisfied, he didn't care how much vanished.

Timing their landing so the passengers would disembark soon after nightfall, in accordance with Rick's careful instructions, Paul headed for the shore by way of unoccupied Catalina Island, and they soon came to a natural harbor known only to a few coastal fishermen. Here the process of landing was begun.

Rick had already gone ahead and, mounted on his stallion, had made a quick reconnaissance of the area in the immediate vicinity of the harbor. Someday a settlement might spring up here, but for the present the entire region was deserted. A few monasteries established by members of various Spanish religious orders still existed inland, but he intended to avoid them as he led his companions toward the east.

The landing took over two hours. Then Paul, still following Rick's suggestions, weighed anchor and slipped out to sea. Now it no longer mattered if the commander of a Mexican gunboat halted him and came on board to inspect the schooner. Scores of American traders sailed in these waters, and there was no way the Mexicans might discover that he had landed a party of Americans who intended to travel to Texas.

Rick's strict discipline prevailed on shore. The horses were watered at a small pond and, having been cooped up on the ship for the better part of a week, were allowed to graze on the high, sweet grass of a pasture near the harbor's edge. The men sat in a circle, and Rick addressed them in quiet tones. "We'll light no fire tonight. If you're chilly, wrap yourselves in your blankets. And we'll eat cold food for supper and again for breakfast. I don't think it's likely that there are any Mexican patrols in the vicinity. This godforsaken area is pretty useless. But we'll take no chances. We'll light fires only in daylight and only when the wind is strong enough to blow away the smoke quickly."

His orders made sense, and his charges nodded.

"I have only a few basic rules," Rick continued. "I'll tolerate no loud laughter and no horseplay. There's no sense advertising our presence in any neighborhood. And always keep your rifles close at hand, day and night, awake or asleep. Firearms aren't going to be much use to us if we leave them ten or twenty feet away from us."

Every member of the party immediately checked to make sure his rifle lay on the ground beside him and that the pistols he carried in his belt were loaded.

A large pot of beans and sausages, prepared in advance by the cook on the *Liz Lou*, was passed around, and the men helped themselves, eating the cold meal from the folding plates secured to the backs of their water canteens. These devices had been developed in Oregon and were so helpful to those who traveled through the wilderness that they were being manufactured in large quantities by a New England metal foundry.

Members of the company were mindful of Rick's regulations, and there was little conversation as they ate.

Suddenly Rick raised his head, listened intently, and then sprang to his feet, his rifle in his hand.

The others had heard nothing but lost no time following his example. Apparently Rick, like Whip, had a keener sense of hearing than that with which ordinary mortals were endowed.

A sharp, clicking noise indicated that the Texan's rifle was ready for instant use. "Whoever you are out yonder in the trees," he called, "come forward. Slow and easy, with your hands high in the air over your heads. Now!"

Two shadowy figures emerged from the patch of woods behind the group, and at first glance these buckskin-clad figures appeared to be those of young, slender men.

Harry Canning gasped when he recognized his wife.

Nancy ran to him, bursting into tears as she threw herself into his arms. "I'm sorry, dear," she sobbed. "But I just couldn't bear to be parted from you, even though I knew it was wrong to do this."

Harry was so stunned that, for the moment, he could feel no anger. "What in God's name—"

"I was stupid." His wife made a great effort to control herself. "I just hate being told there's something I can't do. I've always been independent, as I'm afraid you know. Too independent for my own good. Except I'm not really that way at all. I lean on you more than I ever realized, and when Melissa and I decided on this lark, I couldn't resist."

He was badly upset. "What lies ahead for us is no lark.

You heard Rick explain what may be in store. Mexicans who hate all Americans and will shoot on sight. Some of the nastiest, most ruthless Indians alive, especially the Apache. Long stretches of desert. Snakes and scorpions and the Lord only knows what other enemies of human beings."

Ashamed of her impulsive behavior, she knew she had to face reality. "It wasn't until we had sneaked ashore that I began to think I had made a terrible mistake, and by then it was too late."

A cold fury welled up in him, and he waited until it subsided somewhat before he replied. "You behaved like a spoiled child."

"There's nothing you can say that I'm not saying myself," Nancy declared. "I know it does no good to apologize."

"This party is stuck with you. For better or worse."

She looked up at him earnestly. "For whatever good this will do, Harry, I swear to you that I'll change. If we survive. I—I'm not your daughter, rebelling against a strict parent. I'm your wife, and I'll try to act like a wife."

Perhaps something could be salvaged from the disaster, Harry thought. It was possible, if they lived through the weeks ahead, Nancy would live up to the potential he had seen in her and would become a responsible, mature wife.

Melissa Austin was as defiant as she was calm. Removing her hat and allowing her red hair to tumble down across her shoulders, she stared directly at Rick as she said, "We planned for a long time to stow away on board the ship. There was just no way we were going to be left behind in Oregon. Now Paul Thoman has sailed away, so you'll have to take us with you. We know you have extra horses, so you can't abandon us here." Softening deliberately, she tried to flatter Rick with her most dazzling smile.

The Ranger showed no reaction of any kind. He stood unmoving, his eyes looking as though they were made of marble, his face drained of all expression.

Danny Taylor was elated, and so was Chet Harris, but both were afraid to let the coldly angry Rick see how they felt.

"Rick," Harry Canning said somberly, one arm encircling Nancy's narrow waist, "I apologize to you on behalf of my wife. God knows what problems the presence of these girls may cause us—"

"They'll be damn few, I promise you," Rick said. "Nancy, can you ride?"

Nancy Canning nodded.

"What about you, Melissa?"

"Of course," she replied, tossing her head.

His expression remained unchanged. "Can you handle firearms?"

Nancy was tempted to lie, thought better of it, and murmured, "Not really."

"I'm as good a shot as most men," Melissa said, her manner changing and her tone of quiet confidence indicating that she was telling the truth.

"I hope you won't have cause to demonstrate your talents with a rifle." Rick was still grim. "I also hope you can keep up the pace I'm going to set. I'm under orders to bring Harry Canning safely to Texas, and when Sam Houston tells me to do something, I do it. That means I'll sacrifice all the rest of you, if I must, including you, Nancy Canning."

Rick frowned. "Harry, you're responsible for both ladies on this journey. Boys, I'm going to make plain talk, and if the ladies are embarrassed by it, that's too damn bad. All of you know Miss Austin is single, and you don't need me to tell you there are many who are worse looking."

His feeble compliment was the first he had ever paid Melissa, and she brightened.

"I'll tolerate no shenanigans on the trail. After we reach Texas, I don't care what she does. Or who she does it with."

Melissa stiffened indignantly.

"You'll mind your manners while you're under my

command," Rick continued, the ring in his soft-spoken statement indicating that he meant precisely what he said. "I'll put a knife into any man who tries to make love to her. As for you, Melissa, I'll expect you to control that natural tendency of yours to flirt with every man you see. We face dangers on this journey more terrible than any of you know, and I'll not have our existence complicated."

Outraged by Rick's blunt statement, Melissa obviously intended to retort in kind, but Harry tapped her on the shoulder and shook his head.

Nancy silently begged her friend not to cause more trouble. They had already won the most significant of victories: they were being permitted to accompany the expedition. Rick had no choice, to be sure, which was just as they had planned. But any open show of opposition to him now would make him an enemy.

Melissa grasped the meaning of her friend's unspoken entreaty and shrugged. She would desist, but only because Nancy and Harry had her best interests at heart. How dare Rick hint that she might be willing to sleep with Danny or Chet, like some common trollop. Eventually she would force Rick Miller to apologize to her.

In the meantime there were practical matters to consider. "Please," she asked in a deceptively small, meek voice, "may we have some food? We've eaten nothing since we stole the remains of last night's supper from the ship's galley."

In spite of Harry's upset state, he had to laugh. Now he knew the ship's cook had been telling the truth when he had complained that food on board had been disappearing.

"Help yourselves," Rick growled.

The two young women needed no second invitation. Carrying field equipment identical to that of the men, they piled beans and sausage onto their plates and ate ravenously.

Nancy looked sideways at her husband. "Am I forgiven?" she murmured.

Harry smiled helplessly. "You don't give me much of an alternative. You're here in California, on Mexican soil. You'll be coming to Texas with me. So I don't know whether to kiss you or wring your neck."

"Darling," she said, moving closer to him as she continued to eat, "it will be far more pleasing to both of us if you kiss me."

"I know." Harry sighed, needing no one to tell him that his wife had triumphed.

Danny became bold enough to sit beside Melissa, and Chet promptly moved to her other side. They interrupted each other repeatedly as they told her how delighted they were to see her.

Still scowling, Rick Miller stayed away from his charges. He was willing to admit that these willful, headstrong young women had forced him to accept them in his band. All the same, he could make no allowances because they were females. There were hazards to be overcome on the long ride to Texas, and they would adapt to his ways and obey his sometimes necessarily harsh commands or perish. It gave the veteran Ranger no pleasure to realize that what these girls regarded as an adventure would be no lark.

Anthony Roberts was well pleased with himself as he sat opposite Sir Michael Edison in the tiny room at British Legation headquarters that the Minister used as his private study. By no stretch of anyone's imagination were there any truly comfortable, expensively furnished homes or offices in the frontier town of Austin. But the urbane British envoy seemed unmindful of his surroundings as he jotted notes on a sheet of paper, occasionally bending over the table of raw pine that served as his desk. "You've really accumulated a mass of information that London will find fascinating, Roberts," he murmured.

Anthony was not above boasting. "I haven't been cultivating these crude Texas officials because I enjoy their company, Sir Michael," he said, laughing. "And I've saved the best items for the last. I can tell you the precise size of the so-called regiment of Rangers, if you don't already have it."

Sir Michael leaned forward in his hard chair. "Ah, that would be helpful. The bloody Texans take such pride in their Rangers that we've guessed there must be at least one thousand of them."

Anthony's laugh was scornful. "In all, they have fewer than one hundred and sixty men, including headquarters personnel. The Rangers have three companies, each with a total complement of fifty officers and men."

"Surely you're joking!" the Minister declared. "Why, the Royal Marines stationed on board just one of our ships-of-the-line would outnumber their entire force."

"During a recent evening at my house, the chairman of the military affairs committee of their House of Representatives had a few drops too many of that dreadful corn whiskey they drink. He was the first to give me that figure. It was corroborated only last night by their Assistant Secretary of War, who is also fond of whiskey."

"You are truly doing well, Roberts."

Anthony raised a hand. "Now for the real gem. No Texas official with whom I've spoken believes that Texas will be annexed by the United States until the Americans elect their new President in the autumn. If Polk should be elected, there's little doubt that the annexation will take place. If Clay wins, however, they may have to wait an additional four years, and in that time anything can happen."

"I've heard similar opinions expressed."

"The man who told it to me was quoting none other than President Sam Houston."

"I shall pass that news along to London without delay," Sir Michael said as he jotted another note on the paper. "Our legation in Washington City is doing everything it can to support Clay, including providing funds for his campaign. But these Americans are a strange breed. Would you believe, Roberts, that we must give money in a roundabout way because Clay and those who are managing his campaign are so honest they would refuse the gifts if they knew?"

Both men laughed heartily.

"You've more than earned your retainer again this month," the envoy said.

"Perhaps you might agree to do a small favor for me in return," Anthony declared.

"Anything within reason," the cautious diplomat replied.

"I'd very much like to know any data that may be in your files on Senator Woodrow Blount, who represents a district in the northeastern part of the state."

"That's simple," the envoy said. He stood and walked out of the room, returning a short time later with a single sheet of paper. "May I ask why you want this information, Roberts?"

Anthony would never reveal that he believed the Texas Senator had been a member of the lynch mob that had murdered his father. "I'm—ah—curious about him," he said. "He walks past my house at sunset every day of the week. I'm not acquainted with him, as it happens."

The request seemed harmless enough, and Sir Michael studied the sheet of paper. "The Senator owns a large ranch about six or seven hundred miles from Austin—a distance Texans regard as trivial. He has a wife, two sons, and a daughter—"

"Does your information include his place of origin, Sir Michael?" the impatient Anthony interrupted.

"Let me see. Yes. He came to Texas from Hartford, Connecticut, migrating here fourteen years ago. He was one of the early Texas settlers."

"Thank you. That's all I want to know." Anthony felt a sense of deep satisfaction as he shook hands with Sir Michael and took his leave. Now he knew for certain that Woodrow Blount had been one of his father's killers.

Returning to his own house by a roundabout route, Anthony first rode out of town to the woods, where he placed an unsigned message in the hollow tree used as a letterbox by the couriers from Mexico City. His month's payment from President Santa Anna awaited him in the tree, and he reflected that he knew of no easier way to augment his income. The information he sent along to Mexico was identical to the reports he made to the British.

Now he could devote his thoughts exclusively to Woodrow Blount. He pondered on his ride home, saying nothing about the matter to Elisabeta Manuel, in whom he no longer confided. His relationship with her was still pleasant enough, at least on the surface, but he knew she was afraid of him, and that suited his purposes. They had not been intimate for a long time, and she now served him exclusively as his housekeeper and cook, which would make it easier for him to make stringent demands on her in the future. It was far easier to handle a housekeeper than a mistress, and if his hunch was right, Elisabeta would have important work to do for him very soon.

Late that afternoon Anthony kept watch from a window in the parlor, and he was not disappointed. The silver-haired, somewhat overweight Senator Blount made his appearance at sundown, his walk brisk for a man in his sixties. He bowed to acquaintances and seemed completely at peace within himself.

It was obvious, the grim Anthony thought as he left the house and followed the Senator at a discreet distance, that the lynching of an innocent man in Hartford a generation earlier did not weigh on his soul.

Blount did not break his stride as he entered a building about a half-mile from Anthony's rented house. Quickly reducing his own pace, Anthony looked carefully at the house and was elated when he saw an oil lamp with a bright red shade covering it burning in the parlor window. The place was a bordello, and the Senator, separated by hundreds of miles from his wife when the Senate was in session, was indulging his appetite. This knowledge of his habits was priceless.

Wanting to be certain, however, Anthony carefully

followed him the next evening, and again the Senator
went to the bordello. He didn't yet know it, but his lust
was responsible for his death warrant.

Keeping his own counsel until the following afternoon,
Anthony waited until Elisabeta returned home from a
marketing expedition and then followed her into the
kitchen. "You can put away the food later," he said
genially. "I want to have a little chat with you."

His amiability made her uneasy, but she nevertheless
followed him into the parlor. She would have followed
the usual practice of pouring him a drink of the sack that
he imported from Spain by way of Cuba, but he waved
her to a chair.

"In about an hour," he said, smiling, "I want you to
change into one of your more attractive dresses. The
green velvet with the very low neckline will be best, I
think. And don't spare the cosmetics. I want you to look
as dazzling as possible."

"Are you entertaining someone of importance this
evening?" Elisabeta asked.

Anthony laughed. "No, my dear. You are."

She was puzzled.

"A short time before sundown, an elderly man with
gray hair who carries a walking stick with an ivory
handle will stroll past the house. Smile at him. Use your
wiles in any way you please. I want you to entice him
into the house."

Elisabeta was indignant. "Surely you aren't asking me
to—"

"I ask nothing," he interrupted savagely. "I'm giving
instructions, which you will follow." He saw the fear
appear in her eyes and glared harder at her. "All you will
do will be to lure Senator Blount into this room. Then
you'll make an excuse to leave the room, allowing him to
think you'll return in a few minutes. Instead, you'll
mount your horse, which will be saddled and ready, and
you'll ride to the Lone Star Inn. Go to the taproom,
where you'll be seen, and have a cup of tea or coffee.
Have a glass of whiskey, for all I care. Just be sure you

absent yourself for an hour before you come back here."

"But I don't understand," she said.

"There's no need for you to understand," Anthony replied brusquely. "Just do as you're told!"

"How can I entice this man into the house?"

"Are you a simpleton? Sit out on the porch and wait until he passes!"

"Sit on the porch—in my green velvet—and flirt with a man I don't know? Why, he'll think I—I'm a strumpet!"

"I hope he does," Anthony said, smiling again. "In fact, that's the point of the whole exercise. Wear a cloak, if you wish, when you ride to the Lone Star Inn," he added carelessly. "I dare say you'll be more comfortable if you're exposing less of your incomparable breasts there."

All Elisabeta knew was that he was up to no good. "Why do you wish me to act as a lure for you, Anthony?"

He leaped to his feet, his chair toppling over backward. Catching hold of her arm, he twisted it savagely behind her back. The shock of his assault startled her, and the pain he caused her was so intense that she could not stifle a scream.

"If you don't want your arm broken," he said in a low, angry voice, "you'll do precisely what I direct you to do, and you'll stop annoying me with your stupid questions. Are we in agreement?"

"Yes, Anthony! Please, you're hurting me badly."

He released her suddenly, then shoved her into a chair. "Very well. Remember what I've told you to do. If any detail isn't clear, I'll go over the instructions again."

She shook her head, unable to speak for fear she would burst into tears. She wanted to salvage what was left of her pride by not weeping in his presence.

"I'm depending on you," he said harshly, then stalked out of the room.

Elisabeta waited until she reached her own bedchamber before she wept. She felt no better after she regained her poise; her mind continued to whirl. She had no idea why Anthony wanted her to lure the Texas Senator into the house, although it was plain enough that he was expecting her to utilize her feminine appeal for the purpose.

There had been a time when, recognizing her unusual beauty, she had rejoiced because the Almighty had been kind to her. But her beauty had become a curse. She changed into her green velvet gown without pleasure, then applied her cosmetics with a heavy hand, as Anthony had directed, hating him for being a bully and hating herself for giving in to him so meekly.

But common sense told her that she had to obey his wishes. If she walked out of the house now, never returning to it, she would be penniless in this alien world. She had no vocation, and she had seen enough of Austin, where the men vastly outnumbered the women, to know what would become of her. There was little doubt in her mind that necessity would force her to become the harlot that Anthony wanted her to simulate this very evening.

A sense of hopelessness enveloping her, Elisabeta returned to the parlor a short time before sunset.

Anthony was waiting and led her to a window, where he carefully inspected her. "You look the part," he said. "Now act accordingly. And don't forget to leave the house quickly after you've brought the Senator in here. Make sure you're seen at the Lone Star Inn. That's important. If you see anyone we know, just tell him the truth, that you're idling away an hour because I'm busy elsewhere. You understand?"

Her trepidation was so great that she could only nod.

Anthony's expression did not change as he left the room without waiting for her reply.

A deep sense of shame burned within Elisabeta as she forced herself to take a straightbacked chair out to the small porch and seat herself there. It was useless to guess what Anthony had in mind, and she couldn't imagine why he had chosen to utilize this strange method of luring Senator Blount into the house when it would have been easy enough to meet him through some of his other acquaintances in the Texas government and then invite him to spend an evening with some of the others in the parlor. But she warned herself that it was no longer her place to wonder. She had been reduced to a role little better than that of a servant, and now she was being pushed even lower.

Fortunately for Elisabeta, there were few people about at this hour, and those who did pass by took little note of her. Still, she felt dreadfully conspicuous in her daring gown and cosmetics. Her spirits sank even lower.

After sitting for what seemed to be a long time, she saw a man approaching who had to be Senator Blount. He was silver-haired, carried a walking stick, and was strolling slowly, apparently savoring the evening breeze that usually sprang up in Austin at sundown.

Elisabeta felt as though her face were cracking as she compelled herself to smile at the man. When their eyes met, Elisabeta wanted to look away, but could not permit herself the luxury. He studied her intently, and she continued to return his gaze, the smile frozen on her face. Never had she felt so cheap.

Senator Blount sauntered toward her and raised his hat. "Good evening," he said somewhat tentatively.

Elisabeta hated herself for being so nervous. "It is a good evening isn't it?" she managed to reply.

"It could be. Indeed."

She realized that his gaze had shifted and that he was now ogling her half-exposed breasts. Wanting to cringe, to run to her room and lock herself in it, she nevertheless made no move.

"You are Mexican?" he inquired politely.

Elisabeta had to hide her annoyance. Many Texans thought she was Mexican because of her accent, and she had learned there was no love lost between the people of the two nations. "No," she said pointedly, "I am Spanish. I have never visited Mexico."

"So much the better," Blount said jovially. "I take it you're enjoying a breath of air."

"Yes," she said, "but the night is growing chilly. So I

think I'll go inside. Would you care to accompany me?"
It was difficult, almost impossible, for her to make the
little speech she had been rehearsing.

The invitation was precisely what he had wanted. "I'd
be delighted," he said promptly.

Leaving the chair near the porch railing, she rose and
led him inside, taking him directly to the parlor.

Wasting no time, the Senator immediately reached for
her. Elisabeta's last hope faded. There was no shred of
doubt that he thought her a strumpet. All the same, she
instinctively took a step backward in order to avoid the
man's embrace.

For a moment Blount frowned, and then his brow
cleared. "Of course," he said. "You want us to reach a
financial agreement first."

She knew that color was burning in her already
rouged cheeks, and she could only nod.

"What is your fee?" he demanded bluntly.

Elisabeta didn't quite know what to reply. "That—that
depends," she stammered lamely.

"Well," he said, "as I dare say you know, the girls in
the house down the road charge one American dollar.
But you're obviously someone special, so I'll double the
amount."

"That will be fine," she said, and could tolerate no
more. "Will you excuse me for a few moments?"

The Senator nodded, apparently thinking she intended
to change into more informal attire.

Somehow, Elisabeta managed to walk to the door,
then closed it behind her. Thoroughly disgusted, she
snatched her cloak from a peg in the entrance hall,
then almost made the mistake of bolting out the front
door.

Anthony loomed up behind her and silently pointed
toward the kitchen.

Of course! Senator Blount could see her through the
parlor windows if she fled down the road in front of the
house. She left hurriedly by way of the kitchen and was
not surprised to see her mare, already saddled, tied to a
hitching post. She undid the reins, mounted, and rode

sidesaddle to the Lone Star Inn, which she reached in a very short time.

There she sat at an inconspicuous corner table, as far from the bar as possible, and looked down miserably at the sawdust on the floor. When the barmaid approached, Elisabeta asked for a cup of tea, taking great care to keep her cloak wrapped around her to conceal the low neckline of her gown.

The taproom was fairly crowded, and several men who had been entertained at the Roberts house recognized her and came to the table to greet her.

She dutifully repeated what Anthony had instructed her to say, telling the various Texans that she was indulging herself by coming here for a cup of tea while her "husband" was busy elsewhere. Two or three of the men continued to linger at the table, but she did not make the error of asking anyone to join her.

Not until her tea was served did it dawn on her that perhaps Anthony had brought her to Texas because he wanted to use her as bait for whatever schemes he was planning. Surely, as a man of the world, he knew there were relatively few women here and that an uncommonly attractive one would be certain to become a center of attention. Somehow, she had to find a way to leave Anthony and return to Madrid, even though she knew of no one there who would offer her more than a very temporary refuge. But she didn't know how to begin. The obstacles in the path of such a journey seemed insurmountable.

The tea cooled, but Elisabeta could not drink it. After she had huddled at her pine-topped table for what she hoped was an hour, she paid for her tea, then rode slowly back to the house that she was beginning to regard as a prison rather than a home.

The front door was bolted now, so she went to the rear, first taking her horse to the stable and removing the saddle. Then she entered the place fearfully by way of the kitchen. Anthony was nowhere to be seen, and neither was Senator Blount. The parlor was undisturbed and looked precisely as she had left it.

Common sense told Elisabeta to eat something, but she had no appetite and went directly to her own room, where she took the precaution of bolting the door. Perhaps she was making too much of this evening's incident, she reflected. What Anthony had forced her to do was harmless enough, even though she felt cheapened by the incident. It was possible that she was reading too much into the episode, and she tried to put it out of her mind.

After brooding for a long time, she undressed and went to bed, but sleep would not come. It was late when she heard the front door open and close. A few moments later Anthony mounted the stairs, whistling tunelessly.

Elisabeta stiffened, but he made no attempt to come to her, and she relaxed somewhat when he went off to his own room. Her reaction told her something that she hadn't realized previously: the mere prospect of allowing him to make love to her again made her flesh crawl.

The following morning she prepared breakfast, as usual, and Anthony was in a pleasant mood when he joined her. He was not particularly communicative, however, and made no mention of the previous evening's episode. Under the circumstances, she decided not to bring up the subject, either.

Soon thereafter it occurred to her that this was market day, when freshly butchered beef, lamb, and pork were available each week. So she saddled her mare, taking two large wicker baskets with her, and went off to the market.

"Good morning, Mr. Staudt," she said, greeting the butcher whose stall she visited regularly.

"Mornin', ma'am. You want your usual?"

"Yes, please."

The man began to chop off a chunk of beef for her from a quarter, then paused in his labors. "Terrible about poor old Senator Blount, ain't it?"

"I—I haven't heard anything about it," Elisabeta said faintly.

"He was murdered last night. Choked to death, from

what folks are sayin'. His body was found at dawn this mornin' in a gully off the new South Road, a few miles out of town. The killer strangled him with a cord that was still around his neck."

Elisabeta was so dizzy and ill she was afraid she would faint.

"Funny thing," the butcher continued in a hushed tone. "They say the cord was fixed so it looked like a hangin' noose. Peculiar, ain't it? The Rangers will be investigatin', of course, but with Cap'n Rick Miller off somewheres on a special job for old Sam Houston, I don't know if the boys runnin' his office for him can handle this. The Senator, poor old feller, didn't have an enemy in the world. Except, maybe, he really did." He resumed chopping off the chunk of beef.

With a desperate effort Elisabeta managed to regain partial control of herself. Horrified and sickened, she knew that she had unwittingly participated in a premeditated murder. She hadn't dreamed that Anthony was capable of killing a fellow human being in cold blood, but there was no doubt whatever in her mind that he had perpetrated the grisly deed.

After she concluded her business at the market, she forced herself to ride back to the Roberts house, her mind spinning wildly. She wanted to flee, but there was no place to go.

For her own protection, she realized, she could not mention the Senator or his death to Anthony. And if he brought up the subject, she didn't know what she could say. All she knew for certain was that the man whose false promises had enabled him to bed her and bring her on the long journey to the distant New World was evil.

To her infinite relief she found that Anthony had gone out by the time she returned home. She put her purchases in the larder, then forced herself to eat after she realized she had touched no food since noon of the previous day. The bread, butter, and leftover cold meat she managed to choke down were tasteless, and she brewed a pot of tea, hoping the beverage would calm her.

As Elisabeta continued to sit in the kitchen, brooding and sipping her tea, a knock sounded at the front door.

A man carrying a brace of pistols in a double holster hanging from a belt around his waist removed his broad-brimmed hat. "Sergeant Ted Haight, Rangers special division, ma'am," he said. "May I come in for a few minutes?"

Elisabeta froze but managed to nod.

"I hope I'm not interrupting something important," he said politely as he walked into the house, his spurs jingling musically.

Elisabeta made a tremendous effort to speak calmly. "Not at all. I was just drinking some tea in the kitchen. May I offer you a cup?"

"That's right nice of you."

She led him into the kitchen, hoping he didn't see her hand shaking as she poured him some tea.

"I'm visiting every house on this road," Sergeant Haight told her. "Old Senator Blount was killed last night—"

"So I was told at the meat market this morning," she said.

He nodded gravely. "We've established that he walked down this road every evening at nightfall, and I wonder if you happened to see him last night."

"I'm not—I wasn't acquainted with Senator Blount." She hated herself for lying.

"Silver hair," Haight said briskly. "Medium build, with a fat stomach. Always carried an ivory-handled walking stick."

Desperately afraid that the Ranger had learned she had conducted the Senator into the house, Elisabeta's instinct for survival dominated her desire to tell the whole truth. "He sounds vaguely familiar," she said, hoping against hope that he wouldn't challenge her. "I may have seen him once or twice, although I can't say for certain." She pretended to ponder, then shook her head. "And I can't tell you whether he came past the house last night, either. There was no special reason I should have noticed him."

"That's what your neighbors say, too." Sergeant Haight took some folded papers from a shirt pocket and jotted down a few words.

"As a matter fact," Elisabeta said, suddenly understanding why Anthony had insisted she establish an alibi for the previous evening, "I went to the Lone Star Inn around sundown last night. Mr. Roberts was away from the house on business, so I went there for a cup of tea."

"Not as good a brew as the tea you make, ma'am," he replied politely. "Am I right in assuming that Mr. Roberts won't be able to help us, either?"

"I cannot speak for him," Elisabeta said. "I don't recall the exact time he went out, but he was away for some hours, so it isn't likely that he would have seen the Senator."

Furious at herself for providing a story for Anthony, too, she was on the verge of blurting out everything she knew.

The Sergeant chose that moment to ask, "I take it that you're Mexican, Mrs. Roberts?"

"I am Spanish," she said primly, irritated by the question. "I was born and grew up in Madrid, and until I came to Texas, I had never spent any time in the New World. I am not Mexican, and I have never spent a single minute in that country."

Haight was afraid he might have offended her but decided not to make matters worse by apologizing to her. Instead, he finished his tea and politely took his leave.

Elisabeta continued to sit at the kitchen table, the experience having rendered her weak and numb. She was still there when Anthony returned home a short time later. "I just saw a Ranger down the street," he said. "Has he called here?"

She nodded and, trying to speak normally, repeated the conversation as best she could.

Anthony listened carefully, then grinned at her. "You're improving rapidly," he said. "You did well." Unexpectedly digging into his purse, he flipped a gold coin in his hand, then handed it to her. "Keep up the good work," he said and left the room.

Elisabeta was so furious she wanted to throw the coin out the window—or through it. By accepting it she had become Anthony's accomplice in a vile business. She raised her hand, then let it fall to her side again.

The angry gesture wouldn't bring Senator Blount back to life. But it did provide the beginning of a nest egg. If she could accumulate more money in one way or another, she would be able to leave this loathsome man.

VI

A report reaching Austin from the western Texas
frontier indicated that a Mexican cavalry patrol of unde-
termined size had crossed the border and was remaining
in an area claimed by the Republic of Texas. Some
officials wanted to dispatch a punitive expedition without delay, but President Houston decided to wait for
more precise information. Another war with Mexico, if
fought prematurely, inevitably would delay the annexation of the nation by the United States. Besides, Houston well knew, as did his principal subordinates, that the
western borders separating Texas from the province of
New Mexico had never been sharply and clearly defined.

Three similar reports were received within the span of
a single week, and Houston knew he could not procrastinate any longer. So he decided to send half a battalion
of volunteer cavalry to the area, the unit consisting of
two troops, each of seventy-five men. He gave the command to an old comrade, Major Roger Ebert, a cool-
headed, dependable veteran who would not grow panicky in a crisis.

"It doesn't suit our national purpose to start a new war
with Santa Anna," Houston told him, "so don't start
shooting if combat can be avoided. In the first place,
make sure the Mexicans are actually encroaching on our

133

territory and find out, if you can, whether they're doing it deliberately. Maybe you can persuade them to withdraw, but don't ask me how you can manage that feat. I simply don't know. If they're tough or otherwise unpleasant, however, you'll have no choice. Blast them off the face of the earth and leave just enough survivors to take the word back to Mexico City. Under no circumstances can we permit Mexican soldiers to roam at will on our land."

The half-battalion left the same day, and Major Ebert set a grueling pace as he led his men westward. An encounter with a herd of buffalo on the third day out of Austin provided the troops with all the meat they required, and they made such good time that they reached the border area a week later. As yet no farms had been claimed in the region, and no villages had been established, so the entire border country was still an uninhabited wilderness. Occasionally the Apache set hunting expeditions into the area, but, otherwise, few people ventured into the sector, where there were low-lying mountains, rolling hills, and vast stretches of plains and valleys.

Major Ebert established his base camp beside a creek east of a chain of mountains known as Mescalero Ridge, in what later would become part of the state of New Mexico. The following morning he instituted a methodical search for the Mexican patrol. He and his men had no luck when they rode southward, and after spending a fruitless week, Ebert led his half-battalion to the north.

It was his private opinion that the entire region wasn't worth the loss of a single Texan's life. The soil was sandy, obviously unproductive, and a lack of rainfall had created a near-desert. Wooded areas were few, and grass grew only near creeks and rivers. It was not easy finding fodder for the horses, and the Major could not understand why any patrol would venture into the inhospitable sector.

His probes carried him farther and farther northward, and on the third day of the exploratory journey, one of his officers found evidence indicating that a body of soldiers, at least one hundred strong, had made their camp the previous night near the bank of a small, unnamed river. Thanks to a prolonged dry spell, the waters of the stream had been reduced to a trickle.

The cavalrymen filled their canteens, took water for their horses, and pressed on with renewed vigor. Not until late the following morning did they sight a body of men in the distance. Ebert studied the intruders through a telescope, their gray uniforms revealing that they were indeed Mexican cavalry. He counted approximately one hundred and thirty riders, so he knew the opposing forces were about evenly matched.

"Get ready for a fight," he told his troop commanders, "but I don't want one man to fire until I've given the word myself. President Houston wants us to avoid a battle, if we can."

The column started to ride in the direction of the Mexicans, who had seen the Texas unit and were advancing toward it, too. Major Ebert rode at the head of the column with the standard-bearer, and when no more than a half mile separated the two forces, he gave the order to spread out. The Mexicans engaged in a similar maneuver.

When no more than one hundred and fifty yards separated the two forces, Ebert called a halt. The Mexicans immediately stopped short, too.

"Hold your lines firm, but do nothing until I give the signal," the Major told his troop commanders. "If I draw my sword, open fire. Or if they shoot me down, you'll know how to take care of them."

Accompanied only by his standard-bearer, he moved forward. A Mexican officer did the same, escorted by his own flag-carrier and a sergeant. The two groups halted only a few feet apart, and polite salutes were exchanged. Then Major Ebert introduced himself.

"Lieutenant Rodolfo Cordova," the handsome Mexican officer, a man in his early thirties, replied in excellent English. "Commanding the Twenty-seventh Mexican Cavalry."

"I hope you realize, Lieutenant, that you're encroach-

ing on territory under the jurisdiction of the Republic of
Texas."

The officer was surprised. "I am?" he asked, then
turned to the part-Indian noncommissioned officer, who
muttered something to him. "Sergeant Taloco swears this
is the sacred soil of the Republic of Mexico."

"He's mistaken," the Major declared as he took a map
from an inner tunic pocket. "The border," he said, hand-
ing the map to the Mexican officer, "is marked in red."

Lieutenant Cordova unfolded the map and studied it
in silence, with Sergeant Taloco alternately peering over
his shoulder and glaring at the commander of the Texas
half-battalion.

The Major waited patiently. "Your own district commander should have a map that shows roughly the same
boundary," he said.

After a long, tense pause, Lieutenant Cordova nodded.
"You're correct, Major."

Sergeant Taloco glowered at his superior, obviously
regarding him as a weakling, and, perhaps, a coward.

The relieved Ebert did not fail to note that the Mexican troops were mounted on superb horses, as always,
and that they carried the latest model of British musket.
Both sides would suffer if a battle developed.

"It appears to me," Cordova said, "that the boundary
lies twenty-five or thirty miles to the west."

"That's more or less the way I read it," the Texan
replied. "We're in agreement."

"We must be in agreement," Cordova declared. "I
have two small sons, and I teach them that the Texans
are our neighbors."

"My son is already full grown," Ebert said, "but I'd
sure hate to lose him in a new war."

"I fear that our nations will fight again in the years
ahead," Lieutenant Cordova said. "There is so much
bitterness on both sides that only more bloodletting will
clear the air. Unfortunately, that is the way of men
everywhere. But eventually there will be peace between
us."

"There must be peace between neighbors," Ebert said, extending his hand.

The Mexican grasped it. "I shall not forget this occasion, Major," he said. "It may be that we will meet again. In battle. But I assure you that, for the present, I shall immediately withdraw my troops to our own side of the boundary."

They exchanged salutes again, then returned to their respective lines.

Sergeant Taloco waited until they were out of earshot before he said, "That was clever of you, Lieutenant. You pretend to withdraw but will prepare an ambush for the Texans after they make camp for the night."

"You are mistaken, Taloco," Lieutenant Cordova said coldly. "We have strayed into Texas and will return to the Mexican side of the border."

"All of this land belongs to Mexico," the junior said hotly. "The Texans stole it from us when they captured President Santa Anna and forced him to sue for peace."

"I have received no orders instructing me to go beyond our own border," Cordova said, his voice firm.

Major Ebert's principal subordinates waited anxiously for him to return to the positions they had taken, and he grinned as he told them, "We'll have no fireworks today. The Mexican commander is a civilized man, and I believe he was making an honest mistake. He's agreed to pull back behind the boundary."

"When, sir?" one of the captains wanted to know.

"At once." Ebert gestured toward the Mexican column, which was moving into formation, then starting off toward the west.

"I can't help wondering if this is a trick," the other troop commander mused. "It would be just like them to make a loop and double back toward us."

"In my opinion," the Major said, "Lieutenant Cordova is a gentleman and will keep his word to me. He would have a right to be insulted if we followed him closely, and a single shot from either side would cause a battle. On the other hand, as much as I believe we must learn to live at peace with our neighbors, I don't intend to be carried away by this new spirit of unexpected friendship. We'll give the Mexicans a start of an hour or two, and then I'll send a small patrol of scouts to see if their tracks—which are easy enough to follow in the sand—take them back across the actual border. All I can say right now is that President Houston will be very pleased when he finds out there are Mexicans no more eager to fight us than we are to go to war again with them."

Under the able leadership of Lee Blake, the wagon train traveling on rafts reached the point at which the Red River flows into the Mississippi. There the members of the train disembarked and prepared to travel overland. On the first night they formed their wagons in a large circle in an empty field on the west bank of the great river. Then they led their horses, oxen, and mules into the circle, and Lee summoned the entire company to a meeting.

"From now on," he told the future Texas settlers, "the wagons will be placed in a circle every night, and your animals will be inside it. We'll always camp near a lake or river, in a place where your animals can graze. There are so many of you that you're being divided into two groups, those on the far side of the circle and those on the near side. Five men of my cavalry will go ahead of the column each day as scouts, and the rest will act as monitors."

Most of the company nodded in agreement.

"Right now," Lee said, "you'll need to elect your own president. He'll arrange chore assignments and will work with me to keep order."

To the astonishment of Innes MacGregor, he was the first nominated and was elected by an overwhelming majority. He was pushed forward, and after exchanging a few words with Lee, he mounted a wagon stoop. "I thank ye for your confidence," he said. "I'll try to live up to it. In a minute or two I'll ask for volunteers for work details. But first, I have one more announcement. Nobody is allowed to wander outside the circle of wagons after dark. General Blake's cavalry troopers will be standing sentry duty, and I tell ye plain, I'll fine anybody who breaks this rule!"

There were more than enough volunteers for each of the daily chores necessary for the group's survival and comfort, and they went to work with a vengeance. Soon buckets of water were lined up, huge piles of wood had been gathered, and when the fires had been lighted, the women who would be cooking the meals came forward.

Cathy Blake surveyed the familiar scene and smiled at Ginny Mullins. "I cooked my way across North America, last time," she said. "I can't tell you how relieved I am that my husband says I don't need to do it again."

Lee gathered a few key men while the meal was being prepared. "Teng Chu and Sergeant Mullins," he said, "will ride with me at the head of the train. We'll use existing roads wherever possible and will try not to go across open countryside until we leave civilization behind. For the present, we can permit no hunting and will have to depend on the food in the supply wagons that the financial supporters of this expedition provided for us. Rivers are public property, so fishing will be allowed at the end of each day, but not during the nooning hour.

"I've covered just about everything except one minor problem. Mrs. Blake will drive our wagon, and Mrs. Mullins will drive the Sergeant Major's wagon. But we need to find a driver for the wagon that the U.S. Government has made available to Teng Chu. He prefers to ride up front with me, and I can't blame him. He'll get more of a feel for what we're doing that way."

"My oldest daughter, Heather, would love to drive that wagon," Innes said.

Lee raised an eyebrow. "How old is she?"

"Only fifteen, General, but she's been around horses all her life. I give ye my word, she can handle any team!"

"Your word is good enough for me," Lee replied.

Heather MacGregor was ecstatic when her father told her about her new assignment.

Her younger sisters clamored for the right to ride with her, and Matilda had to intervene. "One of you may ride with Heather," she said, "but only one."

Little Wallace had the last word. "Then I'll go with her," she said solemnly, "because Teng Chu is my friend."

Rick Miller had a sixth sense for avoiding danger, and he encountered no Mexican patrols as he led his party eastward from the California coast. They rode through fertile valleys and thick forests, traveled north of the San Bernardino Mountains, and moved on rapidly through country where the vegetation became increasingly sparse.

He was the first to admit that his techniques were unorthodox. The day's march always began at daybreak, after a small breakfast of leftover food, eaten cold. The party halted an hour or two before sundown, in ample time to light a cooking fire, then extinguish it when night came. After supper the march was resumed, and a halt was not called until midnight or later, when the exhausted members of the group were permitted to sleep for a few hours.

Most of the men, being young and healthy, bore up well and experienced few difficulties. Harry Canning, who was older, was nevertheless hearty and strong, and he, too, managed to hold his own. But the two young women became bone-weary, and each day's long journey was harder than that of the previous day.

Nancy Canning made no protest. "I know Rick wants to lead us safely to Texas as quickly as he can," she said privately to her husband. "And no matter how tired I am every night, I keep remembering that I brought this situation on myself."

"I don't want you to kill yourself," Harry told her. "Maybe I'd better have a few words with Rick and urge him to slow our pace a bit."

She shook her head. "I'll survive," she replied grimly.

"Besides, I want no accusing finger pointed at me if we run into trouble because we're traveling more slowly."

He considered the problem, then said reluctantly, "All right. I'll accept your position. But only on condition that you'll tell me if you really start to feel sick. I'll grant that you shouldn't have come with us, but you're here. And the well-being of my wife means more to me than setting up a shipyard in Texas."

Melissa Austin's attitude was far different from that of her friend. "I'm convinced," she murmured to Danny Taylor at supper one night, "that Captain Miller is deliberately trying to punish Nancy and me for daring to force ourselves on this company. Why, even our horses are showing the strain."

Danny was in no position to pass judgment, but he nodded sympathetically.

"I'm trying to stay calm," she said, "but I don't have red hair for nothing, and one of these days I'm going to explode."

"Let me know when it's going to happen," he said, "and I'll give you my support."

A couple of evenings later Melissa made substantially the same remarks to Chet Harris, and he, too, swore to give her all the assistance she needed.

As Melissa herself well knew, she was weathering the swift journey better than Nancy was managing it. Her pride was hurt, however, partly because she had concluded that Rick was avenging himself at her expense and in part because he had failed to react to her as an attractive young woman.

In her more honest moments of self-examination, she had to admit that she was spoiled, that she expected every man she met to admire her. She had to concede, too, that she wasn't particularly interested in Captain Rick Miller. He was too hard, too practical, too much of a realist in his approach to life. She was attracted to romantic men, and for that reason she far preferred the company of Danny and Chet.

All the same, she was determined to force Rick to acknowledge her charms, even though she was wearing a man's clothing on the trail. Perhaps she was being childish, but she wouldn't be satisfied until he paid her a compliment or two, at the very least.

They came to the Colorado River, a roaring torrent at this season, when the melting snows of the Rocky Mountains were added to the volume of the water that was spilling over its banks and cutting deeper into the soil.

Rick called a halt for twenty-four hours, the first real rest period he had allowed, and permitted most of the men to go hunting in the forest on the west bank of the mighty stream. Then, accompanied by Harry, he walked to the edge of the plateau and looked down at the churning water below.

"I suppose we can build a couple of rafts to carry us across the river," Harry said. "But as a man who has spent most of his life at sea, I don't advise it. We'd be swept downstream, and we'd be almost sure to founder."

"There is no way we'll cross by raft," Rick said grimly. "That would be catastrophic, and we'd be lucky if half of our company survived."

"How will we manage, then?"

"I've been thinking about it a great deal in these past few days," Rick replied. "We'll talk about it after supper."

That meal proved to be even heartier than they had anticipated. Chet had brought down a huge brown bear that he estimated weighed at least three hundred and fifty pounds. It was so heavy that three of his companions had to help him carry the beast to the campsite. There, under Rick's direction, the carcass was skinned and butchered. Then they cooked over the fire what they needed for that night and banked the flames to smoke the rest, a task that would require the better part of the night.

After they had eaten, Rick said, "I want to talk about something that won't be easy for any of us, the crossing of the Colorado tomorrow. Who's the best rider among you?"

The young men exchanged glances. Bill Devlin, who

had arrived in Oregon less than a year earlier and had found it too tame for his liking, raised his voice. "None of us is in a class with Danny," he said.

"I'm not too bad," Danny declared modestly, "but I don't think I'm all that good, either."

"I disagree," Rick said. "I was hoping the rest of you would settle on Danny. I didn't want to do it by myself. Do you think Danny is the best horseman?"

"No doubt about it," Harry said firmly, and that settled the matter.

"I've purposely picked a spot for the crossing where the river is fairly narrow. The water runs pretty deep there, and the current is strong, so it wouldn't be too difficult to drown." Rick paused to let his words sink in.

"Don't tell me you want us to swim across that river!" Melissa exclaimed.

Rick ignored the interruption. "Danny and I will ride across the river on our horses," he said. "Harry, I'll ask you to pay out a line to us, little by little, as our mounts make the passage. You'll anchor it securely on this side. Then you'll ride your own horses across, one by one, holding onto the rope as you make your passage."

They absorbed the information in silence.

Melissa was the first to speak. "Why won't we cross in a group?" she demanded.

"A horse can get pretty panicky if he sees the horse in front of him floundering and having a rough time," he replied curtly. "All of you, hang on to that rope! But don't lose your seat, either. Your horses are strong enough to swim across the river if you give them their heads. Lose your seat, and you'll not only have to make your way across the river hand by hand, which is almost impossible, but you'll also take the risk of losing your mount. And let me remind you that, thanks to the presence of the women, we have only one spare horse left."

Melissa felt certain he was making a deliberate, cutting observation, but she remained silent.

The entire party retired immediately after supper,

aware that the following day's exercise would be critical. Melissa, as always, rolled up in her blanket only a short distance from Harry and Nancy, who had assumed the burden of acting as her chaperones.

Rick was awake before dawn. Removing the meat from the fire, he divided it into chunks small enough to be carried by each member of the group, and he left enough for breakfast.

Tensions mounted, and the party ate in silence.

"We'll be on our way," Rick announced, and the fire was extinguished.

He tied one end of the rope around his middle, then handed the line to Danny. "Stay a good forty or fifty feet behind me on the crossing," he said. "Harry will pay out the line little by little. You have the hardest job of any of us, so be alert."

Danny nodded somberly.

They walked their horses down the embankment and paused at the river bank. Harry looked around and found a cedar tree with a thick trunk that stood only a few feet from the water's edge. "This looks pretty strong to me," he said.

Rick studied the tree, then nodded. "Bill," he said to young Devlin, "shinny up that tree and tie the near end of the rope around it. Make sure the knot faces directly toward the far side of the river."

Devlin obeyed at once, asking no questions.

"I'll signal to you when we have the line made secure at the other side," Rick said, raising his voice above the roar of the water sounding from a canyon somewhere below them.

Harry nodded, then shook hands with the pair who would make the initial crossing. "Good luck," he said.

Rick had a final word for the entire party. "When your turn comes," he said, "stay calm and everything will go just fine. Don't lose your head, or your horse will lose his." He mounted his powerful stallion and plunged into the swift-moving Colorado. His stallion seemed to understand what was expected of him and began to swim across the stream, his legs thrashing, his head held high.

Harry payed out the rope inch by inch, trying not to allow it to become slack, and soon he realized why Rick needed Danny's help. The current was so strong that Harry himself needed two men to help hold the coiled rope so all of it wouldn't be payed out at once.

Danny carefully waited until he estimated that Rick had gone about fifty feet. Then he leaped into his saddle, took hold of the rope, and, glancing briefly at Melissa, started toward the river.

The water was icy, and his gelding halted abruptly, raising one front hoof and then the other. It was obvious the animal disliked the cold. Danny spurred forward, and the gelding inched slowly, then plunged into the swiftly flowing Colorado and began to swim. It was apparent to those who were left behind on the shore that the beast, if given its own way, would have followed the course of least resistance and moved downstream.

Harry was mindful of the boiling, churning canyon below them. So he called to Nancy and Melissa but deliberately spoke loudly enough for the young men to hear him, too. "Look at the way Danny keeps his horse's head angled up the river! That's the only way he can avoid moving down. When your turn comes, keep the pressure on your left-hand reins!"

By now Rick Miller was nearing the opposite bank, while Danny approached midstream. Their mounts were struggling, although firmly controlled by their riders. Rick had been right when he had said that the animals had the strength to make the crossing.

When Rick reached the east bank, he remained in the saddle until Danny joined him. Together they pulled on the rope until it grew fairly taut, and then Rick climbed a cedar, untied the loose end from his waist, and, looping it twice around the trunk, hauled it still tighter.

He did not stop until the line spanned the Colorado at a height of about three to four feet above the waterline. When the line had been secured at the proper height, he signaled to Harry and the others waiting on the opposite shore.

"That's perfect!" Harry declared, then turned to the others. "When you cross, hold to the line with one hand and keep a tight grip on your reins with the other. Who wants to go first?"

"I do," Nancy said, "provided you don't mind, dear. I—I'm anxious to cross before I lose my nerve."

He hesitated briefly before he nodded. "All right. Give me your rifle and your meat pack so you won't be encumbered unnecessarily." He refrained from kissing her because he didn't want her to think he was bidding her farewell. Then he forced a broad, encouraging smile.

Nancy's return smile was apprehensive. She mounted her gelding without assistance and did not look at Harry again as she started toward the river.

"Take hold of the line before you go into the water!" her husband called.

She did as he directed, then urged her horse into the water. The gelding was the smallest of the mounts but was spirited and swam even more rapidly than had the horses of the two men who had already crossed.

Harry tried in vain to conquer the anxiety that gnawed at him, and he caught his breath when, at midstream, Nancy lost her grip on the rope for a moment. Then she grasped it again, and he breathed a trifle more easily.

Rick and Danny stood on the far bank, calling encouragement to her. Everyone was relieved when the gelding reached the far side of the river, and Danny, catching hold of the reins, led it up to the rocky ground where the footing was secure.

"It's my turn now," Melissa said calmly.

Chet urged her to give him her rifle and meat pack.

"Thanks, anyway," she replied airily, "but I can manage just fine." She started forward, her wave flippant.

When she reached the water, however, she sobered quickly, then had difficulty as her gelding began to buck.

Chet immediately sprinted forward, intending to help her bring the animal under control, but Melissa waved him away. She was determined to accept no assistance so she could prove her worth to every man present. Her craving for attention was only one side of her nature; she was also fiercely independent, and that streak was in the ascendancy right now.

She mastered the gelding, forcing the animal into the river, and laughed aloud in triumph as she grasped the steadying rope beside her. The gelding fought her all the way across the river, but Melissa won the battle. Then, before Danny could reach her side, she rode up the bank, dismounted, and hugged him exuberantly.

Those who remained on the west bank cheered her.

"Harry," Chet said, "I think you should go next, and the others can follow you. I'm riding my own horse, and we know each other pretty well after four years. Neither of us is inclined to panic."

Harry Canning was eager to rejoin his wife, so he did not argue. He knew ships far better than he knew horses, but his understanding of currents was vast. He knew precisely the right moments to exert pressure on his gelding, just as he knew when to relax briefly and allow the animal to take charge. Consequently, he negotiated the crossing more rapidly than had any of those who had preceded him.

One by one the others crossed. The young men were confident but careful, and none encountered serious problems. Rick had chosen well when he had accepted these pioneers as members of the party.

By the time Chet joined his comrades, they had gathered wood and built a roaring fire. Everyone huddled as close to it as possible so clothes could dry, and Rick offered sound advice. "Let your boots dry on your feet," he said. "You won't be as comfortable, but if you take them off, they'll shrink and crack."

Not even Melissa disputed the suggestion.

A short time later Danny stared off toward the river and said softly, "Oh-oh."

The others looked at him.

"Our rope is still suspended above the river. Any Mexican cavalry who come this way are sure to see it, and they'll know that a crossing was made here in one direction or the other."

Rick smiled faintly. "I hope you don't think I aim to leave all that rope behind," he said. "It may come in handy before we reach Austin. In all kinds of ways."

"You can cut it down on this bank," Chet said, "but there's no way to salvage it."

"You think so? Just watch," Rick said. "And remember I had Bill Devlin tie the knots over yonder facing this bank."

He picked up his rifle, took careful aim, and fired, the shot echoing through the wilderness. Everyone strained, but the distance was too great for anyone to determine whether his aim had been accurate or wild.

"One more should do the trick," Rick said as he reloaded. "There were three or four knots tied in the rope." Again he fired.

To the astonishment of the entire party, the rope fell clear at the base of the tree at the far side of the river.

"Give me a hand, some of you, before the rope gets waterlogged and becomes much heavier," Rick said.

Bill and Chet promptly began to haul in the line.

"I reckon that's the best marksmanship I've ever seen," an awed Harry Canning said. "I'm a pretty fair shot myself, but I'm not in your class, Rick. I doubt if Whip Holt or Kit Carson could have done better."

Rick was embarrassed by the praise. He glanced up at the cloudless, pale-blue sky and saw that the sun was almost directly overhead. "It's nearly noon," he said. "So eat some cold meat, if you like, and we'll be on our way. I know of a couple of spots where we can stop for water, so—with luck—maybe we can travel straight through until midnight tonight."

Melissa was outraged by the change in schedule. "Captain Miller," she said angrily, "you must be joking. All of us have taken great risks crossing the river, and you surely don't intend to have us spend hours and hours on the trail today and tonight!"

"We're still fresh, ma'am, and so are our horses," Rick

replied in a mild tone. "I'll grant you the river crossing may have been scary for a short time, but it didn't tire us or our mounts. We rested for a whole day and night over yonder on the west bank, and now we've got to make up for lost time."

"You're just being an obstinate bully!" Melissa cried as her rage increased. Nancy put a restraining hand on her friend's arm, but Melissa was so furious she shook her off. "I refuse to budge until tomorrow!"

There was a long moment of stunned silence.

Rick jammed his thumbs into his broad belt, planted his feet apart, and looked at the girl, his expression still benign. "When you lead a party, Miss Austin," he said in a deceptively soft voice, "folks will do things your way. I happen to be in charge of this party, and all of you agreed to put yourselves under my command—"

"I didn't!" Melissa interrupted.

Still amiable, he grinned at her. "Now you mention it, Miss Austin, you didn't. Some might say you butted in where you weren't wanted, but seeing as how you're a lady, I'll just say you joined us of your own free will. Well, ma'am, you can leave us the same way, and I won't try to stop you. But I hope you realize you won't get far alone across the deserts and mountains that stand between us and Texas."

The frustrated Melissa burst into tears. Rick realized, as did Harry and Nancy, that she was finding release after the tensions caused by the crossing of the Colorado. But Danny and Chet were in complete sympathy with Melissa and turned to Rick, their fists clenched. "You're being too rough on her," Danny said. "You can't talk to Melissa that way!"

"Nobody can," Chet added, his teeth clenched.

Rick looked them up and down. Certainly he knew, better than anyone else, that his basic authority was being challenged, but he remained unperturbed. He handed his rifle to Bill Devlin, then drew his pistols and gave them to Harry. "Mind these for me," he said.

Danny and Chet braced themselves.

The ranger turned back to them and grinned. "Boys," he said, "I'm bigger and stronger than either of you, I'll grant you. But put the two of you together, and I'm outweighed as well as outnumbered. You're healthy lads, both of you, so I'll make you a sporting offer. I'll take you on right here and now in a free-for-all, with no holds barred. Beat me, and we'll do as Miss Austin says. We'll delay our journey until tomorrow. But I warn you, if I win, as I aim to, no one will dispute my word again before we get to Texas."

Chet and Danny exchanged an uneasy glance. The offer was more than fair, but both of them had spent years on the Oregon trail with Whip Holt, and they knew that Rick Miller belonged to that same class of resilient frontiersman. Consequently, they were as reluctant to fight him in a free-for-all match as they would have been to attack a cornered wildcat with their bare hands.

Harry wanted to intervene but wisely refrained, realizing he had to allow Rick to handle the insurrection as he saw fit. If he administered a severe drubbing, as he probably would, Chet and Danny would learn a lesson they wouldn't forget, and Melissa might be less inclined to stir up trouble.

Nancy lacked her husband's ability to take a long-term view of the situation, however, and she moved between the potential combatants. "Have you taken leave of your senses, Danny Taylor?" she demanded. "Have you lost your wits, Chet Harris? We're in the middle of a wilderness, and only the Lord and Captain Miller know where we are! Can you two lead us safely to Texas? Hardly! Can you avoid pitfalls and overcome the dangers and threats that may await us? I wouldn't care to put myself under your leadership, thank you! As for you, Melissa Austin, the time has come for you to close your pretty mouth and keep it closed. Stop acting like a nasty brat. Behave like the grown woman you like to think you are!"

The admonished trio gaped at her, too astonished to reply.

Rick chuckled quietly, retrieved his pistols, and took his rifle from Bill, then tipped his hat to Nancy. "I'm obliged to you, ma'am," he said. "I'll give all of you fifteen minutes to eat, and then we'll be on our way."

Neither Danny nor Chet ever revealed to each other or to anyone else that they felt an infinite sense of relief. Both were courageous, as they had demonstrated repeatedly on the Oregon trail, but, having become adults, they were no longer foolhardy. They knew they stood no chance of winning a free-for-all contest with Rick, and they knew there was nothing to be gained by fighting him. They realized only dimly, however, that Melissa had goaded them into challenging the Texan. The time had not yet come when they would be cautious in their dealings with the headstrong girl who loved to have her own will prevail.

Melissa herself felt she had been betrayed by her closest friend, and she vowed not to speak to Nancy for days, even though she well understood that living conditions in the wilderness would make it impossible to keep that pledge. At the same time, however, she finally admitted to herself that her attitude had been foolish and reckless. Danny and Chet would have been willing to suffer severe beatings as the penalty for acting as her champion, and that was flattering.

If the experience had taught her anything, she had learned it was not wise to cross Rick Miller. Perhaps she was strong, as she liked to think, but he was stronger.

For a number of days the wagon train followed the course of the Red River, one of the Mississippi's major western tributaries, but when it twisted to the north, they continued to follow the rutted dirt roads that took them due west across Louisiana. Although it had been a state for more than three decades, ever since 1812, most of Louisiana's larger communities were located farther south. The country through which the Texas-bound pioneers were traveling had been sparsely settled until recent years, when plantations had been established in

ever-growing numbers. The train passed through no
cities of consequence, and residents of the small towns
paid scant attention to the wagons. Over the course of
several years, they had become accustomed to the sight
of covered wagons heading for Texas, and their only
reaction was to keep a sharp watch on their livestock
and poultry.

Certainly the members of the huge wagon train were
no better and no worse than those who had preceded
them on the route. But General Lee Blake and his
cavalrymen made a difference. "The old man," Sergeant
Major Hector Mullins told the soldiers, "wants to make
damn good and certain that no chickens, ducks, or cows
start disappearing from farms hereabouts. He's holding
you responsible for thefts, and you know what that
means. If you don't, I'll tell you plain. Any man in this
troop who closes his eyes when somebody from the
wagons starts to steal from the locals will be sent to one
of the loneliest outpost forts on the Oregon trail, and
there he'll stay until his tour of active duty in the army
expires."

The soldiers were vigilant, permitting no stragglers,
and at night, when they stood sentry duty, they were
firm in allowing no member of the company to wander
after dark beyond the confines of the circle of wagons.
Consequently, the word soon spread through Louisiana
that this train of wagons was "different."

Thanks to the good will that was engendered, Lee
Blake was able to send Innes MacGregor off to nearby
plantations at the end of each day's march to purchase
food. Plantation owners and farmers responded generously, and the company acquired ample quantities of
beef, ham and bacon, flour, beans, and a large variety of
fresh vegetables.

"The people of this train don't know they're well off,"
Ginny Mullins said to Cathy Blake one evening after a
supper that included green peas, blueberries, and mel-
ons.

Cathy smiled. "They're living in luxury—for however

long these conditions last. I doubt if we'll eat any better than this in Austin."

The mere mention of their destination cast a shadow across Ginny's face. Instead of ignoring the issue, Cathy attacked it directly. "Ginny," she said, "you're causing your own misery. You may be very pleasantly surprised by the people you meet in Austin. Why don't you reserve judgment until you get there and settle down?"

"That's good advice, and I know I should." Ginny made an effort to look and feel less forlorn. "I'll try."

"No one asks for more than that," Cathy said, then went off to the MacGregor wagon to pick up Beth, who was playing with Wallace.

Matilda MacGregor was sitting outside her wagon, enjoying the balmy night air, and appeared to be absorbed in her knitting. But as her children well knew, she was aware of everything that took place around her. She greeted Cathy with a quick smile and invited her to sit beside her.

They chatted about inconsequential matters for a time, and Cathy, giving in to an impulse based on instinct, told the Scotswoman in detail about Ginny's background and her depressed state of mind.

Matilda's knitting needles clicked rhythmically. "How does the lass get along with children?"

The question was surprising. "I don't really know," Cathy admitted. "She's looked after Beth for me on occasions when General Blake and I have had official functions to attend, but it isn't fair to judge her by her relations with us. After all, General Blake is her husband's commanding officer, and—"

"Aye." Matilda understood completely. "Mrs. Blake," she said, "I'm not one of them fancy doctors that trains at the medical school in Edinburgh. But I've brought five young ones into this world, so it may be I know something about a woman's heart and mind."

Cathy nodded, feeling that her hunch had been right. "If ye had been an orphan, ye might feel as Mrs. Mullins does," Matilda said. "She needs young of her own, ye

know. But I'd say she's afraid to have them, nae doubt
because she has many a bitter memory of her own
childhood."

"I think you have a point there. In fact, she's said as
much herself."

"There's nothing like a wee one of her own to cure a
woman who has a heart of lead."

"I believe you're right," Cathy said.

Matilda stopped knitting and lowered her voice so the
children would not hear her. "At breakfast tomorrow,"
she said, "I'll start a campaign. My youngsters will go to
Mrs. Mullins for all kinds of help and favors and advice.
When they've a mind to it, these girls of mine can melt
stones, I tell ye. And once Mrs. Mullins warms to them,
she'll begin to think how nice and comforting it would
be to have a family of her own."

"Wonderful! How may I help?"

"Stand clear," Matilda said brusquely. "Ye be the
General's lady."

Taking Beth with her, Cathy was heartened as she
returned to her own wagon.

The following morning Matilda MacGregor was as
good as her word. Observing the scene at breakfast,
Cathy saw seven-year-old Cara and five-year-old Wallace hurrying back and forth from their own wagon to
that in which Ginny and Hector lived. The campaign
was underway.

Progress was even more rapid than Cathy had anticipated. A scant forty-eight hours later Beth came to her,
saying that Wallace and Cara were going to ride in Mrs.
Mullins's wagon and begging for the privilege of accompanying them. "Can I, Mama? Please!"

"May I, not can I. And you certainly may."

All through the day Cathy glanced back from her own
boards to the wagon behind her in the line and saw
Ginny laughing with the three little girls. Matilda was
wise, she concluded, and for the first time she entertained real hope that Ginny would recover her buoy-
ancy.

Meanwhile, the wagon train rolled on. The weather

remained favorable, too, the spring rains holding off, and although the local planters were unhappy, the commander of the wagon train was pleased. Few obstacles were encountered, the vehicles traveled through flat countryside, and the dirt roads remained dry.

Therefore, the train was able to cover more than the ten miles per day that Lee had wanted to make, and on some days they were able to stretch the journey to fifteen miles. "I don't know how long we can maintain the pace," he told Innes and Hector, "but at this rate we'll reach Austin in less than six weeks."

One night, when Lee sat late at the fire with Innes MacGregor, checking off the food supplies that would need to be purchased the following day, one of his blue-clad troopers approached, spurs jangling.

"Corporal of the guard at report, sir."

Lee returned his salute, looking up with interest because this was the first time on the journey that the guards had come to him at night.

"One of my troopers—Private Krause—just caught a civilian who was violating the curfew, sir."

Innes MacGregor also stared at the Corporal.

"He was trying to sneak back into camp, making his way between two of the parked wagons, sir. He won't tell us where he had been or why he left the camp." The trooper sounded aggrieved.

"Bring him to me," Lee directed. "Mr. MacGregor and I will have a few words with him."

The Corporal saluted again, then went off into the dark.

"This was bound to happen, Innes," Lee said philosophically. "It's inevitable, in a group of individualists like this, that someone will rebel and break regulations. Particularly when we're traveling through a region where threats to our security are light. We need to take a firm stand, of course, because we'll be moving through long stretches of wilderness after we cross the Texas border."

The Corporal returned with two troopers, one on either side of Asa Phipps.

The Kentucky dirt farmer was incensed. "These goddamn soldiers have no right to treat me like a criminal!"
he shouted. "I'm a free citizen of the United States, and I
have the right to go where I please and do what I
please."

Displaying great patience, Lee dismissed the military
detail, then looked the man up and down. "You're in
error, Mr. Phipps," he said. "Certain rules have been
established for the good of this entire company. Our
people have been requested not to leave camp after dark
for a very sound reason. We don't want burglars sneaking in and out, as I'm sure you'll realize if you stop to
think about it."

"Are you accusing me of being a burglar, General?"
Phipps demanded.

Innes MacGregor grew tense, but his demeanor did
not change. "Not at all. But you must have had a good
reason for leaving camp. I hope you'll be good enough to
give us an explanation."

"Where I went is none of your business!"

Innes could remain quiet no longer. "Phipps," he said,
"I was elected president of this company, a post I didn't
seek. Now that I hold it, I'll do my duty. Tell us plain
what ye were doing—or suffer the consequences."

"What consequences, MacGregor?" The Kentuckian
was defiant.

"We have the authority," Lee said quietly, "to have
you stripped and searched. But that won't be necessary
if you'll just behave civilly and tell us where you've
been."

Trembling with rage, Phipps was forced to back
down. "If you must know," he said, becoming surly, "I
saw a tavern in that village we passed a couple of miles
down the road this afternoon. I went there for a few
pints of ale."

Lee was silent for a moment. "I strongly urge you not
to leave the wagons again after dark."

The man turned on his heel and stamped off.

"Innes," Lee said, "he was lying to us."

"So, General?"

"There was no tavern in that village, but I didn't want to expose him. I suspect he's following a pattern that has been noted on other wagon trains. I'm willing to wager that he stole some property from one of the wagons, then went off to the village to sell it for whatever price he could get. The problem is that the belongings of most people are piled up in a jumbled mess in their wagons. Many days may pass before the victims realize that something is missing."

"Ye didna' call him out, Lee!" MacGregor protested.

"I couldn't, because I have no proof. Suppose we found a dollar or two in his purse. For all we know, it was his money all along."

The Scotsman became thoughtful and nodded. "I see what ye mean. The only way we could prove he sold stolen goods would be to question everybody in the village."

"Right, and whoever bought the property from him would likely become frightened and lie, too."

"Then what do we do, Lee?"

"From now on, we'll keep a closer watch on Asa Phipps after nightfall, without his knowing it. I'll give instructions to Sergeant Mullins first thing in the morning. But don't let it worry you overly much. In a large barrel you often find one rotten apple."

VII

Rick Miller demonstrated why he had risen to the rank of captain in the exclusive regiment of Texas Rangers. He was tireless, a tower of strength, as he led his small party through mountain passes and vast stretches of semi-arid land in that portion of provincial Mexico that one day would become Arizona. Where there were no rivers or lakes, he had a "nose for water" that enabled him to find springs where the men, the two women, and their horses could drink. He spotted antelope tracks, then sent Chet and Danny hunting. But he allowed no campfires to be built, ever, until he had scaled the heights near a campsite and assured himself that no Mexican cavalry patrols would see the smoke.

One day he saw a small village in the distance from the top of a cliff, and he carefully made a wide detour around it. Questioned by his charges, he replied succinctly. "Anybody who lives in these parts is scared to death of the Mexican cavalry."

Melissa Austin adopted an air of bravado. After her confrontation with Rick, she stopped complaining and, instead, put up a defiant front. At times she seemed to be challenging him and all of the other men in the band, daring them to make still greater demands on her strength. Under no circumstances would she admit that on most nights she was so exhausted she felt ill.

158

One night Danny thought he heard her weeping. Aroused from his sleep, he sat upright and stared at the girl, who was wrapped in her blanket on the far side of Harry and Nancy. But he could not see her clearly enough to determine whether she was actually shedding tears.

Chet heard his friend stir, and he, too, sat upright, then realized why Danny was concerned. He was tempted to go to Melissa but was afraid the gesture would be misunderstood at this time of night. So he remained beneath his own blanket.

At breakfast the next morning, however, he said to her in a low tone, "I was upset last night when I heard you crying."

Melissa looked at him sharply, then saw that Danny also was watching her, concern in his eyes. Color flamed in her cheeks beneath her tan, and she took refuge in anger. "I've never heard anything so absurd!" she exclaimed. "I never cry!"

Others, who had not heard Chet's remark, looked at her curiously. She offered no explanation, however, and began to joke with Bill Devlin.

The incident was forgotten by most of the travelers, although Nancy looked occasionally at her friend throughout the day. Melissa was behaving recklessly, laughing too loudly, and twice she spurred forward, overtaking Rick. On both occasions he had to send her back to her regular place in the single-file line.

By mid-afternoon, when a halt was called to light a fire and cook antelope steaks, Melissa was more on edge than anyone realized. Her gelding suddenly sidestepped in alarm as the girl was about to dismount. Looking down, Melissa saw a rattlesnake slowly coiling itself to strike, the diamondlike pattern of its scales glistening in the sun as it sounded the ominous rattle in its tail.

No longer able to control her emotions, she screamed.

The others stopped whatever they were doing and stared at her. Unable to speak, she could only point.

Rick, showing his usual calm in a moment of crisis,

drew one of his pistols, waited until the snake was about to strike the gelding, and then squeezed the trigger.

The snake's head was parted from its still-writhing body.

Melissa had bottled up her feelings for so long that she overreacted and began to weep hysterically. Irritated without measure with herself, she was unable to stifle her sobs, and the tears streamed unheeded down her cheeks.

Rick stood helplessly, shifting his weight from one foot to the other as he pushed his broad-brimmed hat back from his forehead. He was capable of handling almost any emergency in this desolate land, but he had no idea how to calm the weeping girl.

Chet Harris intervened. Lifting Melissa from her saddle, he held her gently until she was able to control herself. Danny handed her a bandanna, and she wiped her eyes, sniffed loudly, and moved away from the dead snake.

"I'll make the skin into a belt for you, if you like," Danny said.

"No! I can't abide snakes!"

They were afraid she would begin to weep again, but her self-discipline had asserted itself, and she managed to smile somewhat stiffly at Rick. "Thank you," she said simply.

"Glad to be helpful," he muttered, then busied himself gathering what little firewood he could find in the area. Melissa Austin was a handful, no question about it, and he felt sorry for the man she would marry. He knew one thing for certain: there was no way he would be that man.

Major General Winfield Scott braced himself as he entered President Tyler's private office. The Secretary of War should have handled this unsavory assignment but had been unwilling to face the wrath of the Chief Executive, so he had given the task to the Chief of Staff. Oh, well. The worst that would happen would be a tongue-lashing, and anyone who was stationed in Washington City had to be prepared for such treatment from time to time.

The General couldn't help wishing he would be transferred to the field, but that would happen only if the United States went to war with a major foe. He regarded himself as a soldier, not an administrator, and he hated meetings like this.

Nevertheless, he smiled amiably as he shook John Tyler's hand and seated himself opposite the oversized desk.

"You wanted to see me on what your note said was a fairly urgent matter, Scott?"

"Yes, Mr. President. It concerns the shipment of arms and munitions to Texas." The Chief of Staff could feel perspiration gathering under the collar of his tunic. "I'm afraid, sir, there's going to be a delay."

Furrows appeared in Tyler's smooth brow.

"As you may know, both the army and the navy have increased their orders of gunpowder recently from the plant in Delaware. Our general staff doesn't know what may lie ahead for us, and I know the commodores feel the same way."

"Come to the point!" the President snapped.

"Yes, sir." Long experience enabled Scott to speak smoothly, almost confidently. "The plant in Delaware is already operating at capacity. We've reached an agreement with the navy that will channel all powder made in the next two months for Texas—"

"You're saying there will be a delay of two more months before we can send off a wagon train of munitions to Sam Houston?" The President raised his voice, a sure sign of danger.

"There's no alternative, sir."

"Can't you get powder from New England or Pennsylvania?"

"I'd rather not, Mr. President. They do well enough when they're making powder for small arms use. But only the people in Delaware provide a product that's adequate for rifles. And particularly for cannon."

Tyler drummed on the desk. "What about arms?"

"There's also a slight delay there, Mr. President. Our own Ordinance Division has just completed its field tests of the new pistol invented by Samuel Colt. It's a remarkable weapon. I know because I've tried it myself. Colt calls it a six-shooter, which means it can fire six bullets without being reloaded. An incredible improvement, when you think about it. We've ordered one hundred thousand of these pistols for the army—"

"Now you're saying that the order must be filled before any will be made available for Sam Houston?"

"In a nutshell, that's about it, sir."

"Nonsense! I want the first ten thousand of those pistols set aside and packed in the wagon train that we're sending to Texas."

General Scott was incredulous. "Before we fill our own needs, sir?"

Tyler sighed. "You're like all the rest. You insist on thinking of Texas as a foreign country. Every last citizen there is an American! A fact that will be reconfirmed when we annex her and admit her to statehood!"

A man who had spent his entire adult life in military service could not remain on the defensive indefinitely. "Unless," the Chief of Staff declared, "the Whigs manage to elect Henry Clay as President."

Tyler compressed his lips. "You misjudge the mood of the country. I would have been elected had my party seen fit to nominate me. There's no doubt in my mind that Polk will succeed me. And even if Clay should win through some accident, the Congress is determined to annex Texas—no matter what Mexico does, no matter how strongly Great Britain may be opposed to the idea."

General Scott had to admit defeat. His own troops would be forced to wait for Samuel Colt's marvelous new pistol. "As you've ordered, Mr. President, the first ten thousand of the new weapons will be set aside for Texas."

"I'll put that directive in writing." Tyler was familiar with the demands of the bureaucrats in his government. "I assume the cannon and rifles we're sending to Texas are ready?"

"Yes, sir. They've been stored in our arms depot across the Potomac."

"And these new pistols will be ready for delivery when the gunpowder has been manufactured?"

"At more or less the same time, sir."

"Very well. I'll write to Houston, asking him to be patient a little longer. I'm not forgetting that his militiamen are actually stationed on the Mexican border, while the nearest units of our own army are sitting in barracks hundreds of miles away. If my interpretation of Santa Anna's nature is accurate—and it's the same as Andrew Jackson's—we're virtually certain to be at war with Mexico. So don't stand for any procrastination anywhere. We—and I include Texas when I say this—must be ready to retaliate immediately when Santa Anna declares war!"

Anthony Roberts was pleased with himself. The New Orleans–Texas freight company in which he had invested was showing a handsome profit that was growing monthly, but he was taking no active role in the operations of the concern, which left him free to do as he pleased. He continued to entertain Texas officials in his home, and they were happy to accept him socially because he had acquired a reputation as a successful businessman whose efforts were beneficial to the Lone Star Republic.

The information he gleaned from these talkative gentlemen enabled him to make full reports to the British Legation, where his efforts were appreciated, and to send off a long report every month to Mexico City. He was amused, after doing a little arithmetic, to discover that his various activities were actually showing a small profit. He had been prepared to lose money while he pursued his private plan of vengeance against his father's murderers, but when he returned to London, he would have more money in his purse than he had had when he had left for the New World by way of Spain.

Now he was ready to strike again, and he smiled broadly at Elisabeta Manuel as she placed his breakfast steak before him. "My dear," he said jovially, "I hope you realize that you're leading a very pleasant life here."

Something in his tone made the woman uneasy. "In some ways it is pleasant enough," she admitted as she took her place opposite him and poured herself a cup of tea, her sole concession to breakfast.

Anthony began to eat with relish. "I'll grant that you keep house for me. But now that I've generously provided you with funds to hire a woman to do the heavy cleaning, you need only prepare our meals and do a bit of light housekeeping. In return you have free room and board, and I'm going to give you money to have some new clothes made for yourself."

She tried to rid herself of a nagging sense of apprehension. "That's generous of you," she murmured. It might be necessary to have one dress made in order to satisfy him, but, depending on what he gave her, she would hide the rest in the cache that would bring her the freedom she craved.

"I make no demands on you other than to ask you to be present when I entertain our friends in the Texas government. A small chore. Surely you know I'm making no personal demands on you."

Elisabeta nodded, grateful that he no longer made love to her. Certainly she had no intention of reminding him of his promise to marry her, which he—fortunately—seemed to have forgotten.

Anthony chose his words carefully. "I don't suppose you've heard of an elderly man named Victor Burgess."

She shook her head.

"He is a grain dealer who lives in a small town northeast of Austin. I'm told that no one sells more wheat and corn to President Houston than he does. Burgess arrived in town last evening and intends to spend several days here."

Elisabeta listened vaguely.

"Unfortunately, I am not acquainted with Victor Burgess. But that is a state that you can remedy for me."

A chill crawled slowly up her spine when she recognized the significance of his words. "Not again!" she cried, unable to conceal her horror.

Anthony ignored her outburst. Reaching into his purse, he carelessly pushed two gold coins across the table to her. "For your clothes," he said, smiling.

She knew he was trying to bribe her to persuade her to prepare another trap, and she wanted to throw the money in his face. But he would beat her, then force her to obey, and she wouldn't have the gold, either. So she took the coins, even though they felt red hot in her hands.

"Burgess, I understand, dines very early, which seems to be a habit of Americans and Texans who live in rural places. I want you to go to the Lone Star Inn, where he's staying, and arrange to have him follow you here. Make certain he doesn't accompany you back to the house, however. That could create awkward complications."

She was overwhelmed by memories of Senator Blount's murder. "No, Anthony! Please!"

"I do so much for you, yet I ask so little in return," he said. "No one else will be in the taproom of the Lone Star at that hour. What I'm asking is mere child's play for a woman of your great beauty and intelligence."

Elisabeta's whole body was turning to ice, and she shivered.

Anthony wiped his sharp knife with his napkin, then tested the blade with the ball of his thumb. "You cannot imagine how much I would regret the marring of your perfect beauty," he said.

The expression in his eyes told her he was making no idle threat. Tears came to her eyes and rolled slowly down her face. "Why do you do these terrible things, Anthony? Why did you come to Texas?"

"Terrible things, my dear? I merely ask you to help me make the acquaintance of a prominent citizen of this country." His voice hardened and became grating. "Do I ask too much? Speak quickly, before I lose patience with you."

She lowered her head, unable to meet his piercing,

hostile gaze. "You—you don't ask too much," she said in a broken voice.

He scooped up the last of the food on his plate. "I neglected to tell you these potatoes are delicious," he said calmly.

Unable to remain in his presence any longer, Elisabeta jumped up from the table.

"Remember that I'm depending on you," he called as she fled from the dining room.

The day dragged, and Elisabeta would have been willing to sacrifice years of her life to avoid the onerous chore that awaited her. But, for the second time, there was no escape.

Her spirits leaden, she waited until afternoon before she bathed, dressed in her provocative green velvet gown, and daubed her face heavily with cosmetics. Anthony was nowhere to be seen, but she found her mare saddled and waiting outside the kitchen door.

She rode to the Lone Star Inn, where she found the taproom unoccupied, and in a dead voice she ordered tea from a new barmaid, a middle-aged woman whose expression indicated she disapproved of strumpets. Elisabeta was so uncomfortable that she paid for her tea when it was served to her.

A few moments later an elderly, bald man came into the taproom, took a seat directly in Elisabeta's line of vision, and ordered a hearty supper from the barmaid.

When the woman left the room, Elisabeta opened her cloak to reveal her low-cut neckline, then forced herself to smile. She could see the startled expression in the man's eyes, but he promptly averted his gaze.

She sipped her tea as she waited, wishing the ground would open beneath her feet and swallow her. Inevitably, the man—who almost certainly was Victor Burgess—glanced in her direction again. Again she smiled.

He rose from his chair abruptly, then changed to another seat so he would no longer be facing her. Elisabeta's shame was so great that she wrapped herself in her cloak and returned without delay to the Roberts house.

Anthony was waiting for her in the kitchen. "Well?" he demanded. "Speak quickly, and then leave the house for at least an hour."

Stammering and terrified, she told him what had happened. He listened carefully but did not threaten her, afraid she would become hysterical. "Don't worry about it," he said calmly. "You'll have to try again tomorrow."

"How can I?" she cried. "I did my best today—but he was disgusted!"

Anthony pondered for a few moments. "You'll have to take a different approach," he said. "Win his sympathy."

"How?"

"I leave the details to you," he said vaguely, then left the house.

Elisabeta spent a sleepless, despairing night. She was convinced that Anthony intended to commit another murder, and for reasons she was unable to fathom. There was no doubt whatever in her mind that he was going to use her—again—to further his evil design, and the knowledge made her heartsick.

There seemed to be no way she could avoid serving as his accomplice. The funds she had managed to scrape together since making up her mind to escape would take her as far as New Orleans and pay her room and board there for a few days, but that wouldn't suffice. She needed more, far more, to obtain passage for Spain, where she would find real refuge. She knew no one in New Orleans, and there was no way she could earn an honorable living there. So, for the present, she was compelled to continue to do Anthony's bidding and would have to accept the inevitability of her fate. The next afternoon she scrubbed her face clean, applying no cosmetics, pulled back her hair severely, and arranged it in a tight bun at the nape of her neck. Then she put on the simple, loose-fitting, high-necked dress she had worn the day she met Anthony, and over it she threw her old, shabby cape, which she usually wore only on rainy days.

She could only pray that she looked like a different person.

Late in the afternoon, after passing Anthony's chuckling, approving inspection, she returned to the Lone Star Inn. She had no idea whether the barmaid recognized her, but the woman made no comment, which she found encouraging.

Taking a place directly opposite the second seat that Victor Burgess had occupied the previous evening, she ordered tea and steeled herself. She did not have long to wait.

Burgess came into the taproom, placed himself opposite Elisabeta as she had hoped, and ordered his meal.

Elisabeta waited until the barmaid disappeared into the kitchen with his order, and then, following the plan she had devised, she addressed him.

"Mr. Burgess." She wished her pulse would not race so fast. The man looked up at her. "Mr. Burgess," she said, "I have not come here today by accident. My—my father recently acquired a large amount of wheat in a barter deal." She spoke rapidly, hoping her nerve would not fail her. "He is ill, and he doesn't know how to dispose of it. We heard you had come to Austin, and we were informed you were the best grain broker in Texas, so we hoped you could help us. I hope I'm not imposing on you."

Burgess peered hard at her, frowning slightly. "Do I know you, young lady?" he asked. "For some reason you look very familiar to me."

"We have never met, sir," she replied, and that much, at least, was the truth.

He continued to search his memory, then shrugged and smiled, as if to indicate it didn't really matter if he had seen her somewhere previously.

"We have been hoping, sir," she continued, "that you might be willing to meet with my father for a few minutes after you finish your supper."

The man's smile broadened. "I'm never opposed to making a profit," he said.

Her heart pounding wildly, Elisabeta told him the

location of the house, describing it carefully. Then, before the barmaid returned with his supper, she placed the money for her tea on the table, gathered her cloak around her, and departed. "We will be waiting for you, sir," she said as she left.

A tense Anthony Roberts awaited her at the house. Elisabeta was forced to give him a word-for-word account of the conversation.

"Did you mention my name?" he demanded.

"Neither your name nor mine," she told him.

He nodded in approval. "Good," he said. "Now make yourself conspicuous so people in the neighborhood will remember they've seen you at this time of day. Go to the people who live next door and borrow something."

Elisabeta did as she was told. She walked across the yard to the adjoining dwelling, where she borrowed a half-cup of salt, which sometimes was in short supply. The neighbors, a middle-aged couple with whom she was on vaguely friendly terms, chatted with her briefly before she returned home.

Anthony was standing at the front gate, using a sledgehammer to pound the fence posts enclosing the property deeper into the ground. The sound had attracted the notice of the people who lived directly across the road, and he was exchanging a few words with them. Then he followed Elisabeta into the house.

"You've done your part well," he told her. "Now leave the house for an hour, at the very least."

"Where shall I go?"

"Just ride somewhere. Anywhere. But be sure you take the North Road, the old road out of town." He spoke with slow, deliberate emphasis.

"The North Road," she repeated, certain in her mind that he wanted her to avoid the area south of Austin. Then, glancing out the window, she became panicky. "It will be dark soon!"

"So much the better." His smile was cryptic.

"I—I don't know if it is safe for me to be out alone after nightfall."

"Of course you'll be safe." He was even more annoyed.

"I'm not suggesting that you ride far out into the open countryside. Let it appear that you're going out for a little fresh air. Walk your horse rather than canter. The more people who see you, the better it will be. Now go quickly." He laughed dryly. "I'm expecting a visitor very shortly, and it will be best all around if you aren't here when he arrives."

Elisabeta was grateful that she wouldn't face Victor Burgess again. Losing no time, she departed quickly. Following Anthony's instructions, she rode slowly toward the old North Road, taking it to the end of town and beyond. Only when she came to the open spaces of the ranches located beyond the confines of the community did she become apprehensive, but she was more afraid of Anthony's wrath than of what might happen to her here. She took care not to go back to the house until an hour and a half had elapsed.

As she had anticipated, the place was empty, and she could find no signs of a struggle. How Anthony had persuaded Burgess to accompany him elsewhere was something she didn't want to learn, now or ever.

In spite of her trepidation she felt empty, so she forced herself to eat something, although the food tasted like sour cardboard. Hastily washing the dishes, she hurried off to her own room, barring the door behind her, and when she went to bed, she pulled the covers high and buried her head beneath the pillow. She didn't want to hear Anthony returning home, and she didn't, but it was very late before she dozed off.

At breakfast the following morning, Anthony was so cheerful she felt certain that his latest grisly mission had been successful.

Before he went off on unexplained business, which he said would keep him occupied most of the day, he fished in his leather purse and handed her a gold coin. "You deserve some more new clothes," he told her.

Adding the money to her secret fund, Elisabeta was grateful that he failed to observe what she wore. She had not had any dresses made because she had better use for the money, but she prayed that he would not use her as a decoy again.

She remained indoors all morning, but by midday she could tolerate the loneliness no longer, so she went next door with the same half-cup of salt she had borrowed the previous evening. The woman was alone and invited her to sit down for a cup of tea in the kitchen. Elisabeta accepted reluctantly, dreading what she might hear.

Her worst fears were confirmed when the woman said, "I'm sure you've heard about the latest murder."

Elisabeta could only shake her head.

"I don't rightly recall the man's name, but my husband says he was a very prominent grain dealer. His body was found in a ditch near the South Road this morning."

There was no need for Elisabeta to simulate the horror that filled her.

"The most terrible part is that the people who killed poor Senator Blount are the very ones who did this poor fellow in."

Somehow, Elisabeta found her voice. "How do you know that?"

"My husband says he was choked to death and that the Rangers found some kind of strong string around his neck, fixed so it looked like a hangman's noose."

Although Elisabeta had been prepared for the news of the murder, she couldn't withhold a gasp.

"From time to time there are violent deaths here," the woman said. "Somehow, you have to learn to expect that in frontier country. But this seems to be a special kind of killing with a special kind of meaning."

The girl nodded, and the room swam dizzily.

"Oh, how the Rangers miss Captain Miller! Sergeant Haight is a fine young man, but they say he found no clues when Senator Blount was killed. You can just bet that folks hereabouts can hardly wait until Rick Miller comes back to his regular duty!"

"Is—is this Captain Miller all that good?"

"He's a human bloodhound! He has a real instinct for ferreting out lawbreakers, I can tell you! The people who put pretend nooses around the necks of the old men they murder may think they're being funny, but it won't take Captain Miller long to discover who they are. Then they'll find out for themselves what it's like to have a noose over their heads!" The woman spoke grimly.

Elisabeta took her leave as quickly as she could, and thereafter, she performed the rest of her day's chores in a daze. She had no intention of asking Anthony why he placed miniature nooses around the necks of his victims. The less she knew about his terrible pastime, the better off she would be.

She tried to put the frightful killings out of her mind, but her efforts failed. For many days her sleep was disturbed by the same recurring nightmare: a shadowy, faceless figure called Captain Miller pursued her down a long, dark corridor. Each time he caught her, and when he clapped a heavy hand on her shoulder, she awakened with a start, bathed in perspiration.

The realization that the territory that lay between California and Texas was extremely hazardous was driven home, one morning, to the party Rick Miller was escorting, when the tracks of two men, traveling on foot, were found in the desert. Rick ordered Bill Devlin, one of the best horsemen in the group, to follow the trail and rejoin the party late in the day at a water hole on the far side of a small but jagged peak that was visible in the distance.

Devlin did not appear, nor did he return the next morning, so Rick delayed the day's march and set out in search of the missing Oregonian. Riding at a gallop, he returned to the place where they had parted, and encountered no difficulty in following the tracks of Devlin's gelding.

An hour or two later he came upon a grisly scene. The body of Bill Devlin was sprawled on the ground, his rifle still clutched in his hand. Less than one hundred feet from him was the body of his horse.

Studying the footprints in the vicinity, Rick soon figured out what had happened. Two men who were wear-

ing boots, which indicated they were whites rather than
moccasin-clad Indians, had lain in ambush, shot Devlin,
and stolen his horse. But the dying Devlin had managed
to fire a single shot at his murderers before he expired,
had missed them as they had started off on the stolen
mount, and instead had killed the horse. The killers had
been obliged to flee from the scene on foot.

The travelers were sober and subdued when Rick
reported the unhappy news to them.

An immediate change in their routines was instituted,
and thereafter, the men took turns standing sentry duty
every night. Rick had been depending on his instinct to
wake him if danger threatened, but now, he decided,
greater precautions were needed. The members of the
party accepted their new responsibility without complaint.

For the next week, as the group moved across the
rugged, inhospitable country, nothing unusual occurred,
and gradually tensions were eased. Bill Devlin was
mourned, but his murderers appeared to have vanished.

Then, one night when Chet Harris had the first sentry
watch, Melissa Austin felt restless and could not sleep.
In spite of the dangers that were very real, she was
bored by the routines, even though she well knew she
should be thankful. Certainly she saw no reason to
remain wrapped in her blanket when she was wide
awake, so she sat upright, combed her red hair, and then
strolled to the place where Chet sat on a boulder,
keeping watch. The horses grazed nearby on scrub grass,
a half-moon shed its light on the raw, bare peaks of the
mountains in the distance, and Chet, although alert,
appeared to be daydreaming as, from time to time, he
looked around him.

"I hope I'm not disturbing you," Melissa said with the
provocative smile that was second nature to her.

The stocky young man beamed. "Why aren't you
sleeping?"

"I guess I preferred to keep you company. It must be
so dull for you, keeping watch hour after hour."

"I reckon it is," the flattered Chet replied. "But there's still a job to be done."

Melissa, knowing she was impressing him, said, "I do admire you for your sense of responsibility. I'd find it so dull to do what you're doing that I think I'd scream. I'm so glad I'm not a man."

He swallowed hard, then dared to say, "I'm mighty glad, too."

"Oh, Chet," she said, her eyes bright.

His heart pounded, and he wondered if it was possible that he was winning her favor. Less sensitive than Danny, he was more inclined to take people and what they did at face value. Clearly, Melissa thought highly of him. How much he didn't know, but maybe he could summon the nerve to find out. He cleared his throat, then said in a rush, "I was thinking about you just now, when all of a sudden you showed up."

Her eyelids fluttered. "What were you thinking?"

"You might not like it if I told you."

"That's impossible. Unless they were bad thoughts."

"I was kind of imagining what it would be like to be married to you," he said.

She pretended to be coy. "That's sweet, but we can't think about such things until we've established ourselves in Texas."

Chet looked crestfallen. Perhaps, Melissa thought, she had applied too strong a damper and should encourage him somewhat. "I'm not sure what I want," she said softly, "but I must admit that sometimes I wonder what it would be like if I were married to you."

Rick Miller awakened from a light sleep, disturbed by sounds that neither the sentry nor the girl heard. He opened his eyes. Two scruffy, unshaven men in faded, stained buckskins were stealing a pair of their horses. One had already mounted, and dug his heels into the gelding's sides, spurring the animal to action.

Rick instantly reached for the rifle he kept beside him at all times. But by the time he raised it to his shoulder, while still lying prone, the beast had traveled more than a hundred feet. A single shot had to be effective, and he took aim as best he could, then squeezed the trigger. The thief toppled from the horse's back, and fell to the ground dead. The frightened gelding continued to run. Rick sprang to his feet, leaped onto the bare back of his own stallion, and went in pursuit of the runaway.

Meanwhile, Chet was jarred back to the present. He saw the second thief, slower and clumsier than his companion, climbing onto the back of another gelding. Aiming carefully but swiftly, he brought down the intruder with his shot.

The entire camp was in an uproar. By the time most of the party realized what had happened, Rick had retrieved the runaway and was riding back to the campsite, coldy furious.

"It was my fault," Chet told him before he could speak. "I—I wasn't paying attention like I should have been doing."

"You sure as hell weren't," Rick replied curtly. Aware of the younger man's deep chagrin, he knew a further lecture would be unnecessary. Chet had learned a lesson he wouldn't forget. Instead, Rick turned to Melissa. The girl was recovering from her initial shock, and her eyes were innocent.

This was too much. Rick had neither the inclination nor the time to spend hours explaining to someone who should have known better that it was sheer stupidity to distract a sentry. "Young lady," he said, his voice harsh, "you'll be doing this whole company a favor if you'll tend to your own business."

"I beg your pardon!" Her temper flared. "You have no call to blame me for what happened!"

In a strange way, Rick realized, she was innocent. Apparently she was so self-centered, so conscious of her appeal to men, that she was incapable of understanding she had placed the entire company in jeopardy. But this was not a moment to look dispassionately at her side of the matter. It was his duty to escort Harry Canning safely to Texas. Nothing else mattered, including the feelings of this beautiful but immature girl. "You weren't invited to make the journey with us," he said, "so I'll make my position plain. From now on you'll behave yourself. Step out of line just once more, and I'll be forced to let you fend for yourself."

Now Melissa's temper exploded. "If there's one thing I can't tolerate, it's a man who has a little power and behaves like a tyrant. You can go to hell, Rick Miller!"

Surprisingly, Rick paid no more attention to her. He turned and walked away. A further tongue-lashing was beyond her ability to understand, and a hard spanking, which she deserved, would have made her hysterical. Somehow, he would manage to deliver Harry Canning to Austin, even with Melissa in the party. Meanwhile, his resolve to remain a bachelor for the rest of his days was confirmed.

Members of the wagon train company celebrated with a special supper when they reached the east bank of the Sabine River, which marked the boundary between Louisiana and the Republic of Texas. Hunters sent out by Lee Blake had shot a number of buffalo. The cooking detail urged people to eat their fill, and ample supplies of meat were left for future meals.

The next day was spent constructing several sturdy rafts, which were used to ferry the wagons and animals across the river. The flow of the Sabine was gentle, so no serious difficulties were encountered, but there were so many wagons in the train that the feat required two days to accomplish.

It was mid-afternoon of the second day when the last of the wagons, its occupants, and their mules were ferried to the west bank of the Sabine, and the hundreds who watched the operation cheered spontaneously. A few, like the MacGregors, had come from the far side of the Atlantic, and there were some who had traveled overland from the seaboard states. All had made sacrifices, and, although a long journey still awaited them, the knowledge that they stood at last on the soil of Texas was infinitely helpful to their spirits.

That night the wagon train members celebrated again. With all the activity, it was impossible for Matilda Mac-

Gregor to keep watch over her entire brood, and she had to trust in the good sense of her children not to become involved in mischief. But when seven-year-old Cara happened to notice Asa Phipps hiding something beneath his frayed coat and quietly leaving the campfire with two other men, she was naturally curious, and beckoning silently to little Wallace, who willingly went with her, Cara followed them. Thistle, the family collie, instantly joined the girls, who crept out of the wagon circle into the open prairie, where the grass was so high that it hid them from view.

Phipps and his companions headed toward the Sabine River, then disappeared from the children's sight.

"I think they went to the river," Cara said.

Wallace was no longer certain that the game offered a pleasant time. "We better go back," she said. "Or Ma will yell, and Pa will thrash us."

Cara wanted to show her independence. "I'm going to see if I can find them at the river. You go back if you want to, baby."

Wallace hated being called a baby. "I'm coming, too," she announced firmly.

The children advanced cautiously, parting the tall grass in front of them. Thistle walked happily beside them, pausing to sniff occasionally when she caught the scent of a gopher or a field mouse.

The little girls had no way of knowing that Phipps and his cronies, having filled a container with river water, were making themselves comfortable in the high grass as they shared a bottle of corn whiskey that the Kentuckian had been saving for some special occasion.

In places, the grass grew to the river's edge, and Cara, who took the lead, went too far. Before she could halt herself, she stumbled forward and toppled head first into the water.

The Sabine was only five feet deep, but it rose higher than the top of the little girl's head, and she was unable to swim. So terrified she could not utter a sound, she tried to stand but could not, and instead of paddling the few feet toward the shore, which might have been within her capability, she thrashed wildly, the current dragging her downstream.

Wallace screamed.

The collie, whose tail had stopped wagging and whose body had become tense, leaped into the water and began to swim toward the floundering child.

Wallace wanted to hurry back to the campfire and fetch her parents, but her limited common sense told her they would arrive at the scene too late. She, like her sister, could not swim, and she had no alternative, so she screamed again.

Phipps and his friends either did not hear the little girl's cry or ignored it. Neither then nor later did anyone ever learn that they were close enough to intervene and save the badly frightened child.

Cara thrashed madly, swallowing large quantities of water. Thistle swam as rapidly as she could, and Wallace stood close to the bank, tears streaming down her face as she watched. She herself was incapable of intervening, and she could only hope that the collie would reach her sister in time.

Cara disappeared beneath the surface of the water.

The dog, after twice missing, managed to catch hold of the back of Cara's shirt in her teeth. Wasting no time, Thistle fought against the current and started to swim toward the shore.

In her desperation Cara, choking and gasping, caught hold of the long hair of the dog's coat. Her head freed, Thistle swam with greater confidence and strength. Fortunately, the current was not strong, but the child and dog nevertheless were carried more than twenty feet downstream before Thistle could reach the bank and try to climb it.

Wallace ran as fast as she could down the river bank. In her haste she pitched headlong into the grass but scrambled to her feet again and continued to race. Thistle tried to make her way up the bank, but she was encumbered by the weight of her burden and could not manage the feat. Wallace arrived at the spot and reached out as far as she could, but her arms were too short for her to touch the animal. She caught a glimpse of her sister's pale face and knew Cara could not climb up the bank unaided.

"Come to me, Thistle," Wallace pleaded, showing remarkable poise for one of her age. "Come on, Thistle. That's a good girl."

The collie tried again with all her might, gained a foothold, and ultimately succeeded in dragging Cara to safety.

The child relaxed her grip when she knew she was safe, and for a long time she lay motionless on the ground, utterly spent. Thistle shook herself and stood panting, her tail in motion again as she hovered protectively over the exhausted girl.

"Are you dead, Cara?" Wallace asked.

"I'm not sure." Slowly she dragged herself to her feet, then hugged the collie. Thistle joyously licked her face. But sensing that her work was not yet done, the collie nudged one girl, then the other, in the direction of the wagons.

Wallace, catching hold of her sister's hand, started back toward the safety of the beckoning campfire. The collie circled the children as they walked, taking no chance that harm might come to either of them.

Not until they had squeezed through the opening between two parked wagons did it occur to the girls that they might be in trouble because of their adventure. The only way to escape parental discipline was to return at once to their own wagon, where Cara could change into dry clothes.

But that feat was more difficult to accomplish than either had been able to anticipate. Staying close to the wagons, they tried to creep toward that of their family, while Thistle trotted beside them.

Matilda and Innes were chatting and drinking after-supper tea with the Howells near the fire when Matilda caught a glimpse of Thistle, her hair plastered to her body. The woman looked more closely, saw Wallace's guilty little face, and then realized that Cara, like the dog, was sopping wet. Not remembering to excuse her-

self, Matilda bolted toward the children and was followed by Innes.

"What's all this?" she demanded, hands on her hips.

The girls knew they had been caught and, stopping
short, began to speak simultaneously.

"One at a time," Matilda said sternly and pointed a
forefinger at Cara.

Thistle complicated the situation by rubbing against
Innes, soaking his trousers.

Cara's gibberish made no sense. The finger pointed
toward Wallace. The youngest of the MacGregor girls
seemed to have lost the power of speech.

Innes tried to rub the moisture from the side of his
trousers. "Let me guess," he said. "You went fishing."

Cara shook her head. By now she had forgotten their
reason for leaving the campsite.

"Cara fell in the river," Wallace said, able to speak at
last. "Thistle saved her."

To the astonishment of both girls, they were neither
lectured nor spanked. Matilda gathered Cara in her
arms, unmindful of the child's wet clothes and hair,
while Innes patted and commended the dog.

"Wallace," he asked, "what say ye to a reward for
Thistle?" She nodded eagerly. He went quickly to the
fire, returning with a chunk of dripping buffalo meat,
which the collie began to eat.

"To bed with ye now," Matilda ordered. "And Cara,
give me every stitch ye be wearing so your clothes can
be dried at the fire." Without further ado she shepherded
both children to the wagon.

Within moments Matilda was hanging her daughter's
apparel on the side of the wagon that faced toward the
fire. "I hadna' the heart to chastise them," she told her
husband when he joined her. "From the looks of them,
they were afrighted bad enough."

Together they led Thistle to the fire so she, too, could
dry out. "The hand of Providence still guides us," Innes
said somberly. "Five thousand miles we've come, and the
Almighty continues to protect us, just as He shielded the

ancient Israelites when He parted the waters of the Red Sea for them."

No one noticed the return of Asa Phipps and his cronies just before Sergeant Major Mullins posted the cavalry sentries for the night's watch.

Hector reported to his commanding officer that the posting was completed, and Lee nodded thoughtfully. "Now we've reached Texas, we'll triple the sentinels, Mullins," he said. "Ask Innes MacGregor for his list and start with the first group of sentries. We're pretty far from any civilized community here, and we don't have any idea where robber bands may be operating. We've heard confused stories about their whereabouts, and all I know for certain is that this train is going to draw robbers the way an overly ripe piece of fruit draws flies."

Hector saluted, went off to obtain the list from Innes, then stood near the fire and called out the names of those who would be required to join the bulk of the cavalry detachment in standing watch through the night.

Asa Phipps, somewhat the worse for wear after consuming considerable quantities of corn liquor, was dismayed when his name was called.

When his friends began to tease him, he cut them short by cursing them. "Go ahead, laugh," he told them. "In no time at all, you'll be asleep. I'm damned if I know why I've got to play at being a soldier."

"Them's the rules," one of the men said. "I don't know the reasons, neither, but General Blake made it plain for all to hear when he said that any man who shirks sentry duty when he's called will be punished."

"Damn him and damn his stupid rules," Phipps replied. All the same, he went to his wagon for his rifle, then placed himself in the open space between his own vehicle and the one that stood next to it in the circle.

A short time later Hector Mullins appeared, making the rounds as he placed the civilian sentries in position.

"I'm stayin' right here," Phipps told him. "I don't see why I've got to do all this in the first place."

"Because we could be robbed of everything we own, all of us," Hector replied curtly. "General Blake has explained it to everybody, and so has Innes MacGregor."

At the mention of the pair he hated, Phipps let loose with a stream of epithets.

Had Phipps been a soldier, Hector would have given him a beating rather than report him to higher authority. General Blake had made a point of ordering his troops not to become embroiled in fights with civilian members of the company, however. He supposed he would leave well enough alone, even though he would have given the disagreeable Kentuckian a place several wagons farther down the line. Controlling his temper, he moved away.

Asa Phipps leaned his rifle against the side of his wagon, propped his back against the rim of a rear wheel, and, in spite of the uncomfortable position, soon drifted off to sleep. The corn liquor had taken effect, and he was no longer able to stay awake.

By now most of the travelers had gone off to their wagons. Members of the wood detail tamped the fire, and soon the entire camp was quiet, with the silence occasionally broken only by the soft whinnying of a workhorse.

The moon disappeared beneath thick, black clouds, and the stars also vanished. The wind freshened, and a light drizzle began to fall. Some of the civilian sentries returned briefly to their wagons to obtain covering.

Phipps was dead to the world, unaware of the light rainfall. He had no idea that a band of a dozen men, attracted to his position by his soft snores, were crawling toward the opening between wagons through the high grass. Experience with past wagon trains had taught the robbers they could steal considerable quantities of goods if they entered a circle past a sentry who had dropped off to sleep, took what they could find very quickly, then left again by the same route.

Two men in the group broke into the circle by stepping over Phipps, who had slumped to the ground. A cavalryman posted farther down the sentry line caught a glimpse of several dark, alien shadows. "Who's there?" he called. "Identify yourselves!"

There was no reply, and the robbers tried to flatten themselves in the tall grass. But they were too late. Their reaction to the challenge branded them as guilty, and the cavalryman followed his instructions to the letter by firing a warning shot.

The sharp crack of his rifle so alarmed the two robbers who had entered the compound that they fled the way they had come, leaping over Phipps as they sprinted for safety.

Their appearance caused a half-dozen sentries to open fire, and one of the civilians, trying to do more than force the intruders to withdraw, took careful aim and squeezed the trigger of his rifle. The bandit stumbled and pitched forward. He lay motionless in the grass.

The entire band was so alarmed that all pretense was discarded. The men jumped to their feet and raced off to a dimly seen patch of woods, where they had left their horses. They were sent on their way by volleys of rifle shots. The fire of the cavalrymen was deliberately high, while that of most civilians was wild.

The Corporal was the first to examine the body of the dead bandit. He was soon joined by Sergeant Major Mullins, and a few moments later General Blake, carrying a pistol, and Innes MacGregor, a rifle in one hand, arrived simultaneously.

"The no-good bastards couldn't even wait until we pushed a way into Texas," the Corporal said, nudging the body at his feet with the toe of a boot. "This one paid with his life."

"The others got away?" Lee wanted to know.

"I believe so, sir. This is the only one I know for sure was hit."

"We'll leave his body," Lee said. "People who see it before we break camp tomorrow will know we weren't exaggerating about the dangers of the wilderness. It may be his friends will come in search of him and find his body. If not," he added, his voice hardening, "he'll feed the crows."

"Good work," Lee told the Corporal. "Keep your detail alert, although I think it highly unlikely that any robbers will return tonight, no matter how great their greed for loot."

"Yes, sir. It never pays for sentries to let down their guard." The Corporal saluted and returned to his duty post.

"That gunfire waked a good many people," Innes said, peering into the circle between two wagons.

"Before we go off to bed, we'll explain to them what's happened," Lee replied. "Otherwise, they'll soon be telling each other that we're under attack by rogue Indians, and the whole company will be in an uproar."

They laughed, then started back into the compound, but Hector Mullins halted abruptly and pointed. "Oh-oh," he said. "Look yonder, General."

Lee saw another body sprawled on the ground. "It appears our marksmen got more than one," he said.

Hector saw that the man's chest was moving up and down. "He's still breathing, sir," he said and dropped to one knee beside the body.

"He's been wounded, then?" Lee wanted to know.

The rancid smell of whiskey filled Hector's nostrils. "No, sir, he's dead drunk." He moved a shielding arm from the man's face. "It's that Phipps from Kentucky, General."

Lee and Innes stared down at Phipps, who continued to sleep, blissfully unaware of all that had been happening around him.

Hector rose to his feet and was unable to contain his indignation. "Sir, if one of our men got drunk on duty and passed out, you'd either send him before a firing squad or, at the least, ask a court-martial board to lock him away for twenty years!"

"I'm sorry to say that Phipps isn't in the army. Remove his name from the sentry roster. This is the point where two of the robbers broke into the camp, according to the Corporal's report. So it isn't too difficult to pin the blame for what might have turned into a disaster for our whole company." He sighed. "We'd better start passing along the news to the people who are milling around in there."

Hector immediately went off to attend to the task, but Innes touched Lee on the arm, delaying him. "Is there nought ye can do to give Phipps what he deserves?"

"As president of the wagon train," Lee said, "you could fine him. But I'd be surprised if he has any money in his purse. I suspect he owns nothing but his clothes and the few sticks of furniture he carries in his wagon."

"We can't let him go unpunished, Lee! Other men accept their responsibilities!"

"We still have a long way to go before we reach Austin," Lee said, "and it's true that the whole company will be upset if Phipps isn't rapped hard across the knuckles." He was lost in thought for some moments. "This is drastic, Innes, but it may do the trick. Give him a solemn, final warning. In the presence of every man, woman, and child in this train. Make it clear to him— and everyone else—that the very next time he breaks any rules or fails to fulfill his obligations to the rest of us, he'll be expelled from the wagon train."

Innes MacGregor was startled, but the thought appealed to him. "Ye be right when ye say that would be drastic. What would a man do if he was expelled?"

Lee shrugged. "He might fall in with bandits or be killed by them. He might go on alone to Austin, assuming he could make the rest of the journey by himself. Or he might die of starvation on the way. Countless fates await such a man, all of them unpleasant. Make all of that plain to Asa Phipps tomorrow, and there's at least a possibility he may behave until we disband."

VIII

Rick Miller led his band through a valley where, thanks to the exceptionally rich soil and spring rains, the grass was lush and thick, perfect for grazing. "The day will come," he said, "when immigrants from the United States will settle here and grow fine crops. This land is just begging to be settled."

They moved on to higher ground, a rocky plateau dotted with patches of pine woods as well as areas where nothing grew except clumps of cacti. The air was dry and clear, the days were hot beneath a burning sun, and the nights were as cold as the snow on the ever-present mountain peaks the party could see in the distance.

The scenery of New Mexico Province was breathtaking, but the men and the two weary women anxious to reach Texas were in no mood to enjoy the views as they rode steadily toward the east. The only aspect of the area that did impress the travelers was its isolation. There were no humans and few animals to be seen anywhere. The group lived principally on the fruits of their previous hunting, but when they finally drew closer to Texas, Rick allowed them to use limited quantities of their bacon, flour, and beans. Some food, he insisted, must be kept for possible emergencies.

Melissa and Nancy were fascinated by what Rick told

them were mesas. These were hills, many of them high, all with flat tops, looking as though a giant knife had sliced off their peaks. "When you see hills like these," he said, "you know you're in Arizona or New Mexico. I've hunted and trapped all over the West, and there's nothing like the mesas anyplace."

Gradually, as he pointed out to the party, there were subtle changes in the scenery. This was most evident in the woods; yellow pine continued to predominate, but now they also saw spruce, red fir, box elder, cedar, cottonwood, and occasionally scrub oaks.

Riding on a plateau, they made their way through a forest that was more lush than any they had encountered previously, then came to a slope that would take them into a river valley where the grass was thick enough for their mounts to graze. As they emerged from the wooded area, they were astonished to see a large party of Indians, armed with bows and arrows and wearing buckskins and clothes made of buffalo hide, sitting on the height opposite them. Even at a distance it was possible to make out the black and white war paint smeared on their faces. It was apparent that these men also intended to ride into the valley in order to feed their horses.

Melissa reacted instantly, instinctively, and raised her rifle to her shoulder. Before she could fire, however, an irritated Rick reached out and knocked the weapon from her hands. "Never shoot until I give you the word," he said angrily. "If you have eyes in your head, girl, you can see plain as day that we're badly outnumbered."

Melissa tried to defend herself. "They've seen us, too, you know. Our rifles are effective at a far longer range than their primitive weapons. Are you telling me we ought to wait until they slaughter us?"

"Just do what you're told," he said bluntly. "Now, follow me down into the valley, all of you. Forget you carry firearms. Don't make a single hostile gesture, or it will be our undoing."

He moved forward, slowly riding down into the valley. The thoroughly confused members of the party did the same, wanting to ask questions but knowing the time was inappropriate. The Indians, meantime, rode rapidly down the opposite slope.

"Wait here," Rick commanded.

He rode alone to the near bank of the small stream that meandered through the valley, then dismounted. A single Indian did the same. Each raised one arm in greeting, and then they began to speak in a tongue that neither Harry Canning nor any other member of the group could understand. Each made a long speech.

"What do you suppose they're saying?" Nancy whispered.

"As near as I can tell, they're exchanging greetings," her husband replied. "There's always a rigamarole like this when you talk with Indians instead of fighting them."

To the surprise of the entire party, Rick drew a knife from his belt and extended it hilt first across the narrow stream.

The Indian took it, then handed a knife to Rick.

The Ranger turned to his party. "Graze your horses now," he called. "But don't cross the river and don't stare at the warriors. They'll think you're being rude."

With great reluctance the group from Oregon dismounted and allowed their mounts to nibble on the green, thick grass. The Indians, scrupulously staying on their own side of the river, did the same. What made the situation stranger was that no one on either side of the river said a word. The silence was as deafening as it was extraordinary.

"Fill your canteens with water and water your mounts," Rick finally ordered. The party again followed instructions.

Then the Indians drank from the stream, led their horses to the river, and watered them. At a signal from their leader they mounted, crossed the stream, and, still not paying the slightest attention to the white men and women, rode away.

Rick waited until they were out of earshot before he spoke. "Those warriors," he said, "are Apache. I know of no tribe that's more warlike or more aggressive."

"They had no quarrel with you or with us, I take it," Harry said.

A glint of humor appeared in Rick's eyes. "That's because I convinced them we're all Texans. If they had thought we were Mexicans—if they'd even suspected the possibility—there would have been holy hell to pay. They have a grudge against Santa Anna, and when they see Mexicans, they start shooting without waiting to find out any details."

Nancy's sigh of relief was loud. "I was afraid we were in for trouble," she said.

Melissa made no comment but looked sheepish, able to understand now why Rick had been so annoyed when she had been on the verge of opening fire.

"They gave me a heap of valuable information," Rick said. "We're only a short distance from the Texas border now—about fifteen miles closer than I had estimated. Anyway, the senior warrior in charge of the party told me there are two Mexican cavalry units patrolling the area. One of them is dangerous. The Captain in charge believes all Texans who wander across the border, even innocently, are spies. If we run across his unit, we'll either have to try to make a dash across the border or stand and fight. I lean toward the probability that we'll have to exchange fire with them. A lot of fire."

"Why can't we outride them?" Melissa demanded.

The Ranger stared at her for a moment, his eyes cold. "If you really want to know," he said, "it's because you and Nancy are with us. There might be a chance for men to outride them. But there are no better horsemen on earth than Mexican cavalry. They can ride faster than old Beelzebub himself."

"I'm as good a rider as any man!" Melissa declared, flushing beneath her tan.

Rick refused to dispute the matter with her. Deliberately ignoring her, he spoke quietly. "The other patrol," he said, "is commanded by one of the most civilized men I've ever met. Lieutenant Cordova and I crossed swords twice when Texas fought Mexico and won her independence. I wouldn't call him a friend, exactly, but we'll

have a chance to get out of a scrape with our hides intact
if we run across him."

The members of the party listened intently.

"You're civilians, all of you," he went on, "but in the
present situation I want you to think of yourselves as
members of a military unit. Obey orders instantly and to
the letter. We're not going to rest for food or drink again
until we reach the soil of Texas. I want no talk. And,
Harry, I'll have to ask you not to smoke your pipe. We'll
be threading a needle for the rest of the day. And into
the night, too, if need be."

They were in a somber mood as they mounted their
horses and started forward again, with Rick, as usual, in
the lead. For several hours the countryside remained as
desolate as the countryside through which they had been
riding for so many days. In spite of the emptiness of
these open spaces, however, they became more tense,
realizing that at any moment a confrontation that could
mean life or death might develop.

Suddenly, as they were riding through the hills where
the vegetation was sparse, Rick halted. "There's cavalry
up ahead," he said.

For some moments his companions could see nothing,
and they wondered if his imagination had confused him.
Then they caught sight of faint clouds of dust that were
rising in the air, seemingly on the horizon. A few seconds later they were able to make out a party of horsemen, approaching at a full gallop.

"There are about fifty of them," Rick said, speaking as
though to himself. The others became even more uneasy.
"Check your firearms and make sure they're loaded," he
directed them. "Spread out. Allow about ten feet between those on your left and those on your right. Have
your arms ready to use, but don't even make a threat-
ening gesture unless I tell you to fire. Once I tell you to
open fire, do it! And when I tell you to press forward,
spur as fast as you can to a gallop. Any questions?"

They shook their heads, and no one spoke.

Melissa looked as though she relished the prospect of

taking part in a battle. After making certain that her rifle was loaded and ready for instant use, she also checked the pistol she carried in her belt. Then she grinned at Danny and winked at Chet. If she was frightened, she was doing a beautiful job of hiding her emotions.

"I hardly need to explain," Rick said, "that if the Mexicans open fire, you don't need any orders from me. Return that fire! And make every bullet count! If anything happens to me, Harry, you're in command, and good luck to you. Now, spread out!"

He watched them as they awkwardly accomplished the maneuver. Then Rick unslung his rifle and held it in both hands as he walked his horse forward slowly. As the cavalry troop continued to approach at a canter, he toyed with the idea of attaching a white handkerchief to the muzzle of his rifle and raising it so that unnecessary bloodshed could be avoided. Then he abandoned any thought of making the gesture. The Mexicans might misread it, thinking that he was surrendering to them.

The riders slowed their pace, then formed into a single, long line. As they drew to a halt they picked up their muskets, obviously ready for any trouble that might develop.

A single rider, wearing the insignia of an officer, moved forward to meet the Ranger. Rick breathed more easily when he saw that the man was a lieutenant rather than a captain. That meant the unit was Cordova's, so there was at least some hope that there would be no battle.

Rick raised his right hand in a gesture that was more of a friendly greeting than it was a salute.

Lieutenant Cordova responded with a crisp salute as he drew to a halt within speaking distance.

"We meet again," Rick said, sounding amiable.

"Indeed we do, Captain Miller. As usual, on the soil of my country." Cordova was not antagonistic, but his remark was nevertheless pointed.

Rick managed to look dismayed. "I must offer you my apologies and those of Texas, Lieutenant. I didn't realize we had strayed across the border until I saw your troop approaching us from the east. Then I knew."

The Lieutenant had a right to raise an eyebrow. If only a small fraction of the stories told about Captain Miller were true, he had a map of the border engraved in his mind, and it was unlikely that his crossing of the line had been accidental.

Rick guessed what the Mexican was thinking. "You will note, Lieutenant, that there are two ladies in my party." He paused to give the man time to confirm his statement.

Cordova studied the party that faced him, and realized that the Ranger was telling him the truth. "Never have I seen women in this region!"

"I'm embarrassed to tell you that they're the advance group for a new settlement we're establishing not far from the border," Rick explained.

"All are Texans?"

"I can't think of anybody else who'd consent to travel in these parts." Rick grinned, hoping that the officer would accept his bald lies.

Cordova knew something was amiss, but he was reluctant to place the Texans under arrest and take them to his immediate superior, much less to the headquarters of his regimental commander, which were located about one hundred miles to the south. The men might be tortured, and it was certain that the women would be violated. Texas would protest vigorously, and the precarious peace that existed between Mexico and Texas well might collapse. Cordova, who regarded himself as cultivated, didn't want to be responsible for the start of a new war in which thousands on both sides might be killed and wounded.

"I will confess to you, Captain Miller," he said, "that not long ago I myself ventured across the border into Texas by mistake. A half-battalion of troops was sent from Austin to expel me, but the major in command was kind enough to accept my apologies and explanation. I do not recall his name, but when you see him, be good enough to extend to him my regards and concern for his welfare. Tell him I am returning the compliment he paid to me."

Rick realized that, even though his story had been received skeptically, the Lieutenant was repaying Texas in kind for the treatment he himself had received.

Cordova raised his hand to the brim of his hat, then returned to his own line, where Sergeant Taloco spat on the ground in disgust when he learned that no attempt would be made to take this small party as prisoners.

Watching the Mexicans form a double rank and ride off, Rick was relieved that the troop was not passing close to his own party. Only Cordova knew he was escorting two women, and the soldiers might not have maintained their disciplined behavior if they had seen two attractive women so close at hand. Now his charges would be safe, and most important of all, he would be able to conduct Harry Canning to President Houston, fulfilling his assignment to the letter.

Melissa's eyes sparkled as they started forward again. Nancy fell in beside her. Most of the time she thought she understood Melissa, but there were moments—and this was one of them—when she felt perplexed. "You look as though you really enjoyed that near-battle."

"I did, every minute of it. I'd love to know what Rick said to the Mexican officer to convince him we weren't dangerous. But I'll never find out from Rick! I may not be able to decide the kind of man I want for the rest of my life, but I certainly know the type I don't want. Ugh!"

Nancy was still curious about her reaction to the confrontation. "What would you have done if the shooting had started?"

"I'd have shown Rick Miller and the rest of these men that I'm as good a marksman as any of them!" was the emphatic reply.

It was strange, Nancy thought. Melissa had the face and body of an adult, but in some ways she was still a child. Apparently she hadn't been in the least concerned that they had been in grave danger and well might have lost their lives.

* * *

John Tyler knew only too well, in spite of his dedication to his country and his hard work, that his term as President—one month short of four full years—would not go down in history as one of the most distinguished. But he was determined to leave his mark and, in the closing months of his presidency, was beginning to deal privately with the leaders of Congress. Regardless of whether James K. Polk or Henry Clay succeeded him, he wanted to be remembered as the man who brought Texas into the Union. With luck and the cooperation of the Senate and House of Representatives, he would succeed in achieving that goal.

In the meantime there were ways in which he could show his fellow citizens, as well as the rest of the world, that he was continuing to do everything in his power to help Texas defend herself and prepare for coming statehood. So he seized an opportunity to make an important, symbolic gesture.

A large presidential party that included Mrs. Tyler, Cabinet members and their wives, army officers, and members of the Congress who were sympathetic to the cause of Texas, left Washington City in a caravan of carriages. Escorted by a regiment of cavalry, the party traveled to the small town of Stroudsburg, Pennsylvania, where they stayed overnight, then traveled to nearby Kittatinny Mountain, where the Delaware River cut through solid rock to form the so-called Delaware Water Gap, regarded by many Americans as the gateway to the West. There thirty enormous, canvas-covered wagons, each of them double the size of an ordinary covered wagon and each pulled by a team of twenty mules, had been assembled.

In the wagons were the arms and munitions that the United States was sending to the Republic of Texas.

A score of reporters representing some of the most influential newspapers in the country had been persuaded to accompany the President, and before the formal ceremonies began, they were allowed to examine the contents of the wagons. Later they would write in glowing terms about the stacks of rifles and boxes of Colt revolving pistols, the cannon ranging from tiny three-pounders to fifteen-pounder howitzers, the largest guns ever manufactured in the United States. Only the wagons containing gunpowder were off-limits to the press, and pleasant but firm cavalrymen not only prevented anyone from peering into these wagons but also prevented the smoking of cigars or pipes in their vicinity.

Tyler's speech, like all of his public addresses, was short and graceful. "The people of America send greetings to their American brothers across the Texas border," he said. "The contents of these wagons are expressions of our hope and conviction that Texas soon will join the Union as our twenty-eighth state."

Then the President asked Major General Winfield Scott to send the wagons on their way. No one had ever accused the General of being modest, and he lived up to his customary image. The regiment of cavalry that would guard the wagons as far as the Texas border already sat in formation, the drivers and their assistants had mounted their boxlike seats, and the mules were ready to move. But, thanks to the presence of the press, General Scott felt compelled to make a rambling, thirty-minute oration before he shouted the awaited order, "Colonel, you may begin your march!"

The regimental adjutant shouted a command, and the cavalry started forward. Then the huge wagons began to roll as whips cracked over the heads of the mule teams. Soon the entire wagon train was moving slowly toward the southwest.

The formal ceremonies were at an end. A mild wine punch and sandwiches were served to the ladies, while a stronger libation was offered to the gentlemen. Members of the press were invited to join in the celebration, and every politician present cornered the reporters long enough to express his hearty approval of the arms shipment. Several of the newsmen made it unnecessary for General Scott to seek them out by going to him, instead.

"General," one of them wanted to know, "how will Santa Anna react when this train arrives in Texas?"

"I'm afraid I can't speak for President Santa Anna," the Army Chief of Staff replied, smiling.

"Do you suppose Mexico will declare war?"

"I would hope not. Texas is already an independent nation, and we have every right to negotiate with her concerning her admission to the Union. As you gentlemen already know, the President and the State Department are trying to purchase California from Mexico. You'll have to get the latest news on those talks from either the White House or the Secretary of State."

"Then you don't think we'll have war?"

"I sincerely hope not," Scott replied, but could not refrain from adding, "If it should come in spite of all our efforts to prevent it, however, you can rest assured that we'll be ready. Just as Texas also will be ready, thanks to this munitions train!"

Neither the immigrants to Texas from the East nor those from the Old World, like the MacGregors, had ever seen any country that was like this vast, unpopulated land. As far as anyone could see, looking in every direction toward the horizon across the endless prairie, there was no sign of human habitation. Teng was reminded of parts of China, but there was a significant difference.

"In the Middle Kingdom," he said, "there is much flat land, as much as in Texas. But there, also, are millions of people."

"The day may come when Texas is heavily populated," Lee Blake replied as they started toward the head of the column after the noon rest. "But this particular area is even emptier than the Nebraska country. Not one person lives within at least one hundred miles in any direction from this spot!"

As the wagons moved into line, a frowning Cathy came to her husband. "Beth isn't feeling well," she said.

"What's wrong with her?"

"An upset stomach, probably, I really don't know."

"Let's hope she'll get over it by tonight," he said, and a few moments later the caravan was under way.

By the time the wagons halted and formed into a circle late in the afternoon, however, Beth's condition was much worse. Her face was flushed, she was running a high fever, and her eyes were glazed. Too sick to communicate, she huddled beneath her blankets in the wagon, shivering and moaning.

"Have you given her any medicine?" Lee asked as he joined his wife and stood looking down at the little girl.

"I wouldn't know what to give her," Cathy said.

He knew what she was thinking. Having lost one baby, she was apprehensive for Beth.

A short time later they were joined by Matilda Mac-Gregor, who seemed to know what she was doing as she examined the sick child. "When my Cara was a wee one, about Beth's age," she said, "she had a fever that seemed to have been much like this."

Cathy could only nod. "We didn't realize how lucky we were to have Dr. Bob Martin with us on the wagon train to Oregon. How I miss a physician on this train."

Lee knew it would serve no useful purpose to remind her that most wagon trains made their journeys without enjoying the presence of a doctor. "What was Cara's ailment?" he asked Matilda.

The Scotswoman shrugged. "We never did find out. All I can tell ye is that we wrapped her in wet blankets for a whole night to bring down her fever."

"Obviously the treatment was effective," Cathy said.

"Aye." Matilda seemed reluctant to pursue the matter.

Her uneasiness increasing, Cathy said, "She's a healthy girl now."

"There's none healthier."

"Matilda, you're holding something from us."

"Aye, that I am. I didn't want ye overly worried, but ye have a right to know the truth. About a year after Cara was ill—maybe a bit longer than that—a physician from Edinburgh was visiting our district, so Innes and I made it our business to see him. He told us we enjoyed God's good grace, that Cara well might have died that night. I don't want to frighten ye, but it would be wrong not to tell ye."

Cathy paled and clenched her fists.

"What medication would the physician from Edinburgh have given Cara if he'd seen her when she was ill?" Lee asked.

The Scotswoman shrugged. "He didna say. This is a sickness that strikes young girls more than boys, when they be two or three. That's all I know."

Lee hurried off, returning with two pails of water.

"I'll help ye wrap her," Matilda said. "After ye've soaked a blanket in water, make sure ye squeeze the liquid from it before ye bundle the child."

"Why is that?" Cathy asked, trying to prevent her voice from trembling.

"Now ye know all I know." Matilda showed her how to prepare a blanket, supervised the wrapping of the little girl, and then, not wanting to intrude, returned to her own wagon. "If ye need me," she said, "I'll be back."

Lee lighted an oil lamp, which he placed inside the wagon, then sat on the back steps beside his wife as they watched Beth, whose face was even more flushed and whose breathing was shallow and labored. "Do you want me to bring you some supper from the cooking fire?"

Cathy shook her head. "You go and eat."

"I'm not hungry, either." He placed an arm around her shoulders.

They sat in silence for a long time, and then, when the damp blanket became warm and they replaced it with another they had cooled, Cathy finally spoke. "Oh, Lee—" She broke off, steadying herself. "I'm no coward, but I'm so frightened. If only we had a physician on this train."

"I've been debating whether to ride off in search of one. I'd send someone, but no one has my stamina, and even my troops might get lost in this prairie. I'd have to do it myself."

"Do you suppose you could find a physician?'"

He sighed. "That's the problem. I'd have to ride at least one hundred miles before I'd come to the first farms and ranches, and perhaps as far again before finding a physician. It might take days to bring him back here with me. Besides, I'm responsible for all the people on the train. I'd be neglecting my duty if I let them sit here in the middle of nowhere, while I hunt for a doctor."

Cathy, realizing he faced an impossible dilemma, put her hand in his. "Do whatever you think best," she said. "I'll support that decision."

No man could have asked for greater loyalty.

Again neither spoke for a long period. "I'm not sure whether she's sleeping or unconscious," Cathy ultimately said.

"Well, she's resting."

Lee's attempt to comfort her was clumsy, but she was grateful for it and smiled at him.

His grin was equally feeble. "One way or another, Cathy, things will work out for us," he said without conviction.

"They will!" He was strong in so many ways, but now she had to show the strength that only a woman could display in this kind of a crisis.

Lee studied the sick child again, noting that she was no better but did not seem worse. "I'm damned if I stay and damned if I go off to find a doctor," he said.

Cathy replied in a low but surprisingly steady voice. "Stay," she said. "If Beth is going to die, she'll be gone long before you can bring a physician back with you."

"I could never stop blaming myself if she doesn't pull through."

Cathy had seen him face physical danger without flinching on many occasions, yet in this situation his uncertainty seemed greater than her own. "You'll blame no one, any more than I would. Besides, I'm not giving up hope."

His jaw jutted forward. "Neither am I."

"Time to change the blanket again."

They took temporary refuge in activity.

It was odd, Cathy reflected as they seated themselves on the steps again and resumed their vigil, that in spite of all their intimacy, she and Lee had never been closer than they were right now. This crisis, in ways she could not understand, was making their relationship even deeper and more enduring than it had been.

Others in the train were aware of the situation but refrained from disturbing the concerned parents.

For hour after endless hour Cathy and Lee sat and watched Beth, their hands clasped, neither of them moving except when it was time to dampen another blanket. Shortly before dawn, while Lee finished wringing a blanket and Cathy began to unwrap the child, she said, "Her fever has gone down." She spoke quietly.

Lee was drained, too. He felt Beth, then nodded. "She feels normal to me."

Before she could reply, Beth opened her eyes. "Mama," she announced in a weak but clear voice, "I'm hungry."

Cathy's peal of relieved laughter awakened Matilda MacGregor in the adjoining wagon. "I'll give you a drink of water, Bethie," she said.

The little girl drank thirstily, then repeated, "I'm hungry!"

Matilda heard the demand as she approached. "Bless her," she said. "She'll be fit again before the day ends. Give her some bread. And when breakfast is ready," she added, pointing toward the fires, where some of the women were already at work preparing the morning meal, "you might let her have a bowl of porridge."

Lee hastily fetched a slice of bread. Beth sat up, munched happily, and then said, "Mama, you're crying."

Cathy hastily brushed tears from her face.

"So are you, Papa," the child said in wonder. Never had she known her father to weep.

Lee was unashamed. "Bethie," he said, "when you grow older, you'll understand there are times that adults are so filled with joy they can't help crying." He turned to Cathy, a lift in his voice. "Do you want me to find someone who'll drive the wagon for you so you can rest this morning?"

"I should say not! I've never felt better in my life." She looked at him anxiously. "Perhaps you should give instructions to someone who can take the lead. You ought to take a nap."

"I'm the wagonmaster of this train, and I'll ride in my usual place," he replied exuberantly. "I don't know when I've had more energy."

Others in the company later remarked, in private, that the General and his wife were remarkable people. The march went on, Beth recovered quickly, and the wagons slowly inched their way through the prairie wilderness.

As Lee Blake led the wagon train ever closer to Austin, the pioneers saw increasing signs of civilization. One day they rode past a ranch, and some cheered when they saw cattle in the fields. Forty-eight hours later they halted their day's march at the side of a small lake, and a number of the pioneers became aware of a farmhouse in the distance. A short time later the farmer himself made an appearance, giving the future settlers their first taste of Texas hospitality when he invited all those who intended to go into farming themselves to accompany him on an inspection of his property before sundown.

Innes and Matilda MacGregor were among the first to accept, and they spent the remaining daylight hours going through the fields, then joining the farmer and his wife in the oversized kitchen of their large, sparsely furnished house, asking many questions. Night was falling by the time they returned to the circle of wagons.

Innes went to find Lee for their daily, brief conference regarding the planned march for the following day, and Matilda returned to their wagon. The cooking fires had been lighted, and the Scotswoman frowned when she saw two small fires already burning near the wagon. The children had no authority to light fires of their own, and her concern deepened as she increased her pace.

Two of the girls were busily stirring the contents of

large iron pots under Heather's direction, while Cara
and Wallace, each armed with a sharply pointed stick,
occasionally jabbed at a prone figure.

Matilda stopped short, stunned when she saw Asa
Phipps lying face down, his ankles and wrists tightly
bound. She was horrified and outraged when she saw
that his breeches and underwear had been pulled down
to his calves, exposing his bare buttocks.

"Miz MacGregor," he pleaded, "make these young
she-devils let me loose."

"We told you to be quiet!" Cara exclaimed, and she
and Wallace jabbed him enthusiastically with their sharp
sticks.

Matilda found her voice. "Heather, what's the meaning of this disgraceful scene?"

Fifteen-year-old Heather smiled beatifically. "Good
evening, Ma," she said in a tranquil voice. "In this pot
we're making a purple dye out of some plants that Mrs.
Mullins showed us. And in the other pot we're boiling
pitch. When we're ready, we're going to vote." She
pointed in the direction of the helpless Phipps. "We'll
decide whether to dye him or tar and feather him.
Maybe," she added brightly, "we'll do both."

Matilda spluttered, unable to find the right words.

Ginny Mullins emerged from her own wagon and
sauntered toward the Scotswoman. "I had a hand in all
this, Matilda," she said, and she, too, was tranquil.

"You did? I don't understand!" Matilda was ashen. "I
don't know what kind of a game the girls—"

"It's no game, Ma," Heather interrupted.

"I'd best explain," Ginny said. "That vile worm,
Phipps, made advances to Heather. The younger children came to me for help. So I diverted his attention
by—by flirting with him myself." She paused, then gig-
gled. "While he was paying attention to me, the girls
threw him to the ground and tied him up. It was quite a
sight. I told them about making the dye from some
wildflowers growing over yonder, but the pitch was
their own idea. Your daughters are wonderfully inven-
tive and imaginative, Matilda. You have every right to be

proud of them. Now you know why I enjoy their company so much."

Phipps groaned. "Please, Miz MacGregor. Have mercy
on me."

Wallace and Cara poked him hard with their
sticks.

Thistle edged closer to the man, growling menacingly
as she stood near his head, ready to leap on him if he
tried to escape.

Matilda digested what she had heard, shook her head,
and then turned to her eldest daughter. "He actually
made advances to ye, Heather?" she demanded.

"Yes, Ma." The girl spoke quietly, a hint of deep anger
in her voice. "He came up behind me and grabbed me. I
couldn't have fought him off alone, but the girls and
Thistle heard me, and they went to fetch Mrs. Mullins.
You know the rest."

The tiny Scotswoman stood erect. "Ginny," she said,
"I'm much obliged to ye for the assistance ye've rendered."

"Stir harder," Heather told her sisters.

Matilda stared off into space across the vast Texas
plains. "Does the purple dye last, Ginny?"

"Well, I used a batch some years ago to dye an old
dress. I got a bit of the dye on my hands, and it took
weeks to wash off, even though I scrubbed my hands
more times a day than I could count."

"Use the dye first," Matilda said, making a decision.
"Then ye can tar and feather him. I'll give ye an old
pillow that's near worn out. It still has feathers a-plenty
in it."

"No!" the tormented Phipps screamed.

Thistle barked at him, and Wallace gave him an even
harder jab with her stick.

Innes approached. "What's all this?" he called, his
smile fading as he took in the scene.

Matilda and Ginny hastened to explain. The Scotsman
stood very still, listening intently, his face wooden.
When the women stopped speaking, he turned to his
eldest daughter, his manner stern. "Ye tell the truth,

child? This isn't just mischief that ye've dreamed up for the entertainment of your sisters?"

Heather was upset. "I've never lied to ye since I was Wallace's age and ye took a strap to me, Pa. And well do ye know it."

The other children began to clamor, supporting their sister, but Innes silenced them with a curt gesture. "Matilda," he said, speaking so softly that they could barely hear him, "get ye into the wagon. Girls, go wi' Ma. Ginny, I'll be obliged if ye will withdraw, too."

No one moved.

"There will be no dyes used and no pitch boiled today," he said. "Now do what ye've been told."

Matilda reluctantly shepherded her daughters into their wagon, and Ginny accompanied them.

"Call Thistle, too," Innes called. "I wouldn't want her to do any damage to Mr. Phipps."

Heather sounded pained as she called the dog.

Innes drew a knife, then swiftly cut the ropes that bound the Kentuckian's ankles and wrists. "Haul up your breeches, man," he ordered.

Asa Phipps scrambled to his feet, his mud-caked face scarlet as he pulled up his breeches and buckled his belt. "Thanks, MacGregor," he said. "The females in your family have mighty warped senses of humor. They'll be in real trouble if you don't control them." He started to sidle away.

Innes reached out quickly, a heavy hand descending onto the man's bony shoulder. "Not so fast," he thundered, raising his voice for the first time.

Phipps saw his expression and became alarmed. "Let me go!"

The Scotsman examined him slowly, looking him up and down in obvious disgust.

"It was all a mistake. A misunderstanding," Phipps stammered. "I was being playful, that's all, and the girl jumped to the wrong conclusions."

"Ye made advances to my daughter." Innes sounded as though he were pronouncing a sentence. "And her still a wee one who has ne'er been kissed by a man."

Badly frightened, Phipps tried to break free, but the huge hand continued to grasp his shoulder.

"I hate bullies," Innes declared. "So I've ne'er used my fists in anger on one who is smaller and weaker than I am. But I've ne'er known a man so low that he'd assault a girl child. Defend yourself, Phipps!" Suddenly he released his grip.

The Kentuckian tried to dart away, but Innes grasped him by the front of his shirt with one hand. "I warned ye," he said, and his other fist smashed into the man's face with such force that he drew blood. "If ye be a man, fight like a man!" Again he loosened his grip.

Phipps tried to defend himself, but he was facing an infuriated father whose wrath would not be denied. A hard punch in his stomach doubled Phipps over, and a blow to the chin promptly straightened him. Innes showed him no mercy, rocking him with solid lefts and rights to the face, then sending him crashing to the ground with a devastating blow that smashed into his cheekbone.

Phipps lay still on the ground, moaning loudly.

Innes made certain, however, he had not lost consciousness. "Ye were told the last time ye caused a bother," he said, "that ye'd be expelled from this train the next time ye made trouble. I'll give ye until suppertime to hitch up your team, take your wagon, and be gone. Aye, and good riddance to ye, man. If ye should still be here when we're called to supper, spoiling the appetite of decent people, I'll have ye clapped in chains for the rest of our journey."

Phipps painfully dragged himself to his feet, then tottered off in the direction of his own wagon. He did not doubt that MacGregor had meant every word. Somehow, he had to pull himself together and leave this accursed wagon train without delay, or he would arrive at Austin in manacles. Cursing under his breath, he vowed vengeance against his assailant, but he knew that his threats were hollow.

Innes stood with his arms folded, making no move until he saw the Kentuckian round up his mules, harness

them, and, not daring to look back, pull out of his place
in the circle. "Girls!" the Scotsman bellowed.

The children appeared so quickly that he knew they
had been watching from the safety of the wagon. "Empty the vile brews from those pots before ye ruin honest
metal," he said sharply. "We'll have need of the pots
when we make our new home."

His daughters immediately busied themselves, with
Heather directing the operation, as usual, and doing the
better part of the work herself. She, like her sisters,
couldn't help giggling. Their father watched them, his
gaze stern, but he could not keep a straight face, and at
last he chuckled.

Heather threw herself into his arms. "Oh, Pa! Ye were
wonderful! Every time ye hit him it made me feel less
embarrassed."

"Now, now," Innes said, patting her. "There's no need
to make a fuss." He held her at arm's length. "Would ye
really have painted the rogue's backside purple and then
tarred and feathered him?"

"Aye," she replied calmly.

He shook his head, then laughed more loudly. "Wife,"
he called, "Ginny and ye may come out now. Just knowing this young spitfire is our daughter gives me an
appetite fit for a king. Lass, I'm proud of ye, but I don't
envy the man ye'll marry when ye be full grown. He'll
ne'er tame ye, that's for certain!"

Two church steeples stood out against the horizon,
and soon the buildings of bustling, growing Austin could
be seen by Rick Miller and his weary companions. The
Ranger rode into town at the head of the little procession
and, waving to a number of acquaintances, took his
party directly to headquarters. There he learned about
rooms available for them in a new barracks for a company of Rangers just being formed, so he conducted them
to the place, then hurried to the office of President
Houston to report their arrival.

Sam Houston listened without comment to the succinct recital, but it was obvious that he was pleased.

"Well done, Miller," he said. "How soon can I see Harry Canning?"

"I'll fetch him right now, sir."

A short time later Harry was ushered into the bare, plain room.

Houston grinned at him. "You have no idea how happy I am to see you," he boomed.

Harry smiled in return. "No happier than I am to be here, Mr. President," he replied.

"Tonight I want you and your wife to have supper with me. And bring along the other young lady who stowed away. I'm eager to meet women with that kind of courage. They sound like they're already Texans." Wasting no time, he got down to business. "How soon will you be ready to start to work?"

"I'm ready now, Mr. President."

"Good. I'll escort you to Galveston Island myself. We'll leave first thing tomorrow." Houston leaned forward in his chair. "How long will it take you to start producing warships for me?"

It was evident to Harry that the President knew nothing about the building of ships. "That depends on how much help I have, the size of the ships you want, and the availability of raw material, sir."

"We've been collecting oak timber for you. I know very little about ships, but I've been told oak is the best. I think we've stored enough of it to keep you busy for a long time to come. As to trained manpower, my recruiters have been searching for shipwrights and carpenters for the past ninety days. Will almost five hundred men be enough for you?"

Harry began to realize that everything in Texas was done on a mammoth scale, and he laughed. "With five hundred men, sir, I can build a whale of a lot of ships by early next year."

Nancy Canning was astonished when her husband returned to their temporary quarters wearing a gold-braided bicorne and a loose-fitting tunic with the twin silver epaulets of a commodore on his shoulders.

"A tailor has taken my measurements," he told her, "and my uniforms will be sent to me. They do things in a hurry in Texas, but it appears that I'll be in more of a rush than anybody else!"

The following morning the Oregonians left Austin with Sam Houston and a small cavalry escort. The road that led to the Gulf of Mexico was broad and in fairly good condition; according to the President, it was the best in the country.

After an uneventful journey, the party arrived at the Gulf and saw heavily wooded Galveston Island standing a short distance off the shore.

"The harbor is first-rate," Houston said as they were ferried to the island. "I've allowed no permanent construction work to be done until you got here and could pick your own sites for shipbuilding, the location of the harbor, and so forth. The men are all living temporarily in tents." He doffed his hat to Nancy and Melissa. "As you'll be doing, ladies, with my apologies, until more substantial houses can be raised for you."

"After sleeping on the ground every night, all the way from California to Texas, Mr. President," Nancy replied, "I can assure you a tent will be positively luxurious."

The men who would build the ships of the Texas navy and the men who would sail them lined the shore, cheering when they recognized Sam Houston on board the raft. Nancy and Melissa attracted immediate attention, and Harry frowned when he realized they were the only women on the island. Their presence could create complications, but he had to devote himself exclusively to the task ahead, at least for the present.

Sam Houston took his leave after assuring Harry that supplies of food and water, nails, and any other hardware he might require would be sent daily from the mainland. "If there's anything you want but don't have," he said, "just let me know. And one way or another, I'll see you get it. Good luck, and may you prosper here."

Now there was work to be started, and Harry summoned all of the volunteers to a meeting. "The regular workday will begin at dawn and end at sunset," he announced. "Bonuses will be paid to anybody who wants to keep going for a few more hours." Turning slightly, he addressed only the shipwrights and carpenters. "How many of you are married?"

About fifty men raised their hands.

"Send for your wives, if you like," he told them. "The ferry that will bring us supplies tomorrow will take your letters. And by the time the ladies get here, I hope we'll have ample housing for them." Not only would the spirits of the married men improve, Harry reasoned, but the presence of Nancy and Melissa would become a far less acute problem.

Nancy and Melissa helped the men who served as cooks prepare the evening meal, but it was long after dark when Harry finally appeared at the tent they had been given.

"I've saved some beef stew for you," Nancy told him. "Shall we go to the cooking fire?"

"I'll be with you shortly," he replied. "I want to make some notes to myself about tomorrow."

Nancy watched him for a moment, smiled, and went off for his meal, returning shortly with a large bowl of stew and a mug of steaming coffee.

Harry ate hungrily but somewhat absently, still reviewing the day's activities in his mind, and not until he had eaten did he begin to relax. "Well," he asked, "how do you like your new home?"

"I'll like it—once we move into it," Nancy said.

He grinned at her. "It won't take as long as you think. We have two hundred men working on housing and almost five hundred on the shipyard." He paused, then asked sharply, "Where's Melissa?"

"In her own tent," she replied, "right next to this one."

He rose to his feet. "I want to make good and sure that she stays there for the night. With seven hundred men roaming the island, she could get into all kinds of trouble."

"She isn't that foolish," Nancy replied. "Besides, Danny and Chet have put up their tent only a few feet from

Melissa's. They came back here a little earlier, and they haven't allowed her out of their sight."

Harry pondered for a time. "I've already given orders," he said, "that our cabin is to be twice the size of any other house. Not only because of my rank and responsibility. Melissa," he said authoritatively, "is going to live with us."

The keels of the first two miniature clippers were laid less than a week after Harry's arrival, and he put the more experienced shipwrights and carpenters to work on these vessels. Thanks to the size of his work crews, the clippers began to take shape quickly.

The Canning house was ready for occupancy a scant ten days after the arrival of the new Commodore. Nancy and Harry moved in, heartened by the arrival of a brass bed, a sofa, and other luxuries that the always thoughtful Sam Houston sent them as gifts.

Melissa moved in with them, and Nancy had a word with her in private. "Harry will send you packing if you don't behave yourself, and he means it," Nancy warned her.

Suddenly frightened, Melissa asked, "Where would I go?"

"He doesn't know, and he doesn't care. He's building ships now, and soon he'll start training his crews, so nothing else matters to him. When Harry has something on his mind, he becomes a demon. So watch what you do, Melissa."

The redheaded girl made no protest, doing her best not to flirt with anyone other than the faithful Chet and Danny. For the present she was taking great care to behave properly.

During the next few days, the wives of the married men began to arrive at the island, sometimes as many as three or four on a single day. So Melissa felt less exposed. An expert seamstress, she went to work with the sailmakers and tried hard to remain as inconspicuous as she could.

Those efforts were not completely successful, howev-

er. She was exceptionally attractive and continued to
draw the attention of the single men. Their interest in
her aroused Chet Harris's concern and jealousy, and at
times, as he functioned as one of Harry's roving foremen,
he heard some of the workers discussing the girl.

His tension mounting, Chet went to her one day at
sundown and was pleased to find she was alone in the
large main room of the Canning cabin, lighting a pair of
oil lamps. She greeted him warmly, which encouraged
him, and as soon as she finished lighting the lamps and
sat down opposite him, he lost no time expressing the
thoughts that were on his mind.

"Melissa," he said, "I'm earning only token pay here,
as you know."

"Your food and housing are paid for," she replied
without guile, "so you don't really need much money."

"But I do. For what I have in mind. All I'm trying to
say is that by this time next year, after I establish a claim
of my own to land and begin to work it, I should be in
good financial shape."

"I imagine you will." She had no idea why he was
confiding in her.

"You agree that I have a future. Good." Chet clenched
his fists and leaned forward tensely in his chair. "You
know how I feel about you. So I'm asking you right
out—will you marry me?"

His blunt proposal was so unexpected that, for a
moment, Melissa was at a loss for words. "I—I don't
know what to answer," she murmured.

"One word will take care of it," he replied, trying to
smile. "Yes."

She took a deep breath to steady herself. "You—you
know how much I like you and enjoy being with you,
Chet. And there's nobody I like more than you. But I'm
not ready to settle down yet."

He was bitterly disappointed.

"I wouldn't be honest if I pretended I'm in love with
you," Melissa went on, speaking more rapidly now that
she had started to explain. "I'm not in love with any-

body. Which isn't to say I'll always feel this way. For all I know I could fall in love with you next month or next week or even tomorrow."

Chet tried to speak calmly. "You mean there's a chance you'll marry me eventually?"

"Of course. A very good chance. In the meantime, I'm flattered, naturally."

He sprang to his feet and hooked his thumbs in his belt. "Just so nobody else has an advantage over me, I reckon I'll have to be satisfied. For now."

Melissa stood, too, and walked with him to the door. "I won't forget this, Chet. And if it should happen that I fall in love with someone else, which I don't expect to happen, I'll be honest and tell you right off."

"That's fair." He stood at the door for a moment, wondering whether he dared to kiss her.

She knew what was going through his mind, but offered him no encouragement. It was fun to flirt, but this was a serious situation, and her private code of honor would not permit her to fool someone who was vulnerable. With slow deliberation she extended a hand to him, and her smile, for once, was demure.

Ordinarily Chet told Danny Taylor virtually everything about his activities and feelings. But the relationship with Melissa was different. Chet well knew that Danny's interest in her was as great as his own, so he made no mention of his proposal or Melissa's response. His good friend was his rival, and he wasn't forgetting it.

So Danny, unaware of what had taken place, struggled with his own emotions. Slower to act and far more careful in his approach to other people, he was as sensitive as his friend to the interest of the bachelors on Galveston Island to the flamboyantly pretty Melissa Austin. Examining his own feelings as analytically as he could, he guessed that he loved her. At least, he knew, he had never been drawn so forcibly to any other girl.

Ultimately, he decided the time had come to clear the air. So he made it his business, one day at noon, to end his morning's work as a roving foreman near the cabin where the sailmakers were cutting and sewing canvas. And when Melissa stopped her morning's labors for the pause when everyone halted to eat, he was on hand.

"I've already picked up your food for you," he told her. "Let's go off to a little clearing in the woods to eat."

"How nice," Melissa said. "That will be like a picnic."

When they reached the clearing, he spread a bandanna on the grass for her, then produced a container of tea. "This is only lukewarm," he said, "but it's better to drink than nothing."

"You're very thoughtful," Melissa said. He was even more somber than usual, and her instinct told her this was not a time to flirt with him.

"I've had to be thoughtful of others," he replied modestly. "I guess you know I was an orphan—"

"You mentioned it once, but that's about all you said."

"Well, I never knew my parents. The first things I remember were at the orphanage. I stayed there for a few years. Then they got rid of me by selling me as a bound boy. To an old, no-good miser. I ran away and joined the first wagon train to Oregon. Ted Woods, who is now the top blacksmith out in Oregon, was good to me. And so was Chet's Ma. Mrs. Harris, she was back then."

Melissa wondered why he was telling her in detail about the past, which he had always taken care not to discuss.

"I've always looked forward to the day when I'd have a home and family of my own," he said. "That's one of the reasons, really, that I left Oregon. Oh, I was getting my fair share of the profits from the Harris farm. But I've had it in the back of my head that maybe I could do better for myself down here in Texas. And I will. Although it may take some time before I get organized. First off, I've got to help Harry Canning as long as he needs me."

Melissa had the uncomfortable feeling that he, like Chet, was going to propose to her.

"I want to tell you something and ask you something," Danny said awkwardly. "Melissa, I think I'm in love with you. I wouldn't swear it for sure because I've never been in love before. I thought you ought to know."

Her heart went out to him, and she nodded gravely. "Thank you, Danny."

"If you fancy somebody else—Chet, for instance— that's your right and your privilege. Naturally, I hope you lean in my direction. I can tell that you aren't in love with me. Or with Chet. Or with anybody else—"

"How do you know all that?" She couldn't help challenging him.

Danny shrugged. "Blamed if I know. But it's easy enough to study people and get a pretty fair idea of what they're really thinking and feeling."

He was a far shrewder judge of human nature than she had suspected. That was what came of having had to depend only on himself nearly all his life.

"Anyway," he said, "I figured it was only right and proper to tell you how I feel."

"You've been honest with me, and I've got to be the same with you." Melissa's meat and bread were forgotten. "You're right, Danny. I'm not in love with you or anyone else. But there's no one I like more than you. Or Chet, either. I'd be hard put to it if somebody held a gun to my head right this minute and said I had to marry one of you right off. I don't think I could make that choice."

Danny looked hard at her. "That's good enough for me," he said. "There's no way of telling what's going to happen here after we get the ships built for the Texans. Maybe there will be a war, and maybe there won't. Maybe I'll decide to throw in my lot with Harry and stay in shipbuilding. Or I might want to get myself some property and start a ranch. I'd like that better than farming. By the time I'm settled, I reckon you'll have a better idea of where you stand. So will I. If you and I ever get married, it will be just for one reason. Because we want to spend the rest of our lives together."

Impulsively she reached for his hand, squeezed it, and smiled at him without artifice. One thought that came to her mind forcibly was that Danny was more mature than Chet and more adult in his approach to life than she herself had ever been. Marriage to Chet might be more pleasurable, but she knew that no woman could hope for a steadier, more reliable husband than Danny. The woman who won him would be getting a prize, and she hoped her heart would respond to him as her mind had already done. Harry might think her fickle, but he had no idea how difficult it was for her to decide what she really wanted in life.

In his eagerness to send vessels to sea, Harry had virtually forgotten the personal needs of his crews. But in response to Nancy's urging, he finally gave his men a two-day holiday, the first rest period they had known since he had joined them. A number of the workers, including some of the married men and their wives, celebrated by going off to the mainland. Harry elected to remain on the island, however, so he could utilize the lull to good advantage by determining what timber, copper, and other materials he would require in the weeks ahead.

At his request, Chet Harris and Danny Taylor stayed on the island, too, in order to help him make his inventory. As usual, they were at work soon after daybreak.

Melissa enjoyed the almost-forgotten luxury of sleeping very late. The house seemed deserted when she awakened. A short time later, after she had dressed, she was surprised to find Nancy in the kitchen outbuilding, which they ordinarily used only to prepare simple breakfasts. At the moment Nancy was very busy scrubbing potatoes.

"Are we having a party?" Melissa asked, thinking she was being amusing.

"You guessed right," her friend replied. "We've been eating those tasteless suppers at the mess hall almost every night. Today you and I have the time to prepare a real meal for Harry and his chief helpers, so we're going to surprise them this evening. Yesterday I paid the boatman who brings the supplies by ferry for some

extras, and he had everything here early, soon after
Harry went off to work."

"Potatoes. Lettuce. Peas. Steak."

"Yes, and a vanilla and chocolate cake for dessert.
Suppose you pound the beefsteak and shell the peas. I'll
have another job for you a little later."

Melissa rolled up the sleeves of her shirtdress and
plunged in, shelling peas with a vengeance before she
took a mallet to the fresh beef.

At noon the two young women paused for a light meal
of salad greens, and Nancy said, "I wonder if you'd mind
taking a walk to the fishing village for some shrimp. Get
about four or five pounds, and be sure you don't let them
charge you more than five cents a pound."

"Indeed I won't! We had shellfish in Oregon, remember, so the fishermen can't cheat me the way they do the
farm folk."

A path had been worn through the woods to the
village where the dilapidated shacks of the fishermen
were located, and Melissa walked there briskly. The sky
overhead was clear, the air was balmy, and the sun was
shining in a cloudless sky. This would have been a
perfect day for a picnic on the vast expanses of yellow
sand that faced the Gulf of Mexico. Perhaps, after the
first warships for the Texas navy were built, manned,
and went to sea, there would be time for such personal
outings.

In the village Melissa haggled with two fishermen,
playing one against the other, and was pleased with
herself because she was able to buy five pounds of
large shrimp for a total price of twenty-two cents. The
transaction took only a few minutes, so she decided to
treat herself by returning to the Canning house by way
of the beach on the south shore of the island.

The water was even calmer than usual, and there was
almost no surf. The sand was so warm underfoot that
Melissa gave in to impulse, removed her shoes and
stockings, and walked barefooted. Weather like this
made her glad she had come to Texas, although, much as
she hated to admit it to herself, she sometimes regretted

having left Oregon. Life here was basic, far more primitive than it had been in the growing town on the Columbia River, which was what she had anticipated. What she hadn't expected was the daily drudgery, the endless hours of hemming stiff canvas with a heavy needle and thick thread until her fingers ached. Others might regard life on the Texas frontier as romantic, but there had been no real excitement since Rick Miller had conducted his party here from California.

Lost in thought and basking in the sun, Melissa paid scant attention to her surroundings until she heard the shouts of men and the sounds of axes biting into wood. Too late she realized she had come upon a work party of volunteers who were using their holiday to cut down trees that would be used as planking on the decks of Harry's ships.

"Look who's here, boys! The redhead!" a man shouted in a deep baritone.

Someone cheered, all work halted, and within a few moments Melissa found herself surrounded by ten or twelve grinning men, most of them still carrying their axes, all of them stripped to the waist.

Aware that her hair was in disarray, she made a futile attempt to pat it into place, then hastily closed a button that had popped open at the neckline of her dress.

On second thought, perhaps she should have left it open. She enjoyed being surrounded by so many admirers. Impulsively, she smiled first at one, then at another, flirting effectively but impartially. The men began to edge closer.

This was fun, Melissa thought, and although an inner voice warned her not to become too friendly, she ignored the thought. There were so many men in the crowd that no harm could come to her.

"I've had my eye on you for a long time," one of the men said.

"Well," she replied, "I'm flattered."

Another muttered something she couldn't hear, and several of his companions laughed coarsely.

All at once Melissa realized there was a great more

than innocent interest in her. These men, who had not spent time with women for many weeks, were looking at her hungrily.

A slow chill traveled up her spine. Perhaps she had gone too far. She was the better part of two miles from the Canning cabin, separated from the main town of the shipyard settlement by the woods, and she had to concentrate on extricating herself before serious trouble developed.

"You came all this way to pay us a visit," a grizzled worker said, leering at her. "Ain't that nice?"

"We were just talkin' about you, and all of a sudden here you are," another declared. "We're in luck, boys!"

Afraid she would offend them and create additional complications for herself if she adopted a haughty attitude, Melissa spoke impersonally. "I was bringing some shellfish home from the village and decided to take a little stroll," she said, hoping the circle would open so she could pass.

"Ain't that great?" one of them shouted. "She's bringin' us food as well as herself."

The atmosphere was taking a decided turn for the worse, so Melissa took a tighter grip on her bag of shrimp and her shoes, then started forward resolutely.

The men facing her locked arms. Several guffawed, and soon the others locked arms, too.

Caught inside the circle, Melissa knew that a show of good humor was her only hope. She could not let them see that she was afraid. "The joke is on me, boys," she said. "But I've got to cook these shrimp for Mr. Canning's supper now, so let me pass, please." She hoped the mention of Harry's name would tame the men.

They continued to hold their ground, however, and the worker who spoke in a deep baritone said, "Canning already has a wife. He don't need two women. Which is lucky, because now we got you."

"And we ain't letting loose of you in a hurry, neither," the man next to him in the circle declared.

The amiable grins slowly vanished, and Melissa realized her danger had become real and immediate. There was no way she could break free of a dozen determined, work-hardened men. "Where is your foreman?" she asked, her manner becoming chilly.

"Don't you worry your pretty head none about him," one of the crew replied. "He went off to eat his noontime meat and bread."

Melissa guessed that either Chet or Danny had taken charge of the wood-cutting detail after completing his share of taking inventory. Perhaps both of them were within earshot. She could only pray that was the situation, for she knew she needed all the help she could get. Before the men could silence her, she screamed as loudly as she could. The high-pitched sound echoed through the woods.

"You cut that out!" one of the men growled.

"Shut up, or we'll shut you up," another said.

Melissa screamed again.

The heavyset man with the deep baritone voice broke ranks and advanced toward her, his eyes hard and menacing. "You was warned," he said and reached for her.

Dropping her belongings, Melissa clawed at his face with her nails, and when he caught hold of her wrists, cursing her, she brought up a knee hard, striking him in the groin.

The man was in pain and threw her roughly to the ground. The circle grew tighter and smaller around her.

Panting for breath, the frightened girl tried to rise. The same man shoved her hard, and she stumbled, then fell onto her back. There was no escape possible now, and she braced herself for the inevitable.

"What in the devil is going on here?" Chet Harris called from the edge of the clearing as he came onto the broad beach.

Recognizing his voice instantly, Melissa managed to stand. Several of the men also turned in the direction of the voice of authority and after a moment's silence, began to offer lame excuses simultaneously.

Melissa tried to speak, but for an instant she was still

so terrified she could not. Then she managed to say, "They were trying to keep me here against my will. I—I know they were going to rape me."

Chet's eyes burned. "They were, eh?"

The heavyset man picked up his ax, which he placed on the hard sand. "Harris," he said, "we take orders from you in our work because Mr. Canning made you our boss. But this here is private. So go someplace else. In a hurry, if you know what's good for you."

"I'm making this my business," Chet said. "Miss Austin is under my protection."

"That's too damn bad for Miss Austin and too damn bad for you," one of the men declared.

A speeding figure raced out of the woods, leaped onto the heavyset man, and knocked him to the ground. Landing on top of him, Danny Taylor pounded the man mercilessly with both fists, drawing blood. Then he jumped to his feet, and his boot landed in the heavyset man's side. "I stand with Chet Harris," he said, his voice surprisingly calm. Drawing a pistol from his belt and cocking it in the same motion, he demanded, "Anybody want to argue the matter?"

Chet drew his pistol, too, and together the pair went to Melissa.

"My trigger finger itches something awful," Danny said. "The only thing that will cure it will be to see you lads going back to work. Fast. Chet and I both know how to shoot straight, and we'll soon have a chance to decide which of us is the better marksman if one of you makes a single false move with an ax."

"Get going," Chet added, then prodded the prone man with his toe. "If you were well enough to intimidate a girl, you're well enough to work."

The man dragged himself to his feet, looked murderously at Melissa, and groaning as he picked up his ax, limped off toward the woods. The others, sullen and silent, followed him.

Danny kept his pistol trained on them.

"Thank you," Melissa said to the pair. "I don't know what I would have done without you."

"Well, we got here in time," Chet said soothingly.

Danny was more critical. "You should have given these men wide berth," he said. "You know there would be trouble if you came near them."

Melissa's pride prevented her from telling him the meeting had been accidental, that she had been paying too little attention to her surroundings.

Danny's mind was on practical matters, however, so he ignored her silence. "Chet," he said, "you'd best escort Melissa home. I'll find Harry and report this incident to him."

"Good enough." Chet, too, continued to grip his pistol. "Come along," he told her.

Melissa quickly put on her shoes, stuffing her stockings into her pocket, then picked up her string bag of shrimp.

Danny stalked off without another word.

Chet took care to avoid the work detail as he walked beside Melissa. "Is Danny angry with me?" she asked him.

He shook his head. "That was a near call," he said, "first for you and then for us."

"The way you and Danny made them behave so fast made it look easy." She laughed in relief.

Chet remained grim. "Danny and I were outnumbered by about six to one, and all of them were armed with axes. I knew I had to draw my pistol, but Danny was still smarter. By taking care of the ringleader, he knocked the fight out of all of them."

"Well, the two of you are formidable," she said, then fell silent for a time. "What will Harry do?"

He shrugged. "That's hard to say. These men stayed in camp to work as volunteers on a holiday. So that's in their favor." He sounded dubious.

Melissa knew she had no control over any decision that Harry Canning might make, but she wanted her own part in the incident made clear. "I didn't go near the men on purpose, Chet," she said. "I was in the fisherman's village, and it was such a lovely day I decided to walk home by way of the beach. I was careless, that's all."

To her surprise he continued to frown. "We've got so much going on here that Galveston Island doesn't seem much of a wilderness these days. But it is, just as all of the Republic of Texas is, still frontier country."

"I wanted adventure, which is why I came to Texas in the first place," she said, giving him a rueful smile. "But I didn't want this much or this kind."

"Forget the primary rule of the frontier at your peril," Chet told her. "Always be alert to danger. The Oregon Trail from Independence to the Pacific is littered with the bleached bones of the careless, and so are the prairies of Texas."

A chastened Melissa made no reply because there was nothing she could say.

Harry Canning reacted instantly when Danny brought him word of the incident. Leaving the three shipbuilding foremen with whom he had been conferring, he accompanied Danny to the scene, where he ordered the work halted, then called the men around him.

"I've heard one version of what happened here a short time ago. Now I want your account, in your own words."

Some of the men looked down at the ground and others stared out at the tranquil Gulf of Mexico, but no one spoke.

Harry looked hard at the battered heavyset man. "Suppose you tell me."

"It was all a misunderstanding, Mr. Canning."

"You didn't molest or threaten Melissa Austin?"

"No, sir."

"Then why did Danny Taylor here give you such a beating?"

"He—he attacked me from behind, Mr. Canning. Or he'd be the one with the black eye and cuts on his face."

Harry refused to be sidetracked. "Why did he attack you?"

"Damned if I know, sir."

"You lie," Danny declared. "Put up your fists here and now, and I'll beat the truth out of you."

Some members of the detail were becoming restless. "There's no need for another fight," one of them said. "I don't know what you've been told, Mr. Canning. But we started to tease the redhead. She's a lively one, and a lot of us have had an eye on her for a long spell. Then, all of a sudden, things got out of hand."

"Who was responsible for that?" Harry demanded curtly.

Three of the men jabbed their forefingers in the direction of their heavyset companion. The man completely lost his composure. "You wanted her as bad as I did. Don't put all the blame on me!"

"So you admit you threatened her?" Harry's voice was metallic.

"Well, yeah. Something like that," the man mumbled.

"He threw her down onto the beach, too," one of the others said. "After she clawed at him and kicked him when he grabbed her."

"None of the rest of you touched her?"

A tall, bearded man cleared his throat. "No, sir. But that ain't to say what we might have done after Gus here had his way with her."

"At least you're honest." Harry looked slowly at each of the men in turn. "You have all their names, Danny?"

"Chet has them."

"Very well." He pointed at the heavyset man. "You," he said, "collect your gear and go to the paymaster for whatever is owed you. You'll leave the island in about an hour from now on the afternoon ferry, and you won't come back. If you know what's good for you, you'll also leave Texas. I'm sending President Houston a full report of this matter, and I can assure you that Texans don't have much sympathy for men who treat ladies like whores. The rest of you will have one more chance, but only one. Now, either go back to your work or take the rest of the holiday off, as you see fit."

He stalked off without another word, Danny beside him.

That evening it seemed for a time as though Nancy's surprise feast was a failure. But the meal was so deli-

cious that spirits gradually improved, and only Melissa
remained subdued.

Chet tried to cheer her but failed, and then Danny
went to her. "Forget about this afternoon," he told her.
"Provided you learned that Galveston Island isn't Pittsburgh. Or Chicago. Or even one of the new towns in
Oregon. This is a rough country, and you have to obey
the rules of self-protection here in order to survive."

"So I'm finding out," she said, sounding tearful. "Maybe it was a mistake for me to come to Texas."

She looked and sounded so forlorn that Danny melted.
"Don't tell Rick Miller," he said, "but I'm glad you
came."

The sympathy in his voice sparked Melissa, and she
rallied quickly. "From now on," she said, "I'm never
leaving the house without a pistol and a knife. If I'd had
them this afternoon I might not have needed help from
you and Chet."

Danny couldn't help smiling. The Melissa he knew
had come back to life.

IX

Sir Michael Edison, K.B., Queen Victoria's Minister Plenipotentiary to the Republic of Texas, had been knighted for valor in combat when he had been very young and naive. Now he was cynical after spending the better part of his adult life in the diplomatic service. Weary and looking forward to retirement once the future of Texas was determined, he was still cautious in his maneuvers.

He was frowning as he admitted Anthony Roberts to the small, cramped room in his legation that he used as an office. "It makes me apprehensive," he said irritably, "when you come here in broad daylight, Roberts. This road is one of the principal streets in Austin. A great many people might see you entering or leaving."

"Let them, Sir Michael," Anthony replied insolently as he lowered himself into the only comfortable chair in the room. "Everyone I've met here assumes I'm English because of my accent, and no one knows I'm actually an American citizen. My business investments have been as good for Texas as they've been for me. So I can think of nothing more natural than a successful British man of business paying a visit to his country's legation. Only you and I know the real reasons I come here, and both of us have good cause not to talk out of turn."

The Minister sighed as he seated himself opposite his

guest. Unfortunately, he had to admit, Roberts was right. All the same, Sir Michael didn't approve of these flaunting visits. Perhaps his real reason was that he disliked Roberts personally and felt only contempt for the man's vocation. All spies were lowly and despicable, but the worst of them was the man who was a traitor to his native land.

It wasn't Sir Michael's place to pass moral judgment on the man, however. Roberts performed useful functions for him, and no other agents were as farsighted, intelligent, or malleable. "I trust you destroyed the brief note that I sent via my clerk, asking you to call on me?"

Anthony yawned. "I burned it at once, as I burn all such messages," he said. "I take only the risks that cannot be avoided in a delicate profession."

Ignoring his distaste for the man, Sir Michael became crisp. "I received a nugget of information today in a letter brought to me from our legation in Washington City by special courier," he said. "President Tyler has sent the Texans a huge munitions train that includes rifles, cannon, vast quantities of gunpowder, and a remarkable new revolver that fires six shots without reloading."

Anthony whistled softly. Texas would become far more self-reliant now. "You're certain this data is accurate?"

Sir Michael stiffened. "Our Minister in Washington City wrote to me in his own hand. But the contents of the freight wagon are no state secret, I assure you. He enclosed a number of newspaper cuttings. The major American press enumerates the various weapons and the quantities of powder. They positively gloat."

"Do you happen to have a spare cutting that I might see?"

Sir Michael handed one to him, and Anthony glanced through the article, read it more carefully a second time, then handed it back to the diplomat, the contents already memorized. "Three huge wagons filled with powder could blow the entire Republic of Texas off the face of the earth," he said. "There's enough to destroy every town, farm, and ranch house in the country."

"It will be used to defend Texas if a new war should break out, obviously. Not only does this gift bind the Texans more closely to the United States, but it now will become possible for them to adopt a far more independent attitude toward us."

"Could you be more specific, Sir Michael?"

"I've recognized their need for warships and have offered to sell them some of our older vessels for a very low price, charging them no interest on the loan. Instead, they're building their own fleet now and obviously will have good use for the cannon and powder in the wagon train."

"How soon will the train arrive here?"

"Our people in Washington City don't know how rapidly or slowly a train of that size can travel. The best estimate is another two to three months."

"Then we have only that long to drive a wedge between the Texans and the Americans?" Anthony asked.

The Minister's smile was frigid. "You delude yourself. Texans are Americans, my dear Roberts. Neither you nor I nor all the Queen's horses and all the Queen's men could drive such a wedge. The very most we can hope to achieve is a postponement of the annexation of Texas by the United States. A series of such postponements might cool the ardor for the marriage on both sides. Long enough, perhaps, for us to accomplish other goals."

The seeming complexity of the problem caused Anthony to frown.

"We're playing for high stakes, Roberts. The question of the Oregon border hasn't yet been settled. The Americans will be in a far stronger position to insist that the line be drawn anywhere from the forty-ninth to the fifty-fourth parallel if the Texas issue has already been settled. If it hasn't been resolved, Britain stands to gain a vastly larger territory."

Anthony understood the game that Great Britain was playing now, but he still had no idea what part he was expected to play. "You haven't summoned me here to listen to a lecture on high diplomacy or to hear a sermon on the exercise of international power. Precisely what do you want of me, Sir Michael?"

The Minister's smile was as cold as it was faint. "We've already discussed the arms and munitions train the Americans are sending to Texas. Surely you can use your imagination."

Anthony suspected what was wanted, but hints were not enough. He wanted specific orders so that his efforts could not be disavowed in the event he failed. "My imagination is boundless, which I sometimes find a problem," he replied, matching the diplomat's smile.

"It would be a pity for both the United States and Texas if something happened and the delivery of those arms just happened to be disrupted."

"I see." His suspicions were correct.

"No—ah—accidents must be allowed to take place on the American side of the border, mind you. The United States is proud of her growing physical strength and is inclined to flex her muscles. The administration in Washington City is sensitive to insults, and there would be an outcry for a break in diplomatic relations with Britain if it were learned that we instigated such an accident."

"You're saying that any incident should take place after the munitions train reaches Texas."

"Exactly. This country may be large, but it is very thinly populated, and Texas is in no position to break with us, much less declare war against us."

Anthony pondered for a time. "The action you've suggested would be difficult to arrange and might cost a very considerable sum of money."

"Hang the expense!"

"How much are you willing to spend, Sir Michael?"

"Whatever may be necessary," the diplomat replied succinctly, "provided the source of the funds is never traced to me or to anyone else in this compound."

"Of course." Anthony paused for a moment. "An enterprise of that delicacy and magnitude would involve certain risks on my part, you know. I'd require adequate compensation."

"I am willing to pay you a full year's worth of your present monthly fee. And I'm quite sure that, in addition, a handsome bonus would be waiting for you on your return to London."

It was apparent that the British desire to see the munitions train sabotaged was urgent. "This is very generous of you, Sir Michael."

"We've struck a bargain, then?"

"We have." Anthony extended his hand.

Conquering a feeling of repugnance, the Minister took the proffered hand and shook it.

"I should also like to ask a small personal favor."

Sir Michael braced himself.

"You maintain files on all British companies that do business with the Texans. It's my understanding that one of the shipping firms that engages in trade between New Orleans and the Texas coast has hired a number of American schooners and their crews."

"That's correct." Sir Michael remained wary.

"I'll be grateful for any background information you can give me on a ship's master named Homer Smith. The name is a common one, and I'm trying to determine whether this person is the same Homer Smith I may have known some years ago."

The diplomat relaxed. The request was harmless, and he was willing to accommodate the man on whom the successful destruction of the munitions train depended. Sir Michael went to an adjoining room, returning shortly with a single sheet of paper. "What would you like to know about Captain Smith?"

"Anything you can tell me that might help me to identify him, Sir Michael."

"He's rather elderly; from our data he appears to be in his sixties." Anthony nodded. "He owns his own ship, and his home port is the town of New Haven, in Connecticut."

"I don't suppose you know whether he's a native of New Haven? The Homer Smith I knew came from the capital of the state. Hartford."

Sir Michael glanced at the paper. "Captain Smith

seems to be your man, Roberts. He was born in Hartford and lived there until he inherited a part interest in a shipping company and first went to sea about thirty years ago."

"He is my man," Anthony said, concealing his surge of elation.

After leaving the British Legation, Anthony mounted his horse and took his time returning to his own house. The task of sabotaging the munitions train would not be easy, and he postponed a detailed consideration of the problem until a later time. His mind was filled with the personal vengeance he could exact on another of his father's killers.

This time, he reflected, he would utilize a somewhat different technique. Twice he had left the bodies of his victims in ditches near the South Road, and it might be too dangerous to do the same thing for a third time.

Elisabeta, in spite of her horror and repugnance, would be required to play a more active part in his confrontation with Captain Homer Smith. He was reluctant to use her because she might grow panicky in a crisis, but he would have to run that risk. She was already too deeply involved in his affairs to refuse, and his hold over her was absolute. The risks would be far fewer if she cooperated with him, and one way or another he would force her to do his bidding.

Certainly he knew she despised him, and he grinned as a thought—a brilliant notion—occurred to him. If she worked with him to dispose of Captain Homer Smith, he would offer her passage back to Spain. That would insure her help, and if he failed to keep his end of the bargain, there was literally nothing she could do about it.

He timed his move perfectly, allowing Elisabeta Manuel as little time as possible to protest against the plan he intended to reveal to her. Waiting until mid-afternoon, when she came down to the parlor from her chamber, he told her casually, "I think you'd be wise to change into one of your more attractive gowns. We're going to be entertaining a guest shortly before nightfall."

Many visitors still came to the house, but something sly and cold in Anthony's manner turned Elisabeta's blood to ice. "As you wish," she murmured.

He called her back as she started to leave the parlor. "One moment, my dear. Today's guest is no ordinary person, and he won't be accorded ordinary treatment."

Now she knew for certain that there would be more trouble.

"All you need to do," he said, "is to sit with the gentleman in the parlor for a time. I want him sitting there." He pointed to a chair that stood with its back to the door.

He was plotting another murder, Elisabeta realized, and this time he intended to kill his victim right here, under their roof.

"Entertain him in any way you see fit, provided you gain and hold his attention for a short time," Anthony directed. "It doesn't matter whether you dazzle him with your beauty, your wit, or your conversation. Just make certain he doesn't look around at the wrong moment."

"I—I don't understand." Surely this madman didn't intend to keep her in the room while he killed a man!

"This is all you need to know." Anthony drew a length of strong, thin cord from his pocket and dangled it before her. "I'll dispose of the body without help from you, never fear."

"I—I can't do it," Elisabeta cried.

He caught hold of her shoulders and shook her until her head ached. "You'll do as I tell you, no more and no less."

"I refuse to help you murder innocent people!" she screamed. "You are insane!"

"Who says they're innocent? And who says I've murdered anyone? As soon as Captain Smith finds his attention diverted from you, my dear, you're free to leave the room. What you don't see and don't know won't hurt you. Or me. And this time you shall have the best of all possible rewards." He paused, then said slowly, "I shall engage passage for you to Spain from New Orleans and will pay all of your traveling expenses."

Elisabeta stood very still. Freedom was beckoning, and she stared hard at her tormentor. "You—you're not joking, Anthony? You're not making promises you don't plan to keep?"

"Hardly." His sincere, earnest smile reminded her of their early relationship. "At one time we thought of marriage, but we've drifted apart. Far apart. You'll be much happier in Spain than you are here, with me. I'd be a boor if I tried to keep you here by force, you know. So you'll help me voluntarily—and earn your reward. Or you'll submit unwillingly and receive nothing. Which shall it be?"

The prospect of escape blotted everything else from her mind. "I accept your terms," she said at last.

His smile broadened. "Splendid. You don't disappoint me. Now hurry, and make certain you look ravishing enough to capture the complete attention of our honored guest."

Elisabeta thought she was dreaming as she changed her clothes, then applied cosmetics. She still had no idea why Anthony was murdering elderly men, but she didn't want to know. It was enough that she would be leaving him in the immediate future and would not set eyes on him again. Soon her nightmare would be ended, and she could not think beyond that time.

Less than an hour later Elisabeta was seated in the parlor opposite Homer Smith, a sinewy man with a rocklike face, whose braided, old-fashioned bicorne, pea jacket, and short boots identified him as a merchant mariner.

In no way struck by her beauty, Smith made polite conversation. "Have you settled in Texas to stay, Mrs. Roberts?"

The girl shook her head, then forced herself to speak. She hated being called Mrs. Roberts. "No, I'm quite sure that Anthony's business will take us back to Europe eventually."

"Ah, then you don't own this house."

"No, we rent it." She didn't know how much longer this horrid ordeal would last.

"Your husband tells me he can offer me a lucrative contract for cargo carrying. Do you know what kind of cargo he intends to ship, ma'am?" The elderly man was speaking casually, but his shrewd eyes were alert.

"I—I know very little about the details of his business affairs," Elisabeta said faintly, telling the truth.

At that moment Anthony appeared on the threshold behind the visitor, the ends of his silken cord securely wrapped around both of his hands.

Elisabeta made a supreme effort not to give away his presence by raising her eyes. "All I can tell you, really, is that Anthony has been very successful here. As I'm sure you know, he has invested in several trading enterprises."

"I'm afraid I know nothing about his investments. All I know is that he's told me he wants to do business with me—"

The sentence remained unfinished. The cord was looped over Smith's head, cutting him short.

Before Anthony could draw it taut, however, the merchant mariner reacted violently, tipping the chair backward. He and his attacker fell to the floor together and began to struggle there. In spite of Smith's age he was in superb physical condition, and now that the man who had assaulted him had lost the advantage of surprise, they were far more equally matched.

For a moment Elisabeta stared aghast at the pair who were punching, kicking, and wrestling on the floor. Then she lifted her skirts, fled from the parlor, and raced up the stairs to her own chamber, bolting the door behind her. She could hear banging, crashing sounds emanating from the parlor, so she clapped her hands over her ears and pulled her pillow over her head as she threw herself onto the bed.

Eventually she realized that there were no more sounds below. Timidly, experimentally, she rose, then tiptoed to the door and listened, straining hard.

The silence on the ground floor was total.

The unexpected sound of a horse's hoofbeats caused her to start. But she could not force herself to go to the window in order to see who was leaving the premises. There was so much about this dreadful incident that she didn't want to know, now or ever.

She returned to the bed, blotting the fiasco from her mind by falling asleep for a time. It was dark when she awakened, so she reluctantly lighted a lamp, unbolted her door, and crept down the stairs, afraid of what she would find.

No one was in the house with her, and the parlor had been more or less straightened. The furniture had been righted, and there was a damp spot that covered about a square foot of the hardwood floor. She was afraid it might be blood, but a closer investigation indicated that it was water. Perhaps, she surmised, water had been used to wipe away blood.

A mirror hanging on the wall adjacent to the entrance was askew, and a porcelain figure of a frog that Anthony had bought for her in New Orleans—ages ago—when she had found it amusing, was missing from the table on which it had stood. But Elisabeta intended neither to straighten the mirror nor search for the porcelain object. She never wanted to set foot in this room again.

Forcing herself to eat before she retired, she locked herself into her room once more. It was difficult to refrain from speculating on what might have happened in the fight between Anthony and the American sea captain, but she felt the urgent need to block the whole matter from her mind, and she took refuge in sleep.

It was daylight when she awakened, and she had no idea of the time, but the position of the sun told her it was not early. All the same she dawdled as long as she could before going downstairs. With any luck Anthony would not be there.

She found no sign of him. There was no indication that he had eaten breakfast, and when she went up the stairs again, she saw that his bedroom door was ajar. She peeked in apprehensively and saw that, if he had returned during the night, he had taken care to make his bed again.

The girl shrugged, then shuddered. Her sole, over-whelming desire was to leave Austin at once, and she prayed that Anthony would return long enough to give her the passage money he had promised her.

In the meantime, while Elisabeta was roaming through the empty house, Captain Rick Miller was spending a very busy morning in his almost bare office at Ranger headquarters. When he had arrived at work, he had been informed that the body of an American merchant mariner named Homer Smith had been found on the North Road several miles from town. A miniature noose hung from his neck, but the man obviously had been in a fight before being murdered, for there were several welts and cuts on his face.

Still digesting the information, Rick was interrupted by the arrival of his second in command, whose expression indicated that he had picked up some news.

"Sir," Sergeant Haight said, "the body has been positively identified by Captain Smith's mate." He paused. "The mate also told me that Smith left him a little before sundown to meet with an Englishman named Anthony Roberts, who claimed he wanted to do business with him."

Rick merely nodded. "Do we have a file on this Roberts?"

"Yes, sir." Haight went off and returned with a two-page document.

"You questioned Roberts and his wife after the other noose murders?"

"Yes, Captain. And they came out clean."

"Well, if the mate is right and Roberts wanted to do business with Smith, we might have a clue that will lead to something."

The Ranger who was on duty in the outer office tapped on the closed door, then came into the room. "Captain," he said, "there's a man calls himself Anthony Roberts here to see you."

Rick and Haight exchanged glances. "Show him in, please. And stay right where you are, Haight. This promises to be interesting."

Anthony came into the room, exuding his utmost charm and ignoring a cut on one cheek near his eye.

Introductory amenities were exchanged, and Rick lost no time in observing, "That's rather a nasty cut under your eye, Mr. Roberts."

"My own fault, I'm afraid. I spent the evening at President Houston's reception last night. I was one of the first to arrive, soon after sundown, and must have been one of the last to leave, too many hours later. I'm not accustomed to drinking your American corn liquor, and I'm sorry to say I fell off my horse on my way home."

Rick's polite laugh was guarded.

"I've come to see you, Captain, because I learned something disturbing a short time ago. I've been told that Captain Homer Smith, who charters his ship and crew to one of our British companies, has been murdered. Strangled to death."

"I'm afraid the story is true." Rick was watching him closely. Either the man was totally innocent or an accomplished actor and liar, he thought.

"That's dreadful." Anthony looked stricken. "I expected him to call at my house late yesterday to discuss a business deal I intended to offer him. When he didn't appear—after I'd waited about three-quarters of an hour for him—I went off to President Houston's reception."

It would be an easy matter for Haight to determine when Roberts had arrived at the President's party and when he had departed. Certainly there wouldn't have been time for him to deposit a body on the North Road before being one of the early party-goers.

"I'm so sorry," Anthony said. "I met him only briefly, earlier in the day, but he seemed to be a very nice chap." He stood and picked up his hat. "Do let me know if there's anything I can do to help you, Captain." His alibi having been established, Anthony took his leave.

Haight sighed. "When I saw that cut on his face, I thought sure we had our murderer."

"Check out his story. If he was one of the first to arrive at the President's reception and one of the last to leave, there will be a dozen or so people who will corroborate what he's just told us."

"I'm sure they will. A man wouldn't relate facts like those if they couldn't be corroborated."

"We'll see."

Haight looked at him and raised an eyebrow.

"Roberts's story may hold water, and it may not," Rick said. "I'm going off to do a little snooping on my own."

"You still suspect him, Captain?"

"Yes. Because his alibi is so neat, so airtight. I'll meet you back here."

Wasting no time, Rick saddled his horse and rode directly to the Roberts house.

Elisabeta answered his tap at the door.

"Captain Miller, Texas Rangers," he said. "May I come in?"

"Of course," she said faintly, growing pale. The feared Rick Miller had actually come here. Today. Her worst nightmare was being realized.

Rick followed her into the parlor, struck by her great beauty. Haight's report had called her "attractive," but that didn't do the lady justice.

Elisabeta's hand trembled slightly as she waved him to a chair.

He immediately noted that a mirror hanging on one wall was crooked, and then, behind a small table, he saw several shards of broken procelain. Unless the lady was a sloppy housekeeper in spite of her immaculate grooming, which was possible, there had been a fight in this room.

"You're Mrs. Roberts?"

"Well, yes." She hated to lie to an officer of high rank, and she had been totally unprepared for Rick Miller's rugged good looks or the great force of his personality. She folded her hands tightly in her lap, so tightly that the knuckles turned white.

Rick knew at once that she was under great tension. Interesting. "Mrs. Roberts, can you tell me where your husband spent the evening last night?"

"I'm afraid not." That was the truth.

"What time did he go out?"

"I—I'm not sure. I had a very bad headache, and I fell asleep in my own room."

He found it odd that she and her husband slept in separate rooms. If he had such a great beauty for a wife, they would sleep in the same bed. "Can you tell me what time he came home?"

Elisabeta shook her head, and when her gleaming hair fell forward across her face, she pushed it away absently.

"Please, Mrs. Roberts, I'm asking for your cooperation. Can you tell me when your husband went out this morning?"

"I don't keep count of his movements." She was finding it difficult to breathe.

"Mrs. Roberts," Rick said sternly, "you're making it hard for me to believe you. You're trying to tell me your husband comes and goes without your knowledge?"

Elisabeta took a deep breath and knew she could lie no more. "Captain Miller," she said, "I am not Mrs. Roberts. I am Elisabeta Manuel. It has been simpler, because of the entertaining Anthony does, for me to be known as his wife. But we—we do not live together here." That, too, was the truth, and bringing it into the open made her feel a little better. "We have separate bedchambers. I am employed by Anthony as his housekeeper."

He was fascinated by her revelations, and, if his experience meant anything, he could tell she was not lying to him. He could read the relief in her liquid eyes.

She anticipated further questions. "We met in Madrid long ago. He knew my family there before they died." The words were pouring out in a rush now. "Anthony knew he would need someone to keep house for him and act as his hostess, so he hired me for the position." What she could not admit was that he had promised to marry her and that, as a consequence, she had slept with him for a time.

Rick guessed the unspoken part of her story when he

saw how forlorn she looked, but this was not the moment to press her for the details. When he was engaging in an investigation, he was noted for his hard-bitten, unyielding attitude, but this case was different. He felt great sympathy for this lovely young woman who was so tortured and frightened.

Elisabeta thought his silence meant that he doubted what she had told him. "If you wish," she said earnestly, "I can show you the bedchambers upstairs."

He was embarrassed for her sake and shook his head. "That won't be necessary, Miss Manuel." He paused, gestured in the direction of the small, vacant table, and spoke casually. "I see you've had an accident."

For the first time Elisabeta became aware of the bits of shattered porcelain on the floor that Anthony, in his haste, had failed to remove after his fight with Captain Smith. She stared at the shards for a moment, her blood congealing.

He saw the expression of pure fright in her eyes and quickly added facts. Homer Smith had been in a fight before he had been murdered. Anthony Roberts had a nasty cut under one eye, and his explanation had been almost too glib. Now, in this room, he saw the mirror that had not been straightened and the remains of a shattered porcelain object on the floor.

"I knocked over the table by accident last night on my way to bed," Elisabeta said, an edge of desperation in her voice. "I thought I picked up all the pieces of my broken porcelain frog, but it appears that I missed some because my oil lamp was burning low."

The woman was one of the most inept liars Rick had ever encountered. There was no doubt in his mind that she was making a great effort to conceal something from him. But his years of service as a Ranger had taught him that some people became hysterical and revealed nothing of consequence when they were pushed too hard.

So he smiled blandly, rose to his feet, and said, "Thank you for your time and cooperation, Miss Manuel."

She hesitated, then asked, "May I know why you've come here to see me?"

"I'm seeing many people," he replied, watching her closely. "An American sea captain named Homer Smith was strangled to death last night or early this morning, and I'm trying to account for the whereabouts last evening of everyone who knew him or might have done business with him."

Elisabeta stared at him open-mouthed for an instant. So Anthony was suspected, and her own part in the killing might come to light!

Rick saw that her terror had increased. Obviously she knew much more than she had told him. But he was in no hurry. Walking to the front door with her, he said, "I appreciate your candor." He extended his hand, immediately noting that her palm was moist. Her fear was overwhelming her. "Perhaps we'll meet again one day, Austin is a small town, you know."

"I don't expect to be living here much longer," Elisabeta blurted. "Anthony has promised me passage back to Spain, and I hope he keeps his word soon."

So she wanted to leave Texas but was uncertain whether Roberts would provide the funds for the purpose. Why was she so eager to leave, and if she had a strictly business relationship with Roberts, why was there a possibility to finance her journey? The situation under this roof was strange, and Rick needed to sort out what he had just learned.

He remained bland as he took his leave. Once outside, he pretended not to notice the beautiful, anxious face, half-concealed by the parlor curtains, watching him leave.

Certainly he would intensify his investigation of Anthony Roberts now. And in one way or another, he would make it his business to see Elisabeta Manuel again. Not that he minded that part of the task. She was the most attractive young woman he had ever met, and he had to warn himself sternly that he could not allow his personal feelings to interfere with the performance of his duty.

*   *   *

The arrival of the wagon train brought employees of the Texas government, numbers of elected officials, and scores of private citizens out of their homes. Some of the younger members of the train fired rifles and pistols in the air in their exuberance, and the established residents cheered the newcomers.

The settlers were conducted to a bare, sparsely furnished building, and there it was learned that most heads of households were choosing to settle in the vicinity of Austin, where ample land was still available. As they signed their names to the land claims for the property where they would make their homes as ranchers or farmers, they automatically became citizens of the Republic of Texas.

President Houston made a brief appearance to greet the new arrivals and promptly invited General Blake, his wife, and Teng Chu to dine with him that evening. Then Lee and Cathy, along with their little daughter and the Chinese warrior, were conducted to the compound of the United States Legation by the chargé d'affaires, Wilford Teller of Boston, who was the head of the office, pending the appointment of a new minister.

The compound, the largest of its kind in the town, was a complex of nine buildings, surrounded by a palisade, that included offices, dormitories, a meeting hall, and several private homes. Lee and Cathy promptly occupied one of these houses, which was fully furnished, and Teng Chu moved in with them as their guest. Hector and Ginny Mullins were given another of the private dwellings, much to their delight, while the cavalrymen were conducted to their own dormitory quarters. At once, the first time the legation had ever enjoyed such an impressive luxury.

Sitting with Wilford Teller for a chat, Lee was quickly brought up to date, the chargé telling him in detail about the huge munitions train currently making its way to Texas.

Lee was impressed by the formidable statistics. "President Tyler and General Scott told me the arms were being sent," he said, "but I had no idea the quantity would be so great. When are the supplies due to arrive here?"

"You'll get word on that via a courier when they approach the Texas border, General," Teller replied. "Until then, there's one aspect of the matter that you should know. In spite of all the publicity that has appeared in American newspapers, President Houston is making no statements about the train here. Many people in Texas inevitably know about it, of course, but he prefers that the details—particularly the arrival date—be kept as confidential as possible."

"That's wise," Lee said. "Enormous quantities of arms and powder would tempt desperadoes to make attacks on the train. I think we've provided enough guards, and I dare say the Texans will do the same when the wagons cross the border. But it's far better to avoid trouble."

At supper that evening Sam Houston brought the new American military attaché up to date on Harry Canning's progress on Galveston Island. "Canning hasn't had an easy time of it because we've had to send so much of what he needs from the mainland. Tools, copper sheathing, kegs of nails. Not to mention the food he and his people need. But he's doing remarkably well, and I expect the first ships to be launched in another month."

"Good." Lee thought for a moment. "What are you doing about officers and crews?"

"We have them," Houston said proudly. "We advertised in the major American newspapers, and we have officers and seamen in training right now on Galveston Island, too."

"Do the Mexicans and the British know about the shipbuilding program, Mr. President?"

"I'm sure they do. We've made no secret of it. But I'm also sure they don't attach much importance to it. The British are blinded by what they regard as the world-wide superiority of the Royal Navy to all others. And Santa Anna is so arrogant that he undoubtedly thinks the old tubs he calls warships could handle anything that we send to sea. He has some surprises in store if he raises his hand against us, I can tell you."

"You think he'll go to war, sir?"

"I look at it this way," Houston said slowly. "I'm keeping my powder dry and preparing for the worst, but at the same time I'm hoping for the best. My principal worry is that Santa Anna may go to war *now* if he stops to think of the significance of the munitions train that's on the trail to us, because, with all of those arms, we'll be in a good position to defend ourselves. By the way, General, have you seen the new Colt revolver?"

"I was shown one in Washington City, but I haven't had the chance to try it."

"Andy Jackson sent me a revolver as a personal gift, and I turned it over to Captain Rick Miller of our Rangers as soon as he returned to Texas. I'm sure he'll let you try it."

"I can wait until the munitions train gets here," Lee replied, smiling.

They chatted for hours, enjoying the simple but hearty meal prepared by Houston's landlady. Cathy found it difficult to believe that the Texans were so unpretentious that they provided no home for the President of the young nation, forcing him to live in a boardinghouse during the better part of the year he spent in Austin. And she was startled when the President revealed that Nancy Canning and Melissa Austin had stowed away on the voyage to California, then accompanied Rick and Harry to Texas.

"Nancy should have known better!" she said.

Sam Houston grinned at her. "Everything has worked out for the best," he said. "Mrs. Canning is a hard worker, and her husband has greater peace of mind, having her with him."

"Has Melissa adjusted to her new life?" Cathy asked.

"Harry Canning is loyal and makes no complaints," Houston said, "but I've had private reports of a few flurries she's caused."

"Melissa is too pretty and attracts too much attention for her own good," Cathy said severely. "She'll be a far better person when she grows up."

Lee tactfully changed the subject. "How is President Jackson these days, sir?"

Houston sighed deeply. "He's fading fast, from what his niece writes me. As soon as the munitions train arrives here, I intend to take my young son up to visit him. I want the boy to meet the greatest American of our age, and I just pray I get there in time. His vision is responsible for the settlement of Texas and Oregon, and I never let myself forget it!"

Lee nodded in solemn agreement. Other, younger, men might claim the credit, but it was Andrew Jackson who was responsible for making the United States a major power that stretched from the Atlantic Ocean to the Pacific.

Later that night, as the Blakes were on their way to bed for the first time in their new house, Cathy asked, "Will there be a new war, Lee?"

"I don't see how it can be avoided," he replied. "Santa Anna still feels disgraced because Texas broke away and became independent. And although Mexico has more wilderness than she can fill with people, the annexation of Texas by the United States will be a blow to Santa Anna's prestige. Even tyrants and dictators can't ignore their people, and Santa Anna—whose position has been shaky ever since he came back and made himself President again—can win popular support for a time by rallying his people. A declaration of war is the easiest way to do it."

She heard him out in silence, then came to the heart of the matter. "Will you stay on here in your assignment?"

Lee smiled and shook his head. "Once Texas becomes a state, the legation will be closed, and there will be no need for an American military attaché here. I imagine all these buildings will be turned over to the new state for whatever purposes it wishes."

"What will you do then?" she persisted.

"I hope I'll be given a brigade of my own or be appointed as second-in-command of a full division."

Cathy looked dismayed.

He put his arms around her. "I'm a soldier, dear. It's my profession. We had an instructor at West Point who told us that times of peace, for men trained to fight, are waiting periods between wars."

She tried to display the stolid courage that was expected of a general's wife. "Were you given this post so you'd be—well, closer to the scene of the action when the time comes?"

"Neither General Scott nor anybody else at the War Department even mentioned that possibility. But I'm sure it was in their minds, as it has been in the back of mine ever since I learned I was being sent to Texas."

Cathy's façade broke down, and she looked stricken.

"As long as I remain on active duty," Lee said gently, still holding her, "we must learn to enjoy and appreciate each day for its own sake. For our sakes, too, and for Beth's."

"That's easier said than done when I face the prospect of becoming a widow."

"Not a very likely prospect." Lee released her and, unbuckling his dress sword belt, decided to take a light approach. "We had another saying at the Military Academy. Most generals die in bed."

"You won't! If I know you, you'll be at the head of the column, leading your men into battle."

"You're probably right," he admitted, knowing he wouldn't allow his troops to do anything he didn't do himself.

Anthony Roberts didn't enjoy slapping a woman, but there had been no other way to silence Elisabeta that morning, to stop her repeated, nagging requests for her passage to Spain. Now, perhaps, she'd leave him in peace for a time.

He intended to keep her with him in Austin because she was still useful to him. It was unlikely that she would be of any further assistance to him if he located another of his father's murderers—she had been on the thin edge of panic in the Homer Smith affair—but she continued to supply him with an aura of respectability that he could achieve in no other way, and that cloak would be vitally important to him in the days and weeks ahead. He wanted to have no suspicion thrown on him when he sabotaged the munitions train.

Riding slowly into the center of town, Anthony analyzed that situation carefully. His plan would be effective, he knew, provided he obtained the services of people on whom he could rely. And that was his major problem. Every Texan he met was an unqualified patriot, and the new immigrants from the United States were equally firm in their devotion to their country—which, in their minds, already included Texas.

There was always a possibility, no matter how remote, that he might encounter a newcomer willing to sell his services if the price was right. For that reason he had been spending several hours each day in the vicinity of the immigration center, where the new arrivals were registered and given their land claims.

Looping his reins over a hitching post, Anthony wandered into a saloon directly opposite the center, then took his usual place near the window, where he could keep watch on the comings and goings of people across the street.

Slowly sipping a mug of ale, he smiled to himself at the sight of a raggedly attired man with a week's stubble on his face. The canvas of his covered wagon was in tatters, and his mules looked as though they were on the verge of starvation. The man dismounted stiffly from his wagon board, then dragged himself into the building. He emerged a short time later, cursing loudly.

Anthony quickly paid for his ale, then sauntered across the road. "You seem unhappy, my friend," he said.

Asa Phipps glared at him with bloodshot eyes. "I wish to hell I hadn't come to Texas!" he said. "Those idiots in there want to give me a claim to farmland. Hell, I left

Kentucky because I'm sick and tired of grubbin' on a farm!"

Studying him, Anthony told himself that the man's reliability might be questionable, but he looked impoverished, so he might be amenable to a deal. "What do you want to do here?" he inquired lightly.

"Back home folks were sayin' the streets of Texas are lined with gold! What a laugh that is! They're made of mud, just like roads everywheres else."

"There's a possibility," Anthony said slowly, "that I might have work for you that you'd enjoy. You'd have very little to do, and the pay will be good."

"I'm your man!" Asa exclaimed. "What's the work?"

"We'll talk about it in detail later. Right now, it appears to me, you need a decent meal."

"Do I! The day afore yesterday I used the last of my flour and bacon!"

"I suggest you follow me to my house, where I can assure you of a fine dinner—as well as fodder for your mules."

"Lead the way, mister!" Asa hoisted himself onto the boards and picked up his reins.

The man did not appear to be too bright, Anthony reflected, which was all to the good. He would reveal as little as possible until the time came to take decisive action, and in the meantime, if he guessed correctly, the fellow would be satisfied with just enough money to provide him with food and shelter.

They soon arrived at the house, where the mules were unharnessed and led to the stable, where they could feast on oats. Then Anthony led Phipps, with whom he had exchanged introductions, into the house. "Let me find out how soon dinner will be ready."

Elisabeta was seated at the kitchen table, her eyes red, her face tear-stained, with a suggestion of a red welt on one cheek, where Anthony had slapped her. She did not look up as he came into the room.

He wasted no time on preambles. "I've brought a guest home with me," he said. "When will dinner be cooked?"

"Whenever you want it."

"Now!"

She rose, listlessly but obediently, and as she crossed the kitchen she caught a glimpse of the visitor. "He looks like a beggar," she said but refrained from adding that she could smell him, even at a distance.

"I'm thinking of hiring him," Anthony said curtly.

Elisabeta shrugged wearily. "I'll serve you," she said, "but I don't intend to eat with you. Not now, and not ever again. When you struck me this morning, it was the last straw."

"Do what you please," he replied, then stalked out.

A short time later he and an overwhelmed Asa Phipps, who clutched a glass of whiskey and water in one hand, seated themselves at the table.

"I'll pay you three dollars a week," Anthony said, "and in return you'll only wait until I have further orders for you. How does that strike you?"

Asa showed two rows of yellow teeth as he grinned. "It's too good to be true!"

Anthony reached into his purse and handed him three American dollars worth of silver. Asa stared at the money, then thrust it into his pocket. He was dreaming, perhaps, but the cash was real.

Elisabeta came into the room, carrying two steaming bowls, which she placed on the table before withdrawing silently. Asa Phipps gaped at her, then continued to stare as she returned with a sizzling beefsteak, which she placed in front of Anthony. Not glancing at either of the men, she vanished a second time.

Asa was as fascinated by the young woman as he was by the sight of the food. "You got yourself a mighty pretty wife, Mr. Roberts," he said.

"I'm unmarried," Anthony replied as he cut a generous slice of beef for the visitor.

"She—uh—stays here with you?" Asa couldn't help leering.

"Our relations aren't personal. She works for me, that's all." Anthony helped himself to a baked potato and wax beans.

Asa heaped food onto his own plate, then began to eat quickly. "That girl now, she ain't your lady?"

Anthony shook his head. "She is not," he said emphatically. Perhaps, he mused, he could use Elisabeta to help him maintain a stronger hold over this unsavory man.

Elisabeta heard the conversation from the kitchen and could tolerate no more. Hurrying upstairs to her own room, she changed into one of her more conservative dresses, made of thin wool, then applied cosmetics lightly and stuffed her small hoard of cash into her purse. If she could, she would return later for the rest of the clothes. If it didn't prove feasible, however, she was prepared to abandon them. There was little doubt in her mind that Anthony planned to force her to give herself to the disgusting person who was dining with him, and she could stay in this house no longer.

She had no idea where she might go, but for the present it didn't matter. She would offer her services to anyone willing to pay a small fee in return for honest, decent labor.

Afraid to carry any luggage with her for fear that Anthony would lock her into the house, she crept quietly down the stairs.

To her horror, the visitor was sprawled in a parlor chair, drinking a glass of whiskey. Asa Phipps hauled himself to his feet when he saw her. "Mr. Roberts had to go out on an errand," he said. "He asked me to make myself at home."

"Please do." She began to edge toward the front door.

"Seeing he ain't here, me and you can get acquainted, seeing as how both of us are workin' for him. He says your name is Liz—or somethin' like that."

"Elisabeta." A few more steps and she would reach the door.

Asa deposited his glass on a table with a thump, raced to the door, and barred her exit. "You ain't bein' the least bit friendly," he said.

Before she could reply, he hurled himself at her, and his breath was so foul it nauseated her.

A wild rage welled up within the girl, giving her

strength she had never before possessed. She clawed at the man's face, her nails drawing blood, then with all of her might drove a knee into his groin.

Asa howled in pain, released her, and fell back.

Not daring to go to the stable for her horse, Elisabeta fled on foot toward the center of town.

X

Rick Miller looked at the meager evidence spread out on his desk, ran his hand through his hair, and sighed. The few clues he had managed to scrape together in what Sergeant Haight now called "the hangman murders" pointed toward Anthony Roberts as the killer, but that evidence was insufficient to persuade any court of law that the man was guilty. The time had come for another chat with Elisabeta Manuel.

But that talk would have to wait until tomorrow. Today the Rangers were giving their jamboree for the fourth consecutive year, and as everyone in the government from President Houston down would be on hand, as would virtually everyone who lived in Austin and its environs, his own presence was required. Slipping his new revolver into its holster, then donning his broad-brimmed hat, Rick sighed again as he closed and locked his door behind him. In a few months his tour of duty as head of the criminal investigation division would come to an end, and it would be a relief to be given command of a troop again.

He was about to mount his waiting stallion, which was tied to a hitching post outside his office, when he caught a glimpse of a young woman walking very rapidly down the road. All at once she halted, and as she looked around in bewilderment, unsure of where to go next, he recognized Elisabeta.

There was no time like the present, particularly as she looked very disturbed, so the jamboree would have to wait. Besides, they would be serving food there for at least another hour. He sauntered up to her, then raised his hat. "Good day, Miss Manuel."

"Captain Miller!" Her expression told him there was no one else she would have preferred to avoid. On the other hand, he thought he detected a sign of relief in her eyes, too.

"You seem distressed. Could I help you?"

"I—I'm a little confused at the moment." She was unwilling to admit she was fleeing but didn't know where she was going.

Rick tried to put her at ease. "You're all dressed up for the jamboree, I see." Her face was blank, so he added, "The jamboree the Rangers are giving today."

Elisabeta's vague smile indicated that she was unaware of the festivities.

He would need time to calm her enough to find out why she was so upset. Then, he might need still more time before he could begin questioning her about Anthony Roberts. At least that was his rationalization as he said, "I'd be happy to escort you there for dinner, the trials of skill, and supper afterwards. If you can tolerate my company that long."

She opened her mouth to refuse but instead heard herself reply, "I—I'd like that very much." Why not? At least Anthony couldn't drag her back to the house when the Ranger officer was at her side. "Is it being held far from here?" she went on lamely. "I'm on foot."

He was surprised but didn't show it. "We have plenty of horses in the Ranger stables, and we even keep a few sidesaddles for emergency use."

By the time they selected and saddled a mare for her then started toward the field on the West Road where the jamboree would be held, Elisabeta began to relax. She realized she was hungry, having eaten nothing all day, and at the very worst she would be given two meals. The prospect heartened her.

Rick noticed the faint red mark on the side of her face, which her cosmetics almost concealed, but he made no comment. That kind of a mark could have been made only by a blow, so he guessed that Roberts had struck her. The hours that lay ahead promised to be interesting.

Elisabeta was astonished when they dismounted at a large field, where temporary wooden bleachers had been erected and a large number of people, perhaps as many as two or three thousand, were happily eating and drinking near several cooking fires. She saw sides of beef, wild turkeys, and meat that, had she been in the New World longer, she would have known was buffalo, turning on spits being cranked by energetic teen-age boys.

"Everything here is free, for everybody," Rick told her. "The Rangers contribute food and drink, of course, and so do people from President Houston to the newest government clerk. Most of what's here, though, has been given by folks who live for miles around. This is a big day for everybody who comes to Austin—and they come from all over the country."

She was conscious of his hand on her elbow as he piloted her toward one of the fires, but the gesture was natural and protective.

"Ah," Rick said. "We'll start with bowls of this to whet our appetites."

Elisabeta looked at the contents of her bowl, which a smiling women in calico ladled from a huge pot. "What is it? I'm not sure if it's soup or stew."

"Neither," Rick replied, grinning. "Some people are calling it chili because of the chili peppers chopped in it. There's ground-up beef, too, but that's all I can tell you. Some people use beans and some don't. There are no two cooks who use the same recipe."

The girl found herself eating greedily. "Whatever it is, I like it," she said.

"More?"

"Good heavens, no! I couldn't eat anything else!"

"That wouldn't do at all." He moved beside her to another fire, where they were given huge slabs of beef, served on bread that was still warm from the oven.

It was difficult to eat while standing, so they found seats in the bleachers. Then Rick went off and returned with two mugs of still-foaming ale.

Elisabeta wanted to tell him she never drank any alcoholic beverages other than a little wine, but she couldn't be rude. To her surprise the ale complemented the beef and bread perfectly.

"Now," he said when they were finished, "we'll try some potatoes and corn that were roasted in the coals."

Elisabeta laughed aloud for the first time since she had met him. The sound was similar to that of a gentle waterfall tumbling over rocks, and it delighted him.

"I'll burst," she said.

"Rubbish," he replied. "You're even scrawnier than you were the last time I saw you. You look as though you haven't eaten a proper meal for weeks."

That was true, of course. Fear and disgust had robbed her of her appetite. This was the man who could send her to prison for the role she had been forced to play in Anthony's murders, but she no longer cared. Even jail was preferable to life under Anthony's roof, and her mood became reckless. "I've never tasted either potatoes or corn cooked in coals, so I'm willing to try them."

"Good for you!"

As they made their way back to the fires, they were halted repeatedly by friends and acquaintances of Rick's. He appeared to know everyone, and he presented Ranger officers, justices of the appeals court, and so many others to Elisabeta that she couldn't keep them straight in her mind. They also saw various gentlemen who had been entertained at the Roberts house, and without exception they tipped their hats to Elisabeta. If they found it strange that "Mrs. Roberts" was being escorted by Captain Rick Miller, they made no comment, at least to her face.

A large group was gathered around a very tall, broad-shouldered man who wore a wide-brimmed, high-crowned hat of beaver fur. Rick cleared a path for Elisabeta and introduced her to the President of the Republic of Texas.

"Miller, you rascal," Sam Houston boomed, "trust you to show up today with the prettiest girl in the country. Hang onto her! And you, ma'am, latch onto Rick Miller. You won't find a finer man on earth!"

Elisabeta's face was scarlet as they went on to get potatoes and corn, and Rick could feel his own cheeks burning. But the President's remarks swept away many inhibitions, and the couple discovered they could chat easily thereafter.

Elisabeta told Rick in detail about somewhat similar celebrations she had attended in Spain, where they were called fandangos. Then, without meaning to reveal so much about her past, she talked about her childhood, her parents, and their deaths.

Rick replied by describing his own life, first in the mountains as a hunter and trapper, then in Texas, where he had been one of the first company of Rangers. The time passed quickly.

Armchairs, brought to the site in wagons, were unloaded and placed in front of the bleachers for President Houston, his Cabinet, the leaders of the Congress, and members of the diplomatic corps. Because of Rick's rank, he was able to obtain two chairs.

"Make yourself comfortable," he told Elisabeta. "I'll rejoin you shortly."

Alone for the first time in several hours, she searched the crowd, hoping she wouldn't see Anthony.

Bugles blared, drums rolled, and the spectators who hadn't yet found places for themselves hurried into the bleachers or sat near them on the ground. A militia band marched onto the field, a flag-bearer carrying the Lone Star banner at the head of the procession, and everyone stood.

Then people cheered lustily as the Rangers passed in review. All were mounted, and they were led by their commander, a colonel. Directly behind him were two others, one the major, who was the executive officer or deputy commander. The other was Rick Miller. As they rode past the President, they saluted smartly, their military precision more than compensating for their informal attire, their only concessions to uniforms being their armbands. Then Rick, somewhat to his own surprise, found himself raising his hand to the brim of his hat again as his stallion trotted past the woman he had escorted to the jamboree.

His gesture astonished Elisabeta, and at the same time she discovered that it thrilled her. This man whom she had feared for so long was no ogre. He was as gentle as he was ruggedly handsome, certainly the most considerate person she had ever met. On the other hand, she warned herself, he didn't yet know that she had been an accessory to three murders. His attitude would change abruptly when he learned of the role Anthony had forced her to play in luring elderly men to their deaths.

The three Ranger companies rode past the President in formation, and the crowd applauded loudly. Then, suddenly, bedlam broke loose, and people danced up and down in excitement, screaming and shouting.

Brigadier General Leland Blake, finding it difficult to maintain a straight face, led his contingent of troops from the United States Legation onto the field, the men in the precise formation that befitted professional soldiers. The flag-bearer who rode beside Lee carried the Stars and Stripes, and the sight of the banner drove the throng into a frenzy. Even Sam Houston forgot his dignity, removed his hat, and, waving it, cheered lustily. Never had Elisabeta seen so many people showing such depth of feeling simultaneously, and for reasons she could not fathom, she cheered, too. The spirit of these people, who took such pride in their independence, was contagious.

After the Americans had passed in review, Lee Blake joined his wife a short distance from the place where Elisabeta was sitting. He noticed her as he moved past her chair and then said something to Cathy, who turned to look at her. It was obvious to Elisabeta that they were discussing her, but she had no idea what they might be saying.

Sergeant Major Hector Mullins, looking smart in his dress uniform, climbed to a seat in the bleachers that Ginny had saved for him, and the MacGregor girls made a fuss over him as their parents nodded in smiling approval.

Two regiments of Texas militia marched down the field to tunes played by their own band. Their lines were ragged, their uniforms were sloppy, and they made only feeble attempts to walk in step, but the crowd nevertheless loved them. These were the volunteers who had fought Santa Anna successfully and won independence for Texas. Their skills as fighting men far outweighed their lack of precision, and it was plain from the way they carried themselves that they were conscious of their achievements, proud of their past, and confident of what they could do in the future if the need arose.

When the last of the militia left the field, the formal ceremonies came to an end, and the games began. The first was a contest for young men, who were required to remain mounted as long as they could while riding bareback on wild horses. One after another was thrown, to the delight of the spectators, and it was announced that the winner, the owner of a small ranch, had held his seat for more than two minutes. His accomplishment was heartily applauded.

As the applause died away, Rick slipped into the empty chair beside Elisabeta and grinned at her.

"You were very impressive," she told him.

He shrugged. "All in a day's work. We don't much like parades because Rangers don't believe in showing off. We'd rather let what we do speak for itself. But marching like this once a year is expected of us, and folks enjoy it, so we don't mind overly much."

The next contest was announced. Volunteers were asked to mount their horses, then rope cows and steers that were turned loose at one end of the field. Elisabeta watched open-mouthed as the loops were twirled and the riders, moving at a gallop, managed to bring down the animals with their accurate throws. Texans were remarkable people.

There was a change of pace when a race for teen-age girls was announced, the crowd laughing as applause welled up. Heather MacGregor horrified her parents by jumping to her feet, and they could not stop her as she made her way down to the field. Sidesaddled mares were provided, and the girls were told they had to race up and down the length of the field three times. The obvious favorite was a dark-haired girl who waved repeatedly to her admirers.

No one was more grim than Heather, who patted her horse, spoke to it, and seemed to be concentrating her full attention on it as she walked the animal to the starting line. A pistol shot sent the riders into motion.

By the end of the first lap, it was apparent that Heather and the dark-haired girl were the only serious contenders. They far outdistanced the others, and all through the second lap, they rode neck and neck.

When they made the last turn and began the final lap, Heather drew into the lead and gradually increased it, in spite of her opponent's frantic efforts to close the gap. The fickle crowd transferred its affections and loyalties to the girl with flaming red hair and freckles, and they gave her a standing ovation when she won by more than three lengths.

Even before she was awarded her prize, a silver-handled riding crop, Teng Chu leaped from his seat and embraced her. The crowd roared again.

As the next contest was being announced, Elisabeta had the uncomfortable feeling that someone was staring at her. She turned and looked directly into the eyes of Anthony Roberts, who was sitting in the bleachers next to Asa Phipps. Anthony's gaze was cold and full of hate. She was seated beside Captain Rick Miller, the man who could have him hanged for his transgressions, and she knew that if Anthony dared to kill her at this moment, he would not hesitate to shoot her.

A chill traveled slowly up her spine. She was in

immediate mortal danger, and she prayed that Rick would not leave her side again. Henceforth, she had to avoid Anthony at all costs.

A few moments later she could not help looking around again, but by now Anthony had vanished, taking Phipps with him. Probably he would be lying in wait for her somewhere, intending to ambush her. Without quite realizing what she was doing, she inched closer to Rick.

Elisabeta was so disturbed that, later, she could remember nothing about a number of the contests that followed. She was jerked back to the present only when Rick said to her, "Now for the grand climax."

Sam Houston himself made the announcement. "Now we're going to find out what kind of marksmen we have. Militiamen may enter this contest, of course. Only the Rangers are ineligible. Because any Ranger who failed to get a perfect score would disgrace the corps."

The crowd laughed.

"We're setting up two targets, apples mounted at the tops of spiked poles six feet from the ground," the President said. "Contestants may use their own mounts, or we'll provide horses for them if they prefer. All will start at the far end of the field and will come to this end one by one. It doesn't matter how the apples are knocked off the poles. Use pistols, rifles, sabers, or knives, whatever you want, lads. The one requirement is that you ride at a full gallop. Your goal is to get rid of both apples. Anyone in the audience who thinks he can do the trick is welcome to volunteer."

Hector Mullins peeled off his tunic and hurried down the bleachers in his shirt-sleeves to the place where Lee Blake was sitting. "General," he said, "I know I ain't in uniform now, but I've got me a hankering to—"

"By all means, Mullins. Show them what a sergeant major in the U.S. Army can do. And if you'd like, use my stallion."

"Thanks all the same, sir, but me and my horse know each other." Hector hurried down onto the field.

A dozen men were gathering, and suddenly Teng Chu rose and stretched. "In another week's time," he said, "I will leave for New York and my voyage to the Middle Kingdom. I will lose my skills without practice."

People stared at the robed, booted Chinese warrior as he joined the others. Before going off for their horses, the group walked to the two poles, set about fifteen feet apart, each with an apple affixed to the top. Sam Houston accompanied them.

"Mr. President," Hector asked, "are we supposed to ride between the poles?"

"Do it any way you like," Houston said. "Go between them or outside one or the other. Just remember you aren't allowed to double back. You're expected to get rid of both apples on a single run."

Several of the contestants looked dubious. The feat would be far more difficult to accomplish than they had imagined.

Teng Chu, his face expressionless, walked to each of the poles in turn. He carefully examined them, then tested the strength and diameter of each pole. Whatever he had in mind, he appeared satisfied.

The men returned to the opposite end of the field, and the first of the contestants, armed with a rifle and a knife, was given the signal to begin. He spurred forward, and while his mount carried him at a gallop, he raised his rifle. His shot missed the mark, and he swerved closer to the second pole, then threw his knife, but it missed the target by several feet. The crestfallen man retrieved his knife.

Others were equally inaccurate. After the first six riders had taken their chances, the original apples were still intact at the tops of the poles.

Then it was Hector Mullins's turn. Armed with two pistols, he increased his speed gradually, smoothly, then, as he was almost between the poles, shot the pistol in his left hand. The bullet missed by inches. Almost simultaneously, however, he squeezed the trigger of the pistol in his right hand, and the second apple disintegrated.

The crowd cheered loudly.

But Hector was not satisfied with his performance. Turning his horse over to one of his cavalrymen, he went to Lee before returning to his seat. "I'm sorry, General," he said. "I was a mite careless with that first shot."

"You did well, Mullins. I'm proud of you," Lee replied.

One by one the other contestants took their turns, and without exception all of them missed both targets. It appeared that Sergeant Major Mullins would be the winner.

It was no accident that Teng Chu was the last of the contestants, the Ranger commander having held him until the end in order to spare him embarrassment. Now, Teng Chu quickly spurred his stallion to a gallop. The crowd, noting that he carried no weapons, rewarded him with a polite smattering of applause.

When the Chinese was about twenty feet from the poles, riding on a course that would take him directly between them, he reached inside his robe and then hurled his multi-pointed, porcupinelike sphere at the apple to his left. One of the spikes imbedded itself in the flesh, and the weight of the weapon did the rest. The apple fell to the ground, carrying the sphere with it.

As soon as Teng Chu let fly, he put the target to his left out of his mind. Swiftly drawing his strange curved sword, he edged his mount closer to the target on his right, then lopped the apple from the pole with a single, wicked slash.

Then, as the crowd shouted and stomped in approval, he wheeled and somehow picked up the spherical weapon with the tip of his sword, snatching it with his free hand as it rolled down the length of the blade. The unexpected gesture caused the crowd to go wild.

Teng Chu's face was still solemn, but there was laughter in his eyes as he walked his horse toward the President's seat, then held up a hand for quiet. "Accept this as a token from my Emperor, from the people of the Middle Kingdom, and from a grateful Teng Chu, who will leave part of himself in Texas when he returns to his own country."

Sam Houston cleared his throat. "We shall always remember Teng Chu," he said. "I'm going to have copies of this prickly sphere made in a New England foundry.

And before you leave our land, sir, I hope you can find the time to teach our Rangers how to use it effectively."

"Nothing would give me greater pleasure," the Chinese warrior replied, bowing from the waist. Then, not waiting for Houston to extend his hand, he held out his own.

The contests were at an end, and, as the sun sank lower over the hills to the west, people began to drift back to the cooking fires for what Rick called a "light supper."

Elisabeta was no longer surprised by the overwhelming Texas hospitality. The meal included baked ham and baked beans, fried chicken, baked apples, boiled greens, and more chili. She was far too apprehensive to eat again and imagined that at any moment Anthony might fire at her or plunge a knife into her back.

Suddenly she thought she saw him off to her left and peered more intently, but the man only vaguely resembled him.

"What's wrong?" Rick asked, seeing that she had grown deathly pale and was trembling.

At that instant her situation became totally intolerable. "We must get away from all these people," she said urgently. "I've got to talk to you about something very important. Right now."

"Can't it wait until we've eaten?"

She shook her head, feeling miserable.

Realizing she was at a breaking point, for whatever her reasons, Rick filled two plates and, carrying them, led her to the bank of a small stream.

The night was warm and the air was sultry, so others were moving away from the fires while they ate, too, but the place Rick had chosen was located at a bend in the river, near a jumbled pile of rocks, so no one else was in the immediate vicinity.

He placed the plates on a table-high, flat-topped rock, then spread a bandanna on the ground for her.

Paying no attention to the food, Elisabeta poured out her story in a low monotone, punctuated by occasional, shrill bursts of emotion. She told him everything, beginning with Anthony Roberts's courtship and promise to marry her, their affair, and their long journey to the New World. She explained that he had changed after they had reached Texas, relegating her to the role of a servant. And, her voice shaking, she told him about the three murders in which she had been compelled to participate as a lure.

Rick listened quietly, making no comment. He had already assumed that the girl had slept with Roberts at one time or another, so that revelation did not surprise him. Her evidence against Roberts was only circumstantial, as she had not actually witnessed any of the killings. But her story was so damning that he felt certain any court in Texas would find Roberts guilty.

"Arrest me," Elisabeta said. "I am ready to go to prison."

He looked compassionately at this lovely, honest, and badly upset young woman. His deep sympathy was mixed with another feeling that he could not identify. "You won't go to prison, Elisabeta," he said gently. "You've been subjected to cruel pressures and inhuman treatment. You're blameless."

Her relief was so great that tears appeared in her eyes and rolled down her cheeks.

"In fact," Rick went on, "what you've done is rather wonderful. Your life is in danger, but you've increased the risk by telling me your story."

She wept harder.

Giving in to sudden impulse, something he rarely did, he took her hand in his. "I think you're wonderful, and I give you my pledge that no harm will come to you. You're under my protection now." Embarrassed by the intensity of his own fervor, he fumbled in a pocket and handed her another bandanna. "You'd better eat. Quickly. We well may have a long evening ahead of us."

So lighthearted that she was giddy, Elisabeta followed his orders and ate some of the food on her plate. It was a miracle that she would not be prosecuted, even more of a miracle that this solid, reliable man had promised to shield her.

"First off," Rick said, wolfing his own meal, "we've got to find a place where you'll be safe. Then," he added grimly, "I aim to have a little business discussion with Mr. Roberts."

"The very least I can do is carry the plates," Elisabeta said.

Her reply was so unexpected that he laughed, then hugged her, and became even more embarrassed.

As they walked rapidly back toward the cooking fires, Rick was looking for someone he eventually found. "Sergeant Haight!"

His assistant knew that authoritative tone, and stiffened. "Yes, sir!"

"Take three men. Search the jamboree grounds for Anthony Roberts. He probably left hours ago, but I want you to check. Next, go to his house. When you find him, place him under arrest. He's dangerous, so don't hesitate to shoot if he offers any resistance. If he's at the house, hold him until I join you, which may be an hour or so from now. If he hasn't shown up yet, wait for him, but make yourselves inconspicuous. I don't want him to give us the slip. He may or may not have accomplices, so be careful. And although I don't want him questioned before I arrive, take note of anything he may say. Is everything clear?"

"Yes, sir." Haight had only one question. "Is this in connection with the hangman's noose killings, Captain?"

"Could be."

"I've felt in my bones all along that he was the man." Sergeant Haight hurried away.

"Now," Rick said, turning to Elisabeta, "we'll take care of your immediate problems."

"If you're arresting Anthony, I don't have any," she said.

"Really?" He sounded lightly exasperated. "We haven't taken him yet, and there may be others involved with him. Your funds are limited, and you have no safe place to stay. No problems?" He took her arm, his grip firm.

Her confidence in him unexpectedly unbounded, she allowed him to take her wherever he wished.

Rick seemed to wander through the crowd aimlessly, but he was looking for someone, and he was relieved when he saw Lee and Cathy Blake. "General, you're just the person I want to see."

"Can it wait until morning, Captain Miller? Our little girl is so tired we want to take her back to the legation before she falls asleep."

"This won't take long, sir." Rick introduced Elisabeta to the Blakes. "Miss Manuel is in a heap of trouble, General." Rick was speaking for Cathy's benefit as well as Lee's. "She's had hell's own time, if you'll pardon my language, ladies. Right now, she's the only prosecution witness in what promises to be a sensational murder case, and the killer, who will murder her if he can, is still at large. I would have spoken to Mr. Teller, but I saw him leave right after the games. The only safe place in Austin is the U.S. Legation, which is guarded and has a palisade. Is there some place there where Miss Manuel could be sheltered until we can arrange other quarters for her?"

"Of course," Lee replied instantly.

"In fact," Cathy added warmly, "you can stay with us. We have more bedrooms than we're using. We've been admiring you today, Miss Manuel. My husband and I have never seen anyone prettier."

Elisabeta flushed and didn't know what to reply.

"Captain Miller, there will be no need for you to find other quarters for Miss Manuel." Turning back to the young woman, Cathy continued, "We hope you'll make your home with us for as long as you wish."

The kindness of these American strangers was so great that Elisabeta was afraid she would weep again. Instead, she looked down on Beth, who was clutching her mother's hand, her little face sleepy and solemn. Elisabeta smiled at her.

The child grinned in return. "I like you," she announced.

That settled the matter. Elisabeta was accepted.

"Captain," Lee said, "if you're needed elsewhere, we'll take charge of getting Miss Manuel back to the legation."

"Thank you, General, but I'd best be on hand myself. As I mentioned, the killer is still at large."

Teng Chu, who had taken no part in the conversation, took a step forward, bowing to Elisabeta. "I will be responsible for the safety of the lady."

Elisabeta's relief was so great that she laughed. She had seen the Chinese warrior in action, and she could think of no more ferocious a bodyguard. She had been bereft, but her new friends were taking care of her, and her whole outlook on life was changing.

"You'll ride in the carriage with my wife and Beth," Lee told her. "I'll be on one side of the coach, and Teng Chu will be on the other. Are you ready to leave?"

"Oh, yes." Elisabeta turned to Rick, wanting to thank him for all he was doing for her.

He cut her off and spoke brusquely. "I'll stop at the legation later," he said, "and report whatever may develop."

Giving her no chance to reply, he walked rapidly toward the tethered horses, then turned to call, "I'll see to it that your borrowed mare is returned."

His mind seething, he took a quick look around the jamboree grounds, to see if Sergeant Haight was still there. Then, after arranging for Elisabeta's borrowed horse to be returned to the Rangers' stable, he rode into town at a canter, loosening the revolver in his belt as he approached Anthony Roberts's house.

Sergeant Haight was waiting for him on the front porch. "Sir," he said as he saluted, "our buffalo has gone off to find some tall grass somewhere else. The men are in the house, taking inventory of what's there."

Rick was disappointed. "Roberts has pulled out?"

"I'm afraid so, Captain. There were two horses in the stable, and all that's there now is a beat-up, no-good covered wagon. All of Roberts's clothes, his razor, and all his other personal belongings are gone, too. All we can find are a batch of ladies' clothes and cosmetics and such in one of the bedrooms. He left in such an all-fired hurry that the front door was open when we got here."

Rick followed him into the house, made his own inspection, and told his men to pack Elisabeta's belongings in the leather traveling boxes that stood in a corner of the room. Roberts had departed in such a hurry that there had been no time for him to destroy Elisabeta's property. "Take these to Miss Manuel at General Blake's house," he said. "And tell her I'll stop in to see her before the end of the evening." It didn't occur to him that more than a wish to do his duty was responsible for his desire to see her again as soon as he could.

He and Sergeant Haight returned to their office, and there they prepared a full report for higher authority on the day's rapid developments. The key problem now was that of apprehending Anthony Roberts, and the task would not be easy. The law enforcement network throughout Texas was still loosely organized, and there were vast areas where no police force yet existed.

"I reckon all we can do is send out warnings to the sheriffs and hope one of them will see the fugitive," Rick said, sighing. In the morning he would institute inquiries about the owner of the dilapidated covered wagon that had been found in Roberts's barn. A successful search might provide at least some nuggets of information.

There was nothing more that could be done tonight, so he hurried to the United States Legation. Elisabeta had already settled in there, and when she joined Rick in the parlor of the Blake house, her smile was broad. "You don't know how grateful I am to you for saving all of my clothes. When I ran away today, I thought I'd never see any of them again."

"The one thing you haven't mentioned," he said, "is why you chose today to get out of the place."

She told him what little she could about Asa Phipps, indicating to him that the man's crude advances, apparently condoned by Anthony, had been the last straw.

Lee Blake had come into the room quietly during her recital and listened carefully. "You say his name is Phipps?" he asked when she had finished her story.

"I think so, but I wouldn't swear to it," she replied.

"I know the man," Lee told Rick. "He's no good, and we had to throw him off our wagon train." He sketched in the background of his own problems with the Kentuckian.

Rick rubbed his chin. "What all this adds up to," he said, "is that Roberts needs help—for some reason—and is paying this Phipps for it. That brings up the question of what new trouble Roberts has in the back of his mind. I'm afraid we'll find out one of these days, if we don't take both of them into custody first." He turned to Elisabeta and spoke bluntly. "What it means for you is that you'll have to stay right here until the danger is ended. I don't want you to leave the legation grounds at any time, for any reason."

"That's sound advice," Lee agreed. "My troops prevent any trespassers from wandering into the grounds here, and you'll be safer in this house than you'd be anywhere else in Texas."

"I—I don't want to be a burden on you or Mrs. Blake, General," Elisabeta said.

"We're delighted to have you here!" Lee told her.

"Just keep in mind," Rick said, "that you're the only person who can give evidence against Roberts. Without your testimony the prosecution's case against him would collapse. Only the Lord in His wisdom knows why Roberts committed those murders, but we'll need you to make a case against him that will stick."

"I have never hated anyone in all my life," Elisabeta said, "and I always thought that revenge was a base motive. But I do despise that man for all the pain and humiliation he has caused me. I will rejoice when he is brought to justice. But I don't want to be a coward by hiding indefinitely in this house."

"It's common sense for you to stay here," Rick said.

Cathy joined them and insisted that Rick have a cup

of tea with them before he left. She was aware of what
her husband failed to sense, the mutual interest of Elisabeta and Rick in each other, so she lost no time saying, "I
hope we'll see you often while Miss Manuel is staying
with us, Captain."

"Thank you ma'am. I would like to keep her up to date
on whatever we may find out about Roberts. If we
discover anything of significance, she may be able to fill
us in on details that haven't yet come to her mind."

Cathy realized that he might not have analyzed his
reasons for wanting to see Elisabeta. "Come for supper
tomorrow night," she said.

"I sure will!" he said promptly.

Elisabeta's slow smile spoke volumes, and Cathy was
pleased. Later, as she and Lee were preparing for bed,
she said, "Some good comes out of even the most horrible situations. I'm convinced of it. Don't you think those
two would make a wonderful couple?"

"You're incorrigible," Lee said, chuckling.

"Perhaps. But the way they spark to each other makes
me know I'm right. You mark my words, Lee Blake. Rick
Miller is going to be underfoot frequently as long as
Elisabeta Manuel stays here."

"You're a matchmaker."

"In this case I don't need to be," she said. "They've
already found each other, and all they need is a little
time to find out for themselves."

Harry Canning achieved the seemingly impossible by
launching two of his small clipper ships on the same day.
As soon as they were afloat, he supervised the stepping,
or emplacement of the masts, a task that took another
two weeks.

President Houston came to Galveston Island for the
commissioning of the two vessels, which were called the
Texas and the *Lone Star*, and he personally administered
the oath to the ships' officers and crews. Until the cannon
arrived on the munitions train now making its way to
Texas, the little warships would lack teeth, but in the

meantime they were being sent out to sea without delay
to watch for any sign of the Mexican navy in the
vicinity.

A large party accompanied the President, and it included Lee and Cathy Blake, who were present as
Houston's guests. Sergeant Major Mullins stayed behind
in Austin because the presence of Elisabeta Manuel in
the legation made it necessary to maintain a full guard
detail there. But Ginny accompanied the Blakes, and,
like Cathy, she was delighted to be reunited with old
friends from Oregon.

Sam Houston stayed overnight, then left, but the
Blakes and Ginny Mullins agreed to stay on for a few
days. Early in the morning Lee went off with Harry
Canning to the boatyard, and Nancy settled down in her
kitchen with Cathy and Ginny for a chat over mugs of
the first coffee to be exported from the West Indian
islands. Savoring the brew, the three women chatted
amiably.

"You look as though Texas is good for you, Nancy,"
Cathy said.

"Well, day-to-day existence is rougher than I ever
imagined it would be," Nancy admitted. "If I had known
back in Oregon what I know now, I'd have thought
twice before stowing away and forcing myself on the
men who came here. Harry has been wonderful, of
course, and we're closer than ever. But I've learned my
lesson. He's talking about leaving a manager in charge
here after the warships are built, and I think that eventually we'll go back to Oregon."

Ginny smiled, and her words indicated that her own
attitude had changed. "It wasn't so long ago that I would
have envied you, Nancy. I wanted to go back to Oregon
more than anything on earth. Now I honestly don't care,
as long as Hector and I are together."

Cathy knew that the MacGregor girls were responsible for Ginny's new approach to life, but she kept her
own counsel.

"I'm thirty," Ginny said shyly, "but Hector and I have

decided we want to have children. Then, no matter where the army may send us, we'll have our own family with us."

It was a relief to know that Ginny had matured at last and that her future promised to be secure. But Cathy was reminded of someone else, and later in the conversation she asked, "Nancy, may I speak openly about something? I was a little disturbed when I saw Melissa last night. She's prettier than ever, but I didn't like the way she was playing Chet Harris and Danny Taylor against each other at supper and afterward. They're fine young men, both of them, and I'd hate to see either of them hurt."

"I've spoken to Melissa dozens of times," Nancy said, frowning. "She claims she can't make up her mind which of them she wants or whether she wants either of them. I believe she means it. All the same, Harry and I are annoyed by the way she flirts with them and goads them on. I'm afraid she loves being the center of male attention."

"She's still very young, of course," Ginny said. "All of us had known hardships and heartbreak at her age, but all she's ever had to do has been to smile and flap her eyelashes, and the men surround her."

"One of these days," Cathy said, "reality is going to catch up with Melissa Austin. I just hope she's strong enough and has the character to stand up to the problems everyone is forced to face sooner or later."

Anthony Roberts squatted at the campfire, chewing on the tough meat of the buffalo that Asa Phipps had shot earlier in the day. After a lifetime of living in such sophisticated cities as London and Madrid, Anthony loathed every moment he spent in the wilderness. The food was dreadful, and he ate it only because the alternative was starvation. Sleeping in the open on the hard ground was uncomfortable, and the endless travel through unpopulated areas was wearying.

As he well knew, however, he had no choice. He was

no longer in a position to give regular reports on Texas to the British and Mexicans and his world would right itself only if he succeeded in committing the act of sabotage against the munitions train. Then, having been successful in his mission, he would be permitted to live in London again and in time might be given another foreign mission.

Certainly his situation was far from hopeless. He continued to enjoy robust health. He had taken all of his money with him and had enough funds to carry out his present assignment without difficulty. And, although the Rangers surely knew by now that he had killed some of his father's murderers and might well be searching for him, the country was so huge they would have to hunt for months before finding him. By that time he would have left the New World, never to return.

The destruction of the munitions train was a difficult assignment, but Anthony felt confident of succeeding. At the moment he wasn't too concerned about it. What bothered him was a personal matter that had to be resolved before he left this barbaric continent.

"Damn that woman's soul!" he said bitterly.

Asa Phipps had become accustomed to Anthony's diatribes and continued to eat his buffalo steak, sawing at the meat with his knife, spearing chunks, and shoving them into his mouth.

"For the life of me, I can't imagine why she went to the Rangers!" Anthony continued to brood. "She knew she'd be implicated with me, and she's too timid a woman to have taken that kind of initiative. Something must have frightened her badly and caused her to panic."

Phipps ate in silence.

"Perhaps you sparked her in some way and sent her running to Captain Miller!"

"I hardly knew her name. Or your name," Phipps protested uneasily, disturbed by the steady glare of the other's cold, menacing eyes.

"I've been trying to piece this puzzle together, and

there's something I haven't asked you, Phipps. Did you make love to Elisabeta?"

Truly frightened now, the Kentuckian shook his head.

"You made it plain enough before I left the house that you wanted her. What caused you to change your mind?"

Asa Phipps lacked the intelligence to invent a plausible story, so he decided to admit a portion of the truth. "She did."

"Be more specific."

"I tried to get friendly with her," Phipps whined. "But she wouldn't have nothin' to do with me. I tried to tell her I just wanted to talk with her, but she went runnin' out of the house. And the next thing both of us knew, there she was at the jamboree, sittin' with that Ranger officer."

Anthony suspected he was lying, that he had offended or insulted Elisabeta so badly that she had become hysterical and had fled to the authorities. Not that it mattered now. What counted was that she undoubtedly had revealed all she knew about the three murders he had committed. That information would be enough to hang him.

"In a few days," he said slowly, "I'll be finished organizing the plan for the operation we're undertaking. Then I'm going to leave you for a short time."

"Maybe it ain't none of my business, but where be you headin'?" Phipps asked.

"Austin."

The Kentuckian was astonished. "Ever since we left there in an all-fired hurry, you been tellin' me how your life ain't worth a copper there!"

"I think I'm clever enough to go into town and leave again before the Rangers know I've been there. She may have gone into hiding, but in a town the size of Austin, it shouldn't take me long to find her. I owe her for her treachery, and I always pay my debts." He drew a length of silken cord from a pocket, looped it, and then pulled it taut, his face suddenly contorting.

Asa Phipps rarely wasted sympathy for anyone other

than himself, but he couldn't help feeling sorry for the pretty young woman who had become Anthony Roberts's enemy.

The entire MacGregor family worked with a vengeance to prepare the homestead they had claimed. Innes was tireless, cutting down trees from dawn until dusk, while Matilda used her prized spinning wheel to make thread that would be used for the cloth of their curtains, drapes, and furniture coverings. The older girls trimmed the trees, using saws to remove branches, and even Cara and Wallace were kept busy hauling away small pieces of wood that could not be used.

The family continued to live in the covered wagon until the new house was built, and Innes and Matilda were pleased when the owners of neighboring farms, some of whom had settled in the area several years earlier, volunteered their services and those of their sons. A dozen men and older boys helped dig the foundations, then pitched in to make the frame for the dwelling and fill in the sides and roof with logs. Two of the farmers brought their own teams and horses to the property, then plowed the land so it would be ready in time for the spring planting.

"I've ne'er known neighbors like these," Innes said. "We've truly come home."

No one worked harder than Heather, who cut logs into planks, then fashioned tables and chairs from them. Her energy was as great as her mother's, her stamina almost equal to that of her father. She never complained of weariness, and she kept a sharp watch on her younger sisters, too, insisting they attend to their own chores when, from time to time, they wanted to play.

At last the house was ready, and the MacGregors moved in. A celebration was in order, so Innes dipped into his cash reserves to buy food in Austin, and all of the neighbors who had contributed so much time and effort were invited to dinner.

Tables were erected beneath shade trees in the yard, and, to the surprise of the MacGregors, when the neighbors appeared, they brought gifts of still more food. The tables were filled with baked hams and roasted turkeys. There were a number of potato salads, no two alike, each of the contributors proud of her own recipe. Loaves of bread were heaped high, and corn was roasted in a stone-lined pit behind the new house. The children were delighted by the many cakes and pies, as well as by mugs of foaming, sweet cider. The adults drank tea, and there was hard cider for the men who wanted it.

Innes and Matilda wore church-going clothes that had been packed at the bottom of a clothing box and from which it had not been possible to remove all of the creases. The girls had not worn party dresses for a long time, either, and all had grown so much that the problem had to be solved by giving each a dress that formerly had belonged to her next-older sister. This took care of everyone but Heather, who was considerably taller than her mother now, so the girl had made herself a dress of calico, blue-and-white checked, with full sleeves and a ruffled, flounced skirt.

A dozen or more adults sat sedately on unpainted pine chairs that the guests thoughtfully had brought with them for the purpose. The small children ate quickly, then raced off, fortunately out of adult hearing, to play a game of hide-and-seek in a nearby patch of woods.

Heather sat demurely at the base of an oak tree, talking quietly but earnestly and laughing from time to time with a group of her own peers. As it happened, all were boys in their late teens.

Innes paid little attention to his daughters' whereabouts, but as he was sipping tea after eating a hearty meal, he was startled when he noticed Heather. Her eyes sparkled, her conversation was animated, and natural color glowed in her cheeks as she talked with some of the youths who had contributed so much work to the building of the house. They were interrupting each other, trying to gain her full attention, and when she spoke, they fell silent in order to hear what she was saying.

It was difficult for Innes to concentrate on his own talk

with some of the men, and he repeatedly looked in the
direction of his eldest daughter. Then he caught sight of
Matilda, who was emerging from the new kitchen with a
steaming teapot, and he went to her quickly.

"Look ye," he muttered.

She glanced in the direction of the oak, took in the
scene, and nodded calmly.

"Our wee lass is holding court," he declared.

Matilda tried to hide a smile. "Aye."

"But she's just a child!"

"Think ye so, Innes?" She had to allow the smile to
show. "She's sixteen now, and she's no ewe lamb any
longer. If ye haven't noted—and it's plain that ye've been
near blind—our Heather is turning into a woman. Mark
those boys well, because ye'll be finding them underfoot
from this time onward!"

On December 4, 1844, almost three million United
States citizens went to the polls and by a decisive margin
elected James K. Pok as President. Two weeks passed
before all of the ballots were counted and Henry Clay
conceded victory to his opponent. President-elect Polk
promptly told the press that he intended to keep his
campaign promises. He would bring Texas into the
Union as rapidly as possible and would seek a solution
of the Oregon border question by peaceful means if
possible, by force if necessary.

John Tyler remained determined to win his own place
in history, and a scant five days before he left office, he
was successful. Both Houses of the Congress heeded his
urgent request, and on February 28, 1845, they passed a
joint resolution admitting Texas to the Union. The following morning, with Polk's wholehearted concurrence,
Tyler signed the measure that would make Texas the
twenty-eighth state. Two more steps would be required to
complete the annexation process: Texas would be required to make an application for statehood, and the
Congress would have to accept it.

Two days after President Polk's inauguration, the
Mexican Minister to the United States sent a stiff protest

to the White House and ordered his staff to begin packing their belongings. On March 28 the legation closed its doors, and Mexico formally broke diplomatic relations with the United States.

Two messengers had left Washington City with the momentous news on March 1. One traveled to Texas on board a sloop of the U.S. Navy, and the other rode overland to Nashville. Andrew Jackson, whose health was failing rapidly, received the news in bed, and at his urgent request his physicians permitted him a swallow of whiskey.

"I thank God I have lived long enough to see this great day," he said to President Polk in a letter that he was too feeble to write himself and had to dictate to his niece.

The unexpected maneuver caught Texas off guard, but President Houston replied immediately, saying that Texas would respond favorably at the earliest moment. Bonfires were lighted in Austin, and couriers quickly carried the word elsewhere. Houston chose July 4, 1845, as the date on which the Texas congress would vote on the proposal.

In Mexico City President Santa Anna summoned his reserve regiments into duty.

On Galveston Island Harry Canning completed the building of three more small clipper ships, which promptly joined the rest of the growing Texas fleet in doing patrol duty in the Gulf of Mexico.

The badly needed munitions train suffered a series of mishaps, the heavy wagons repeatedly becoming mired in deep mud. Already overdue, the train would spend many more weeks on the dirt roads before reaching Texas.

If President Polk had observed strict legalities, he could have done nothing to help Texas face the coming crisis until her statehood was accomplished. But he was not one to stand on ceremony, and neither was Sam Houston. Two regiments of U.S. infantry and one of cavalry, along with support troops that included engineers and ordnance experts, were sent from New Orleans to Galveston by troop transport. Not wanting to give Santa

Anna an excuse to begin hostilities, Polk ordered the troops to proceed to Austin. There they were placed under the temporary command of Brigadier General Leland Blake.

Late in May Sam Houston put aside his official responsibilities and, accompanied by his young son, traveled to Nashville. He arrived late on June 8, only to learn that Andrew Jackson had died earlier that same day. All America mourned the loss of one of her greatest sons.

President Polk, acting in his role of Commander in Chief, placed Texas under the protection of the United States Navy. This order enabled Harry Canning to alter his program and begin building the merchant ships that Texas urgently needed.

Lee Blake received a confidential message from the War Department informing him that Major General Zachary Taylor was being sent to Texas and directing him to place himself and the units under his command at General Taylor's disposal. An undisclosed number of reinforcements would accompany the new commander, who would station himself "on the Rio Grande or in its vicinity" to await further developments.

Texas increased the pace of her own preparations for war. The Rangers were expanded from one regiment to four, and enlistment was opened to all qualified volunteers, provided they brought their own horses. The Quartermaster General of the U.S. Army thoughtfully sent cavalry uniforms for the Rangers, but they would continue to wear their distinctive, broad-brimmed hats.

Rick Miller was one of a number of regular Rangers given a temporary promotion. He was made an acting colonel and was given command of one of the new regiments.

The American troops from New Orleans arrived and moved into a bivouac area outside of Austin. Lee spent several days in the field with them, conferring with the unit commanders, then inspecting the troops and their equipment. He did not arrive back at the legation until late one evening.

"It's just a matter of time now before the shooting

starts," he told Cathy. "I see no way that a war can be avoided."

"I'm grateful for every day's delay," she replied. "Why hasn't it started yet?"

"I believe Santa Anna is waiting until Texas formally votes to join the Union. Then he'll have the justification he wants, and all hell will break loose."

XI

For a time Rick Miller found some official reason to pay a call almost daily at the home of the military attaché in the U.S. Legation. But these excuses became so transparent that he abandoned them, making it plain that he was calling on Elisabeta Manuel because he wanted to see her. She welcomed his visits, and Cathy Blake eased the path the couple was taking by frequently inviting Rick to supper. Certainly it was no secret to anyone at the legation that the officer and the Spanish refugee were becoming seriously interested in each other.

When Rick received his promotion, he went into the field to expedite the formation of his regiment, and his visits to Elisabeta necessarily halted abruptly. He promised he would see her when he could, but for several weeks she had no word from him.

Teng Chu had stayed on in Austin so he could teach the Rangers to throw the spiked metal sphere that was his favorite weapon, but with the outbreak of war between the United States and Mexico imminent, he knew he could delay his departure no longer. Lee provided him with a cavalry escort to New Orleans, where the navy would take him to New York on a frigate.

He planned to leave at dawn one morning, so the entire Blake household arose early to see him off. Beth clung to him, and he presented the child with a small carved-ivory figure of a mythical creature, half bird and half animal.

"Think of Teng Chu when you grow to be a woman," he said. "May this token remind you of your friend."

The little girl fought back her tears.

The Chinese warrior turned to Cathy. "When I reach my own home, I will send you a gift that properly expresses my appreciation for your hospitality," he told her. "Until then, accept this."

Cathy gasped at the magnificent oblong of polished jade that he handed her. It was exquisite, engraved with Chinese characters. She felt her expressions of thanks were inadequate.

"The characters," Teng Chu said, "are symbols of beauty and wisdom. You have both." Giving her no chance to reply, he gave a similar, slightly smaller piece of polished jade to Elisabeta. "Marry the Ranger," he said. "You are right for each other."

Elisabeta turned scarlet.

The Chinese warrior stalked off abruptly, afraid he would lose control of his own emotions. The cavalry escort, already mounted, was waiting at the legation gate, and Lee gripped his friend's hand. "May we meet again," he said.

"If it is our destiny, we will meet." Teng Chu mounted his horse, waved once, and rode off, surrounded by his escort.

At breakfast everyone was subdued. Cathy and Elisabeta sipped their tea in silence, Beth announced that she didn't want her oatmeal, and although Lee ate his ham steak and eggs, he was anything but buoyant. "We needn't act as though we've lost a dear relative," he said. "Teng always will be our friend."

"I was a complete stranger to him," Elisabeta said, "but he was so kind to me. And I always felt safe when he was near."

Beth examined her carved-ivory piece and snuffled aloud.

Lee's orderly came into the room. "Excuse the interruption, sir," he said. "But Captain—I mean Colonel Miller is here."

"He is? Show him in!"

Elisabeta brightened instantly.

Rick came in, resplendent in his new cavalry uniform, with his silver epaulet on one shoulder. "I'm sorry to break in on you all like this," he said, "but I was called into town, and I have very little time." His remarks were addressed to everyone, but he looked only at Elisabeta, whose eyes shone.

"Join us for breakfast," Cathy said.

"In a few minutes, if I may. This isn't a strictly personal visit. I need a word in private with General Blake."

Lee rose at once, and they went together to the small study at the opposite end of the ground floor.

"You'll be glad to hear, sir, that the munitions train is finally approaching the Texas border," Rick told him. "I've been temporarily detached from duty with my new regiment to take charge of protecting the train from the border to Austin."

"Then I needn't be too concerned about safety problems," Lee said. "Thank the Lord the train is finally arriving. Will the escort troops come all the way with the arms and powder wagons?"

"Apparently not, General. My orders tell me to relieve them at the border."

"That's too bad. I was hoping to snag an extra troop of cavalry when they arrived here. And I'm afraid there isn't time for me to ask the War Department to give them to me. Oh, well." Lee looked at the visitor and became brisk. "What can I do to help you, Colonel?"

"Nothing, thanks. I'm being given enough Rangers to provide the train with what headquarters regards as adequate protection—"

"You don't want help?" Lee interrupted sharply.

"That train is worth many hundreds of thousands of dollars, sir. So, in my opinion, no protection is adequate." Rick grinned. "But I'll make do with the men they give me."

"How soon do you take off for the border?"

"This morning, General. The escort is being assembled at the barracks right now. This has come at a bad time for me, I'll admit. I've just organized a training program for my recruits, but I guess my cadre of veterans will know what to do until I get back."

"In my experience," Lee said, "there's never enough time for training troops." He led the way back to the dining room.

Cathy went out to the kitchen for the ham steaks and eggs she had asked the cook to prepare for Rick. When she returned, she noticed her husband signaling to her surreptitiously, but didn't grasp the meaning.

"I'm trying to tell you," Lee said, "that Rick's time is very limited, so I'm sure he and Elisabeta will appreciate a few minutes of privacy. Come along, Beth." He picked up his daughter, sat her on his shoulder, and left the room.

Cathy left and followed them. "Ordinarily, I'm not all that dense," she said.

Rick salted his eggs and did not look at Elisabeta as he said, "I haven't been able to get you out of my mind."

She tried to speak lightly. "I hope you haven't tried too hard."

"Hard enough. I've been selecting recruits for my new regiment, organizing a training program, and putting our camp in shape. It isn't easy when I find myself day-dreaming about you."

"I'm sorry it hasn't been easy, but I'm glad you've been doing it," she replied, surprised to discover she was breathless. "Because I've been thinking about you, too."

"Good thoughts or bad?"

"I'm not going to tell you," she replied, teasing him.

"There's been no sign of Anthony Roberts here-abouts?" His tone changed.

Elisabeta sobered and shook her head.

"I shouldn't tell you this, but it's only fair to warn you. According to one report at headquarters, he was seen in the vicinity of Austin and then vanished again. So take no chances, and stay in the legation compound."

"I'll do as you say, naturally, but it's so boring never to go anywhere!"

"It's better to be bored and stay alive." He realized he sounded too harsh, so, as he ate, he modified the statement. "This situation won't last forever. I'm hoping we'll have it cleared up for you by the time I get back here."

"You're leaving again?" Elisabeta couldn't hide her dismay.

"For three or four weeks." Rick sounded apologetic. "On a secret assignment."

She knew it would be wrong to ask him any questions, so she poured his tea in silence.

Uncertain whether she was disapproving, but aware of her disappointment, he finished his meal quickly, then pushed his plate away. "I've been wondering all sorts of things about you," he said. "Most of all, I've been thinking of what you'll do when this threat is ended and you've given testimony. By then I reckon we'll have state courts instead of national courts here, but that won't matter. What's important is that you'll be free to do whatever you please once the law has decided how to punish Roberts."

"I have been thinking about the future, too," Elisabeta said, then fell silent again.

"I suppose you'd like to go back to Spain."

"In some ways. But it isn't a practical solution. I don't have nearly enough money for that."

"Maybe you could get a loan," Rick said. "When the story of what you've done for Texas comes out into the open, a lot of folks will sympathize with you. Including our bankers."

She shook her head. "I wouldn't want to be indebted to anyone."

"I can suggest another alternative." Rick steeled himself, looked hard at her, and spoke a trifle too belligerently. "You could marry me."

Elisabeta blinked, then fought back a smile. "Is this a proposal of marriage?"

He nodded, swallowing hard. "I'm not doing it very

gracefully, but I've had no practice. I sure wouldn't blame you for turning me down. The Rangers don't pay much, and I'd be away as much as I'd be at home. Matter of fact, I figure there's a good chance that California will belong to the United States once we've fought this war. I have a hankering to go out there. They'll be organizing a new government, and I'd stand a pretty good chance of getting a good law enforcement job for more money than I can earn here."

"I have some relatives I've never met who own a ranch in California," Elisabeta said politely. "The family has been there a long time. They go back to the time when California was owned by Spain, before it became part of an independent Mexico. But I know nothing about California."

"I reckon you wouldn't like it out there," Rick said.

She curbed a desire to giggle. "So far," she said, "you've told me all sorts of reasons why I shouldn't marry you. Do you know of any reasons I should?"

Rick groped in vain for the right words.

She realized she had to prompt him. "Why do you want to marry me?" she asked gently.

"My God, that's obvious!" he shouted. "Because I love you!"

Her lovely eyes became misty. "That's a fortunate coincidence. I happen to love you, too."

Rick stared at her for a long moment, then, standing so abruptly that his chair toppled backward, he lifted her to her feet and took her into his arms. She returned his kiss with a tender fervor that matched his own feelings.

At last he held her at arm's length, scarcely able to believe his good fortune. "I'll be damned," he muttered.

"I hope not, for both our sakes," Elisabeta said.

"Maybe the air will be cleared by the time I finish this assignment," he said. "Even if Roberts is captured, I wouldn't ask you to live with me in the field."

"You sleep in a tent?"

He nodded. "And we eat field rations, which is no food for a lady."

"This lady would love to live in a tent with you, and she wouldn't care what she ate!"

"I'm so lucky I can't believe it," Rick said as he embraced her again.

Danny Taylor and Chet Harris made their usual after-supper call at the Canning house, and Harry and Nancy started to follow their custom of leaving the parlor so the two young men could chat privately with Melissa. But Danny halted them as they rose to go.

"Hold on," he said. "I want a word or two with both of you, and so does Chet."

His friend nodded, his manner solemn.

Realizing that the pair had something they regarded as important on their minds, Harry sat again.

"The shipbuilding program has settled into a steady routine," Danny said.

"The pressures have been much less since we switched from warships to merchantmen," Chet added. "And you have first-rate supervisors who know their business."

"Some of the younger fellows have been leaving to join the Texas militia," Danny said. "But I've been doing a lot of thinking, and that isn't for me. My gelding hasn't had much exercise since we've been on Galveston Island, but he's plenty strong, and so am I. Riding and shooting are two of the things I do best. So—if you don't have too great a need of me, Harry—I'd like to ask for a leave of absence so I can join that new Ranger regiment that Rick Miller is forming."

"Me, too," Chet said. "When Danny told me his plans, I knew I wouldn't be satisfied to be left behind. The war is sure to start once Texas votes to join the United States, and I'd feel bad if I kept a civilian job instead of going off to fight."

"I'll release both of you, naturally," Harry Canning said. "I don't mind telling you that—in spite of my age—I'm tempted to join you."

"You're needed here," Nancy reminded him succinctly. "They aren't."

He sighed. "Oh, I know. The population of Texas is

growing so fast that she needs all the merchant ships she can get." He stood again. "All the same, I envy these lads. Boys, I'll start breaking in a couple of the supervisors to take your places, so you'll be able to leave almost anytime in the next few weeks."

He got up, and his wife followed him out of the room.

Melissa folded her hands in her lap and did not look at either of her suitors. Danny cleared his throat nervously but said nothing, and Chet felt compelled to break the ice. "You look angry."

"I feel as though I'm being deserted," Melissa said, pouting prettily. "By both of you."

"A man who refuses to fight for his country isn't much of a man," Chet said.

"I wouldn't dream of trying to persuade either of you not to do your duty," Melissa said.

Danny studied her for a moment. "We'd like it far better," he declared, "if you tried to persuade just one of us."

Melissa was startled.

"You've been keeping both of us on the string for a long time," he continued. "I haven't mentioned this to Chet, but I know he'd be more at peace inside himself, just as I would, if you'd say right out which of us you prefer."

"I—I don't want to push her to make up her mind," Chet said hastily, inadvertently revealing his fear of losing her.

"I'm glad you feel that way," Melissa said. "Because I still haven't been able to decide."

Danny took a deep breath, then stood. "Maybe I can help," he said. "If you're still unsure after all this time, I know you don't want me, Melissa. Even if you decided in my favor, I'd always have the sneaking fear that you'd made the wrong choice. I guess I should be saying all this to you privately, but I'd rather clear the air in front of Chet. We've been friends for too long to let any girl come between us."

Color rose in Melissa's face, and her eyes blazed. Chet was too stunned to react.

"I'm bowing out," Danny said flatly. "You're a fine woman, but I'm not for you. And you aren't for me. Not anymore. I wish you every happiness, Melissa. And, Chet, good luck to you in your suit." He took his hat from a wall peg and left the house without a backward glance.

"Well," was all that Melissa could say.

"I had no warning at all," Chet said. "My mind was too full of getting Harry's approval so I could join the new Ranger regiment."

Melissa struggled in vain to suppress her fury. "How dare he reject me and walk out on me like that?"

This was not the moment for Chet to defend his friend, to explain that her procrastination had caused Danny to lose interest in her. "I'm still here," he told her. "And I'm not leaving. Unless you throw me out."

His simple statement forced Melissa to face the reality of the unexpected position in which she found herself. Later, perhaps, she could give vent to her inner rage, but right now she had to encourage her remaining suitor. She smiled at him slowly, provocatively. "I'd never ask you to leave, Chet," she told him, her tone caressing. "Never in a million years."

Fifty Texas Rangers and the troops of the United States Cavalry that had escorted the munitions train on its long journey worked day and night cutting down trees in the forest, making rafts, then lashing them together to form a bridge across the Red River. Rick Miller, who was supervising the operation, was relieved that an early summer dry spell had reduced the current of the river that marked the northern boundary of Texas. The rafts, securely held in place on both banks, would hold the weight of the heavy freight wagons.

The mule teams were driven across the temporary bridge first, and then the task of transporting the wagons began, with the soldiers and Rangers hauling and pushing. The operation was both arduous and delicate, and progress was slow, but the precious cargo was safe.

No one at the Red River had any idea that the work

was being observed from the heavily wooded crest of one of the few hills in the area. Anthony Roberts had good cause to feel pleased and told himself that his gamble was succeeding.

He had spent days in a town of the Waco tribe of Indians, sleeping in one of their miserable huts and eating their nauseating food. But his gold had been persuasive, and so had his clever arguments. It was true that the Waco had signed a peace treaty with Texas, but the lure of rifles and cannon, six-shooter revolvers and vast quantities of gunpowder had proved too great for them. Anthony had sworn to them that they could keep all of the booty they captured, that he himself wanted none of the arms or munitions. It had taken great efforts to persuade them that he had no use for the train's contents himself, that he would be satisfied if the sabotage prevented the train from reaching Austin.

Anthony had coached Asa Phipps carefully, and although the Kentuckian didn't care for the role he was being required to play, his greed had overcome his caution. He was particularly useful in this operation because, thanks to his ability to speak the language of the Indians who lived in his own part of the country, he could grasp what the Waco said, and they could understand him. He rested now on one knee, watching the freight wagons being hauled across the river, and he frowned as he listened to the low-pitched, earnest words of two Waco whose bead-decorated headbands marked them as senior members of the tribe.

"Mr. Roberts," he said, "the chiefs want to know why they can't attack the wagon train right now."

Anthony was exasperated but spoke calmly. "The wagons on the far side of the river would escape. And we'd be pursued by both the American and Texan troops. We'll hold to my original schedule and wait."

The wait lasted for the better part of two and a half more days. Finally, the last of the wagons reached the soil of Texas, the mule teams were hitched, and as the caravan began to crawl southward, Rick had a final word with the commander of the U.S. Cavalry escort.

"I sure wish you were coming the rest of the way with us," he said.

"So do I, Colonel. But our orders were written before we started out from Pennsylvania, and they haven't been changed. It wouldn't surprise me if the war has started by the time we reach Tennessee, and if that happens, we'll be sent back down here on the double."

Armies everywhere were hampered by bureaucratic procedures, so the two officers shrugged, smiled, and went their separate ways. Rick kept the wagon train on the trail until almost sundown, and then, although it had moved only a few miles from the Red River, he ordered the cumbersome vehicles to be drawn into a circle for the night. His mounted Rangers moved up and down the line, supervising the difficult movement, while Rick watched from a vantage point just outside the forming circle.

"Lieutenant Andrews!" he called to one of his aides. "Make sure the powder wagons are separated. The one that's already in the circle can stay put, but don't park this one or the last one anywhere near it. Keep a cushion by placing at least a half-dozen other wagons between each of them."

The driver of the gunpowder wagon that was being maneuvered into its assigned spot was unhappy. "We've come all the way across the U.S.A. without having to go through all that rigamarole, Colonel!"

Rick was unmoved. "You're in the Texas wilderness now, mister," he replied, "and we don't take unnecessary risks here."

Watching the maneuver from the woods off to one side of the bivouac area, Anthony Roberts signaled to Asa Phipps. Instead of telling the Waco to open their attack at once, however, the Kentuckian came to him.

"Can't you follow directions, Phipps?" the angry Anthony demanded. "We've got to strike immediately, before that circle is completed. Tell the braves to attack that last wagon, the one with the gunpowder markings on its canvas. Right now!"

Phipps continued to hesitate. "Where will you be, Mr. Roberts?"

"Right here, watching. Damn you, Phipps, do as you're told, or you won't be paid a penny!"

With great reluctance Phipps returned to the Indians and spoke a few words to them.

The Waco hesitated no longer and went into action. Two of the braves crept forward, to the edge of the woods, and lighted small fires with flints and dried wood. Their companions, who carried bows and quivers full of arrows that were coated with pine tar, crept up behind.

The wagons continued to roll toward their assigned positions, crawling forward slowly.

The braves near the edge of the woods were still too far from the last of the wagons to be able to attack effectively. They would have to dash across open spaces in order to be within firing range of their targets.

Asa Phipps was reluctant to participate in such blatant exposure, and he hesitated. But the leaders of the Waco band were eager to claim the spoils that would give them superiority over all other tribes in the area.

A cold sweat broke out on Asa Phipps's face, and he had to wipe the perspiration from his eyes. The maneuver had sounded simple enough when Anthony had explained it to him, but executing it was another matter, and he was sorry he had agreed.

Still watching from the woods, Anthony hoped his luck would remain good for a few moments longer. The Rangers were so busy directing the movements of the heavy wagons that none had noticed the approaching war party.

One by one the Waco went to the two tiny fires and dipped the points of their arrows in the flames. Then, concealing these flaming brands from the direct view of the wagon train, the braves dashed across the open space between the edge of the woods and the last wagon. Quickly they lifted their bows, and within seconds dozens of flaming arrows were arching through the air toward the last wagon in the train.

The first arrows to be fired missed their target, and one landed only a few feet from a mounted Ranger, who grasped the significance of the arrow at once, but before he could call out a warning, a number of other arrows cut through the canvas covering the wagon's cargo. The flames spread quickly, and then a violent explosion rocked the countryside.

The Ranger, who was close to the rear of the gunpowder wagon, disappeared from sight, as did his mount, both blown to bits by the tremendous explosion.

Asa Phipps never knew his own fate. One moment he saw the flaming arrows striking the top of the wagon, and then the force of the explosion tore him apart. The braves of the vanguard died instantly, too, as did the chiefs.

Huge flames, burning fiercely, leaped toward the sky, and a plume of black smoke rose toward the heavens in the still air.

Rick Miller was knocked to the ground by the blast, but he recovered swiftly and somehow managed to pacify his terrified stallion. "Rangers, come to me!" he shouted as he galloped in the direction of the burning gunpowder wagon.

A second explosion, somewhat less powerful than the first, made the ground shake.

The mules that had been unhitched from the wagons already in the circle tried to bolt, but they were halted by several determined Rangers, who managed to keep their seats in their saddles and drove the frightened mules back into the circle.

Even as Rick rode toward the rear wagon, his mind was functioning coolly. One gunpowder wagon was gone, and he could waste no time now on regrets. Thanks to the precautions he had taken, the others were safe. Rifles and muskets strewn on the ground told him that the wagon nearest the explosion had suffered damage, but the weapons could be retrieved later.

Then he caught sight of Waco warriors, their faces and torsos smeared with war paint, fleeing in the direction of the woods. Raising his rifle, he took quick aim, then brought down a running warrior with a single shot.

About half of the men under his command were behind him by now, and they needed no orders to follow his example. The Rangers fired, reloaded with practiced skill, then fired again. Brave after brave sprawled on the ground.

Rick waved his men forward, then drew his new six-shooter.

Anthony Roberts's feeling of deep satisfaction gave way to consternation when he saw the Waco survivors heading toward the woods. If the Waco failed to kill him in retaliation for the failure of their attack, the Rangers would be certain to shoot him. He turned his horse, then made off through the woods as fast as he could. At least he could report to the British that he had severely crippled the munitions train. Now he had work of his own—personal work—that needed to be done. Far outdistancing the braves, he vanished into the woods.

The disciplined Rangers maintained a steady fire, and at least half of the marauding band were killed. The survivors scattered when they reached the woods, and Rick called off the chase. Posting his troops in a semicircle near the woods so the attack could not be renewed, he rode as close to the still-burning wagon as he dared and surveyed the damage. The gunpowder wagon and its contents were a total loss, the driver and his assistant had been killed, and a dozen of the mules were dead. The animals that had lived through the ordeal had been injured and had to be shot.

The wagon containing rifles and muskets that had been directly in front of the powder wagon was damaged but could be repaired, and most of the contents could be salvaged. Dismounting long enough to examine a dead brave, Rick confirmed his belief that the Indians who had conducted the attack were Waco. The knowledge puzzled him. The tribe had lived up to its treaty obligations for years, and he knew of no reason they should have broken their promise to keep the peace.

He suspected that someone other than the Waco themselves had been responsible for the assault. The timing had been perfect, and only his order to separate the powder wagons had saved the entire train from destruction.

Lieutenant Andrews, his face blackened by fire, joined his superior. "Sir," he said in a choked voice, "we've lost three of our Rangers. The driver of the powder wagon and his assistant are dead, and we've just found what's left of the body of a white man who is neither a Ranger nor one of our civilians."

Rick accompanied him a short distance, and together they looked at the shattered remains of the man who had been Asa Phipps. His face had been blown away by the explosion, and the remains of his body were so mangled that it was impossible to identify him.

"One thing is sure," Rick said grimly. "We know now that whites inspired the Waco attack. We can't spare any men, but you can bet your last dollar that President Houston will send a commission to the main town of the Waco to find out who was behind this conspiracy!"

Rick sent one of his Rangers ahead to Austin with a full report of the attack, and the crippled train moved slowly southward on a journey that lasted more than three weeks. When they were only a two-day march from the capital, President Houston rode out to join them.

"Our losses were bad, but they could have been much worse, sir," Rick told him. "As you can imagine, we couldn't save as much as an ounce of gunpowder from the wagon that exploded. We've taken the best inventory we could under the circumstances, and I estimate we may have lost as many as three hundred muskets and rifles."

"We can replace the powder and the weapons, now that we're about to become part of the United States," Sam Houston said. "I regret the needless loss of life, naturally. But you've done well, Miller. I commend you for saving the better part of the train."

"I hope you're investigating the reasons for the attack, Mr. President."

"I sent a troop of Rangers to the land of the Waco, and they brought the chief of the tribe, his principal medicine man, and two other chiefs back to Austin. All of them swore they knew nothing. Finally they admitted that two white men came to one of their subsidiary towns and bribed the leaders there."

"Two, sir?"

Houston nodded. "You say one was killed in the attack. The other has simply disappeared. The Waco don't know his name or nationality, and they give conflicting descriptions of his appearance. It's my guess that they were agents of Santa Anna's, although they could have been British. We may never find out. The special convention I've called to accept the American offer to become a state will meet next week, and Old Rough and Ready is due to arrive any day now, bringing more than three thousand men with him."

"I had no idea that General Taylor would get here so soon!"

"Zack Taylor has never been one to waste time when he's given an order. The fur will start flying any minute."

Rick knew this was not the time to ask for a leave of absence for even a few days. Besides, it would be unfair to Elisabeta to marry her, then ask her to return to the American Legation compound for protection when he went off to war.

She continued to be ever-present in his mind, to be sure, and when Lee Blake met the arriving munitions train in Austin, Rick seized the first possible opportunity to inquire about her.

"She was afraid you had been hurt when we received the news of the attack and the loss of a powder wagon. But she's delighted you're here. I hope you can come to the house for supper tonight."

"Not even Santa Anna could stop me," Rick said.

A strong guard was thrown around the munitions, and as soon as Lee checked off their contents, distribution of weapons and powder began at once. The small cannon that would be used on board the warships Harry Canning had built would be dispatched to Galveston Island the following morning. The distribution of other weapons was started, and at Houston's insistence every Ranger was to be issued a new rifle and a pair of Colt revolvers. "The days of saber attacks by cavalry are pretty much ended," he told Rick. "Your boys can shoot, so I believe in giving them the weapons they'll need."

The day's work was not finished until long after night came, and a weary Rick accompanied Lee back to the legation.

Elisabeta was so eager to see her betrothed that she came to the compound gate to greet him. The moment he saw her he felt rejuvenated, and jumping to the ground, he ignored the grinning sentinels as he embraced her.

Ordinarily taciturn, Rick dominated the conversation during the early part of supper with his story of the attack on the munitions train. His modesty prohibited him from mentioning the all-important fact that the damage would have been far worse had he not taken advance precautions.

"Speaking as something of an expert on wagon trains," Lee said, "I can't help wondering how it happened that the powder wagons were separated."

"Well," Rick said grudgingly, "the thought of standing them too close together made me nervous."

"Hooray for your nerves," Cathy said.

Lee had news to impart, too. "I had a letter from Ernie von Thalman in the diplomatic pouch that came today," he said. "He and Emily are heading back to Oregon. He says that the certain prospect of war with Mexico has cooled the ardor of Great Britain for the Oregon country, and they're now negotiating in earnest. President Polk is still insisting publicly that he wants a border at fifty-four degrees, forty minutes, but he's told Ernie privately that he'll accept a border at the forty-ninth parallel. He's sure the British will settle amicably after dragging their feet for a time."

Later, when Rick and Elisabeta were alone, he said, "I was hoping I could get a leave for a few days. But with General Taylor due at any time, I've got to make certain my new regiment is in shape. That means I'll go off to the field early tomorrow morning, and I probably won't be coming back to town until General Taylor reviews the regiment and tells me how he wants my men deployed."

"I knew we couldn't be married this soon," Elisabeta said. "The idea was too good to come true."

He gripped her hand. "There's another obstacle. You're still not safe."

"I don't believe it," she said in a dry voice. "For all we know, Anthony Roberts may be back in Europe by now."

"Maybe so, maybe not. I have hunches, based on the years I spent doing criminal investigations. One of them tells me that the attack on the wagon train may be repeated in another form. And the other insists that Roberts won't rest until he's done away with the one person who can put a real noose around his neck!"

"I'll be patient, I promise," Elisabeta told him. "Just knowing we'll be married eventually is enough for now."

Rick left for the field at dawn and immediately began a troop-by-troop inspection of his regiment. His veterans were succeeding in instilling the unique spirit of the Rangers into the newcomers, and Rick was pleased when he saw how well the recruits could ride and shoot.

The demonstrations lasted for two days, and on the second afternoon, when the newest troop put on an exhibition of marksmanship while riding at a canter, he was particularly impressed by two of the men, both of whom scored high marks. An aide was sent to fetch the pair so he could commend them.

Rick was surprised when he saw Danny Taylor and Chet Harris, who saluted him smartly.

"What made you volunteer for my regiment?" he asked them.

"Sir," Danny said seriously, "we got to know you pretty well on the trail from California. So we figured that we'd see more action in an outfit under your command than we would anywhere else!"

"I'm glad to have you with me," Rick told them, and meant it.

On July 4, 1845, the special convention called by President Houston voted in favor of the entry of Texas into the United States. For all practical purposes Texas joined the Union at that moment, although technical and legal problems concerning the transfer of authority to the Federal government delayed the formal admission of the new state for several months.

Sam Houston, who was expected to be the first governor, surprised his friends by indicating that he would prefer service in the United States Senate. It was a foregone conclusion that he would be elected virtually without opposition.

In the meantime Major General Zachary Taylor had left his plantation in Louisiana, placed himself at the head of his troops in Arkansas, and at noon crossed the Texas border.

A scant week later he arrived in Austin, after putting his troops in bivouac near the Ranger training center. He had a reunion with Houston, then set up his headquarters in the still-empty house of the American Minister, it having been decided that the legation would not be disbanded until Texas statehood was complete.

Lee Blake, who had served under Taylor in some of the later Indian Wars, immediately called on the new commander. Over sixty, Old Rough and Ready, as his subordinates called him, looked his age after spending almost four decades in the army. His square face was seamed and leathery, his prominent nose was permanently tanned after a lifetime of outdoor living, and he spoke in the rasping voice of an officer who had shouted countless commands over the years. He had already opened the top buttons at the collar of his tunic and was studying a map as an aide showed Lee into the parlor.

"Brigadier General Blake reporting for duty, sir," Lee said as he saluted.

Taylor returned the salute, jumped to his feet, and grasped the younger man's hand. "Damn my eyes, but it's good to see you, Lee," he said. "I asked for you immediately when I was given this command, and when that idiot hemmed and hawed, I threatened not to take the post unless you were included."

Lee knew that by "that idiot" Taylor meant his arch rival, Winfield Scott. There was no love between the army's two senior commanders.

"I see you've been given temporary command of about a thousand men. How do they shape up?"

"Fairly well, sir. I'm shy of cavalry and artillery, and most of my troops have never fought a battle. I don't have a real brigade, sir. The War Department didn't know what to do with various units, so they lumped them temporarily under my command."

"Typical of the War Department." Taylor frowned for a moment, and then his face creased in a lined smile. "What sort of work do you want?"

"I'm at your disposal, General."

"Well, that raises a question. I've had half a mind to make you my chief of staff, but no fighting man is ever happy with a staff post. Besides, I'd lose one of the best field commanders in the army. How would you like a permanent brigade of your own? Two regiments of regular army infantry. A regiment of cavalry that we'll have to borrow from the Texas Rangers because Washington City is so damned stingy. A half-battalion of sappers I've brought with me. And a battalion of artillery I've been promised in writing by that idiot. How does that sound?"

"Great, sir." Lee beamed at him. "I couldn't ask for more. How soon will we go into the field?"

"As rapidly as we can organize the command and the rest of the army sent to us. Now that Texas has made her move into the Union, Santa Anna is certain to increase the pace of his recruiting, so I'm anxious to get down to the Rio Grande. Long sections of the border have never been properly marked there, so the Mexicans will encroach on our territory. Unless we encroach on them

first. Then they'll have the burden of trying to throw us
out."

Here was a commander, Lee well knew, who never
lost an opportunity to seize an advantage. Suddenly he
reminded himself that the social amenities could not be
ignored. "My wife and I would like the pleasure of your
company at supper this evening," he said. "We live next
door, you know."

"There's nothing I enjoy more than the company of
ladies at a meal," Taylor declared. "It's a luxury I've
been denied through the better part of my career and
will be denied again when we go into the field. As will
you. So I accept with pleasure, General Blake!"

At dinner that evening the guest behaved like a polished gentleman, fascinating Cathy with stories about his
relative, the late President James Madison, who had
been his military sponsor, and amusing Elisabeta with
humorous tales about experiences he had had during the
Black Hawk and Seminole wars. When he chose to be
charming, Old Rough and Ready was a very different
person from the man who could curse a subordinate for
more than three minutes without repeating himself.

"I like General Taylor so much," Cathy said later.
"Just knowing you'll be serving with him makes me a
little less apprehensive about what's ahead for you."

Lee indicated he was pleased she felt relieved, but he
refrained from mentioning that Zachary Taylor was a
hard, demanding taskmaster and that he himself, commanding a brigade of seasoned troops, would be in the
thick of whatever fighting the newly developing army
would see.

Hector Mullins was elated. General Blake had appointed him to the post of brigade sergeant major. He
was now the chief enlisted man in a seasoned force more
than one thousand strong, and when he went off to the
bivouac area to take part in the reorganization of General Taylor's forces, he told his wife, "This is going to be
the greatest time of my life."

Ginny couldn't understand his attitude, and repeating

his words to Cathy and Elisabeta when she joined them for tea in the Blake kitchen, she said, "It doesn't make sense, but I honestly believe he enjoys the prospect of going off to war!"

"Of course he does," Cathy replied. "Men think of war as a great adventure. They have no idea how we wait in dread back home."

"In some ways," Ginny said thoughtfully, "the experience is good for us, too. Even though Hector is only a few miles away at the bivouac, I'm already realizing how much I miss him, how much I took his love for granted. When he comes back to me—and he will—we'll have a stronger, better marriage. We'll be ready for the baby that both of us want so much."

"I know what you mean," Cathy said. "I'll have many more responsibilities with Lee gone, but I accept the challenge. In a strange way, the war is already bringing us closer together."

Elisabeta, who had been listening in silence, looked first at one of her companions, then at the other. "Both of you are already married," she said slowly, "so your feelings aren't like mine. Rick keeps hoping our wedding can be held before he leaves, but I don't see how that will be possible, although I haven't told him that. What frightens me is the possibility he won't come back. How can you be so sure your men will return?"

"We aren't really sure," Cathy told her. "We pray. And we cling to the hope they'll be safe from harm. It's all we can do."

Elisabeta knew she would require all of her courage to see her through the period that loomed ahead.

Meanwhile, Rick Miller was even busier than he had anticipated. The Ranger high command was amenable to the assignment of one of its regiments to Lee Blake's brigade, but General Taylor was disappointed when he learned that the veterans had been split into cadres and that, consequently, all three of the major Ranger units contained many new recruits.

There was only one way Zachary Taylor could satisfy himself, so he and Lee spent a day in the field with

Rick's regiment. "Our cavalry," the Commander in Chief told Lee, "are going to be the heart of our fighting force. There's only one way I can beat the Mexicans, and our horsemen will carry the heaviest burden. I asked Secretary of War Marcy to give me horses for everybody. Including our infantry. I almost had him convinced, but that idiot interfered, and my innovation has been rejected. Damn Winfield Scott!"

Lee, who admired both senior officers, wanted to stay clear of their disputes. "I'm convinced, sir, that Colonel Miller's unit can perform as we hope. Rick Miller is an exceptionally able officer, and from what I've seen of his men, they're first-rate."

"We'll soon find out." Taylor glowered as they took their places on the field where the cavalry regiment would be reviewed. "What in the devil is that?" He pointed to a huge square of cardboard, mounted on a pine frame, that had been erected at one end of the field. On it someone had drawn a crude figure of a man mounted on a horse.

"I have no idea," Lee replied, "but we'll soon find out."

A bugle sounded, and the parade began, with two horsemen in the lead, one carrying the American flag and the other the Lone Star banner. Behind them, alone, rode Colonel Miller, with his men in formation behind him.

Watching the riders carefully, Zachary Taylor growled inarticulately, the sound indicating impatience and, perhaps, disgust. Lee Blake couldn't blame him for feeling as he did. The troops rode in loose formation, unable to keep their lines straight, and they resembled amateur soldiers rather than the trained, disciplined professionals his brigade needed. He had faith in Rick, however, and hoped the Rangers would find some way to compensate for their sloppiness.

The regiment paraded the length of the field, halting at the far end. Then Rick raised his saber, signaling a charge, and the bugle blared.

Suddenly the entire regiment raced up the field at a

gallop, and somehow each troop, made up of fifty men, managed to maintain its separate identity.

Rick set the example for his men. His saber disappeared into its sheath, and he unslung his rifle and shot at the cardboard figure as he raced past it at a distance of about two hundred feet. Then, as the entire unit rode past the target at a gallop, each of the cavalrymen also fired.

Lee, knowing now what Rick had in mind, grinned but made no comment. General Taylor was watching the maneuver closely, his thick eyebrows drawn together.

After the entire regiment had fired at the target, Rick joined his superiors. Saluting as he rode up to them, he said, "I hope you enjoyed our little demonstration, gentlemen."

"That depends on the results," Zachary Taylor replied curtly. "Your men held their seats nicely, I'll grant you. But how accurate was their fire?"

"That's exactly what I intend to show you, sir." Rick raised an arm, and two of his sergeants immediately rode to the target, picked it up, and carried it to the place where the three senior officers were sitting.

"The entire regiment," Rick said, "including my staff and me, consists of two hundred and eleven officers and men. General Taylor, I invite you to examine this target."

The two sergeants, sitting their mounts about six or eight feet apart, held the framed cardboard up for Taylor's inspection.

A rare twinkle appeared in the Commander in Chief's eyes when he saw that fewer than a dozen shots had penetrated the unpainted portion of the cardboard. The figures of the rider and his mount were heavily peppered with bullet holes; the man's face and chest had been virtually obliterated, as had the head of the horse.

Lee was impressed. Even the newest recruits, carefully chosen for their riding ability and marksmanship, were living up to the traditions of the Rangers, who quietly believed they were superior to all other cavalrymen on earth.

A slow smile creased Zachary Taylor's seamed face, and then he laughed aloud. "By God, Miller," he said, "your men may not win any prizes for precision marching, but they sure as hell can shoot. And that's exactly what we need. As of this moment the Third Ranger Regiment is incorporated into my army and assigned to General Blake's First Brigade!"

XII

On the eve of the departure of Zachary Taylor's army for the vicinity of the Rio Grande, Austin was electrified by news from California. Americans had been moving into the northern portion of the province in ever-increasing numbers in recent years, some settling in San Francisco and others establishing farms and ranches. Now they had erupted in a revolt against Mexico and were demanding that the area be ceded to the United States. The flames of their rebellion were fanned by John Frémont, the explorer, making his third journey to the region. Frémont ultimately would present the American Californians with a Bear flag, the symbol of their independence and allegiance to the United States.

It was obvious that President Santa Anna of Mexico could not allow this challenge to go unanswered. "He no longer has a choice," General Taylor said. "Now he's being forced to declare war against us."

Lee Blake spent his last night at home, as did Hector Mullins, and before breakfast the following morning Lee presented Cathy with a new Colt revolver. "This compound is still Federal property," he said, "but the legation is being disbanded, and there won't be any more sentinels on guard duty here. So you may need this."

"To protect Elisabeta?" Cathy examined the revolver carefully.

305

"Whatever," Lee replied. "You and Beth and Elisabeta will be living here alone, without men on hand, and there's no telling what might happen."

"It's a remarkable pistol," she said. "I just hope I'll never have to use it."

"So do I. But if the need arises, shoot straight!"

Rick arrived in time to share a final breakfast with Elisabeta and the Blakes, and after eating hastily, he and his betrothed went into the parlor for a few final, private words.

"Be careful," Rick said. "I'll grant you there's no indication that Anthony Roberts is anywhere in the vicinity of Austin, but you never know when he might show up. Lee is leaving a revolver with Cathy. Would you like one?"

Elisabeta shook her head vehemently. "I've never fired a shot in my life, and I wouldn't know how. Firearms frighten me. Besides, I'm no longer concerned about Anthony. I think he's gone for good. You're the one I'm worried about."

"Don't be," he told her. "I have the best reason in the world to come back safe and sound. You."

For his sake Elisabeta managed to remain dry-eyed when the men took their leave. Not until the army had gone did she go to her room, close the door, and weep quietly.

Eager to reach the border area as soon as possible, the army, now more than four thousand strong, marched south rapidly, with General Taylor insisting they cover at least twenty-five miles each day. "The men need the exercise," he said. "They'll get very little rest in the days ahead."

A base camp was established near the deep V made by the Rio Grande, within sight of the Mexican village of Boquillas in Coahuila Province. Both Texas and Mexico claimed this territory, and the army's arrival was greeted with relief by the few ranch owners in the area. They had been harassed frequently, they said, by Mexican cavalry patrols.

Zachary Taylor immediately called his three briga-
diers to his tent, offering them a supper of beef jerky and
baked beans, which they ate by candlelight.

Lee was conscious of being the youngest by far in the
group. General Robinson, the commander of the Second
Brigade, had held his rank for almost a decade, and
General Delwart, the commander of the Third Brigade,
was junior to him by only a few years. Both had known
long service with the Commander in Chief and were
familiar with his ways.

"Gentlemen," Taylor said, "you'll send your cavalry
regiments across the river tomorrow morning, with orders to rid the area of any Mexican troops they encounter."

General Robinson wanted a clearer directive. "You
mean, sir, they're to open fire?"

"That's why they have firearms," Taylor replied tartly.
"And I never want to see your horsemen in camp. Keep
them on constant patrol duty."

"Won't the Mexicans interpret hostilities as an act of
war, sir?" General Delwart asked.

"Hellfire, General, we *are* at war!" the Commander in
Chief exclaimed. "You heard those ranchers this afternoon. Their cattle have been killed, their horses stam-
peded, and their barns burned. Those are acts of war!
Mind you, I'll court-martial and hang any man in my
army who molests a civilian or causes damage to his
property. But I want to make it plain as day to Santa
Anna that he can't send his patrols into disputed border
territory to intimidate American citizens. Blake!"

"Sir?"

"Right now is as good a time as any to find out if the
Third Rangers can live up to their promise. Send them
on a two-day ride into enemy territory, penetrating as far
as they can. And driving out every last one of Santa
Anna's troops they can unearth."

"When do you want them to start out, sir?"

"I'll leave that up to you."

"Well," Lee said, "the night is dry, without even a
suggestion of rain, so there's no time like the present."

He grinned at his colleagues. "I don't want my cavalry to get rusty. After all, they only rode twenty-one miles today before we made camp."

Rick Miller's regiment quickly became the spearhead of Zachary Taylor's counter-harassment campaign, and in ten days the Texans fought in five skirmishes, each time defeating their foes without suffering even a single casualty.

The other Ranger regiments, jealous of Rick's success, became increasingly daring. Miniature battles were fought everywhere, and the Mexicans, thrown onto the defensive, sent an army corps of ten thousand men marching toward the northern border. This was precisely what Zachary Taylor was seeking.

"An actual declaration of war has become academic," he told his senior commanders. "Both sides are shooting freely now, and it won't be long before the main forces are joined. There's only one way to win a war. Take the battle to the enemy and beat the tar out of him!"

President Polk and his cabinet continued to hope that a negotiated compromise would avert a full-scale war, and an experienced diplomat, John Slidell of Louisiana, was sent to Mexico City with what the Americans and most European diplomats regarded as a generous offer. Slidell proposed that the permanent border be established at the Rio Grande, in return for a cancellation of all American financial claims against Mexico. The staggering sum of five million dollars was offered for New Mexico Province, and the United States was prepared to pay three or four times that sum for California.

The Administration's hand was strengthened by the success of the negotiations with Great Britain. Early in 1846 it was agreed that the Oregon border be established at the forty-ninth parallel, with the Hudson's Bay Company granted the right to free navigation on the Columbia River. Almost six more months would pass before the formal treaty was signed, but Polk was now available to devote himself almost exclusively to the dispute with Mexico.

Santa Anna resolved that problem in his own imperious way. He ignored his own moderates, who believed the American offer was fair and that war could be avoided. Instead, he refused to receive Slidell, announcing that he would not deal with a nation he no longer recognized. At the same time he issued orders publicly, sending an additional five thousand men to crush Zachary Taylor's army.

He miscalculated, however, because the indomitable Taylor refused to be crushed. In short but sharp engagements he defeated armies almost triple the size of his own at Palo Alto and Resaca de la Palma. Santa Anna still refrained from issuing a formal declaration of war, hoping that world opinion would force the United States to call off its troops. But Polk played the international chess game flawlessly, and in May, 1846, the Congress responded to his initiative by officially declaring war.

General Taylor responded to the declaration by defeating some of Mexico's best brigades at Matamoros, then occupying the town long enough to rest his men and enable the supply wagons from Texas to catch up with him. As soon as food and powder, cannonballs and lead reached him, he resumed his drive, and in July he captured the larger town of Camargo. Here his troops again rested, the Commander in Chief issuing strict orders that his troops were not to molest or fraternize with the local population.

Food was purchased in quantity from local merchants, with the American quartermaster paying cash for what he bought, and the night after the battle his troops enjoyed a feast. The commanders of brigades, regiments, and battalions dined with the Commander in Chief at his headquarters in what had been the town hall and were served a sumptuous repast—their first in months—that included soup, fish, and beef, which they washed down with Spanish wines.

Certainly the men of the Third Rangers did not envy the high command. Ravenously hungry, they gathered around their campfires for a meal of fried beefsteak, potatoes roasted in the coals, two kinds of squash, fresh corn, and beans. Sergeant Danny Taylor, twice promoted for gallantry in action, silently concentrated on his food for a long time, then turned to Corporal Chet Harris, who had already finished his gargantuan meal.

"What's the matter with you, Chet?"

"Um. I've been thinking."

It wasn't difficult to guess what was on his mind. "We're a long way from home."

Chet reached into a breast pocket. "I showed you the letter I got today from Ma and Ernie, didn't I?"

"You did." The von Thalmans had written that they were back in Oregon, that the border question with Great Britain had been resolved peacefully, and that, as a consequence, the rate of immigration to Oregon already had more than doubled.

Danny looked out beyond the confines of the town they had captured, and after staring at the dimly seen shapes of the rugged hills, he gazed for a time at the star-filled sky. The night was balmy, the taste of victory was sweet, and there were moments he was glad he had no close ties, that there was no one with whom he corresponded.

Suddenly Chet pounded a fist on the ground in impotent rage. "Damn her," Chet muttered.

"Who?"

"As if you didn't know. Melissa, that's who! I write to her regularly, but I haven't had a word from her in blame near two months. It wouldn't take her all that long to scribble a letter."

Danny felt sorry for him. "The mails aren't very regular, you know. A whole pack of letters could be sitting some place in a postal sack."

Chet shook his head miserably. "Everybody else gets mail from Austin, Galveston Island, all over Texas. I spend twelve hours a day in the saddle, and I've already fought in more battles than I care to remember. But Melissa can't even bother to let me know whether she's well or what she's thinking."

Yes, Danny decided, it was all to the good that no one in Texas, Oregon, or any other place cared whether he was alive or dead. There were times he felt lonely, and he realized his isolation was responsible for the reckless disregard for safety that he had shown in combat. But he was spared the heartache that Chet was suffering, and he knew he had been right when he had called a halt to his pursuit of Melissa Austin.

Eulalia Holt always behaved circumspectly and sedately when she went into town in what she called her "lady's clothes," even riding sidesaddle because of her long, full skirts. So the people whom she passed on the road that led to the Holt ranch were startled when they saw her galloping at full tilt, leaning so far forward that her face almost reached her mare's neck. As anyone could have told her, it was downright dangerous to ride that fast when using a sidesaddle.

Arriving at the ranch, Eulalia threw her reins over a hitching post, not even bothering to remove the mare's saddle, and gathering her skirt around her, hurried to the kitchen.

Little Toby, who was laboriously copying words from a book, looked up in surprise when he saw the excitement in his mother's eyes and her flushed face.

She gave him no chance to speak. "Where is your father?"

"On the range. You're home early, Mama. Papa and I were going to have a picnic. We thought you were going to eat in town with Aunt Cindy, and—"

"Fetch your father!"

The boy responded at once to her tone of command, racing out to his pony, which he had left at the hitching post while he had been engaging in the chore of learning to write.

"Don't tarry!" his mother called after him.

The boy vaulted into the saddle in a style reminiscent of his father, then hurried off, spurring his mount quickly to a rapid canter.

Unable to calm herself, Eulalia paced the length of the kitchen, her heels drumming on the hardwood floor.

Whip burst into the house, the persistent ache in his

hip forgotten in his anxiety. Toby was close behind him. Eulalia flung herself at her husband, then kissed him resoundingly.

After a time he managed to disentangle himself sufficiently to hold her at arm's length. "Did somebody molest you or insult you?" he demanded fiercely. She shook her head, then kissed him again.

Whip was so relieved that he responded in kind before he called over her shoulder. "Toby, your mother has had a touch of the sun. Pull out a chair for her and then put the pot of coffee on the stove to heat."

Eulalia's lighthearted laugh filled the room. "Don't bother, Toby. I've never felt better in all my life!"

Her joy was so contagious that the little boy grinned at her. But Whip regarded her soberly. "I was rounding up the new colt when Toby came flying out to the range like he had Beelzebub at his heels. So you sit yourself down and tell me from the beginning."

She seated herself obediently and looked up at him, her face radiant. "Cindy and Dolores and I were looking for print material to use for summer curtains," she said. "They found what they wanted, but I'm not keen on flowers, and I spent more time looking. Anyway, thanks to my delay, we were next door to the post office when the mail pouch from New York and Washington City arrived. And the word spread faster than I can tell it. Whip, President Polk has settled the border problem with the British!"

He inhaled sharply and held his breath.

"The boundary is being set at the forty-ninth parallel," she said. "The President's only concession is that the Hudson's Bay Company will have the right of free navigation on the Columbia River."

"You're sure this isn't another of those confounded rumors?"

"The announcement was official, made by President Polk himself. There were only a few copies of the New York newspapers in the pouch, and so many people were trying to read them that I couldn't bring you one. The treaty goes into effect six months from the date it was signed, which means four months from now."

Whip's whoop would have aroused an entire wagon train. He hoisted Toby to one shoulder, hauled Eulalia to her feet with his free hand, and began to dance wildly around the room with her.

She gasped. "Your hip—"

"It never felt better!" He did not release her until she was breathless.

"There's sure to be a bonfire and fireworks in town tonight. Son," Whip said, setting him down, "this is the most important day of your life. There will be no war with the British, and we've won a fair share of the Oregon territory. As a special treat, you can come into town with us and stay up past your regular bedtime."

Eulalia sat in a chair, catching her breath. "That reminds me. I saw Tonie and Bob Martin as I was getting my mare. A special committee has been formed already, and they're sending a delegation out here this afternoon to call on you."

"What in blazes for?"

"There will be a formal celebration, including a supper for all, on the day the treaty becomes official. They want you to be the chairman."

"Not me," Whip said. "I'm not one for making speeches."

"But you're the natural choice," she protested. "You've done more than any other person to develop the Oregon territory and make it part of the United States. You should have the credit."

"The results are what count," he said. "I don't give a hang about the credit."

Eulalia stood with her arms akimbo and her feet apart. Her eyes gleamed. "You owe it to Toby and me," she said. "Most of all, you owe it to yourself. You will accept the chairmanship, Michael Holt, and I won't hear another word." She spoke softly but with deep conviction.

Whip returned her gaze for a moment, sighed, and

placed a hand on Toby's shoulder. "Son," he said, "your
mother is the brightest, sweetest, and prettiest woman in
the world. I'll carve the heart out of anybody who tries
to disagree with me. But I don't want you to get the idea
that she's perfect. Oh, no. She can be more cantankerous
and stubborn than the meanest old Rocky Mountain mule
you ever did see. Whether I like it or not, I'll be the
chairman of the Oregon territory celebration. I'll have
to wear my go-to-church suit, a stiff collar, and a cravat.
I'll have to buy enough silk material so your mother will
outshine every other woman there. Which she would
even if she wore an old housedress. I'll even be obliged
to make a speech. Will I do all those things? You just bet
your boots I will!"

Toby laughed uncertainly.

"The reason I'll do what she tells me," Whip continued, "is because I've lived with her long enough to
appreciate how wonderful she is. That's why!"

Anthony Roberts paid in advance for a week's lodging
at an Austin rooming house, certain that no one would
recognize him. And a glance in the tiny mirror on the
wall beside his narrow cot confirmed his confidence. He
looked like an old man, thanks to the tribulations he had
suffered in the months since he had been a fugitive after
sabotaging the munitions train. He had grown a beard
when there had been no chance to shave for days on
end, and it was white, as was the hair on his head. There
were deep hollows beneath his eyes, and his forehead
was as lined as his once-immaculate clothes were shabby
and worn.

The politicians he had known in Austin could pass him
on the street without a flicker of recognition. So he
hadn't been foolish, as he had thought in his more
rational moments, to come back to the town. The British
Legation had closed, so there was no way he could get
the funds owed to him for his services. It would be truly
insane to go to the British Legation in Washington City,
so he would wait until he returned to London to collect
what was owed to him.

But he had been right to return to Austin. He had the strongest of motives, vengeance against the woman who had betrayed him.

His desire to find and dispose of Elisabeta Manuel burned within him, giving him no peace. And his zeal had become all the greater when he had wandered into the United States Post Office and had seen a sign posted on a wall:

WANTED
Alive if Possible, Dead if Necessary
ANTHONY ROBERTS
Strangler

There had been a detailed description of his appearance, and he read it carefully, almost laughing aloud. He no longer even vaguely resembled that man.

A reward of five hundred dollars in gold had been offered for his capture, and he felt flattered. But he was safe, totally safe. The Rangers had gone off to war, their places taken by bumbling, middle-aged farmers and mechanics who called themselves the Texas Legion. Last night he had eaten at a table adjoining that of several of their officers, and one of them in particular, a man named Innes MacGregor, who had to be close to fifty, struck him as being especially ineffectual. If all members of the Legion were like the soft-spoken, fatherly MacGregor, he could stay in Austin for months.

He started his search for Elisabeta at the house he had occupied with her, but its current tenants were a couple with a large brood of children, so he asked them no questions. Instead, he spent all of his daylight hours methodically walking the dirt roads of the town as he hunted for her. He was haunted by the fear that she had left Austin, but his long, successful search for his father's killers convinced him that people who disappeared always left traces. Even if Elisabeta had gone elsewhere, he would dig out the clues, follow her, and obtain his revenge against her.

She alone was responsible for his misery. If she hadn't

gone to the Rangers with the story of what he had done to three elderly men who were now rotting in hell, he would be safe, his purse heavy, and he would be back in London, where he belonged. Instead, he had lived in the wilderness as a fugitive, stealing food from farmhouses and ranches, existing from day to day in constant peril. Now she would be required to pay for his torment.

Occasional flashes of common sense illuminated Anthony's mind, and in those moments he told himself to go without delay to New Orleans and obtain immediate passage back to England. He still had enough money to pay the fare, and he knew he would be wise to put the New World behind him for all time.

Then the dark fog enveloped him again, a cold rage shook him, and he thirsted for Elisabeta's death.

A brief visit to the town hall, where he asked if a register of residents had been compiled, proved fruitless. He was told to try the new Federal government offices in the former United States Legation compound. It was the understanding of the Austin officials that now that Texas had become a state, an all-Texas census was being taken.

As much as Anthony disliked dealing with American authorities, he went to the old legation. There he was sent from office to office by bustling, self-important little people, and after an hour of learning nothing of substance, he concluded that he was wasting his time. He wandered out of the building, then stopped short.

Not fifty feet from him, standing in the yard of a house that had been part of the legation, was Elisabeta! She was rolling a hoop with a little girl who appeared to be about four or five years of age.

His hands suddenly clammy and beads of cold sweat running down his face, Anthony quickly stepped into the shadow cast by the office building so he could observe her quietly.

She looked healthy and alert, lovelier than ever, and she was wearing a demure wool dress that he didn't remember or had never seen. The filthy bitch.

Another young woman, a blonde some years older than Elisabeta, emerged from the house, and the two spoke in low tones. Then the blonde, after glancing casually in Anthony's direction and looking away again indifferently, called to the child. All three went into the house.

Anthony knew he could not stand there indefinitely, or someone would be sure to notice him. Fortunately, the old compound wall had been torn down, and as he made his way to the street, a plan formed slowly in his mind. A tavern that sold food and drink to Federal employees had been opened directly across the road from the former legation, so he entered, found the place almost deserted at this hour, and had no difficulty in seating himself at a small window table.

He ordered a mug of ale, which he sipped slowly as he watched the house. Don't rush, he told himself repeatedly. Stay calm and, above all, take your time.

For the next three days he spent most of his daylight and evening hours in the tavern, eating all three of his meals there, although the food was deplorable and the ale was flat.

The proprietor and the barmaid, who happened to be his wife, made several attempts to converse with the stranger who had taken such a liking to their humble establishment. He was polite, gentle-spoken, but he made it plain from the outset that he had no desire to engage in small talk. So they left him alone, which he preferred, and regarded him as something of an eccentric. He paid for his food and drink in cash, always sitting at the same table.

By the third night of his vigil, Anthony believed he had learned all he needed to know. He knew that Elisabeta was living in the house across the road, as were the blonde woman and the little girl. Every morning they went off to the market together, then returned and spent the rest of the day and evening at the house. Their only callers were several other young women, so Anthony guessed that most of them were the wives or sweethearts of men who had gone off to war. Perhaps Elisabeta had married during his absence. If she had a husband, he would soon have cause to grieve for her.

Tonight he had gleaned the last of the information he so desperately required. Not a quarter of an hour earlier, Elisabeta had opened a window on the second floor, her features easily recognizable in the light of a candle she held in one hand. A few moments later the cande was extinguished, and the chamber was dark.

So that was her bedroom!

Anthony's luck had turned in his favor again. On the outside wall, only a short distance from the window, stood a brick chimney that served a fireplace on the ground floor. The chimney, which was thick, had been clumsily built, and there were many places where a man who wanted to climb to that bedroom could gain a footing and a hand grip.

Finishing his ale, he whistled under his breath as he sauntered back to his boardinghouse.

The next morning he slept late, enjoying the luxury, then went to a nearby tavern for a hearty breakfast. His greatest need was a fresh horse, but he tried in vain for several hours to purchase an animal. So many were needed to carry supplies to General Taylor's army, he was told repeatedly, that they were almost impossible to obtain.

Someone finally suggested that he go to the farm of Innes MacGregor, which was on the West Road outside of town. In spite of his dislike of dealing with an officer of the Legion, he had no choice. He would have to leave town quickly after he disposed of Elisabeta, and he couldn't take the chance of being forced to walk all the way to New Orleans.

Long accustomed to walking, Anthony made his way to the farm without delay. The house was a two-story log cabin, but he paid scant attention as he tapped at the door. A red-haired girl of sixteen or seventeen answered the summons.

Politely removing his hat, Anthony tried to speak in an American accent as he said, "I'd like to see Mr. Mac-Gregor, if you please."

"Pa isn't home right now," Heather told him. "He won't be home until supper, and Ma is in town, too. Is there anything I can do for ye?"

He heard the sounds of children laughing and playing in the house. "I was told he might be able to sell me a horse. I'm in bad need of one."

The girl's brow cleared. "Aye. Ye'll be wanting a workhorse, then."

"Preferably." That was a lie, but even a workhorse that would carry him to New Orleans was far preferable to making the journey slowly on foot.

"Pa bought some horses from the estate of a farmer who died not long ago," she said. "Workhorses. He had to buy all of them, one more than he needed."

"How much does he want for it?"

"Five dollars," Heather said.

Anthony knew by the set of her Scottish jaw that she would not bargain with him. His funds would be running perilously low by the time he reached New Orleans, but he had no alternative.

"Mayhap ye'd like to wait until Pa comes home," she said, inviting him into the house.

"Thank you, but I'd like to be on the road before sundown. That way I can reach my own home before midnight." He fished in his purse, counted out five dollars, and handed it to her.

"I'll have one of my sisters get the horse for ye," she said. "Ye'll forgive me, sir, but I've got to change. I must be on time at the hospital for the war wounded."

He raised an eyebrow politely.

"If I were a man," Heather said, "I'd be in the army. But the best I can do is tend to the injured, so I spend my evenings and some of my days at the hospital."

Anthony had no interest in what the girl did, but he mumbled something, then waited impatiently until another girl, a younger version of the teen-ager, appeared from a barn behind the house leading a sturdy gray workhorse.

Losing no time, Anthony mounted the beast and started back toward Austin. Never before had he ridden bareback, but a saddle would be an extravagance and, what was more, would look too conspicuous on a work-horse. Perhaps it was just as well. He would continue to act the part of a farmer on the road to New Orleans.

He returned to his boardinghouse, then turned the animal loose in the fenced yard behind the building. Only a few tidying details remained. He told the proprietor he would be leaving early the following morning, and then he rumpled his bed so it would appear that he had slept in it.

Evening had come, so he went on foot to the Lone Star Inn, where he indulged in a fine, multi-course dinner, the most satisfying he had enjoyed in a long time. He craved a few strong drinks of gin, too, but knew that hard liquor would dull his mind after his months of abstinence, so he kept a tight rein on his desires and settled for a single mug of ale. It was infinitely superior to the weak brew he had been forced to endure at the tavern opposite the former American Legation, and he enjoyed every drop.

Dawdling deliberately, he did not return to his board-inghouse until fairly late. No lights were burning in the rooms of the other lodgers or the proprietor, so his luck again was good. Throwing his few belongings into his saddlebag, he left the house quietly, went to the yard for his horse, and then slowly rode toward the old legation compound.

The roads were deserted at this hour, as he had guessed they would be. Members of the Legion were family men, and he suspected that unless an emergency arose, they spent their nights at home. The night air was sweet, as sweet as the revenge that awaited him, and he breathed deeply.

Approaching the buildings of the legation, Anthony dismounted, then led the docile workhorse to the lot behind the house he planned to enter. He was so confident of success that he tethered the animal to the hitching post after satisfying himself that the horse could not be seen from the road.

Lights were still burning in what appeared to be the

parlor, so Anthony concealed himself in a patch of thick bushes, and from this vantage point, seeing but unseen, he began his vigil. The moment for which he had longed was at hand, and he couldn't allow himself to spoil it by acting prematurely. It was all-important that Elisabeta enter her bedroom before he struck.

But it was not difficult for him to curb his impulses and wait. After all this time, he knew, the exercise of patience would bring a certain reward.

The unsuspecting Elisabeta sat in the parlor reading a travel book by Washington Irving, and there was no sound in the room but the scratching of Cathy's quill pen as she bent over a sheet of paper. Growing weary, Elisabeta marked her place and looked up. "I finished my letter to Rick right after supper. You're still writing to Lee?"

Cathy nodded. "I'm telling him that Beth is learning to spell, and I know he'll want all the details."

Elisabeta stifled a yawn. "I think I'll go to bed."

"I'll put your letter with mine on the front hall table so it will be ready when the military courier comes tomorrow morning."

Elisabeta paused at the bottom of the staircase. "I'll look in on Beth, if you like."

"Thank you, and good night, Elisabeta."

The young woman mounted the stairs and went first to the child's room, where she placed her candle on the bedside table. She saw that Beth had kicked off her covers in her sleep, so she rearranged the bedclothes, making them secure. Then, picking up the candle, she started back toward the door.

Elisabeta's blood congealed when she heard the window being opened behind her. But she had the presence of mind to blow out her candle before she turned.

In the dim light she was able to make out the figure of a tall man with white hair and beard creeping into the room. Her heart pounded, and she was so paralyzed by fear that she was unable to cry out.

The man stealthily approached the bed. Thinking the sleeping figure in the bed was his intended victim, and not knowing that it was instead Beth Blake, Anthony raised an arm. Elisabeta made out the dull gleam of a knife in his hand. The man was intending to stab Beth!

Reacting instinctively, Elisabeta leaped forward and brought her metal candleholder down onto the man's skull with all of her strength.

The blow stunned him for a moment, but he was still on his feet as he turned to face his unexpected assailant.

The cold, pale eyes that stared into hers could only be those of the man who had defiled, abused, and shamed her. Hatred that had been pent up within Elisabeta for many months boiled to the surface and exploded.

At the same instant Anthony recognized her, and his lips twisted in a smile. He had almost killed the wrong person.

Before he could raise the knife again, however, her fury was so great, so overpowering, that she drove a knee into his groin, then raked his face with her nails. Astonished by the unexpected assault, he took a half-step backward.

Now she had her chance and kicked him squarely in the groin, causing him to double over. Grasping his hair with one hand, she knew only that she wanted to deprive him of his eyesight with the other. Never again would those vicious eyes gleam balefully at her, and she jabbed at them with her fingers.

Anthony grunted in pain and dropped his knife onto the bed beside him. Seeing it fall, Elisabeta snatched it.

The brief respite enabled him to recover somewhat, and he threw himself at her, bearing her to the floor. He was sorry he hadn't brought a length of silken cord with him, but his hands would do instead. They closed around her neck, his grip tightening as he strangled her.

She felt certain she would die within moments, and she realized that the expression in his eyes was crazed. As he looked down at her, gloating, his eyes gave her renewed strength. Conscious at last of the knife she held in one hand, she slashed at him, inflicting a painful wound on his wrist. Anthony pulled back his hand.

Gasping for breath, Elisabeta stabbed him in the chest, then struck him again and again, the blade alternately cutting and plunging deep within him. He bled profusely, his expression one of total bewilderment.

Elisabeta slashed again at the face she loathed, then used all of her remaining strength and drove the steel into his heart. He fell backward onto the floor, already dead as he collapsed.

At that moment the door swung wide open, and Cathy stood in the frame, an oil lamp in one hand and her revolver in the other.

"Don't bother to shoot him," Elisabeta said, her voice taut but seemingly composed. "I've already killed him."

Cathy could only stare at the still, blood-smeared man.

"That was Anthony Roberts," Elisabeta said calmly, showing no remorse. "I'm just sorry he died so quickly. I would have liked to prolong his agony."

Cathy looked at her in wonder. This gentle, quiet young woman was as strong and resilient as the knife she still held in her hand.

Speaking quickly, Elisabeta explained that Anthony had entered through the window, obviously coming into what he thought was her bedroom, and was on the point of killing Beth when she had intervened.

Together they dragged his body into the corridor so the still-sleeping child would not see it if she awakened. Then Cathy hastily summoned the middle-aged night watchman who patrolled the grounds of the Federal buildings. He hurried for help, and a short time later Anthony Roberts's body was carried away.

All that remained now was to clean up Beth's room. Cathy paused as they reached the foot of the stairs. "We'll have to add long postscripts to our letters before they're taken in the morning," she said. "And it just occurs to me. You'll be given the five-hundred-dollar reward for his capture, alive or dead."

Elisabeta's expression did not change, but she sighed. "I've had my reward. Now I can live in peace."

In September the forces of General Zachary Taylor won their most significant and decisive victory to date, storming and capturing Monterrey, a city of more than fifty thousand people located more than one hundred and seventy-five miles south of the border region. The assault was led by the Third Rangers, who advanced against vastly superior forces, the charge enabling the rest of the First Brigade to storm the citadel successfully. Then the other two brigades took up the burden, driving Monterrey's defenders out of the city and sending them fleeing to the south.

General Taylor commended Brigadier General Blake and Colonel Miller in his dispatches. His greatest praise, however, was reserved for Sergeant Danny Taylor, who led his squad against an entrenched enemy position without regard for his own life. His attack was primarily responsible for the American breakthrough.

At Rick's request, heartily endorsed by Lee, the Commander in Chief gave Danny a battlefield promotion, making him an ensign, the lowest commissioned officers' rank.

Everywhere in the United States the press hailed Zachary Taylor as a hero. His unbroken string of victories, capped by the capture of Monterrey, made him the nation's idol, and he was now called "The Invincible Rough and Ready."

In Mexico City, President Santa Anna's concern mounted, and he decided it would be necessary for him to lead an army himself against Taylor.

In Washington City, however, the Administration and the War Department took an overall view of the military situation and were concerned. It was true that Taylor was winning victories. So was Colonel Stephen W. Kearny, who marched from Fort Leavenworth, Missouri, to New Mexico Province, where he captured its capital, Santa Fe, and was ordered to march on to California.

But the war would drag on for years unless a direct attack was made on the enemy heartland.

It would be necessary, Polk decided, to send an expedition to capture Mexico City, with the expedition traveling through the Gulf and first taking the port city of Veracruz. General Scott, eager to win his own share of glory, was given personal command of the new army, and all available regular army troops were assigned to his command. The public heard rumors that a new army was being formed, but the plans remained secret.

A major problem arose when it became clear that there were too few men in uniform for Scott to carry out his mission successfully. There was no time to ask for volunteers, then train the new recruits. Winfield Scott needed veterans if he hoped to take Santa Anna's capital. Meanwhile, pressure had to be maintained by Taylor and Kearny.

After listening to various recommendations, President Polk called in Secretary Marcy. "I've examined this problem from every possible angle," he said. "Scott needs troops if he's going to perform the task we've given him. Kearny's force is tiny. We'll have to give him some of Taylor's."

"He'll scream bloody murder, Mr. President."

"It can't be helped. Unfortunately, Taylor is in the wrong theater of operations to win the war. Only Scott can do that. What unit will you take from Taylor?"

"Scott has requested the First Brigade, Mr. President."

"Blake's brigade?"

Secretary Marcy nodded unhappily.

"We've got to leave Taylor enough air to breathe. *Suggest* that he relinquish the First Brigade but leave the final choice to him. That gives him the chance to salvage his pride."

For several weeks, the Army of Northern Mexico—as Zachary Taylor's command now was being called—rested at Monterrey, waiting for cannonballs, gunpowder, new bullet molds, and lead. The supplies arrived, as

promised, but the relief train was accompanied by a
special courier who brought General Taylor a personal
letter from President Polk and an order from Secretary
Marcy.

He understood Polk's position and could sympathize
with it, but his mood was nevertheless sour, and he
suspected that Winfield Scott was trying to cripple him.
He summoned his brigade and regimental commanders
to a conference, along with the leaders of his smaller,
independent units, and controlled his rage sufficiently to
explain the manpower shortage and its consequences to
them.

The senior officers were experienced soldiers, so they
recognized Scott's need for troops, but they were thun-
derstruck by the decimation of their own ranks after
winning repeated victories.

General Robinson of the Second Brigade, who had
known the Commander in Chief longer than anyone else,
was the only officer present who dared to arouse Taylor's
wrath by asking, "How much will we lose, sir?"

"A full brigade and attached supply troops," Taylor
snapped, volunteering no further information as he dismissed his subordinates. They began to file out of the
room, and he called, "General Blake!"

"Sir?" Lee thought he knew what was in store as he
was waved back to his seat.

Taylor, as always, was succinct. "The President has
informed me," he said, "that Scott, the idiot, has requested the transfer of your unit to his army. He's not as
big an idiot as I've always claimed. He knows enough to
demand the best."

"Then I'm being ordered to join him, General?"

"I didn't say that." Taylor was waspish. "I'm being
allowed the rare privilege of deciding for myself whether I want my right hand or my left chopped off. I wanted
you to know the facts, Lee, because I'm leaving the
decision to you."

Lee knew he was walking a tightrope, that he couldn't
afford to offend Winfield Scott and didn't want to insult
Zachery Taylor. So he spoke with great care. "If the War

Department hasn't asked the transfer of the First Brigade, sir, I'm still under your command. I must defer to your wishes, General."

"Well said and well played, my boy!" Taylor's gloom lifted somewhat, and he managed a smile. "Then you'll damned well stay with me. Much as I hate to lose him, I'll send Delwart."

When Lee returned to his own headquarters, he found his subordinate commanders waiting for him, all of them convinced that the brigade was being transferred. He told them what had been said, and they shared his relief. They were reluctant to leave the Army of Northern Mexico.

Colonel Rick Miller explained their feelings best when he said, "I don't know what it is about Old Rough and Ready, but he has the ability to make us fight beyond our capabilities."

"Which is exactly what we'll have to do, now that we're being weakened," Lee replied.

The reduction of Taylor's forces made it necessary for him to remain in Monterrey longer than he had planned. But late in the autumn he learned that Santa Anna was marching to meet him with an army many times the size of his own, so he again summoned his principal unit commanders.

"Gentlemen," he said, "it's plain that Santa Anna has no idea that Scott is setting out with an expedition to take Mexico City. So this situation is made to order for us. We may be outnumbered by three or four to one, perhaps even more than that, but we can cripple Santa Anna so badly that Scott will have a clear road to Mexico City!"

The Americans resumed their march, and four days after Christmas, 1846, they took the town of Victoria. The march was resumed without delay, and the men were heartened when they were joined, unexpectedly, by volunteer militia units from Texas, Mississippi, and Louisiana. In all, the newcomers numbered fifteen hundred, bringing the total strength of the Army of Northern Mexico to a little more than forty-five hundred men.

In mid-February, after Taylor took the town of Saltillo without opposition and established his bivouac there, his scouts told him that the enemy was approaching rapidly and that Santa Anna himself was leading a force approximately sixteen thousand strong. The Americans were outnumbered by more than three to one.

Under the circumstances, Taylor decided, he would need to select a battleground of his own choice, one that would give him the best protection. All of his senior commanders fanned out the next day, and it was Taylor himself who found what he wanted. The terrain was exceptionally rugged, marked by high hills studded with heavy rock formations, and he chose the heights that faced southward a short distance from the village of Buena Vista.

His army moved forward, with the infantry taking places on the crests of a chain of the highest hills, and the artillery were emplaced directly behind them. All of the cavalry, in an unusual move, were being held in reserve.

The troops moved south from Saltillo to take up their battle line, which was anchored by the First Brigade in the center. To its right was the Second Brigade, with the newly arrived militia units on the left. The recruits were supported by half of the total artillery. The move was completed early on the afternoon of February 21, only a short distance from the still-advancing enemy, and the scouts expressed the certainty that Santa Anna would attack the following day.

The men dug into their positions, and the cooks were ordered to prepare double rations for supper. Each man was also to be issued two ounces of brandywine from a special reserve that had been saved for just such an occasion.

General Taylor established his command post on the summit of a hill directly behind the front lines, and a short time before sundown he summoned all commissioned officers in the Army of Northern Mexico to a full-dress council of war. He absented himself from the scene until they had gathered, with the seniors in the front ranks, and then he approached from the rear, followed by his personal staff, as they stood at attention.

"You may be at ease, gentlemen," he told them.

They seated themselves on the rocks and grass.

"Most of us," Zachary Taylor said, "have come a long way together. Tomorrow will determine whether our precious victories were won in vain. It wasn't accidental that we won those victories. We won because I happen to believe that American soldiers are intelligent men who fight better when they know my overall battle plan and what to expect.

"Tomorrow, gentlemen, we can expect pure hell. A swarm of sixteen thousand armed men, led by superb cavalry, is going into battle against us. Because we're so much smaller and because some of our infantry are recruits, I have decided to take a defensive stance.

"In short, we'll be a metal plate that bends but doesn't break under the blows of the enemy's hammer. I want every captain, lieutenant, and ensign who hears my words to explain this situation fully to his troops. We'll pound the enemy with our artillery, but the key to victory or defeat will be the infantry. *Our foot soldiers must hold firm!* Senior unit commanders already know my detailed scheme of operations. Do the company-grade officers have any questions?"

There was a long silence.

Finally Danny Taylor overcame his shyness. "Sir," he said, "Ensign Taylor, Third Cavalry. You haven't mentioned what's to be expected of the cavalry."

The Commander in Chief remembered the courageous young man well and grinned at him. "Namesake," he said, "you'll have plenty of action before the day is over. Enough, I dare say, for even your hot blood. If the infantry and artillery can hold off the enemy, the cavalry will go forward to slice through the lines and chop him to mincemeat."

"Thank you, sir," Danny said.

Now a score of other junior officers were clamoring for attention, and the Commander in Chief answered their questions patiently.

Brigadier Generals Blake and Robinson exchanged glances. Zachary Taylor had already revealed the key to the extraordinary success he had achieved so far in the war. Every man in his army knew what to expect and what role he himself would be required to play. The supreme individualist treated his subordinates, down to the lowliest privates, as individualists, too.

The senior commanders remained with General Taylor as his supper guests when the others were dismissed, and Danny returned to his own unit. There, over a meal of piping hot beef stew, baked beans, and fresh bread baked that very afternoon in Saltillo, he carefully repeated the Commander in Chief's words to the members of his platoon.

They, too, asked questions until supper was finished, and then he went off alone to sit on a flat rock, smoke his pipe, and put his thoughts in order. The battle, he knew, would be the most difficult by far that the army had yet fought. Not only had the enemy gathered the largest force of the campaign, but Santa Anna was leading his legions in person, which was certain to give his men a boost. Yet the prospect left Danny strangely unmoved. Men would die, but he had seen so much killing by now that he did not shrink from the ordeal, even though he knew the risks he himself would be taking might mean the end for him.

He had reached the point where he no longer worried about what might await him. Life or death in combat, he had discovered, was a matter of chance. A random bullet could snuff out a man's life in a second, or he might escape unscathed. He had come a long way since the days when he had been penniless and abused, a bound boy at the mercy of a callous employer, without the means to defend himself or improve his lot.

Texas had been something of a disappointment to him, and perhaps he should have stayed in Oregon. On the other hand, his country needed him, and he was glad to be given the opportunity to serve an America that had been good to him. Whatever he might suffer or be forced to endure in the hours ahead, his debt was paid in full, and his conscience was clear.

Danny heard footsteps, and when he looked up, he saw Chet Harris approaching. Fraternization between officers and enlisted men was not encouraged, but the old friends found it a simple matter to ignore protocol in their personal relationship.

"I've been looking for you," Chet said. "I reckon you're feeling the way I feel."

"What's that?"

"Scared."

Danny's smile was wry. "Any soldier who says he isn't scared when he's about to go into battle is either stupid or a liar."

"Well, this is the first time I've ever felt like this." Chet looked down at the ground, then raised his head and met his friend's gaze. "Maybe I've got a reason."

Apparently it was not easy for him to express his thoughts, so Danny encouraged him with a quick nod.

"At mail call today I finally got a letter from Melissa. It was a long letter. She kept writing and then putting it aside, so it was like three or four letters in one."

"That must make you feel much better."

"It does. She didn't go as far as to say that she'll marry me, but she sure hinted that maybe she would. She left the door wide open, Danny. I've got reason to hope now that things will work out with her like they should."

"I'm glad for you." That wasn't true, Danny thought. Perhaps he had become overly prejudiced against Melissa, but in his opinion she was still flighty and unstable, her attitudes those of an adolescent, and until she became more mature—if she ever did—Chet was too good for her.

"Now I have a good reason to hope I'll come through this fight," Chet went on. "I just hope I don't turn tail and run."

Danny slapped him on the back affectionately. "You, Chet?" he asked, laughing. "Never! Come along. I'm

about to distribute the liquor that Old Rough and Ready
has authorized. It'll do more than warm your insides. It
will help you put things in perspective again. You'll do
just fine tomorrow. Just as you have in every battle that
we've fought!"

Little by little the bivouac area became quiet as men
settled down, rolling up in their blankets for a few hours
of rest before the struggle began. Each was alone now
with his thoughts, and few were actually able to sleep.

No one was more alert than Lee Blake, whose responsibilities were overwhelming. As he well knew, victory
or defeat might depend, to a large part, on whether his
veterans could hold off the foe. As a professional fighting
man he understood, as did only a handful of others, that
it would be a miracle if the small force could defeat the
army that Santa Anna would lead onto the field.

All of Lee's many years of experience contributed to
the various options that seethed in his mind. He tried to
picture one possible contingency after another, then be
in a position to counter it quickly and decisively, and not
until he had exhausted every possibility was he content
to relax for a short time.

Rick Miller's situation was somewhat different. His
superiors would be responsible for overall strategy, and
the tactics his regiment would employ depended on the
way the battle developed. So he was able to allow his
mind to wander.

His thoughts were centered on Elisabeta. At this hour,
with the climax of the war at hand, he realized more
than ever how much he loved her, how devoted he was
to her. He was eager to be with her again, to begin
planning with her their future.

In the meantime, he had a grim obligation awaiting
him. His regiment had been tried repeatedly during the
long, arduous campaign, and he knew his men were
ready for this final test of their skill and courage. They
would not panic when they faced enemy units many
times their own size, and they would give a good account of themselves. Long accustomed to danger, he

deliberately made his mind a blank and dropped off to sleep.

When he awakened, long before dawn, he was not surprised when he realized he had been dreaming about Elisabeta. He grinned quietly as he pulled on his boots and buckled on his holster belt.

The whole army was stirring, and men ate a cold breakfast of jerked meat and parched corn. The lighting of cooking fires was forbidden now, but it didn't matter. Few of the troops were hungry.

A heavy fog had rolled across the rugged countryside after midnight, and the hills and the narrow valleys below them were still shrouded. The velvet-black sky overhead was hidden from sight, and when Lee Blake, accompanied by the members of his small staff, moved to the crest of the sharp-peaked hill that would be their command post, they could see only a short distance in the direction of the deep valley that lay ahead.

The peak behind them was visible, however, and Lee noted that the Commander in Chief had not yet arrived there, although the officers of his general staff were on hand, waiting for him.

Only the gradual brightening of the thick mist told the Army of Northern Mexico that day was dawning.

Lee peered in vain through his telescope. He could see nothing, and the all-enveloping quiet was intense.

Sergeant Major Hector Mullins finally heard a few, faint noises that his long experience made it possible for him to interpret. "General," he said, "I got me a funny hunch that the enemy infantry are creeping toward us across the valley."

"Don't tell me you can see through this fog," Lee replied.

"No, sir, but my ears tell me what's happening."

Lee listened intently and finally concluded that his sergeant was right. "Corporal Haskell," he told his signals aide, "raise a yellow flag to alert General Taylor."

"He ain't back there yet, sir," the Corporal replied.

Lee realized instantly that, in the continuing absence of the Commander in Chief, he was the senior officer present on the field, and consequently, he was responsible for the decision that would inaugurate the battle. Ordinarily the burden would have fallen on General Robinson, but he was absent, too, apparently conferring back at the base bivouac with General Taylor.

"Couriers," Lee said, and three young officers promptly stepped forward. "In precisely five minutes," he told them, "direct all artillery to concentrate a continuing barrage on the valley ahead of us. We have reason to believe the enemy is already advancing across it."

Time seemed to drag, but at the appointed moment the cannon spoke in unison, their roar echoing across the desolate hill country. The impenetrable fog continued to engulf the entire area, and there was no way to find out whether the fire of the gunners was accurate or wide of the mark, whether the iron spheres were claiming victims or merely digging furrows in the hard earth. Salvo after salvo sent flocks of birds high into the air and brought Zachary Taylor to his command post quickly, but Lee neither knew nor could even guess whether the barrage was being wasted.

The sun rose, drawing wisps of mist toward it and dispelling others, and gradually the fog thinned.

Lee peered through his telescope again, then handed the instrument to his sergeant. "You were right, Mullins!" he declared. "We've pinned them down!"

Hector adjusted the glass and saw a force of enemy infantry that he estimated at two thousand men in the valley below. They had thrown themselves to the ground, pressing close to it as the cannonballs whistled overhead.

Now that the artillery observers could see the field more clearly, they were able to correct the faults of the batteries, and one by one the sights of the individual cannon were adjusted. The fire became increasingly devastating, and soon the men of the two infantry brigades were required to withdraw.

Thanks to the alertness of Sergeant Major Mullins, the initial Mexican advance was an abject failure, and the American infantry had not yet fired a single musket or rifle shot. Everyone in the defending army knew that Santa Anna would be compelled to try again. Having committed his troops to combat, he could not disengage, and while he regrouped his forces, sending forward two fresh infantry brigades that the Americans on the heights could see with ease now, the artillery rested. Then the Mexicans swept into the valley on the run toward their position, and the barrage was resumed.

Santa Anna managed to conceal the bulk of his attackers behind the shield of his own hills, so his opponents were unable to figure out even the ratio of foot soldiers to cavalrymen. Had this been a battle between two evenly matched and equipped armies, the Mexican artillery would have fought a duel with the American gunners, but the continuing silence from the hills to the south indicated that there were few Mexican gunners on the field.

The second infantry drive was repulsed, as was a third. Santa Anna altered his tactics and committed a portion of his cavalry to spearhead the next attack. The American artillery maintained its heavy fire, and the enemy advance was slowed. Some units continued to push forward, however, and drew close enough to the hills for the foot soldiers of the First Brigade to enter the battle.

"Tell our infantry battalions they may fire at will," Lee said to the major who stood beside him. "But caution them to hold their positions. I don't want a single squad to counterattack."

The lighter fire of American muskets and rifles added to the din of the heavier artillery. The horsemanship of the Mexicans was superb, as always, and no matter how many casualties they sustained, their ranks remained unbroken. But the flesh of the men and their mounts was weaker than their resolve, and so many were killed, so many wounded that the cavalry had to be recalled. The bodies of men and horses now littered the valley.

To Lee's surprise the sun now stood directly overhead. Half of the day had already passed, and Santa Anna had yet to deploy his major forces. He tried another cavalry charge, this time sending two full regiments of riders into the fray. But the Americans still held firm, first blunting and then repulsing the assault.

An unhappy Rick came to Lee. "General," he said, "my lads are getting a mite restless. They need some exercise."

"I quite agree," Lee said, then sent a message via his signals aide to the Commander in Chief. *Request permission for Third Cavalry to counterattack*, the flags said.

Zachary Taylor's reply was characteristically brief. *Wait*, he ordered.

Not until two more drives by Mexican cavalry had failed did the patient Taylor alter his tactics. "All cavalry will prepare for action," he directed.

The horsemen moved into place behind their shield of foot soldiers. Then the crisp notes of a bugle blown on the heights of the Commander in Chief's hill sounded a charge.

Rick Miller should have taken his own place in the center of his unit, but instead, he chose to ride with his vanguard, and as the regiment swept down the slope toward the valley, he showed a disregard for his own safety by leading his men. He pointed his saber straight ahead as he thundered into the valley and across it, his troops eagerly following.

Robinson's Rangers rode on their right, with the cavalry of the smaller, semi-trained militia on their left. The breakneck pace that Rick set was so wild Santa Anna did not utilize his own cavalry in a counter-stroke, instead allowing his infantry alone to stem the advancing tide of horsemen.

For a few moments it appeared that the ranks of the Mexicans would break, but most units responded to the hoarse shouts of their officers and did not waver.

The leaders of the Third Cavalry's sub-units had the authority to break ranks and exploit any enemy weakness they might find. Ensign Danny Taylor was quick to note such an opening. Seeing that a company of two hundred enemy infantrymen was pulling back, he led his platoon toward the sector, recklessly ignoring the increasing Mexican fire on both of his flanks as he rode at a canter. The crossfire would die away, he reasoned, when he drew close enough to the Mexican defense position, because the enemy on the flanks would not want to strike their own comrades in the middle.

To an extent Danny was right, although Mexican marksmen still maintained a heavy, steady fire.

Just a little farther, Danny told himself, and all would be well. The infantry company opposite him continued to withdraw, and additional pressure well might cause the defenders to become panicky. If they drew back in confusion, which was already rampant, it might be possible to force the whole line backward.

A Mexican sharpshooter's aim spoiled Danny's tactics. A bullet caught his gelding between the eyes, and when the animal stopped short, Danny was thrown forward onto the ground. Then, when the beast dropped, it landed on Danny's leg before he could escape from its path. He felt an excruciating pain in his left leg, and the agony was so great that he lost consciousness.

The momentum he had established nevertheless enabled most of his platoon to continue the advance. But Chet Harris had seen his friend go down and quickly rode to the spot. He could see at once that Danny had been seriously hurt, although it was impossible to determine whether he was dead or alive.

Chet recklessly paid no heed to his own danger, and leaping to the ground, he began to haul the body of the dead gelding from the inert form of his friend. Bullets whistled past him, but he was impervious to his own danger. Veins stood out on his forehead, and his uniform became soaked with sweat as he labored, but he was heartened when he saw Danny's chest rising and falling. He was still alive, and his comrade had no intention of deserting him.

At last Chet managed to pull the dead gelding far enough to free his friend. But Danny was still unconscious. So Chet picked him up, half ran and half staggered back to his own horse, and mounted. Then, aware for the first time of his own danger, he galloped toward the rear. He guessed that Danny's dangling, crooked leg would have to be amputated, but he was still breathing, and he soon would be safe. The knowledge gave Chet the stamina and strength to keep riding until he was out of range of the enemy.

When the regiment could advance no farther, Rick told his bugler to signal a partial withdrawal. The Rangers rode toward the American hills, then regrouped and charged a second time. Robinson's Rangers followed their example, as did the militia cavalry troops.

Taylor's artillery and infantry remained silent as the horsemen launched two more assaults, and Zachary Taylor moved forward to Lee Blake's command post in order to watch the operation more closely.

"Miller is a madman, Blake," he muttered.

"Well, sir, he sure is a fighting fool," the awed Lee replied. In all of his battlefield experience, he had never witnessed such a demonstration of raw courage and determination.

The cavalry severely dented the enemy's lines before being recalled on the personal command of a concerned General Taylor. Rick retreated with great reluctance, but he had more than accomplished his mission. The enemy had been badly bruised, both physically and in spirit.

Santa Anna soon resumed his own attacks, but his subordinates no longer had the enthusiasm necessary to win. The American infantry and artillery held steady, and the valley was "filled with corpses," as Taylor later wrote in his report to the War Department.

The sun was sinking rapidly behind the hills to the west when a trumpet fanfare sounded from the hills held by the Mexicans, and a small party of horsemen rode slowly into the valley, led by a standard-bearer carrying a white flag.

Zachary Taylor, peering through his telescope, saw that a brigadier general was the ranking member of the group. So he promptly sent Lee Blake at the head of a small party to meet the foe.

Lee followed his own standard-bearer, three senior

officers riding behind him, and came to a halt within speaking distance of the waiting Mexicans. Then swords were drawn and courteous but chilly salutes were exchanged.

"General Santa Anna, President of Mexico and Supreme Commander of her armed forces sends greetings to the American Commander in Chief," the ranking Mexican declared.

"General Taylor returns his greetings," Lee said coolly.

"It is suggested by President Santa Anna that a truce be declared until eight o'clock tomorrow morning. That respite will give both armies the opportunity to remove their wounded from the field of combat and, perhaps, bury their dead. The suggestion is made in the name of humanity."

Lee did not hesitate. "On behalf of General Taylor, I accept," he replied.

The silence at dusk sounded strange to men who had been almost deafened by the roar of cannon and the rattle of muskets, rifles, and pistols. Teams of Americans lighted torches and searched the field, carrying their wounded to the rear and removing the bodies of the dead. The task lasted the better part of the night, but thanks to the zeal of Zachary Taylor and his subordinates, the injured who could be moved were on their way to Texas before daybreak, carried in mule-drawn carts and protected by a strong escort.

Almost three hundred Americans had been killed, and more than twice that number had been wounded. So far, Taylor's losses had been severe, and his only consolation was the knowledge that the enemy's casualties had been far worse.

"We're ahead now, and I intend to stay ahead," a haggard Taylor told his principal subordinates as they ate a breakfast of the usual jerked meat and parched corn at his command post before daylight. "According to our figures, Santa Anna has lost at least five thousand men so far—more than the effective pre-battle strength of our entire army. No force can tolerate casualties like those. So we'll do today exactly what we did yesterday. We'll let him batter himself to pieces against our defense shield, and when it's appropriate, we'll speed that process with our cavalry."

As day was breaking, a breathless Hector Mullins reached the command post. Standing at rigid attention, he said to Zachary Taylor, "Sir, the damn enemy has pulled out! He's gone!"

The startling announcement proved to be true. Rather than run the risk of suffering more devastating casualties and seeing the survivors taken prisoner, Santa Anna had used the truce as a trick to withdraw his entire army under cover of darkness.

The Battle of Buena Vista, as posterity would call it, ended in a triumph for Zachary Taylor.

Within a few days, after sending cavalry patrols on a fruitless search for the fleeing foe, he began his own retreat, going first to Saltillo and then to Monterrey. The campaign in northern Mexico, for all practical purposes, had come to an end.

It was too late now for Taylor to send any more of his victorious veterans to join Winfield Scott's army, which was already at sea, en route to Veracruz. Capturing the seaport in March, Scott won an unbroken succession of victories, and in September, 1847, he captured Mexico City.

Santa Anna had lost his gamble. He was forced to recognize the Rio Grande as the Texas border. New Mexico Province and what was called Upper California were ceded to the United States. President Polk, trying to be fair to a conquered enemy, persuaded the Congress to vote a payment to Mexico of the sum of fifteen million dollars.

The war was at an end, Zachary Taylor was certain to become the Whig candidate for President, and the men who had won the victory were free to resume their civilian pursuits.

XIII

At first glance, from the road that passed its fence, the property outside Austin looked like a farm. Those who observed it closely, however, saw that several large houses of white-painted clapboard were clustered near each other, with a courtyard in the center. Anyone who was admitted through the gate guarded by U.S. Army sentries soon realized that the flag of the United States, into which the Lone Star of Texas now had been incorporated, was flying from a courtyard flagpole.

The establishment, built and maintained by the grateful citizens of Texas, was a hospital and rehabilitation center for veterans who had been wounded in combat in the Mexican War.

Former enlisted men were housed in three of the structures, while those who had been officers lived in the fourth. Some were bedridden and would remain in the place for years, perhaps for the rest of their lives. Others were gradually regaining their health and were permitted to roam the grounds freely.

A side door opened, and an attractive young woman with red hair and freckles, wearing the red, white, and blue scarf around her neck that marked her as a volunteer helper, held it ajar.

"Come along, Lieutenant Taylor," she urged. "It's a lovely day, and we're going for a stroll."

341

Danny Taylor limped forward awkwardly on his new wooden leg, afraid he would fall and hating himself for being so clumsy. "I'm not a lieutentant," he muttered. "For whatever worth it may have, I'm a civilian."

"Of course," Heather MacGregor agreed cheerfully. "But ye're still a retired first lieutenant. I saw General Taylor's citation of promotion myself. Please stop dawdling. I can't hold the door all day."

Danny grumbled but made his way into the yard, and Heather started to walk down a path that led through a garden.

"Not so fast," an irritated Danny said. "I can't possibly keep up with you."

Heather smiled at him. "We'll see about that." She walked beside him, occasionally smiling and touching his arm to encourage him, but making no effort to help him whenever he almost lost his balance and was in danger of falling.

A silent Danny moved doggedly until his collar was soaked with perspiration. Then Heather rewarded him by gesturing toward a conveniently located bench. "Let's sit for a spell," she said.

Danny grunted as he lowered himself to the bench.

"I wonder if ye realize," she said, "that ye're walking twice as far as ye walked only a fortnight ago."

"What of it?" He slapped his wooden leg angrily.

"Really, Lieutenant Taylor. Ye sound like my little sisters when they pout."

"You've been assigned to my case for months, so why in blazes don't you call me Danny?"

"Only if ye'll call me Heather."

He twisted on the bench to face her. "Why are you being so all-fired nice to an invalid who is worth nothing to himself or anybody else?"

"Shame on ye, Danny Taylor," she said severely. "Poor Captain Jablonsky, in the room at the end of your corridor will spend the rest of his days in bed. But he's cheerful. He's trying to learn a trade. He wants to be useful. But look at ye! A strapping lad with a fine mind, one of the most handsome men ever to come to Texas. Ye have the whole world in the palm of yer hand, but ye wallow so hard in self-pity that ye don't even know it!"

Danny had the grace to flush. "Sorry, I had that blistering coming to me. You're right. All except the part about me being so handsome."

Heather's cheeks became as fiery as her hair. "That happens to be a personal opinion, sir."

"Do the doctors teach you to flatter all the patients that outrageously?"

She jumped to her feet, her green eyes blazing. "Ye can walk back alone. I refuse to take such insults!"

Instantly contrite, Danny caught hold of her hand. "Don't go, Heather. I—wasn't hitting out at you. You've been wonderful to me. All that time I just wanted to die, you wouldn't leave me in peace. You bullied me and nagged me and pushed me until I realized I wanted to live, after all. Please, Heather."

She looked hard at him, saw he was sincere, and forgave him.

Not until she sat again did Danny loosen his firm grip on her hand. "Sometimes," he confessed, "I get nasty because I feel so helpless. I don't think I'll ever win this fight to walk right."

"There's no better physician in all of Texas than Dr. Meyers," Heather told him, "and he says the day isn't far off when ye'll forget that one of your legs is made of wood. My pa says the same thing. He knew a shepherd back in Scotland who had a leg frozen, and it had to be taken off in Edinburgh. Less than a year later he was back in the fields tending his sheep, as sound as ever."

"If I thought I could lead a really useful life—"

"Ye will!" she assured him. "Look at all the offers ye've had. With my own eyes I saw the letter from Harry Canning, who wants to train ye to take his place at the shipyard so ye can take over when he goes back to Oregon. The Rangers will give ye a post as an administrator, and a commission to boot. Ye could claim the land next to my pa's place and farm it—"

"No farming, thanks, though I'm tempted by the location." Danny stared off into space, then looked at her again. "Tell me something, Heather, and be honest with me. You spend far more of your time with me than you do with any of the other patients. Is it because you feel sorrier for me?"

"It is not!" she said emphatically.

"Why, then?" he persisted.

Heather faced him defiantly, then suddenly became demure. "A lady," she said in embarrassment, "is entitled to her own private preferences and her own private thoughts."

"I—I don't mean to intrude." He was afraid he would be overwhelmed if he allowed himself to dwell on the implications of what she had just said. For many weeks he had wondered why this pretty, charming young woman bothered with him. When other patients teased him about her, he became so angry he was afraid to admit to himself, much less to her, that he might be falling in love with her. Heather MacGregor, who could have any man she wanted, would have no desire to spend the rest of her life with a cripple.

"I think we'd best start back," she said.

"Hold on," Danny said hastily, as he again reached for her hand.

Heather allowed him to take it for a moment before she withdrew it.

"Dr. Meyers says if I continue to make progress, he'll release me next month. Well, Chet Harris is coming up to fetch me, and I'm going down to Galveston with him to attend to some unfinished business."

She thought he was referring to the shipyard offer. "When ye reach Galveston, ye'll stay there," she said, her voice and manner suddenly bleak.

Danny shook his head and ran his fingers through his hair. There was no way he could tell her that Melissa Austin again was refusing to accept Chet's proposal, claiming she thought she "might" be in love with his closest friend. As a favor to the man who had saved his life, Danny intended to confront Melissa and put her straight. So he just said, "I don't aim to stay in Galveston more than a few days. Then I'd like to come back to

Austin and straighten out my own life. And decide the best way for me to earn a living. My problem is that I don't have much money, and the inns in Austin are mighty expensive."

"Ma and Pa have offered ye a room at our house for as long as ye want to stay," Heather said.

"They've been very kind to me," Danny replied, "but I don't want to impose on them."

She looked at him, her eyes mocking as well as compassionate. "No doubt because ye think they're just taking pity on ye."

It hadn't been difficult for her to divine his reason, and not wanting to dwell on the matter, he could only nod.

Heather's sigh was long and loud. "Danny," she said, "for a man who has brains inside his head, ye be stubborn and stupid. Your life isn't ended, even though ye can't see beyond the end of your nose. Ye're just beginning. Ye can be what ye want, do what ye like. Ye're a war hero, and there are hundreds of people—thousands—who wish ye well. Will ye sulk because ye lost a leg—or will ye face the future like the man ye can become?"

Danny bridled, but his resentment faded when he reflected that this girl, as honest and forthright as she was attractive, was speaking the truth. "When your father comes to take you home this evening," he said slowly, "I'll tell him that I accept his invitation to stay with the MacGregors while I work out my plans for the future. I won't give up, now or ever. As you'll find out when I come back from Galveston."

She averted her face for a moment so he wouldn't see how pleased she was that her goads had been effective. And even though she suspected that another girl was at the root of his coming journey to Galveston, her heart told her he would return.

Rick Miller was one of the last of Zachary Taylor's veterans to come home. Thanks to his achievements, he had been transferred to General Winfield Scott's staff as his principal cavalry consultant. Then, after the military campaign had ended, he had been required to remain in Mexico City as the head of the detail that had provided protection for Nicholas P. Trist, the State Department representative who had negotiated the terms of peace with the defeated Mexicans.

A sloop of the United States Navy landed him at Galveston after a voyage from Veracruz, and pausing only for a polite, overnight stay with Harry and Nancy Canning, he rode to Austin as though his life depended on his arrival at the earliest possible moment. Halting only for brief naps and eating his meals in the saddle, he arrived two days before Christmas, 1847, the dust of the road thick on his boots.

Beth Blake stared for a moment at the officer who hastily threw his reins to an orderly and then alerted the household. "Mama, Papa, Aunt Elisabeta!" she shouted. "Colonel Miller is here!"

Elisabeta raced out to greet her beloved, and they almost collided at the front door. Their embrace was fervent after their long, painful separation and expressed the feelings that, in this moment of joy, neither could speak.

Not until later in the evening, after being welcomed by Lee and Cathy and eating his first hot meal in days, was Rick able to think and talk about the future. He and Elisabeta sat side by side on a sofa in the parlor, their hands tightly clasped, and he told her, "The first order of business is our wedding. We've waited long enough."

Her smile was radiant. "If we can find a clergyman who isn't too busy, I'd love to be married on Christmas Day. I've already bought my trousseau with part of the money I received for the Anthony Roberts reward."

His smile faded. "I still can't believe you killed him."

"Neither can I," Elisabeta said. "But all my hate and resentment exploded when I saw him standing over Beth with a knife—thinking he was going to stab me."

"We won't mention him again," Rick promised. "And I know I can find a minister on short notice."

"Cathy insists that we have the reception here."

His grin returned. "You and Cathy have it all planned,

I take it. You seemed confident I'd be here in time for Christmas."

"Your last letter from Mexico City said you would." Elisabeta's expression as well as her words indicated that she had complete faith in him.

"We have one problem," Rick said. "I know I'm going to be offered the position of deputy commander of the Rangers, but the pay increase is very small, and I might have to wait as long as ten more years before I'd reach the top. So I'm thinking of taking a post in law enforcement somewhere else—where the salary will be better and I can get you some of the things I want for you."

"I don't want you to make a change for my sake," she protested.

"For both of our sakes, then," he said. "I'll have to see what's available, but as I told you before, I'd like to go out to California. Settlers are going there in a steady stream of wagon trains. At a rate faster than Texas and even Oregon have ever enjoyed. If the present rate of immigration continues, and there's no reason it shouldn't, California will become a state in a couple of years. Not much longer than that. In the meantime, there's an opportunity for people in my line of work. There's a crying need for sheriffs and police chiefs. I know because I sent off a half-dozen letters while I was cooling my heels in Mexico City, and I've had favorable responses up and down the line. They write that my credentials are impressive, and I know I can get what I want. But I won't make the move unless you agree to it."

To his surprise Elisabeta laughed. "I want to show you something," she said, then left the room, returning with a letter, which she handed to him.

He discovered it had been sent by the relatives she had once mentioned, who lived in California's Sacramento Valley. They had learned her whereabouts when they had read in the newspapers about the death of Anthony Roberts, who had been wanted for three known murders.

The letter, which was warm, explained that the couple

had no other living relatives. They were growing old, and they hoped Elisabeta would consider coming to join them in their large ranch house. If she had a husband and children, which the newspaper accounts had not mentioned, they would be welcome, too.

"The hand of Providence seems to be guiding us," Elisabeta said when he put the letter aside. "In more ways than one, it seems that we're being nudged toward California."

"Your relatives don't say it in so many words," Rick replied, "but they sure do hint that they'll leave their property to you. I had no idea that I'm marrying an heiress."

"You aren't," she replied, lifting her face to his. "You're marrying me."

Thanks to Danny Taylor's progress in learning to use his new prosthesis, he could ride a horse without difficulty, and he and Chet Harris made good time on their journey to Galveston. But Chet remained silent on the subject that caused him so much concern, and not until they sat at their small campfire on the second night of their travels, did he mention it.

"I thought sure that Melissa would marry me when I came back from the war," he said. "I was even convinced that she'd be impressed because I was discharged from the army as a sergeant. But all she could talk about was that you had been made a first lieutenant. The next thing I knew, she was telling me that she still couldn't make up her mind which of us she wants. She seemed pretty confident you'd come back to her. I know for sure that she still feels that way."

"Are you certain you still want her?" Danny asked.

Chet nodded. "I know she hasn't really settled down yet," he said miserably, "but hard as I've tried, I can't get her out of my system. She's the only girl I've ever loved."

Danny was tight-lipped. "It won't take long to straighten out this situation," was his only reply.

When they reached Galveston, Danny was astonished

by the changes. Portions of the thirty-two-mile-long island were still uninhabited, a wilderness of woods, beaches, and scrub brush. But, thanks at least in part to Harry Canning's efforts, a booming seaport was now flourishing, and merchant ships from the major metropolitan centers of the Eastern Seaboard, as well as from New Orleans, lay at anchor. "Everybody wants to do business with the new state," Chet said proudly, "and Galveston is the fastest growing town in Texas."

The community now boasted three new inns and an even larger structure for transients that called itself a hotel. Danny wanted to stay at one of the hostelries, but an indignant Nancy Canning, who was alone in the newly expanded house when he and Chet arrived, put down her foot. "We'll be mortally insulted if you don't stay here as our guest," she said.

Danny had to give in, and a short time later he arrived at the Thoman & Canning shipyard, now almost twice the size it had been when he had gone off to the war. Even the office of the partner in charge, handsomely furnished now, looked different.

Cordial greetings were exchanged, and Harry wasted no time before getting down to business. "You have no idea how glad I am to see you, Danny," he said. "You're badly needed here. Nancy and I have decided we want to go back to Oregon. I've been corresponding at length with Paul Thoman, and we're agreed we need a substantial, trustworthy general manager here. We've also agreed you're perfect for the job. So I'd like to spend six months training you and then put you in charge."

"Why me, Harry?"

"For many obvious reasons."

"You'd be making a mistake," Danny said. "I'm not denying that I'm competent enough, and I reckon I wouldn't make a mess of things as general manager. What you really need, though, is a man who knows and loves the sea. You must have several people here in the company who could perform ably for you."

"We do. But we prefer you."

"Promote one of them," Danny said. "I could handle

the day-to-day operations, but the company soon would
stop growing. Because I don't have the enthusiasm for
building more and more ships and a general manager
needs that."

Harry sighed. "You have other plans?"

"They haven't formed yet. Just before I was released
from the hospital, I received a tidy sum of money from
the War Department as compensation for the leg I lost.
It's big enough to give me time to look around before I
make up my mind. I also have a couple of personal
matters I want to get settled."

Harry thought how much he had matured. "I can't tell
you how sorry I am that you won't take the position," he
said, "but I respect your decision. Let me know if you
change your mind in the next couple of months."

"Thank you. But I won't." Danny knew Heather would
say his stubborn streak was showing.

That evening Melissa Austin greeted him joyously
when she returned from her own work at the shipyard.
Nancy had invited Chet to supper, too, and the atmosphere was strained. In spite of Melissa's prodding,
Danny was reluctant to discuss his experiences in the
war. Chet was silent, gloomily withdrawn, so Harry and
Nancy had to carry the conversation.

Immediately after the meal Chet excused himself, and
then the Cannings withdrew, too.

"You have no idea how much I've thought about you,"
Melissa said when she and Danny were alone.

He didn't want to hurt her, but at the same time he
knew he had to be candid in return—even brutally frank,
if it should become necessary. Hoping she would understand a subtle response, he merely smiled politely and
made no comment.

She jumped to the conclusion that he was being shy. "I
was so proud of you," she said. "And so thrilled by all
you did!"

"I did my duty," Danny replied flatly. Shifting his
position in his chair, he had to lift his wooden leg.

Melissa winced involuntarily and looked away. He
was reminded of Heather's attitude, and the comparison

of the two girls was startling. All they had in common was their red hair.

Aware that she had evoked no response, Melissa pressed harder. "Aren't you going to admit that you missed me, too?" she demanded.

"I can't admit something that isn't true," Danny said. "I meant what I told you when I went off to join the Rangers, and I haven't changed."

She was stunned, unable to believe that any man could lose interest in her.

"Chet Harris is not only my closest friend," he went on, "but he saved my life. He's in love with you, Melissa, and for his sake I hope you love him in return."

"I—I'm very fond of him."

"I'm not trying to probe. Whatever relationship you may have is his business and your business."

She studied him, her eyes narrowing. "You're taken with somebody else," she said at last.

"That's a matter I prefer not to discuss," Danny replied, his manner becoming remote. He had said enough and saw no point in prolonging a painful conversation. He rose awkwardly to his feet, bowed, and left the room, limping on his wooden leg as he climbed the stairs to the new second floor.

When Melissa was alone, she gave in to her feelings, and tears stung her eyes. She could scarcely believe that Danny had rejected her, and she was outraged. Now she had to rearrange her life. Perhaps she would marry Chet, but she hoped that—somewhere—she would find a man more exciting, a man of greater stature. Texas had proved to be dull, and she craved a fuller, richer life than she could find here. She was still young, exceptionally attractive, and she had no intention of settling for second best.

Zachary Taylor's exploits so overshadowed the victories won by Winfield Scott that he became the nation's hero, and delegation after delegation of Whigs visited his home in Louisiana to urge him to accept their nomination for President. The news that James K. Polk, the only man who could defeat him decisively, intended to retire added to the pressure. General Taylor went off to Washington City, and it was assumed that he would retire from the army in order to become a candidate for the highest post in the land.

Soon after he reached the capital, he sent a letter to a close friend and former subordinate in Texas, and it arrived in Austin only three weeks later after being carried by ship as far as Galveston. The mail was delivered at noon, and Lee Blake, who was thoroughly enjoying his first leave of absence in many years, broke the seal eagerly. "This should be interesting," he said.

Cathy sat at the dinner table with him, and she waited with the patience that her life as an army wife demanded.

"Well," Lee said, looking up from the letter, "Old Rough and Ready tells me in confidence that he definitely plans to retire from the army to accept the Whig nomination for President. But he isn't making an announcement until the Whigs hold their convention this coming summer, so the news is private."

"I'm not surprised," Cathy said, "and no one else will be, either. But I won't mention his plans to anyone."

"Ah, he's writing about me now." Lee returned to the letter and read it with great care. "We aren't going to be separated again!" he announced jubilantly.

They had been afraid he would be given a field command, and Cathy felt great relief.

"If he's elected President," Lee said, still reading, "he's prepared to give me a post at the War Department. If you and I want to live in Washington City."

"Not if it can be helped," Cathy said. "You'd be subjected to so many political pressures there."

"In the meantime," Lee continued, "he's secured another place for me. A real plum." He paused and laughed. "He says my appointment is one of the few matters on which he and General Scott can agree."

"Where are we going?"

He teased her by prolonging the suspense. "We're going to a very old fort that is being modernized, now that it comes under American jurisdiction. The War Department is giving me the command of the presidio in San Francisco, and if we like it there, we can stay right through General Taylor's term as President."

Cathy was elated. "I'll miss people we've come to know here, but we won't be too far from our dear friends in Oregon. And Elisabeta and Rick will be in the Sacramento Valley, which can't be too far from San Francisco."

"It isn't," he assured her.

Suddenly it occurred to her that he hadn't expressed his own reaction to the appointment. "Do you want to go there, Lee?"

He smiled. "I'd be an idiot if I didn't. The presidio is going to be the most important army post on the Pacific, and with both California and Oregon growing rapidly, the command is the best that the army can offer to an officer of my rank. I'll get a letter off to General Taylor today. Oregon is quiet these days, and I can't imagine any reason why California shouldn't be equally peaceful."

"It sounds wonderful," she said, but her smile gradually faded. "Are you intending to take Sergeant Mullins with you?"

"Of course! He's the finest non-commissioned officer I've ever known."

"I just hope Ginny won't become upset all over again," she said, remembering the young woman's reaction when they had left Oregon.

Her fears soon proved groundless. As soon as Hector Mullins heard the news from General Blake, he went straight to his own quarters to inform his wife. "I know you didn't like San Francisco because you had some nasty experiences there before you joined the first Oregon wagon train," he said tentatively.

"This time it will be different," Ginny replied. "You'll be there with me. How soon will we go?"

"We won't know until General Blake gets his formal orders. But I'd guess it won't be too long."

"In that case," she said with a mischievous smile, "I imagine our baby will be born in California."

Hector could only stare at her.

"I guessed it a few weeks ago," she said. "Now the doctor says I'm right."

He picked her up, hugged her fiercely but gently, and then, still holding her off the floor, began to dance around the room.

Ginny wasn't certain whether she was laughing or weeping. Not that it mattered. She and Hector had each other, and when the baby came, their joy would be complete.

The youngest MacGregor girls went to their rooms after supper to do their homework, but Innes and Matilda seemed to be in no mood to leave the kitchen table. When Heather started to clear away platters, her mother halted her.

"The dishes can wait, girl," she said.

Heather looked at her parents, then returned to her seat. "Have I done something to displease ye?"

"How could ye?" Innes asked, chuckling. "We hold ye up to the others as a shining example."

"Sometimes, Pa, I think they resent me for it."

"They'll get over it. Your ma and I want some words with ye in confidence." He fell silent, and it was evident that he was uncertain what to say next.

Matilda took charge and, as always, was not one to mince words. "Ye be sweet on Danny Taylor," she said, sounding as though she were making an accusation.

"Aye," Heather responded calmly.

"How sweet?" her father boomed.

Heather laughed. "I don't know that I can measure it, Pa," she said. "But if Danny asks for my hand—and ye approve—I aim to marry him."

Husband and wife exchanged a swift glance. "That's what we've feared," Matilda muttered.

Heather became concerned.

Innes cleared his throat. "In the months I served with the Legion, I made many a new friend, and there's two that came here from Galveston. They've seen the road ye were taking, and they warned me there's a lass in Galveston who has had his eye. A lass with hair almost as red as yours."

Heather wished her stomach would stop churning. "I knew when he went there that he had more on his mind than a meeting with Harry Canning," she said slowly.

"He may not come back," Matilda warned her. "Ye have little knowledge of men, lass, and even less of the world's ways."

Innes could haul a heavy plow across a field, chop down huge trees, and build a house with his own hands, but he didn't know how to deal with this slender, delicate creature, the eldest of his brood. "We don't want to see ye with your heart broken into bits," he said lamely.

"Is that the problem?" In her relief Heather laughed merrily.

"A joke, is it?" Matilda asked, sniffing.

"No, Ma. It's just that ye dinna understand Danny. He'll be back."

"Is that what he told ye, lass?" Her father glowered at her.

Before Heather could reply, they were interrupted by the sound of approaching hoofbeats. Her heart raced, and she smiled as she said, "There's few who come here at this time of evening. This could be the answer to your question."

Wallace, who was growing rapidly and now was nearly as high as her eldest sister's shoulder, raced down the stairs. "I looked out of my window just now," she said breathlessly, "and I'm sure Danny Taylor is here."

Heather leaped to her feet, frantically smoothing her cotton housedress and trying to pat her hair into shape. "Go to your room this instant," she ordered, "and if I catch ye or any of the others eavesdropping on the stairs, I'll take a hairbrush to yer backsides!" Wallace exploded in giggles as she hurried back up the stairs.

Innes quickly pulled himself to his feet. "Ma, as ye said just minutes ago, the dishes can wait. Come along."

Matilda's brow had cleared, and her footsteps were light as she preceded her husband up the stairs.

Innes followed her for a few steps, then paused and

chuckled. "Lass," he said, "I'll even be surprised when he asks to speak to me." He vanished up the stairs.

Heather could hear Danny limping toward the kitchen door, and a sudden feeling of panic overcame her. Perhaps he was returning only so he could keep his promise and was intending to tell her that he planned on marrying someone else. She wished with all her heart that she hadn't sounded so certain of her future when her parents had questioned her.

A tap sounded at the door.

Heather caught her breath, then raised the latch, and the light of the fire in the kitchen hearth played on her hair, then shone on Danny's face. His expression told her all she needed to know.

She raised her arms slowly, her smile radiant.

LOUIS L'AMOUR

BANTAM'S #1
ALL-TIME BESTSELLING AUTHOR
AMERICA'S FAVORITE FRONTIER WRITER

☐ 27739 **JUBAL SACKETT** $4.95

Be sure to read the rest of the titles in the Sackett series:
follow them from the Tennessee mountains as they head
west to ride the trails, pan the gold, work the ranches, and
make the laws.